The patient rolled into the operating room with Casey's right hand pushing on the young man's neck. Before this timely and simple maneuver, a red geyser had decorated the emergency-room ceiling.

"Bullet or knife?" Zach asked as he rinsed his hands.

"Ice pick," she replied. "It's in Zone Three."

"Great, that'll keep things interesting. Well, let's see what you can do, Dr. Brenner."

Casey had her plan. She looked over at Zach. "I'm assuming it's the internal carotid. If I can't primarily repair it, I can put the shunt in and sew in a vein graft around the shunt."

She had brains, too. "Sewing way up in the neck around the shunt is tough," Zach cautioned.

He could see the outline of a smile beneath her mask. "Let me show you," she said softly.

Zach stared at her in disbelief for a split second, then returned the smile. *Pretty cocky,* he thought. *Cocky, smart, and beautiful. There is a God. . . .*

She sewed in the distal graft. It took her twelve minutes with Zach doing no more than following her suture and staying out of the way.

"No leaks, Dr. Brenner. I'm very impressed." Zach paused for a moment. "For a fourth-year resident, that's excellent."

She looked up and formed another smile under the mask. "Could *you* do it faster?" She couldn't help herself—she knew Zach could dish it out; now she wanted to see if he could take it.

FORBIDDEN RESEARCH

HOWARD SIMON, M.D.

POCKET BOOKS
New York London Toronto Sydney Tokyo Singapore

This book is a work of fiction. Names, characters, places and incidents are products of the author's imagination or are used fictitiously. Any resemblance to actual events or locales or persons, living or dead, is entirely coincidental.

An *Original* Publication of POCKET BOOKS

POCKET BOOKS, a division of Simon & Schuster Inc. 1230 Avenue of the Americas, New York, NY 10020

ISBN: 0-671-02184-2

First Pocket Books printing October 1998

10 9 8 7 6 5 4 3 2

POCKET and colophon are registered trademarks of Simon & Schuster Inc.

Cover design and illustration by James Wang

Printed in the U.S.A.

To my best friend and wife, Barbara.

ACKNOWLEDGMENTS

When writing a novel for the first time, I suspect that most authors worry they will never complete a finished product. Along the lengthy path of this book's creation, dozens of people encouraged me that it could be done. I owe the greatest debt to my parents, Seymour and Shirley Simon and Irene and Bernard Feuerstein, who convinced me that I could do it. My wife, Barbara, and my daughters, Rachel, Hannah, and Carly, tolerated my affair with my laptop computer, even on vacations, and without their indulgence, I would never have been able to finish the book.

Many of the views represented in this book are derived from animal rights and medical ethics literature. A search of Medline will provide a bibliography for anyone interested in this controversial topic. Particular thanks go to Professor Carl Cohen of the University of Michigan Department of Philosophy, whom I met at an ethics seminar on animal research at Georgetown University two years ago. In my opinion, his concept of rights and obligations offers a clarity and succinctness not seen in most philosophical discourse. I also thank the medical students, with whom I met once a month as part of their Medicine and Society

ACKNOWLEDGMENTS

ethics course, for tolerating my obsession with the ethics of animal research.

Included in the legions who read the manuscript in its various forms are Karen Gibbs, Chuck Lutz, Kara Kort, Richard Glowaki, Christine Finck, Anne Loosmann, Sharon Heintz, Robert Kellman, Michelle Baum, Tammy Congelli, Shawn Terry, Phyllis Simon, Seymour Simon, Bernard Feuerstein, Irene Feuerstein, and my mother, Shirley, who actually read the manuscript five times. What's a mother for?

I was told that getting an agent is one of the most difficult hurdles for a novice writer and I am grateful to have Kim Witherspoon as mine. Many thanks to Gideon at Witherspoon Associates for spending hours on the telephone with me and indulging my inexperience. My editor at Pocket Books, Gary Goldstein, and Max Greenhut guided me painlessly (for the most part) through the editing process that continues even as I compose these acknowledgments.

FORBIDDEN RESEARCH

PROLOGUE

======

James Scott was finishing up yet another eighteen-hour
day. It was getting easier to put in these kinds of hours,
because he was sure he was close to a breakthrough. For
three years, he had been growing brain tumors in cats and
trying to develop monoclonal antibodies to fight the tumor
cells. There were two advantages to his approach over
standard chemotherapy. While chemotherapy kills tumor
cells, it also kills healthy cells, causing significant side
effects. These monoclonal antibodies would attack only
the tumor cells. A second advantage was that they would
wipe out all of the tumor cells, unlike chemo, which
always left some cells behind. The most aggressive and
common brain tumor, *glioblastoma multiforme,* was treat-
able with surgery, radiotherapy, and chemotherapy—but
it wasn't curable. Its victims all died, eventually.

A glioblastoma was an equal-opportunity cancer. Unlike lung cancer, where most of those afflicted were smok-
ers or victims of secondary smoke, glioblastoma had no
obvious cause or association. Children were afflicted as
often as adults were—James Scott's brother Terrence had
died from a glioblastoma twelve years ago when he was
only nine years old.

1

Scott had received a Ph.D. from Princeton in molecular biology and immunology. Despite his research abilities, he was forced to endure several years of postdoctoral work in another scientist's lab before he was offered the job at the Institute. It had taken nine years after college to land this position and had been a tremendous financial struggle. As a fully trained Ph.D., he had been paid only twenty-one thousand dollars a year until he landed his current job. Even now, he earned only thirty-four thousand dollars a year. His roommate from college, whom he had coached through biochemistry and genetics, had gone to medical school and received an M.D. Now, just a few years later, his roommate worked thirty-five hours a week in an emergency room and earned one hundred forty thousand dollars a year. *At least no one bleeds and vomits on me,* Scott rationalized.

He looked at his watch. It was eight o'clock. If he didn't get home soon, his wife would kill him. She was seven and a half months pregnant and tired easily, so she needed help getting the kids to sleep. He made a last entry in his notebook and turned the lights off. As he headed out of his lab, three people wearing stocking masks burst through the steel door, knocking him over.

"What the hell are you doing in here?" Scott cried, struggling to his feet.

"We are here to liberate your prisoners," a woman's voice announced as the other two fanned out and moved toward the animal cages in a room adjoining the lab.

"Like hell you are." Scott lunged toward the telephone to call security, but he was slammed to the ground and held down by two of the intruders.

Scott saw the woman's cold stare through the slits of her mask and tried desperately to wrestle free.

"There will be no more innocent victims! This project has been terminated," she said. She reached into her vest pocket and retrieved a 9mm handgun with a silencer. "So are you, you bastard." Four shots into the head of James

2

Scott ended not only his life but also the country's most promising hope of finding a cure for cancer of the brain.

Twelve hours later, Dr. Gabrielle Norton, the director of the NIH, the National Institutes of Health, received an Express Mail delivery. She read the letter and was seized by a wave of panic and nausea. She threw the letter down on her desk. One of her worst nightmares had come true. She read the letter again and broke into a cold sweat.

> The ABP claims responsibility for the death of Dr. James Scott. Animals Before People demands the immediate cessation of all animal-based research. Man's domination of animals in the laboratories of this country must end. Participation, in any capacity, in these atrocities shall be considered an act of unprovoked aggression against the nonhuman animal community punishable by execution.

During her tenure, Dr. Norton had received dozens of letters threatening such violence. Now, the war had begun.

1

Traffic was even worse than usual on this hot, muggy Wednesday morning in July. Even at six in the morning, the FDR was backed up for a mile. The commute from Zach Green's co-op on Manhattan's Upper East Side to University Hospital Center, better known as UHC, normally took thirty minutes if he left before six-thirty in the morning. He tried to be patient but was constitutionally incapable. Though he knew blowing his horn didn't get him to the hospital two seconds sooner, he blasted it anyway.

Zach Green was a trauma surgeon at UHC, the busiest trauma center in the city. Located in lower Manhattan, UHC had the best reputation for trauma care in the area and received victims not only from Manhattan but also from the other boroughs. Green was reasonably intelligent but never let that get in the way of his real talent—an extraordinary ability to stop people from bleeding to death.

He finally arrived at the UHC parking lot at seventhirty, only to find all the obvious spots taken. Cars were crammed into every imaginable corner, but his eyes, trained by years of this primal early-morning warfare, spotted a tiny space in an alley. He managed to wedge his 1984 Honda Civic into an area next to a loading dock with only a few decisive maneuvers.

His beat-up Honda was an anomaly in a doctors' lot stocked with expensive foreign cars. Zach could certainly afford an expensive car with M.D. plates, but he couldn't see spending fifty thousand dollars for a symbol of what was bad about medicine. He preferred to drive and park with impunity, free from having to worry about his car getting smashed or stolen.

Before he went to his office, he stopped, as was his custom, in the emergency department to see what had come in the night before. There were four trauma surgeons on the faculty at UHC, so every fourth night, the hospital was Zach's home.

"What did you get last night, Tim?" he asked Timothy Sloan, the second-year resident assigned to the emergency room.

"Not too busy. Couple of gunshot wounds to the chest that, unfortunately, didn't require surgery, and a gunshot wound to the trachea that came in dead and stayed dead."

"Came in dead and stayed dead" referred to a patient who was dead at the scene of an accident or who had suffered cardiac arrest before reaching UHC. Occasionally, a patient would be stabbed or shot in the heart, suffer cardiac arrest, and then be saved in the ER. The patient's survival depended on two factors: luck and the right surgeon. Absence of either of these resulted in death, or, in UHC slang, the patient "boxed."

"Did you crack his chest? Practice makes perfect," Zach said.

"Yeah, of course," replied Tim, grinning. "Had his chest cracked and his aorta cross-clamped in ninety seconds. Close to a record, I believe."

Zach shook his head. "Forget the record and slow down."

"You're right," Tim admitted. "Oh, yeah, Zach, I almost forgot, there was a great case that you would have loved. They brought some guy, exsanguinating, in from an alley. Glen operated on him. He had a retrohepatic vena caval injury."

"How did he do?"

"What do you think?" Tim snickered. "Box city."

Zach shook his head in disgust. "There has to be a better way to try to save those patients. We can't possibly do any worse."

On the way to his office, Zach stopped and bought the *New York Times,* the *New York Post,* the *New York News,* a garlic bagel, and a bottle—never a can—of Coke. He began every morning eating and reading the papers before he made rounds. When he got to his office, he noticed that the door was ajar. The janitors and security people were compulsive about locking doors, so this was unusual. Slowly, he opened the door and ran his eyes over his desk piled with papers, the couch on which he slept a couple of nights a week, and his gym locker, where he stuck his coat in the winter. He figured one of the residents must have borrowed a book and forgotten to lock the door.

Zach sat in his reclining chair, unscrewed the Coke cap, and leaned back to read the paper. This was the most peaceful moment of his day.

A scream from behind made him jump, and his chair tipped over, sending the Coke into the air. His tormentor, who had been hiding in the locker, stood above him.

"Do you expect me to talk, Goldfinger?" Zach gasped.

"No, Mr. Bond, I expect you to die," Glen Brinkman replied.

Glen extended his hand and helped Zach up. "Gotcha!"

"Christ, you left my door open. I should have known something was up," Zach said as he rubbed his neck. Ever since Zach and Glen had been roommates in college, they had thought up new ways to terrify each other. They had popped out of closets, exploded from under beds, lunged out of trunks, and even dropped out of trees.

Ron Stewart, a fellow trauma surgeon, lumbered into the suite and threw his briefcase into his office. He noticed Zach's chair lying on its side near a puddle of Coke.

"You two morons are at it again, huh?" Ron chuckled in a bass voice at least an octave below middle C. He was a six-foot-two-inch black man who weighed in at well over two hundred pounds. Nothing bothered Ron. Shortly after becoming the first black surgeon at UHC, one of the urologists threw his dirty scrubs at him, assuming he was the janitor. Ron just laughed and calmly introduced himself. With five patients in the ER, all of whom needed surgery, he still retained his sense of humor.

Looking at the mess on Zach's floor, Ron shook his head.

"You're just mad because we don't include you in our training exercises," Glen shot back.

"If you ever pulled that shit on me, I'd stuff your head up your ass."

"Now, there would be a great case. We could write it up for the *Journal of Trauma:* cranial rectal intussusception," Zach said as he wiped up the Coke from his floor.

"Zachary, does anything interest you besides operating and fornicating?"

While Zach—with difficulty—was thinking of an answer to the question, he heard a high-pitched beep and grabbed his pager. "Got to run, partners, I told Double-oh-seven I would cover for him until two o'clock. He has another interview to give and needs time to get his hair moussed. What do you guys have today?" he asked as he put on his white coat.

"Ron and I are doing a laparoscopic cholecystectomy together."

"What are you doing that shit for? That's not real surgery," Zach insisted. Taking a gallbladder out through tiny incisions using a fiber-optic camera and specially designed instruments had become one of the most commonly performed general surgical operations. It required an entirely different technique from conventional open surgery. Zach disliked general surgery, particularly if it was done through a camera. If the patient wasn't bleeding to death, he quickly lost interest.

The emergency department looked like Jonestown—all it needed was a vat of Kool-Aid. Every corner of the trauma area contained patients whose injuries ranged from mild to mortal. The trick was to figure out which was which.

The trauma section of the ER was a huge space subdivided into eight separate bays arranged around the room's circumference. Each bay contained all the equipment required to resuscitate and support a trauma victim. The center of the room contained a collection of desks and counters. There were machines for blood chemistry analysis, arterial blood gas determination, ultrasound, and urinalysis. Having the diagnostic equipment in the trauma room enabled the surgeons to get the results faster and save time in making life-or-death decisions.

As Zach walked in, the chief resident was frantically pushing a gurney. The patient on it was pale and sweaty, clearly in shock. He had multiple intravenous lines infusing blood and fluid into him.

"What do you have?" Zach shouted, trying to be heard above the noise of the ER.

"Two shots in the belly, no exit wounds. His BP is fifty!" Joe yelled, wiping sweat from his face as he pushed the gurney toward the operating room.

Joe Farrell was a good resident, although he tended to become mildly hysterical during emergencies. He was as dedicated to his patients as any resident Zach had ever seen. Many nights, though not on call, Joe would stay to care for an unstable patient on whom he had operated.

"OK, Joe, I'll meet you in the OR. Open and get things started. And Jesus, stay calm, you didn't shoot the bastard," Zach called out.

In the operating room, the patient was quickly placed on the table. The nurses stripped off his clothes and put a sticky pad on his leg to ground the surgical electrocautery unit. The scrub nurse, Shirley Parker, was getting her table in order. She made sure all the necessary sutures, instruments, and retractors were available. A twenty-year veteran at UHC, Shirley had served in Vietnam before taking this job. She had seen it all. She had the unique ability to suggest to a resident which instrument he needed, or where the bleeding might be coming from, without threatening the young doctor. Very few residents were egotistical enough not to take her timely and helpful advice.

Hal Cody, an anesthesiologist, was hooking up monitoring lines to measure pulse, blood pressure, oxygen saturation, and cardiac output. Another one was putting the patient to sleep. A third was pumping in blood and fluid to support his sagging blood pressure. The residents scrubbed quickly while the circulating nurse painted the unconscious man from groin to neck with Betadine antiseptic.

Joe Farrell was gowned and gloved first, followed by Terry Bains, a third-year resident, and Sam Silverstein, a medical student. Farrell placed the sterile towels and drapes on the patient so he could expose the entire abdomen and chest, if needed.

Farrell stood up to the table. "OK, get two suckers ready. Knife, please. All right to start, Hal?"

"Please go ahead. His BP is only forty, and we're running him on oxygen and a little nitrous oxide."

Farrell made an incision from the sternum down to the pubic bone. He used the electrocautery to minimize bleeding from the subcutaneous tissues, although since the patient's blood pressure was so low, there wasn't much bleeding—at least, not until he entered the abdomen.

"Holy shit! Suck! Use both suckers," Farrell commanded nervously. He could see multiple holes in the small bowel, colon, and stomach, as nearly four liters of blood were evacuated.

"BP is thirty," Hal anxiously reminded him.

Farrell saw torrential hemorrhage from the lower abdomen and pelvis, although the amount of blood prevented him from seeing exactly what was bleeding. He quickly packed the lower abdomen with several absorbent sponges and placed the bewildered medical student's hand on top of the packs. "Hold this and don't move," he directed.

"Aortic compressor." Shirley handed him the instrument, which allowed the aorta to be occluded high in the abdomen. This would prevent whatever blood the patient had left from circulating to the injured blood vessels and, at least temporarily, raise the patient's blood pressure to the heart and the brain. Farrell pressed the tool against the aorta.

"BP is one hundred now," related Hal, a bit happier.

"OK, the bleeding is relatively controlled. Why don't you catch up with the blood before I come off the aorta and try to fix things," Farrell replied, acting much calmer. At that moment, Zach popped into the room.

"Mmm, love that aroma. Let's see," he said, sniffing the air. "I smell rice and beans, Budweiser, and shit. The bullet must have gotten his stomach and colon."

"Not to mention his small bowel in about ten places, and I think his vena cava or iliacs," Farrell responded, while checking to make certain the medical student continued to hold the sponges firmly on the largest veins in the body.

"The nose knows," Zach said. "Need some help with the cava?"

"Please," Farrell replied, relieved that Zach was there. While Zach was scrubbed, Farrell was able to release the pressure from the aorta with no drop in blood pressure. The patient was resuscitated.

"Hello, Shirley," Zach said as she gowned and gloved him. "Keeping Joe out of trouble?"

"He's doing just fine, Doctor. Now, get going and close those holes. The smell is getting to me," Shirley replied.

Zach took his place directly across from Farrell. "All right, let's get to work."

The bleeding was well controlled with pressure, so Zach and Joe methodically closed all the holes in the patient's intestines and stomach. They then turned their attention to the pelvis, where all the bleeding had begun.

"What do you want to do, Joe?" Zach asked.

"Well, I think the injury is to the cava, so I need to control the vessel, proximal and distal to the injury. I'll dissect around the . . ."

Zach shook his head. "No need. Just use sponge sticks for pressure." Zach had learned that lesson long ago. Rather than waste a lot of time to completely dissect out the huge veins and clamp them, he preferred to apply pressure above and below the injury. It was faster and safer.

Shirley had them ready. She had folded up small four-by-four squares of gauze into tight wads and placed them between the jaws of the sponge stick. She handed Zach the instruments, and he guided one of them into the abdomen, pressing on the vena cava just as it divided into the iliac veins that drained the lower extremities. Then he took the second sponge stick and occluded the right iliac vein. The bleeding stopped, and the hole in the iliac vein became obvious.

"Why don't you sew up that hole?" Zach directed. "Give the doctor some four-zero proline, please."

"That's slick, Zach, thanks." Joe began to suture the laceration that actually not only involved the iliac vein but extended into the vena cava.

"Just be gentle. That vein is fragile, and if you torque the needle, you'll rip it more."

Joe sewed the hole carefully. Zach released the pressure from the veins. There was a small amount of bleeding, but the repair looked good.

"Thanks, Zach, I couldn't have done it without you."

"Bullshit. It would have just taken you a little longer. Besides, in less than a year, no one will be holding your hand. Just be glad the hole wasn't in the retrohepatic portion of the cava. I still haven't saved one of those bastards. Glen lost one last night."

Zach turned away from the table and removed his bloody gown. He snapped off his gloves and belatedly wrote the obligatory preoperative note in the patient's chart. "Let me know if there any problems with this guy," Zach said, as he left the OR suite. "Later, Shirley."

Joe and his junior resident began to close the patient's abdomen. "Shirley, do you think I could have fixed that vena cava without Zach's help?" Joe asked.

"Honey, I have no doubt. You just needed some confidence."

Joe felt good. Shirley never lied.

Zach had finished his cases, rounds, and all his paperwork for the day. He wasn't on call tonight and was itching to get onto the river. He made his exit through the ER but was intercepted before he got out.

"Please, Zach, give me a break." Tim Adams, one of the interns in the emergency department, had just seen a seventeen-year-old boy with a hot appendix. An intern's dream come true. Usually.

"Are you sure he has it?"

"He's been sick two days, is only tender in the right lower quadrant, has a temperature of one-oh-one and a white blood cell count of seventeen thousand. His urine is clean. What else could it be?"

"In a seventeen-year-old boy, not much," Zach conceded.

"So please do it with me. Double-oh-seven is on call, and I'm not good enough yet to get him through an operation."

"No one's that good," Zach admitted. "Is the OR ready?"

"They said they could be ready in fifteen minutes."

"All right, let me see the kid." It was four-thirty. He would be out by five-thirty. Still plenty of time for the river and to get to Glen's for dinner.

The twenty-minute operation took more than an hour. The appendix was retrocecal and was tough to deliver out of the wound. It was only the second appendix that Tim had done, and he had no clue what to do. Zach yelled through the whole procedure, trying to get Tim to move his hands more efficiently, but it was a struggle. Still, Zach let him do the case, from start to finish.

The sweat was visible on Tim's forehead. "Sorry I was so clumsy."

"You'll get better with practice. And faster. If you want to operate with me on big cases, you need to move. Life is too short to spend an hour watching you put in a stitch."

"I know. I'm just a little tired from being on call last night. After I'm done, I can go home and lay down."

Zach angrily glared at him over his surgical mask. "Timothy! I can tolerate you taking all day to make the incision. It doesn't bother me that you still can't tie a knot worth a damn. I didn't say a thing when you missed the fascia by half an inch. But do you know what really pisses me off?"

"No, sir."

"Don't call me sir. You're not in the fucking army."

"Sorry. What else did I do, Zach?"

"You mixed up the transitive verb *lay* with the intransitive verb *lie*. You don't *lay* down. You *lie* down." Zach's vocabulary may have been laced with four-letter words, but he was a stickler for the proper syntax. He was disappointed when he had offered to write a scatological version of William Safire's *New York Times* column, "On Language," and the *Times* had respectfully declined the opportunity.

"Huh?"

"Didn't you take a fucking English course in college? *Lay* is a transitive verb. It takes an object."

"Zach."

"Yeah, Tim."

"Can I ask you one more question?"

"Sure."

"Could you explain when you use *who* and *whom?*"

"Next time. I'm off to the river. I'll talk to the kid's mother on the way out."

At seven o'clock, Zach exited the way he had come in twelve hours earlier, through the ER. The body count was rising, and it was still early. He would have loved to stay, but he hadn't been over to Debby and Glen's in a while. Double-oh-seven was on call, and Zach hoped he wouldn't generate too many cases for the morbidity and mortality conference next week.

THE NATIONAL INSTITUTES OF HEALTH,
BETHESDA, MARYLAND
JULY 7

"It's the first verifiable case of a medical researcher being murdered," Lew Mason announced ominously. With James Scott's murder and the ABP's threat of continued terrorism, the FBI had entered the case. Mason had been at the scene in Vermont but had found little to build a case on.

"Do you have any leads?" Gabrielle Norton asked. Norton had been the director of the NIH for five years. Dressed conservatively in a dark blue pants suit, with dark brown hair cropped in a no-nonsense cut, she looked the part of the serious medical professional. She had graduated from the University of Pennsylvania Medical School with an M.D. and a Ph.D. and completed her residency in internal medicine and cardiology at Hopkins. During her career, she had published more than seventy-five papers. Now, at forty-four, her *curriculum vitae* was measured in pounds. She had a teenage daughter from a first marriage to a young resident that failed when neither partner was willing to compromise their own ambitions. A second go-round at marriage had worked much better. Gabrielle had two young sons and a relatively happy husband whose hours were saner than hers. Although she was still driven, she worked hard to balance her family's needs with her career.

Mason stared at the note Gabrielle handed him. "No. No leads. There was minimal security, and nobody saw anything. No fingerprints. We're running the slugs to get the make of the gun, see if we can trace where it was purchased. Animals Before People," he said, looking at the note again. "Have you heard of them, Doctor?"

She shook her head as she handed him a file of threats they'd received over the last twelve months. "There are more than three hundred known animal rights groups in this country alone. At least thirty of them have been involved in active disruption of ongoing research, and several have publicly threatened violence, but this murder is a first, as far as I know."

"Have you had any other threatening letters recently?"

"We get hundreds of letters protesting our funding of animal research, some angry, others worse. I guess it was only a matter of time before we got an ultimatum."

Mason glanced at the letter again and added it to the file. "I think we should keep this to ourselves for now and hope it was an isolated incident. I'd like to see your list of the groups or people who have threatened researchers."

Gabrielle gestured toward the file. "A copy of everything I've received is in there. You can keep it."

"Could you shut down research, even if you wanted to?" Mason asked, his icy blue stare boring into her.

Gabrielle sighed. The question alone made her feel exhausted; she'd fielded so many interrogations from the press lately. "The National Institutes of Health is the largest government funder of research, so we attract protest from these types of groups," she said, slipping into the standard speech that she always gave the media. "The truth is that there are billions of dollars in private funds that go into basic and applied science. The NIH could defund every lab doing animal-based research, and there would still be money for that work."

"But how many scientists would do the work if the NIH stopped its funding, and if they thought there was a chance they would be murdered?"

She nodded and sipped some tea. "Apparently, that's what this group is trying to find out."

"What do you think would happen if it did stop? I mean animal research?"

She laughed dryly. "Well, contrary to what some might tell you, the world wouldn't immediately come to an end. Only sixty-five percent of our grants fund animal-based research. As alternative methods become available, the number will shrink some more. It's expensive, and the results are often disappointing."

"So, why do it?" he asked, surprised by her answer.

"Because despite what the scientifically challenged will tell you, research on animals has, does, and will continue to advance medicine. There is no doubt that without animal research, the quality and longevity of our lives would be diminished. I participated in a debate over at the Kennedy School of Ethics last summer, and my opponent spent fifteen minutes listing five examples of animal research that cost millions of dollars and misled the scientists. I told the audience that I could give them many more examples of nonproductive research. That is the reality of science. Not all research, animal or otherwise, eventually leads to some substantive gain. "

"The average person doesn't like to hear that," Mason said.

She shrugged her shoulders. "That's research. We never know which one percent will lead somewhere, and yet without it, we go nowhere. I can't emphasize enough how important it is that you stop this group before this escalates any further."

Mason briskly walked down the corridor. He ran his hand through his sandy hair and contemplated his next move.

He had come to the FBI directly out of Fordham law school and never really considered practicing law. His father had been a New York City cop, and he'd wanted his son to transcend his own exemplary if undistinguished career, so he pushed him to get a law degree and shoot for the FBI.

Mason was dogged and compulsive. His discipline stemmed from a three-year stint in the Marines, which transformed a lackadaisical high school pupil into a straight-A college student. Since everyone was constrained by the same twenty-four-hour day, he had vowed never to waste a minute.

After rising at five o'clock each morning, he did one hundred push-ups and two hundred sit-ups and got on an exercise bike for twenty minutes—a routine that kept between one hundred seventy and one hundred seventy-three pounds on his six-foot-two frame. By six-thirty, he had logged onto his computer for an hour and could have discussed national or international current events with the president. Shaving in the shower saved time, and it always took him exactly twenty strokes. His blond hair required no combing or brushing because it remained the same quarter inch in length that it had been on Paris Island. At the office by seven, when he got an assignment, he did more research and knew the subject better than agents with years more experience.

This was his first case as the primary agent in charge, and he had a load of work to do.

2

Zach arrived at Glen's apartment at eight, after a brutal rowing workout on the East River. Glen lived in a new building on Seventy-third Street between Park and Madison. Debby, Glen's wife, had grown up in Scarsdale and had always had money. Despite her inherited wealth, she dressed plainly, used coupons, and volunteered at the Metropolitan Museum of Art. Glen's family was middle-class, but he definitely enjoyed money. He drove a BMW and bought his suits at Barney's. But money hadn't changed Glen. He loved being a doctor and knew that his work and his family were what counted. Nevertheless, as he told Zach, money may not make you happy, but if you are already happy, it's a great mood elevator.

Zach was met at the door by Rebecca and Rachel, Glen and Debby's four-year-old twin girls.

"Uncle Zach!" Rebecca screamed. "I missed you so much." Both girls jumped on Zach as he tumbled to the ground. They hugged and kissed him as if they hadn't seen him in a year.

"What a greeting! I missed you guys, too."

Glen and Debby laughed at the twins' affectionate display. Zach was part of the family. He never missed a birthday and was over for dinner at least once a week. When he was between girlfriends, he came over several times a week.

"So, Zach, you and Lauren are no more?" Debby asked, giving him a knowing smile.

"Well . . ." He pondered the question. "Lauren and I decided that we would see other people for a while."

"What a work of art! Would I love to have had an hour alone with her!" Glen teased.

"You should *both* have your gonads cut off." Debby groaned.

"Just numb me up first, sweetheart." Glen laughed.

"Zach, when the hell are you going to look at women as something other than sperm banks? And you," she said, pointing her finger at her husband, "you egg him on."

"I'm just looking for Ms. Right." Zach smiled as he winked at Glen. "I just don't think my wife has been born yet."

"Yeah, I guess Lauren was a little old at twenty-three. What did you two do, go to FAO Schwarz and play with the electric trains?"

"Actually, she was twenty-two. Look at it from my perspective, Deb. When I turned fifty-five, Lauren would have been almost forty. I'd be in my prime, and she'd be trying to cover up her new wrinkles."

Debby decided to quit while she was ahead. They all knew perfectly well that after eighteen it was all downhill for men. "All right, Don Juan, dinner is ready."

Dinner, as usual, had been ordered from a Chinese restaurant and delivered to their door just ten minutes after the order was placed. Quick but not a record.

"Once, we got our food from the Second Wok in seven and a half minutes," Glen recalled. He liked to track such important details. "I love fresh food," he added sarcastically.

Debby opened the cardboard boxes. Everyone scrambled to a seat, with the twins on either side of Zach. Debby served the twins some chicken fried rice, while the adults helped themselves.

The adults finished in less than fifteen minutes. Glen and Zach were used to gobbling their meals from years of eating on the run as residents. Debby didn't sit down for a leisurely meal unless she could get a baby-sitter and Glen was free—an event that occurred about as frequently as a solar eclipse.

After dessert—some freezer-burned ice cream—Zach went into the twins' room. Rebecca and Rachel were infatuated with their collection of Barbie dolls and their matching accessories. Zach joined them to play his own demented version of Barbie, while Debby and Glen did the dishes. Zach had brought along a stuffed velociraptor and was teaching the girls the finer points of disembowelment. Rebecca took the velociraptor and pounced on an unsuspecting Barbie as Glen and Debby walked in.

"Rrrrr. I'll rip your guts out," Rebecca shouted as menacingly as a four-year-old could.

"You're such a bad influence, Zach," Debby said.

Glen was thrilled. "Those are my girls," he announced with pride.

"You two guys need help. I know you rented *Jurassic Park* the last time you stayed home with the girls. They should lock you up for child abuse."

"I thought I told you not to tell Mom," Glen whispered as he huddled with his daughters.

"We didn't tell, Daddy," Rachel whispered loudly. "She figured it out."

Debby tried to hold her stern expression. "Yeah, it was really tough. I was sitting on the toilet when Rachel comes in and pretends to bite me in half. My mother told me surgeons were sadists, and I didn't believe her."

Soon, Debby announced bedtime, and the girls, with some protest, kissed Zach and Glen good night and climbed into their beds.

Glen and Zach retired to watch a Mets game, leaving Debby the task of reading one book—seven times—before the girls would go to bed. Glen had probably only put the girls to bed a dozen times in their entire lives. One out of four nights he wasn't home, and the night after

21

being on call he was so tired that he went to bed before his daughters.

"The girls get smarter and more beautiful every time I see them," Zach said. "Sometimes I'm jealous."

"So find a nice girl, get married, and make your own." Glen shrugged. "How long can you screw around?"

"I haven't been going out as much lately." He poured himself some coffee and slumped into the chair. "You know what I really worry about, Glen?"

"Well, let's see," Glen replied, scratching his head. "Must be either world peace or your dick falling off."

"Hilarious. No, it's getting married and becoming bored sexually. You've been married ten years, right? How often do you and Debby do it?"

Glen shook his head. "It's the chase for you, Zach. It always has been. Getting women into bed is more fun for you than the actual act."

"That's not always true," Zach protested. "It wasn't true with Susan. You didn't answer my question."

"Sex is different after ten years of marriage and two kids," Glen responded.

"Different better or worse?"

"Different. It's not as exciting as the first time with someone you hardly know. But ultimately, I think it's better. You appreciate it more."

"How often?" Zach persisted.

Glen smiled. "You know that pregnant woman on Four-C? The one whose car crashed on the way to the hospital? It took us ninety minutes to close her lacerations while they delivered her baby."

"Yeah, so what?" Zach replied.

"Well, that was the only look I have had at a vagina in about a month."

"Come on. In a month?"

Glen picked up one of the girls' Barbie dolls. "These dolls are looking really good to me. I mean, look at those tits."

"Not bad," Zach agreed. "I guess I really haven't met the right woman yet. When I remember what happened with Susan . . . I don't need to be tortured like that again."

Susan Grogan was one of Zach's classmates in medical school, and he had succumbed to her violet eyes and willowy body. They were inseparable during their second year, and he thought they were going to get married. But several months after the third year clerkships had begun, the relationship faltered. Zach figured it was all the time they spent apart, but the truth was that Susan had begun seeing one of the radiology residents. Zach abruptly discovered this one night when, while on call, he went to the radiology department to review some films. He noticed two sets of feet, one of which proved to be Susan's, protruding from the CT scanner tube. Susan's repetitive chant of "Fuck me harder" immediately convinced Zach that he should find a new girlfriend.

"The CT scanner—that was real class," Glen recalled.

"Yeah, it's funny now, but she made me miserable for years. Susan was the girl I was going to marry."

"Listen, Debby and I both told you she was bad news. That relationship never had a chance. Susan was not going to marry a medical student and struggle for ten more years. Look who she eventually married, some football star turned Wall Street hotshot."

"He's now in jail for insider trading," Zach added triumphantly. "You really lucked out with Debby. Still, you're always talking about other women."

"Sure, I talk. If you think when you put that ring on your finger, your testosterone level falls outside of your bedroom, forget it. Debby knows I look at other women. The butcher knife in the bedroom is for if I ever do more than look."

Zach thought for a minute. "What if you knew you wouldn't get caught?"

"I don't think I would do it."

Zach pressed for a different answer. "Okay, let's say Sharon Stone came to the ER with a bellyache, and you took care of her. It ends up being the flu or something, and in a couple of days she's fine. So she's in her suite at the

Plaza, calls you up, and wants you to come up to her room so she can rehearse her part in the sequel to *Basic Instinct* with you. You get to be Michael Douglas."

"Does she have an ice pick?"

"No ice pick. She only wants to fuck you to death."

"If she was a patient, that would be unethical."

"Fine, forget that, she's not a patient, but you can screw her, and Debby would never find out."

"I don't think I would do it."

"You could actually pass her up?" Zach said, shaking his head. "I'm not sure I could, even if I was married."

"Zach, at some point in your life, you are going to have to develop at least some rudimentary neural pathway between your dick and your conscience."

Debby came back into the room. "The girls are down, and I think I'm going to turn in, too. One of the girls will be up later."

"Really? I thought they slept pretty well now," Glen said naively.

"That's because you never wake up with them," Debby responded.

"On that note, I'm going to bolt. I need to finish a paper by next week," Zach said. He kissed Debby good-bye and poked Glen in his abdomen, which protruded slightly over his belt. "Too much home cooking. See you in the A.M., buddy."

"I'll ride down on the elevator with you," Glen said, while checking to make sure he had his keys, which he was always forgetting.

In the elevator, Glen shuffled his feet and looked down at the floor for a second. "I got an offer from that group in Westchester," he said as nonchalantly as he could.

"Yeah? Are you serious about it?" Zach knew that Glen had been looking but didn't think he would ever seriously consider leaving UHC.

"It's a great offer. Seven surgeons. The group does twenty-five hundred cases a year. Call is every seventh night, and you can take it from home."

"No trauma?"

"Not much. An occasional car crunch."

"You'll hate it."

"There's nothing wrong with operating in the daytime and sleeping at night. That's what normal people do."

"What about the research? There's nothing academic about Westchester Community Hospital. It's just dialing for dollars."

"Come on, Zach, you know I'm not doing it for the money. I need to spend more time with the girls, and Debby wants to have another kid. I need to have a more normal life. This every fourth night away is murder when you have kids."

"So you're going?"

"I haven't decided. Debby would like me to take it. It would be hard to leave here. To leave our work." He hesitated. "To leave you."

"I guess if I try to talk you out of it, Debby will kill me."

"You know Debby loves you as much as I do. It's not as if we'd be moving to North Dakota."

"You can't get take-out Chinese in less than an hour out there. That's uncivilized," Zach protested.

"You know, two of the guys in the group are in their early sixties. There would be a place for you in a year or two."

Zach shrugged his shoulders. "I can't see myself whacking out gallbladders and lopping off breasts all day."

"Maybe after you get married and have a few kids, your endorphin level will go down."

He shook his head dismissively. "When do you have to decide?"

"They didn't really say. I told them I wouldn't be available until next July, and they told me the offer would still be there."

"So I have almost a year to convince you what a horrible mistake you would be making."

As Zach walked back to his apartment, he thought about how lucky he was to have such good friends. He couldn't fathom the thought of losing them, even though Westchester was only a forty-minute drive from the city. Glen had been his roommate in college until he moved in with Debby after their junior year. They were all close friends. It was the type of friendship that is difficult to develop after college or graduate school, when jobs and real responsibility preclude two-hour dinners, all-night conversations, and lazy days on the beach during spring break. The special and unusual aspect of their friendship was that even after Glen and Debby fell in love, the trio's relationship remained almost unchanged. In fact, Zach and Debby got along nearly as well as Glen and Debby—minus the sex, of course. Glen once remarked that Zach could have been both the best man and the maid of honor at the wedding.

The three of them were inseparable. Glen and Debby were Zach's support system. Whenever he was upset about something, he would lie on their couch, and they would cheer him up. When the girls were born, he was almost as thrilled as Glen and Debby.

Zach wouldn't worry. He had a year to change their minds.

3

JULY 11

Tara McVey pulled into the driveway of her split-level in New Rochelle. The reprints had come today, and she opened the trunk of her Nissan to get the box of five hundred copies of her article in *Nature*. She had fielded calls from reporters all day after being interviewed on the *Today* show. This was big. *Nature* was the Cadillac of scientific journals. It published work from all scientific fields and far surpassed any other medical journal in readership and prestige. She had done landmark work, and now she was famous.

Four years ago, she had received a one-million-dollar NIH grant to study spinal cord regeneration. Using a combination of drugs and nerve-stimulation techniques, she had taken paraplegic mice and restored significant function in their denervated hind limbs. A hundred thousand paraplegic and quadriplegic patients, in the United States alone, had their hopes lifted with publication of her startling results. Next week, she was to be the keynote speaker at a banquet for the Christopher Reeve Foundation.

She lifted the bulky box, balanced it with one hand,

slammed down the trunk, and turned around. She gasped when she saw them and dropped the box.

"You must be very proud, Dr. McVey. Let's see, if I read your article carefully, you used how many animals? Oh, yes, about one thousand. But they were only rats, weren't they?" Cecile pulled out the Browning, while Palmer held McVey's arms, unnecessary since they had already gone totally limp.

"I have a family," McVey said with inaudible resignation.

"So did the animals," Palmer hissed into her ear.

The last thing McVey thought of as the bullets tore through her was Katie Couric asking if she had any apprehension about doing research after the recent episode of animal rights terrorism.

Gabrielle Norton sat at the head of the conference table, her mind drifting, as yet another suit stood up and presented endless statistics. They were going over the budget, an annual chore that she always dreaded. Her mind wandered to her youngest son. Did Timothy finish that math homework last night? As she tried to recall whether her husband had ever gone into the den to help him, she noticed someone signaling to her out of the corner of her eye. It was Marta, her secretary. Annoyed, she got up and walked to the door. Marta knew she wasn't supposed to interrupt this meeting.

"I'm sorry, but it's Mr. Mason on the phone. He says it's urgent."

Gabrielle's heart beat faster as she strode to her office. Perhaps they'd caught the nuts who killed James Scott. She picked up her phone.

"Gabrielle Norton here."

"Bad news, I'm afraid. Another researcher was just shot in her own front yard. No one's claiming responsibility yet, but of course we're thinking ABP. She'd been doing work with paraplegic mice and had had a breakthrough in getting some sensation and motion back into their legs. Apparently, there was an article on this in *Nature*. All the publicity she received made her a setup."

Gabrielle sat down hard. "Tara," she said.

Gabby Norton pounded her desk and wiped her eyes. This one was personal; it hurt. Tara McVey had been her friend. She had approved her first NIH grant and knew then that Tara would make her mark. She finally had, and now she was dead. She shook with anger and saw a Federal Express envelope on her desk. With a depressing sense of repetitiveness, she opened it.

> Did you think we were joking? You have it within your power to stop this war, Dr. Norton. The NIH is to stop the funding of animal research immediately. We are sure that the private sector will follow in kind. You have seen nothing yet.
>
> ABP

"Did you know her?"

"Very well," Gabrielle said, her face crumpling. "I'm going to have to call you back, Mr. Mason."

Gregory Sandstone obsessively devoted fifteen years of his life to CARE, the Coalition for Animal Research Extinction, missing out on family life, including his wife and children's birthday parties, their triumphs and disappointments. Ultimately, his wife divorced him because of his devotion. Greg began as a door-to-door volunteer, soliciting signatures and donations to advance the humane treatment of animals. The organization he started in the basement of his three-bedroom split-level home in Bethpage, New York, had grown from an inchoate dream to a nationally recognized model of political action. He personally sent the message to farmers, pet breeders, zookeepers, and particularly scientists that inhumane treatment of animals would not be tolerated.

CARE was the third-largest group in the United States in both membership and donations. Its huge treasury was the result of Sandstone's unwavering commitment to the organization, and CARE's funds had done much to decrease the suffering of animals. But Greg Sandstone felt they still had a long way to go.

"I don't understand you, John. How could you have expressed sympathy for McVey? Mice spinal cords are significantly different from humans. Her experiments were useless." Sandstone's brown eyes were full of sadness. John Power had been the vice president of CARE for twelve years, but they rarely agreed on the issues.

"I don't think we need to debate this right now," John replied. "Tara McVey is dead. She's the second researcher who's been murdered in a week. That isn't good for us. Our donations are bound to suffer. We need to let the public know we're against the violence."

Greg grimaced. "Are donations all you're worried about?"

John glared at him. "You know exactly what I mean. Every dollar we lose means more suffering for animals."

"When CARE appears to endorse that kind of research, any kind of animal research, we are co-conspirators in cruelty."

John sighed. "I'll give you credit, Greg. You're consistent."

Greg disagreed with John's position, but he still respected him. After his arrest in college, Power had moderated his politics. Though he made no secret of his opposition to all human uses of animals, his rhetoric was gentle and persuasive. A man of intellect and principle, Power was able to sway people's opinions. Greg often chafed at Power's more balanced views, but ultimately they had always agreed that any step to reduce the indiscriminate use of animals was worthwhile.

"There is going to be a lot of scrutiny of animal welfare

and rights groups. Yet we want to keep up the pressure on the researchers. How should we proceed?" Greg asked, feeling him out.

Power looked his friend dead in the eye. "With the truth, Greg. No matter how wrong animal research is, humans still come first."

4

Zach saw Casey Brenner for the first time at the morbidity
and mortality conference, which was held every Thursday
afternoon, and couldn't take his eyes off her. Casey was
about five-foot-five, and although her body was cloaked by
a short white coat, it didn't disguise her graceful lines. She
had large dark eyes, a round cherubic face, and thick black
shoulder-length curly hair. She wasn't wearing much
makeup, except for some muted lipstick that framed a
luminous smile, the centerpiece of a beautiful face. She
laughed at something one of the residents said, and Zach
saw her eyes sparkle. He grabbed his wrist to take his own
pulse.

He turned to Glen and somberly proclaimed, "That, my
friend, is my future wife!"

"Oh, really. Do you know who that is?"

Zach wasn't listening. "Pinch me, so I know this isn't a
dream."

"Well, before you go out and buy the ring, you will recall
that she is one of our residents."

"What are you talking about? I interviewed all the new
interns, and trust me, I would remember her."

"She isn't an intern. We needed an extra R-Four after

Delvechio quit last year. She was somewhere out in the Midwest and wanted to come to New York. Simpson offered her the job last fall. You must have been away."

"That's it, just shoot me," Zach said as he slumped back in his chair. He had never become involved with one of his residents. He took his pedagogical responsibilities seriously and figured that ethically he could not become romantically entwined with a resident whom he was supposed to train and evaluate.

"Not that I want to upset you, but you can bet your ass that our fearless leader, Simpson, will be after her. That slime bag will have his hand up her dress on the first case they do together," Glen added, to cheer him up.

"My wife would never let him get away with that," Zach said as the conference began.

Larry Gordon, a trauma surgeon and the section chief, was presenting the first case of the morning. Gordon was forty-two years old, handsome enough to portray a surgeon on television, and a gifted speaker. Whenever reporters wanted commentary on a story, they could be sure Gordon would give it to them. He relished the limelight, particularly television. He knew the surgical literature cold and could explain medical problems and procedures in a way that anyone could understand. Unfortunately, he was a miserable excuse for a surgeon. His hands were only moderately below average, but his biggest problems came in the judgment department.

Judgment was an ill-defined characteristic that surgeons either did or did not possess. Most surgeons could physically perform all but the most difficult operations. Judgment was knowing who needed surgery and when to do it. Good surgeons knew when to back off and when to be aggressive in the operating room. The clever surgeon knew to quit while he was ahead.

Judgment was the surgical version of common sense. But however one defined it, Larry Gordon did not possess this trait. Hence his nickname: "007, Licensed to Kill."

"The case is that of a fifteen-year-old black female, shot in the right supraclavicular space with no exit wound. She came to the ER in shock with a blood pressure of seventy systolic. She was resuscitated with fluid and blood to a pressure of almost one hundred systolic. A right chest tube was put in place and nine hundred cc of blood was returned. Over the next ten minutes, she remained stable, and she was brought to angiography."

"Here we go," Glen moaned under his breath to Zach. "Sounds like a clean kill." An angiogram was an X-ray of blood vessels. It gave a detailed picture of the arteries in question and was extremely useful for planning an operation. The downside to ordering an angiogram in an emergency was that it took at least an hour to obtain.

"Unfortunately," continued Gordon, "while awaiting her angiogram, she suffered a cardiac arrest and died. An autopsy showed lacerations of the subclavian artery and vein." He paused and took a deep breath. "She exsanguinated. Any questions or comments?"

"Whose turn is it to humiliate him?" Zach whispered.

"I went last week. You're up," Glen replied.

Zach stood up at his seat. "Larry, how big was the patient?"

"She was small, perhaps one hundred pounds."

"Dr. Brenner, would you have angiogrammed this patient?" asked Zach, not quite looking directly at her.

Startled at being called on at her first conference, Casey answered cautiously. "Well, the entrance wound was in Zone One of the neck. Most literature supports performing an angiogram in that location because it's difficult to access surgically."

"What about the blood in the right chest?" Zach was looking at her now, but his even stare offered no clues.

"Well, most of the literature suggests that one thousand to fifteen hundred cc of blood is indication for opening the chest emergently, and this woman only had nine hundred cc."

Zach nodded. "Yes, that's true, but the mistake here is that the patient was small, and nine hundred cc of blood in her chest is the equivalent of fifteen hundred cc in a normal-sized male. She needed to go immediately to the operating room and get her chest opened to fix the vascular injuries."

"But it was important to determine exactly where she was bleeding before rushing in," Gordon protested, realizing he had screwed up once again.

"Come on, Larry. She was shot right here." Zach pointed to the area in the hollow of his clavicle. "It doesn't take a genius to figure out that the bullet must have gotten her subclavian vessels. You should have gone in right away." Turning away from Gordon and addressing the other doctors and residents, Zach summed up the case.

"Listen, people, you've heard me say this before—by now, you must be getting tired of it. Don't make the patient prove he or she is sick. This girl had one chance. She arrived at our hospital alive, and we sent her over to X-ray to die. Young people may have a normal blood pressure and be two minutes away from death. They look fine, until they're dead. You do not get a second chance."

Gordon felt his face burning. He knew he had messed up. Zach, as usual, had extracted the salient facts of the case and made them look obvious. It was always so easy in retrospect. Why did he always have to make him look like such an ass? Gordon knew that he wasn't the greatest surgeon in the world, but he always tried to do the best he could. No patient ever died because Larry Gordon was lazy.

Zach and the other attendings were just as brutal to one another in conference as they were to Gordon. But he bore the brunt of the attacks, due to the indisputable fact that he had the most deaths and complications.

Joe Farrell presented the next case. Farrell was the chief resident and was treated by the other attendings as an equal—a dubious honor in this group.

"The complication is delayed diagnosis of pericardial tamponade . . ."

After the conference, Zach casually made his way over to Casey to introduce himself.

"Sorry to ambush you on your first day here, but we all go after each other pretty hard. It keeps everyone on their toes," Zach explained apologetically. "I'm Zach Green, one of the attendings at UHC." He shook her hand.

"Nice to meet you, Dr. Green," she responded, looking directly into his eyes and smiling. "I think I can take it."

Zach realized that he hadn't let go of her hand and that his palm was sweating. He slowly withdrew it and tried to think of something clever to say. "So why does a nice girl like you want to be a trauma surgeon?"

She stared at him in disbelief and then let him have it. "Dr. Green, I stopped being a girl when I was eighteen, and I'm sure you have no idea whether or not I am nice. As for being a trauma surgeon, I'm supposed to be here to learn to be a good general surgeon. Have a great day." She pivoted and walked out of the room. *Unbelievable,* she thought. *I haven't been here a week, and I'm already getting harassed.*

Nice going, Zach told himself, blushing. Despite his addiction to attractive women, he always treated a female resident as one of the "boys" and had never used his position to coerce a resident into having an affair, which could not be said for some of his colleagues. Why couldn't he ever keep his mouth shut?

Glen had overheard the exchange and could barely contain his laughter. "I think she likes you," he taunted. "Listen, Zach. There's a book by Dale Carnegie I think you should read."

"Can you believe how stupid I sounded? She must think I'm the world's biggest asshole," Zach lamented.

"Well, certainly the biggest asshole in this room." Glen laughed.

"Man, this is going to be torture. If I'm this attracted to her now, what happens when I start working with her?"

"Maybe you can learn to dislike her as much as she apparently dislikes you."

"Glen, how did I get so lucky to have a friend like you?"

Glen just smiled. His best friend had a serious infatuation—again.

Daphne Cates was sitting in the UHC cafeteria, reading the newspaper and slowly eating her lunch—a cup of strawberry yogurt. The cafeteria was crowded, and Casey spied an empty seat across from Daphne.

"OK if I join you?" Casey asked.

"Sure, sit." Daphne noticed Casey's badge identifying her as a resident. "My name is Daphne Cates. I'm a second-year psychiatry resident."

"Casey Brenner, fourth-year surgical resident." They shook hands, and Casey sat down with her lunch: a peach of indeterminate age, a small salad with lettuce, more brown than green, and tepid coffee.

"You must be the resident who replaced Delvechio. Good luck. You had better start sleeping as much as you can. This place takes its toll on surgical residents. Which service did you start on?"

"Trauma," Casey replied, taking a bite out of her peach.

"My goodness, I guess they wanted to give you a trial by fire. That service is brutal. Don't even think of getting sleep while you're on call," Daphne said, rolling her eyes.

"It sounds as if you speak from experience," Casey said. Daphne smiled. She had a Southern drawl but spoke at an allegro pace. She was tall and very pretty. Blue eyes, long blond hair, delicate features—a Southern belle, Casey thought.

"I was a surgical resident for a year. My daddy is a surgeon in South Carolina, and he's had me tying knots and watching operations since I was ten. He always wanted us to practice together someday."

"So what happened?" Casey asked.

"I hated it. The hours were ridiculous, and I really didn't enjoy operating—a bad trait in a surgeon. I always liked talking to people. In fact, I was the only surgical resident who would actually take a social history from the patients. It interested me a lot more than their gallbladder disease. So why did you leave your program and come here?"

"It's a long story. Maybe I can lie down on a couch and tell you sometime," Casey replied.

Daphne laughed. "Do you have a place to live yet?"

"Right now, I'm subletting an apartment over on Twenty-ninth Street. The rents here are surreal. I either need to find something cheaper or start selling insurance on the side."

"My roommate finished her residency in June, and I have a two-bedroom apartment on East Seventy-fifth Street. It's costing me eighteen hundred dollars a month, and I'd love another roommate. We could split the expenses and both have money left over to enjoy the city— although you won't have much free time."

"That's a great offer. Are you sure?" Casey said, her mind racing.

"Sure, you look normal. When do you want to move in?"

Casey hesitated, remembering an unfortunate experience with her first college roommate. "What about boyfriends? Are you seeing anyone now? I don't want to get in the middle of something."

"Well, I have an occasional friend over, but no one steady. I don't think that should be a problem."

"I could move in at the end of the month," Casey replied, excited about having a cheaper place to live and, not knowing a soul in New York, the prospect of having a friend. Looking around the cafeteria, Casey saw Zach eyeing the room for a place to sit and eat. He walked toward their table.

"Hey, Daphne, are you drugging them these days or just hooking them up to old Sparky?" Zach teased as he stopped at their table.

"You know what I miss most about surgery, Zach? It's the books you use. All those pretty pictures."

"I guess I'll quit while I'm ahead. Have a nice lunch, doctors." Zach glanced at Casey, then sat down to eat with some of the surgical residents.

"Another typical Neanderthal, male chauvinist surgeon," Casey muttered contemptuously.

"Zach Green?" Daphne shook her head. "No way, honey. That guy's one of the good ones. He's one of the few attendings who didn't hit on me when I was a surgical resident. And he's one of the few who isn't married. He'll teach you more about operating and patient care than ninety percent of the attendings here. He could operate on me anytime. In or out of the OR."

"Maybe I got the wrong impression," Casey admitted with a quizzical glance over to his table.

"Actually, in a way, you're lucky to start out on trauma. The attendings are all good except for Double-oh-seven."

"Double-oh-seven?" asked Casey.

"Larry Gordon. Smooth talker. Good-looking, but his brain and hands have never gotten along well together. You know, Double-oh-seven, Licensed to Kill," Daphne explained.

"Oh, yeah, he was the one dismembered at M and M conference today."

Daphne smiled wistfully. "M and M conference. That brings back memories. Those trauma surgeons are maniacs. They walk into the meeting like best pals and then spend an hour cussing at each other. Mostly it's harmless. Zach Green, Glen Brinkman, and Ron Stewart are all really good surgeons. But the three of them pick on Double-oh-seven. One night after he screwed up three or four cases, Zach started calling him Dr. Mengele and asking if he had any blood relatives who had been tried in Nuremberg."

"I thought Gordon was the section chief."

"He is, but the other three wouldn't want the job anyway. He's good for show time—the press and everything. The trauma program is high-profile, and Double-oh-seven is magic in front of a camera. If a reporter asked Zach an obnoxious question, he would probably tell the guy to kiss his ass—or worse."

"Bad temper?"

"Not really. When he gets mad, it's usually for show. He

just has no political skills, and he has no tolerance for bullshit."

"Arrogant?"

"More confident than arrogant. Very well-developed self-esteem."

"I can tell you're a shrink."

Daphne laughed and tossed her long blond hair onto her other shoulder. "I'll take that as a compliment." She paused for a minute and smiled, noticing that Casey was still gazing at Zach's table. "Interested in the adorable Dr. Green?"

"One of the attendings?" she asked. "Not in a million years."

"Well, darlin', you'd have to take a number," Daphne added.

Casey didn't like the direction of the conversation and looked down at her watch. "I'm supposed to meet my team in the ICU for rounds. Thanks for your generous offer, Daphne. I can't wait to move in. And thanks for the inside scoop on this place. It might have taken me weeks to figure it out on my own."

"So long, Casey. You can come by anytime to check out the place. I'll get you a key made, and we can set a date when you can move in. It will be fun."

5

Every medical specialty has its unsolved problems—
AIDS in internal medicine and brain tumors in neurosurgery, for instance. In trauma surgery, the most common
cause of death is obvious: patients bleed to death. There
are, however, particular injuries that are more difficult to
fix than others.

Almost always fatal, the injury that most interested
Zach was the retrohepatic vena caval laceration. The vena
cava is the major vein that returns blood from the lower
half of the body to the heart. It runs up the right side of the
abdominal cavity, through the diaphragm, and into the
heart. The portion of the inferior vena cava that lies
behind the liver, the retrohepatic portion, is extremely
difficult to expose and control in an operation.

Zach had not fared much better than most surgeons
with holes in the retrohepatic vena cava, and it drove him
crazy. The liver is a large organ, and moving it out of the
way took several minutes, during which the blood loss was
massive. It was nearly impossible to gain control of the
vessel without opening the chest and clamping the vena
cava as it entered the heart. Clamping it resulted in a huge
reduction of blood flow and often caused cardiac arrest.

The problem could be circumvented by placing a shunt into the vena cava to allow the blood to return to the heart. Cloth ties could then be snugged around the cava above and below the injury, and a clamp applied to the other blood vessels supplying the liver. Theoretically, this would prevent any blood from flowing to the damaged blood vessel and the injury could be repaired.

Although this sounded good in theory, in practice, as Zach succinctly taught the residents, it sucked.

Zach considered any injury that whacked ninety-five percent of its victims well worth studying. He was sitting at his chronically cluttered desk with his feet up, pondering the problem, when Glen walked into their suite toward his own office.

"Glen, I have an idea for a different approach to these retrohepatic cava injuries," he called out. "Just call me Wile E. Coyote—Genius."

"How about Wile E. Coyote—Asshole? I have an idea, too, it's called strict gun control," Glen replied as he began to sort through his mail.

Zach got up and walked into Glen's office. "Listen for a minute. What's the reason these patients die?"

"They bleed to death, you schmuck."

"Obviously, dick-breath. You can bleed to death from a ruptured spleen, too. So why don't patients usually die of a ruptured spleen?"

Glen looked up for a second. "Well, I suppose because it's relatively easy either to take it out or to fix it. Even the technically challenged Double-oh-seven manages that operation."

"Exactly! But with the retrohepatic caval injury, there is so much to do even to expose the injury and get a crack at sewing up the hole, the victim ends up bleeding out first. Remember how many times we practiced placing the atriocaval shunts as residents? We probably did fifty dogs. But as fast as we got, it was never good enough."

"So what's this inspiration, and can we get it through the animal research committee?" Glen asked, his interest finally aroused.

Zach leaned over the desk and began. "The crux of the problem is being able to repair the injury in a bloodless field, without the patient dying first."

"All right already, what is this brilliant idea?" Glen asked with a touch of sarcasm. Zach's ideas were creative but usually impractical because of cost or manpower requirements. Zach hated the details of research; he hated the details of anything. Glen had always possessed the better, more practical research mind and could usually tailor Zach's ideas into a workable experiment. Together, the two were quite productive. Each had published more than fifteen papers, mostly in collaboration, in relatively short academic careers.

"How can you ensure a bloodless operative field?" Zach quizzed.

"You can't, unless the patient doesn't have any blood, in which case he is dead, and then you would be doing an autopsy, not an operation."

Zach pulled up the spare chair next to Glen and sat. "Listen, what do neurosurgeons do when they want to clip an aneurysm in an inaccessible part of the brain and they need a bloodless field? What do the heart surgeons do with an aneurysm of the transverse arch of the aorta when they have to clamp the carotid arteries?"

Glen nodded his head as he grasped what Zach was getting at. "Right—they stop the patient's circulation."

The technique was called hypothermic circulatory arrest and was rarely used. The patient was placed on cardiopulmonary bypass just as if he were undergoing an open-heart operation. But there was an important difference. During routine open-heart surgery, the bypass machine pumped blood everywhere but to the heart and lungs. However, during a period of circulatory arrest, the bypass machine was turned off, and no organ, the brain included, received *any* blood flow.

In operations using circulatory arrest, the patient's temperature was lowered to profoundly hypothermic levels, as low as fifteen degrees Centigrade, before all the blood was drained from the patient and his circulation

43

was stopped. In essence, during an operation done with circulatory arrest, the patient was dead. The time limit before organ damage, brain damage in particular, occurred was about one hour.

"But those operations are all done in elective circumstances," Glen argued. "Our trauma patients are already in shock. Most of them are almost dead. Their organs are already behind the eight ball. We don't know if they could tolerate circulatory arrest or for how long."

"That's what we need to find out." Zach smiled. "Admit it, butthead. It's a great idea."

"Yeah, it's got potential," Glen replied. Zach had the imagination of an eight-year-old, with its attendant pluses and minuses. "But hold on. First, we need to find out if an animal in shock can tolerate circulatory arrest and still be neurologically normal. We also have to worry about the anticoagulation in a—"

Zach cut him off. "OK, there is a lot to do. First, we have to get the project approved by the research committee and the animal use board. Assuming we get it through, we'll need more than just you and me. There's a lot of work in this one. Know of any residents interested in working more than the one hundred hours a week they already log?"

"I can think of one who might be interested. She's already spent time in the lab and tells me she wants to do some research here."

"She?" Zach arched his eyebrows.

"Your current obsession."

"You're kidding. That's great!" He hadn't been this excited about a project in a long time. "I think I'll spend an extra half hour on the river tonight," he said. "Who's on call?"

"Ron."

"You rang?" came a voice from the corridor. Ron Stewart's huge frame filled the doorway of the suite. "Look who I found roaming the halls, poking her little nose into everything."

He stepped aside to reveal a petite woman dressed in a black leather jacket, jeans, and black hightops. A mass of auburn curls ringed her face.

"Oh, no, it's Emily," said Zach.

"That joke was tired the first time you said it," retorted Amy Mendoza. She'd made the mistake of admitting she'd done her master's thesis on Emily Dickinson when she'd interviewed Zach for the *New York News* a year ago, and he'd never let her forget it.

"How did you get in here?" Glen asked.

"Your security is for shit. I smiled at the guy, and he let me through. Of course, I have my fake badge with me, just in case."

Ron and Zach rolled their eyes. Amy was a piece of work: a hard-nosed New Yorker, born and bred in the Bronx, with a habit of pestering politicians, celebrities, and other assorted riffraff with just the questions they hoped to avoid. She'd made waves last year by asking a certain senator about his family's Mafia connections—in the middle of his inaugural party.

"I suppose you've missed me," said Zach. "It's been months since you called."

"Yeah, ever notice how Amy never calls unless she wants something?" said Ron. "Last time she took me out to lunch, she got my drawers off before I knew what was happening. Quotes in the paper I *never* thought I'd say, much less see in print, about Simpson, Attenucci, all the bigwigs. I was lucky I had a job after that."

"That piece didn't do you any harm. A little press is always good for raising the old profile," said Amy. "Besides, you guys never call me, so I gotta come after you when something happens."

"What's happened?" asked Glen. "Simpson dipped below the age limit?"

"You haven't heard about these animal rights loonies offing the brain researcher?" Amy asked. "Don't you guys ever come up for air?"

"Yeah, I saw something about it," Zach said. "So?"

"Another researcher just bought it. They shot her down in front of her own house. I'm doing a piece on it. I think it's part of something bigger."

"Oh-ho, another national conspiracy?" Ron said. Amy was always looking for the big exposé that would win her a Pulitzer and get her into a paper like the *New York Times* or the *Washington Post*.

"Possibly. Well, I'm gonna ask around. It's obvious you guys have your heads up your butts. Do you think if the Chinese nuked us, you'd notice?"

Zach snorted. "We'd have to know, we'd be treating all the scorched meat. Here, I'll walk you out. You must be in a rush to go somewhere."

"I can tell when I'm not wanted. Anyway, I have a deadline for a piece. But I'd keep those furs in the closets, boys. It's sick out there, and it's getting sicker by the minute."

She flipped her card onto Zach's desk. "Call me if you do hear anything," she said as she turned and flounced out.

One of the advantages, if it could be called that, of working at a hospital like UHC was that no one ever said, "I thought I had seen everything."

Casey Brenner was surviving her third night of trauma call when her beeper went off. The code "11111" appeared on the digital display, which meant drop everything and sprint to the emergency room.

When she arrived nearly breathless in the trauma bay, the sight of a baby, no more than eight months old, shot in the chest, surrounded by an intern, a second-year resident, and a terrified pediatric resident, all looking to her for direction, made her deeply question her career choice.

"What's going on?" she asked as calmly as she could. She pulled her hair back and rolled up the sleeves of her white—soon to be red—lab coat.

"The mother," Tim Adams hurriedly explained as he pointed to the adjoining bed where an obviously dead woman lay, "was nursing her baby when the boyfriend shot her, the baby, and himself. He blew his brains out. The paramedics didn't even bring him in. The mother died in the ambulance. The baby has a low pressure and is breathing pretty fast."

"Where's Ron?" Casey asked, praying that he was standing right behind her.

"He's in the OR with another gunshot wound. You're the boss."

She quickly examined the infant. The gunshot wound was about an inch and a half from the baby's left nipple. There were no breathing sounds on the left side of the chest, and the veins in the baby's neck were bulging. The pediatrician and the intern had placed two intravenous lines.

"The blood pressure is forty," said the charge nurse anxiously.

"Get me a number ten chest tube, and let's intubate her," Casey directed, her heart pounding.

Tim Adams put a tube into the baby's trachea so they could breathe for her. At the same time, Casey made a small incision in the infant's chest and placed the tube. Only about five cc of blood returned. No significant bleeding in the chest, she thought.

"She just lost her cardiac rhythm, and her blood pressure is gone," yelled the nurse. "It must be tamponade."

"Get me the thoracotomy tray." Casey's tone was calm and assured. She wanted to vomit. She poured some antiseptic on the lifeless child, took a scalpel, and with one four-inch incision was inside her chest. Taking scissors, she opened the pericardium, the sac that held the kiwi-sized heart, and twenty cc's of blood poured out. Casey found a half-centimeter hole in the front of the right ventricle, which appeared tangential to the chamber. There were no other holes. She grabbed a needle holder, a 5'0 proline suture, and in twenty seconds had repaired the heart. "Transfuse fifty cc's of blood, and get the defibrillator," she said as the final knot went down.

The nurse charged the portable unit, and Casey shocked the motionless heart. It began beating irregularly and then fibrillated. "Give five milligrams of lidocaine and a half an ampule of calcium." She shocked it again, and the beat became regular.

"Blood pressure is eighty," called out the nurse.

"Is that normal for a baby? I don't know much pediatrics."

"Yeah, right. That was the best save I've seen since I've been here." Sara Quinlan had been an ER nurse for twelve years.

"Let's get her up to the OR to close the incision," Casey said. She didn't usually drink, but she could have used one now.

An entourage of physicians, nurses, and respiratory therapists propelled the gurney carrying the infant out of the ER and up to the operating room. Once there, the baby was placed on the table and hooked up to numerous monitors while the anesthesiologist whined about not being given enough time to prepare. Casey began to irrigate the orphan's tiny chest with some antibiotic solution before closing it. Ron had finished his case and popped into the room. When he heard the story, he couldn't believe it.

"You sewed up that little shrimp's heart in the ER?" Ron asked as he looked over Casey's shoulder.

"I was lucky. The hole was small, and the kid arrested right in front of us, so she came back quickly."

"Lucky my ass, that's the save of the year."

"Thanks." The modesty was genuine, but everyone in the room realized that Casey possessed an exceptional skill.

"I'll leave you alone to close. You don't need my miserable help."

In the OR lounge, Ron sat and read the newspaper. Bruce Evans, the cardiothoracic fellow, lumbered in and poured a cup of coffee.

"What's all the excitement?"

"An eight-month-old baby got shot in the heart and arrested in the ER."

"What else is new? Another dead kid," Evans responded.

"Dead my ass. That new surgery resident sewed up her heart. She's gonna do fine."

Bruce's face reddened. "What's that girl doing sewing up hearts? That's my job."

Ron looked at him incredulously. "In the first place, we do the trauma around here. If we need your help, we can ask for it. In the second place, what's this *girl* crap? The last time I checked, surgeons sewed with their hands, not their dicks."

Evans ignored him. "Call me politically incorrect, but all these goddamn women should be pediatricians or something. How can you be a surgeon if you waste half your life being a mommy? Surgery is a full-time job." He slugged down his coffee, threw the cup at the basket, missing the mark by more than a foot, and stormed out.

"And pale white boys shouldn't shoot hoops," Ron shot back before he went through the door.

A hospital is a small world, and information rips along the grapevine at the speed of the fastest computer. By the next day, Casey Brenner's miraculous save was common knowledge.

6

Theodore Simpson was not a happy man. The chief of surgery at UHC, a specialist in cardiac surgery, did not enjoy being screamed at by Chuck Phillips, one of the cardiologists who regularly referred patients to him.

"Listen, Ted," Phillips droned, "if you can't get these cases on the schedule this week, I will find someone who can. I am getting sick and tired of hearing this bullshit about not enough resources. The guys up at Columbia would love to take on more open-heart surgery."

"Chuck, this is a trauma center, and summer is always the worst time for us. OR, the intensive-care unit— everything is backed up."

"Ted, if you want to operate on a bunch of scumbags, most of whom deserved to get shot or stabbed in the first place, then by all means do so. I'll just send my patients somewhere that wants to care for productive human beings."

Simpson bit his tongue. He wanted to tell the bastard off but needed his group's referrals. "Chuck, somehow I will find a spot for them this week," Simpson replied in a controlled voice.

"All right, we'll be talking."

The competition for operating time and intensive-care unit beds was becoming a nightmare. The resources at UHC were always tight, but since it had been designated a Level One trauma center two years ago, the situation had deteriorated. Many hospitals in Manhattan were closing down beds, but at UHC there were never enough. Caring for more than two thousand trauma victims each year meant that there was a lot of open-heart surgery that Simpson could no longer schedule. And at more than five thousand dollars for each operation, he was losing a lot of money. To make matters worse, the revision in Medicare reimbursement had cut the fees for his patients over sixty-five—a large part of his practice—by forty percent. Simpson was desperate. He was a gifted heart surgeon and made almost a million dollars a year, but he was a horrible investor and spent almost as much as he made. Not even his wife had any idea how tenuous their financial picture had become. There was no way he would be able to retire in five years unless he could significantly increase the amount of surgery he did.

He had fought against making UHC a trauma center, realizing long ago what would happen. However, since his appointment as chief of surgery, he had to pretend that trauma was important to the hospital. Yet there was still hope. He was fairly certain that the hospital would build two more rooms dedicated to open-heart surgery.

Simpson leaned back in his soft leather recliner and lit a cigarette. He looked every one of his fifty-nine years. He was balding, and his jowled face was heavily lined, the aging process undoubtedly accelerated by his two-pack-a-day addiction. He was more than six feet tall and was chronically hunched, the result of years spent leaning over an operating table.

He quickly stubbed out his cigarette in an ashtray he kept in his desk drawer when his secretary, Grace, walked in. The remaining smoke from his lungs wafted out of his mouth. He tried not to be seen smoking—a bad image for a heart surgeon—but almost no one who was acquainted with him was fooled by the charade.

"Dr. Simpson, you have your appointment with Ms. Attenucci."

"Come in, Dr. Simpson. Ms. Attenucci will see you right away." A receptionist led the chief of surgery through a set of paneled oak double doors into the office of Lenore Attenucci, the chief executive officer of UHC.

Attenucci got up from behind her desk and extended her hand. She was an imposing figure. Rail-thin, she had straight, short blond hair that was beginning to gray. Pads in her Paul Stuart suit broadened her shoulders. Other than an aquiline nose, her facial features were plain. She neither looked nor acted flashy. But she was effective. When she began at UHC twenty-five years earlier, she was twenty years old and a new nursing graduate with ambitions. Few would have dreamed she could become the CEO. The hospital had paid for her B.A. in marketing, and a senior administrator had suggested she get her M.B.A. It took her four and a half years of night school, but at age twenty-nine she got an M.B.A. from Columbia and worked her way up from there. Her uncanny marketing skills made UHC profitable. While many other hospitals were closing beds, UHC was always full and thriving.

"Good to see you, Ted. It's been a while." She had known Simpson since she was a nursing student.

"Same here, Lenore," Simpson said as they both took their seats. He unbuttoned his double-breasted linen suit and leaned back comfortably.

She glanced at her desk, shuffled a few papers, then looked right at him. "I just wanted to tell you that the board and I have decided against building the additional heart rooms. Actually, we're going to have to cut back open-heart to two rooms on Tuesdays and Thursdays." She braced for the explosion.

"You can't do that." He raised his voice but didn't yell, managing to keep his composure.

"I'm really sorry, Ted, but I think we need to focus our resources on outpatient surgery and preventive programs. That's where the money is going to be. The way the reimbursement has been going for hearts, we'll be lucky to break even in a few years."

"I have brought in millions for this hospital. As well as prestige."

"You've also made millions for yourself. Open-heart isn't a great moneymaker for us anymore. Medicare has ratcheted down the DRG by thirty percent. Also, I hate to mention it, but your statistics weren't as good over the past two years."

"Goddamn it, Lenore!" Simpson shouted, starting to lose control. "I had a two-point-three-percent mortality rate last year!"

She pulled a folder from a pile on her desk, opened it, and took out a paper. "Columbia was less than one percent."

"You know those numbers aren't statistically significant, and besides, I do the hardest cases. The redo-redo cases," he screamed, pounding his fist on the desk.

"We both know that, Ted, but John Q. Public figures less than one percent beats more than two percent. I wouldn't get so exercised. You still have thirteen spots each week plus emergencies. We just don't have any more operating time."

"Jesus Christ, if we just stopped doing all of those trauma cases, I'd have all the operating time I need. That crap loses tons of money for the hospital."

She pushed back in her chair and swiveled around. It wasn't right, but she was enjoying this. "Technically, that's true. But I did a marketing survey last year. The point was to figure out what makes people choose a particular hospital. Well, guess what? Trauma is the most recognizable program in this hospital. People know we're good at it. There have been thirteen newspaper pieces, four television spots, and that *New York* magazine article—all in the last eighteen months. It's millions of dollars of free advertising. If you do the math, the money we lose from trauma is more than recouped by the patients who choose us because of the publicity."

"Well, what the hell I am I supposed to do?"

"Ted, you can still do plenty of operations. I just don't think it's in the hospital's interest to expand open-heart. I mean, how much money do you need?"

Simpson got up and pointed his finger at Attenucci. "That's none of your business."

"Well, you're always free to make arrangements at another hospital."

"We both know that's not possible." He turned and walked out the door.

Attenucci's decision was based strictly on the numbers and the good of the hospital. The irony, however, was inescapable. Twenty years ago, he had screwed her, and now she could return the favor.

Simpson returned to his office, shut the door, and lit a cigarette. Ten years ago, he definitely could have gone uptown to several other hospitals, but not now. That bitch Attenucci thought she had him. Who did she think she was fucking with?

He picked up his intercom and buzzed Grace. "Get me Forrest Wells."

7

Glen, Casey, and Zach met in the surgical library on
Thursday afternoon. Casey, who had been on call the
previous night, was exhausted and felt as if she were going
to collapse. Still, she was excited to get a chance to work
on an innovative, potentially important project. She
hoped Zach had forgotten their initial exchange. She'd
made rounds with him since then, and he had been a
complete gentleman, just as Daphne had predicted.

"Casey, are you sure you can handle all this work?"
Zach asked as he noticed her tired eyes and smelled a hint
of the perfume she had probably put on the day before.
They were seated around the conference table in comfortable leather-backed chairs. Zach was trying to concentrate
on the research, but it was difficult.

"I'm sure I can manage, Dr. Green," Casey replied
confidently. She studied him. He was about five-feet-ten,
had a perpetual five o'clock shadow, and was imperfectly
handsome. He had short-cropped hair, almost a buzzcut,
and looked quite muscular in his scrubs.

"Please just call me Zach."

"Fine, Zach. I think I can manage around ten or fifteen
hours a week."

55

"The initial question we need to ask is: Can a patient already in shock tolerate deep hypothermic arrest without suffering brain damage? Essentially, the patient will be in a state of suspended animation," Glen began. "There's no point in saving the body and ending up with a moron. There are enough gynecologists in the world."

"We need to design the experiment to simulate a real injury. So we subject the animals to varying periods of shock, after which we put them on bypass, cool them down, and do the circulatory arrest, again using varying lengths of time. Simple," Zach said, smiling at Casey.

"What animal should we use?" Casey asked.

"For an experiment like this, pigs or dogs," Zach answered.

"I'd use dogs, Zach. Remember all the trouble we had with the pigs last year? They don't tolerate the shock as well as dogs." Glen made a notation on a pad.

"You're right. Half of them went into pulmonary edema," Zach added.

"But the tougher question is: Experimentally, how do we look at the effects of shock and hypothermic arrest on the brain of a dog?" Glen asked.

Casey interjected. "That's simple enough. I did some research in animal intelligence as an undergraduate. There are lots of methods to evaluate canine intelligence." She was pleased to be able to contribute. "There are a couple of scoring systems we can use to test cognitive function before and after the shock and hypothermic arrest."

"Great. That's what we'll do first. If the dogs get stupid, there's no use in continuing," Zach concluded.

"OK, so we'll get a baseline intelligence test on each animal, then do the experiment. If there are no major changes in Rover's brain, we may have something. We also need to look at the postmortem brains under the microscope. There may be some subtle changes that we can't measure by a subjective intelligence test," Glen added.

Both Zach and Casey nodded in agreement. "How many animals should we use?" Casey asked.

Glen thought for a minute. "We'll need at least twenty

dogs, and we'll vary the length of time that we shock and circulatory-arrest them. I'll write up the research proposal. We shouldn't have much trouble getting it through the research committee, although I heard the hospital administration had to appoint a layperson to it. These animal rights groups are putting on a lot of heat."

"Now we have to explain everything we do to some idiot who probably never even took college biology? They're making research impossible. A fucking dog costs six hundred dollars! We used to get them from the pound for nothing." Zach exploded.

"You must admit, a lot of the animal research is unnecessary," Casey interjected. "I just recently read about a project where the researchers were shooting cats in the head to look at head trauma."

Glen nodded. "Yeah, I read about that experiment, and if you look at the protocol, it was good research. The investigator was a neurosurgeon who watched hundreds of men die from their head injuries during the Vietnam war. He was committed as hell. Some woman turned the guy in for supposedly not anesthetizing the cats, but when one of those pricks from *60 Minutes* got a hold of her, she recanted the whole story. The problem is that most of these people don't understand science or how advances are made in medicine. A small, insignificant finding may lead another worker to a major breakthrough."

"That's not the only example," Casey returned.

"You're right, Casey, I'll admit there is plenty of bad research, and with that, some bad researchers." Glen could always see both sides. He taught the medical students about the ethics of animal use in research and took the side of the animal rights people to play devil's advocate.

"But those guys want everyone to believe that most or all of the research is bad and unnecessary. And once you let those assholes start butting in, where's it going to stop?" retorted Zach, for whom there was only one side.

"The researchers need to police themselves, Zach. We try to do only good stuff, everyone needs to."

"Police?" Zach groaned. "There's no crime, Glen. We're doing this to help save people's lives. Who really gives a shit about dogs and pigs?"

"Mother pigs and dogs," Casey said softly.

Zach looked at her and grinned. "Are you a vegetarian?"

"No," admitted Casey.

He pointed to her pocketbook. "Is that leather?"

She nodded her head yes.

"Then spare me from the Bugs Bunny, Porky Pig, Woody-fucking-Woodpecker anthropomorphic bullshit."

"As you can already tell, Casey, Zach is one of the deep thinkers of our generation," Glen said.

"Don't make me into Dr. Evil." Zach loosened his tie.

"You know how strongly I feel about the need for animal research. We just need to keep what we do in perspective," insisted Glen.

Zach got up and pushed in his chair. "Fine. You two can obsess over the ethics of our little project in your spare time. I'd rather do something more stimulating and less intellectually taxing—like watch Moe poke out Curly's eyes. I'm going back to my office to look at a few videos."

Casey looked at Glen. "He watches the Three Stooges?"

"What's wrong with the Three Stooges?" Zach asked.

She thought for a moment. "Other than being violent and infantile?"

"I'm a trauma surgeon. If it weren't for violent and infantile behavior, I'd have my thumb up my ass."

"I guess you're right about that, Zach," Casey said. She broke into a broad smile and laughed.

"Casey, can you do a computer search and get us all the references?" Zach asked before he left.

"I'll have it by Monday."

"When do we strike again?" Sorrentino asked.

"He has it planned in a couple days. The fake ID cards are ready," Cecile responded.

Palmer was sullen; he wasn't to be part of the next

attack. "So far, we've accomplished nothing. Virtually no labs have closed," he said flatly.

"Be patient, Palmer. We've just begun. Remember what he told us. There are three stages," Sorrentino replied, touching his hand. She pointed her 9mm Ruger at a vase on a table in her apartment and pulled the trigger of the empty gun. "Click," she whispered.

"She's right, Palmer. We're about to make a much bigger impression," Cecile said proudly. The next target was her idea.

8

July 19

Three wasn't always a lucky number.

The animal care facility at Manhattan Medical College had better-equipped operating rooms than many hospitals. More than two thousand surgeons had learned to perform laparoscopic operations at courses sponsored by MMC. Over a period of just five years, the number of patients who required an old-fashioned gallbladder incision had been reduced by ninety percent. Now, with a camera inside the belly and a few tiny nicks in the skin, a gallbladder could be removed and the patient discharged on the same day. The pain was minimal, and most patients were back at work after a week.

As the variety of operations that could be done through the laparoscope grew, so did the business of Creative Surgical Approaches Inc. Tom Howard was a new vice president of CSA. Last year, as a sales representative, he sold more than thirteen million dollars of laparoscopic instruments to Manhattan hospitals, earning close to a quarter of a million dollars for himself. Other companies made laparoscopic instruments, but CSA had a sixty-three-percent market share. Manhattan Medical College used CSA instruments exclusively. In return for the one-

60

point-nine million dollars a year in business, CSA refurbished the MMC animal operating facilities and paid them a percentage of the fees it charged doctors to take their courses. The money was used by the medical school to fund worthy research projects.

The symbiotic relationship between the MMC and CSA had been featured in many investigative journalistic reports, which focused mainly on the ethics of a medical school accepting money from a company with which it did business. CSA's competition labeled the arrangement a "kickback," but since the money the school received was used exclusively to fund research, public outrage was limited.

ABP, on the other hand, was outraged that more than three thousand pigs a year were used so that doctors could practice these new operations.

"That doesn't look too hard," Gail Rich said.

"We'll see," replied Sam Davenport. Along with a dozen other visiting surgeons, Rich and Davenport had just finished watching a video of a laparoscopic hernia repair. They were part of a group learning some new techniques to repair hernias over the next two days. Dr. Rich was a surgeon from Terre Haute, Indiana, and Dr. Davenport was from South Dakota.

"I guess we're partners," said Rich, looking at the group assignments. She was thirty-four years old and had been in practice only two years. Her sweet smile and soft voice fit her petite five-foot frame. Gail's patients loved her. She had learned to do laparoscopic gallbladders as a resident but had continued to operate on hernias using the traditional method. Since surgical groups in Terre Haute had begun fixing hernias through the laparoscope, her partners figured that they had better offer the procedure, too. Gail was excited about learning a new technique, and getting out of town provided a much-needed break.

"Try not to show me up too badly," Davenport requested as they moved from the conference room to the operating suite. "I wasn't brought up as a Nintendo surgeon like you kids were." Actually, for a seventy-seven-year-old, Sam Davenport was extraordinary. He was still a fine surgeon, although he had stopped doing really long operations because he couldn't take the four or five hours of standing anymore. Still, he had the intellectual curiosity of a twenty-year-old and had kept up with modern medicine and surgery. While most of the other surgeons he had trained with were retired or dead, he just kept on going. He had already performed more than three hundred laparoscopic cholecystectomies and hadn't started until he was almost seventy.

"This is some setup they have here. It's gorgeous," Gail said as they put on gowns before beginning.

"Better than a lot of hospital ORs," Davenport agreed.

"I'm glad you like it," responded Tom Howard, who had already changed into scrubs. "You're Dr. Rich," he said, extending his hand. "And Dr. Davenport. Your reputation precedes you."

Davenport shrugged his shoulders. "I'm just trying to keep up like everyone else."

Rich glanced at the setup. Two doctors were assigned to each operating table. The room had eight identical bays, every one complete with an electric operating table, a tray with every conceivable laparoscopic instrument—all made by CSA—and the newest generation of laparoscopic cameras and video monitors. In addition, CSA provided technicians to assist. The techs had been trained at CSA's main corporate headquarters in Tampa, Florida, and each one had practiced the operation hundreds of times. Initially, they were usually better at doing the procedure than the surgeons.

"I can't wait to get started," Rich said as she approached a pig that had already been anesthetized.

"Why don't you go first, Dr. Rich?" Howard said. "Dr. Davenport will assist you, and then you can assist him on the other side. After that, we'll break for lunch."

Rich went ahead, fumbling a bit but able to patch the hernia defect in about twenty minutes. She was pleased and could see that, with more practice, this method would be an improvement over the traditional operation. "The anatomy is a little confusing doing it this way," Rich said as she switched to assistant and Dr. Davenport began the other side.

"I know what you mean," Davenport replied. Deftly, he began to dissect out the hernia defect with almost no help. Within a few minutes, he was done.

"Hey, I thought you hadn't done this before," said Rich.

"Pretty slick, Dr. Davenport," Howard added.

"Not bad for an old geezer, huh?" Davenport replied.

"You two could probably skip the second pig," Howard said as he helped a technician put the pig, which had just been euthanized, into a bag for disposal. In less than two hours, both surgeons had successfully completed their first surgeries using the new technique.

"Oh, no. I want as much practice as I can get before I try this on my own patients," replied Gail Rich, shaking her head. Although Davenport had performed the operation smoothly and was reasonably confident he could repeat it without complication, he agreed with Gail. It would be better to get more experience with the pigs before moving on to human hernias.

"Well, then, you'll get another pig to practice on this afternoon. We'll be done by three o'clock. I hope you'll both join me for dinner tonight. I've gone ahead and made reservations at the Four Seasons." Howard had a special interest in these two surgeons. Each of them worked at a hospital that didn't use CSA instruments. The CSA sales reps from their respective cities had called and asked that he take good care of them. Howard was usually able to snag some business during these courses. Between the impressive facilities and some wining and dining, most surgeons would go back and ask their hospitals to buy CSA instruments.

"I'm free," Rich said as she took off her cover gown.

"Me, too," added Davenport gamely.

Cecile Morgan and Theresa Sorrentino looked like medical students. They were dressed in scrubs underneath white MMC lab coats and carried knapsacks. Their knapsacks, however, didn't contain any books or stethoscopes.

A security guard was posted at the beginning of the corridor that led to the animal care facility. There had been a few threats in the past from animal rights groups, and with millions of dollars' worth of equipment on the premises, the dean didn't want to take any chances.

"What do you want?" the guard asked as they approached his desk.

"We're doing our surgery subinternship, and our attending said we could go watch some animal surgery," Sorrentino answered.

"He said we might even get to do some work," added Cecile, forcing an enthusiastic smile.

"Ya gotta learn sometime," replied the guard. "Go on down."

Cecile and Sorrentino slipped into the operating suite just as the first group of pigs were carted off to the incinerator.

"I think we've had a productive morning. Let's break for lunch, while we re-pig," Howard said, now standing at a podium to address the whole group of visiting doctors. While lunch was being served in the adjacent conference room, the technicians would bring another eight pigs up from the livestock pavilion where they were kept. Because of the large number of courses they taught, the pavilion, which was really a two-thousand-square-foot mini-farm, always housed at least thirty animals.

Gail Rich chuckled. *"Re-pig,* there's a new verb."

Taking Howard's comment as their cue, Sorrentino and Cecile swiftly pulled black elastic masks over their faces, drew silenced 9mm semiautomatic pistols out of their packs, and moved to the center of the room.

"We are members of an army of liberation," Cecile barked as she stepped up to the podium and jammed her gun into Howard's temple.

Initially, the students stood stunned and silent. Then Gail Rich let out a garbled scream as she realized what was happening, and a technician reflexively lunged at Sorrentino, who stood a couple of feet from him. She jumped back a step and put a bullet right through the middle of his chest. Staggering, he knocked over an operating table and fell to the floor. Though surrounded by doctors, he died in seconds. "Any other heroes?" Sorrentino shouted in an eerily controlled manner as she scanned the room with her pistol.

"These animals are treated very well. We have excellent facilities to house them while they are in our care, and I give you my word, they never feel a thing!" Howard said, praying that his skills as a salesman could defuse the situation.

Cecile shoved the barrel of her gun harder into his temple. "Treated well? Every one of those animals is murdered so that you bastards can hone your skills at dismemberment before discarding their carcasses in a furnace."

"The animals are anesthetized. They don't feel anything," Howard said.

"That's so considerate of you." She marched him off the podium. "Lie down on that table," Cecile commanded.

"What?"

She pushed him harder. "Get on the table."

"Please," he begged. "Don't do this." Prodded by the gun, he climbed onto the operating table.

Sorrentino had herded the other dozen or so people into the corner of the room near the table on which Howard lay so she could easily cover them. Cecile put her gun in the pocket of her lab coat and secured Howard's arms and legs to the table.

"Don't, please don't!" Howard screamed.

Cecile drew up twenty cc's of curare, the drug used to paralyze the animals during the time they were anesthetized.

"She's going to . . ." Gail Rich grabbed at Davenport's arm.

"Shh," Davenport whispered, "unless you want to end up like him."

Cecile injected the curare into Howard, and within a minute, he became motionless. He was paralyzed, unable to move or breathe, but remained completely awake.

"Well, Mr. Howard, you'll only be conscious, and alive, for another couple minutes, and since you like operations so much, I'd better get going." Cecile grabbed a scalpel and slit open Howard's abdomen. Then, with one ferocious slice, she reached into his abdominal cavity, pulled out half his intestines, and held them up so he would see them. "I'll bet that hurts," she taunted.

It was Howard's last memory.

Cecile turned to the captive audience. "Who's next?"

Sam Davenport, who was closest to Sorrentino, figured that they weren't going to let anyone escape with their lives. He hoped that if he attacked, the others would react quickly. Impulsively, he threw himself at Sorrentino. As his hand smacked the barrel of her gun, Sorrentino got off a single round, hitting Davenport in the shoulder. Fortunately, two of the doctors followed Davenport's lead and pounced on her. As she struggled with the three men, Sorrentino shot herself in the thigh and lost control of the gun as it skidded toward Cecile.

Cecile instantly reached into the lab coat for her own gun, but her hands were slick from Howard's blood. Her weapon flew to the floor, coming to rest beside Sorrentino's. Holding his shoulder, Davenport shoved Gail Rich and the other participants through the door to the conference room. By the time Cecile got a grip on both weapons and could fire, everyone was safely locked in the other room. Sorrentino staggered toward Cecile.

"Help me, I can't run," Sorrentino demanded. She moved toward Cecile for support. Sorrentino was weak from blood loss and fading. Cecile knew it would only be moments before they notified security. She wouldn't be able to escape with Sorrentino slowing her down. But if she left her behind and Sorrentino lived, there was a chance she might talk to the FBI to save herself. In a split second, Cecile emptied the remains of her 9mm clip into

Sorrentino's chest. Pulling off her mask, she strode out the door and back toward the security guard.

"Get some practice in, Doctor?" he asked.

"A little," Cecile answered.

"You've got some animal blood on your hands, Doctor," he cautioned as the phone began to ring and she disappeared out the main exit.

"I agree," she said as she disappeared out the main exit.

Three retaliations complete—three warnings to stop the cruelty. Cecile Morgan savored the look of horror in the eyes of that eviscerated bastard. She doubted that four killings would be enough to make that bitch at the NIH pay attention, and truthfully, some small part of her hoped they wouldn't stop. For years, she had protested against the inhumane treatment of animals with virtually no success. Her sense of helplessness in the face of such obvious injustice was overwhelming. Now everything had changed. With the initial attack on James Scott, she had tasted blood; for the first time, she clearly understood how sweet revenge could be. Tara McVey, Tom Howard, and the technician were't enough to satisfy her desires. The ABP had so much to do.

Theresa Sorrentino had been a mentor—she'd been trained in the military and had shown Cecile how to load, carry, and fire a weapon. The two women had spent countless hours planning each attack—who would lead, who would follow. She had admired Sorrentino's knowledge of weaponry, but she was never certain that Sorrentino's commitment to ABP matched her own. Cecile didn't regret eliminating her—it was a necessary loss, and she'd gotten the training she needed. Cecile was ready to lead; her apprenticeship was over.

Ed Palmer had been the third member of their team on the McVey assassination. Cecile liked working with him. He was dedicated to their cause yet happy to let the women lead the attacks. His physical stature and upper-body strength made him an asset, but they hadn't included

him in the attack at MMC because he was in his forties,
too old to pass for a medical student. Cecile knew that she
could count on Ed to cover her back on future missions.
Besides, she had been worried that at some point, his
relationship with Sorrentino might jeopardize the mission.

Pumped with adrenaline, she agilely climbed the three
flights of stairs to her studio apartment and unlocked the
door. The small room was sparsely furnished with a bed, a
small dresser, and a chair. The room's stark interior was
lit by a single window.

Cecile was greeted by her closest friend, Otto. Otto was
a large dog of uncertain breed, most likely German
shepherd and Staffordshire terrier. He lurched toward
Cecile, licking her face. The dog was somewhat oafish,
weighing more than one hundred pounds, but he was
unerringly gentle with Cecile. She opened the small refrig-
erator and unwrapped some hamburger meat she had
cooked yesterday. She chopped it up and placed it in a
wooden bowl on the floor. Otto devoured the meal,
unaware that several weeks ago his supper was walking on
four legs on a cattle farm. Though Cecile was a strict
vegetarian and hadn't eaten meat in more than twenty
years, she recognized that dogs, unlike humans, were
natural carnivores. Cecile ate a small salad and drank
some mineral water. When she finished eating, she put her
and Otto's bowls into a sink already overflowing with
unwashed dishes.

After taking Otto out for a walk, Cecile undressed and
crawled into bed. She looked down at Otto and considered
what an exquisite friend he was. Cecile wasn't going to
allow Otto or any other animal to continue to be ex-
ploited. She was going to make it stop.

9

NIH, Bethesda, Maryland
July 20

"My God! That's three attacks in less than two weeks, Mr. Mason. And the media is onto this now. I was on the phone all morning with the press. Someone must have told them I've been getting these letters," Gabrielle said anxiously. "Now that it's out in the papers, other groups may start getting similar ideas. Any leads from the attack at MMC?"

"Actually, yes. The dead woman was named Theresa Sorrentino. Her parents are both dead, and she has one brother who tells us she was quite smart but hadn't been right since high school," Mason said. "We had her fingerprints in the system because she joined the Army when she was nineteen and served for six years. She was good with explosives—had some special weapons training but couldn't make the grade because her psychiatric evaluations were weak. Eventually she left. Her brother didn't have a current address for her, hadn't spoken to her in years. We're still running a background check, but right now it looks like she was living under another identity. There's an image from one of the security cameras of the other woman dressed in a lab coat. It only catches the back of her head and a small portion of her face, but the security guard and the doctors are certain she's the other assailant."

"Any idea who she is?"

Mason shook his head. "She'll be all over the media by tomorrow, along with an old photo of Theresa Sorrentino that her brother provided. Maybe someone will recognize them."

"What are the chances?"

He frowned and ignored the question. "How do you think the research community will react?"

"It depends. I'm afraid a number of labs will close immediately. But most of them will stick it out, at least for now. Most people will figure 'they won't get me,' and keep working. Sort of like an airplane crash or getting hit by lightning."

"If it continues or escalates?"

"Then I see a major change in the way scientists will study certain disease processes." She thought about her children and wished, as she often did, that she could spend more time with them. Her seventeen-year-old daughter, Brooke, was in a summer program at the Bronx High School of Science. She dreamed of going to medical school and finding a cure for AIDS. Gabby wondered what the world would be like for her. Her two sons, Timothy and Paul, were also showing a flair for academics. What if she were next on ABP's list?

"My research is mostly epidemiology, but if I were doing animal stuff, I know I would stop. No job is worth dying for. It's occurred to me that I might be a target, too, since I'm the one getting the letters."

"I've thought of that. In fact, we've had plainclothes agents watching the whole complex here ever since you got the first letter."

Gabrielle was surprised. "Shouldn't you have told me and the rest of the staff, or at least the supervisors? They may be in danger, too, and it seems like they should know."

"We don't want anyone getting hysterical. Everyone

needs to continue behaving exactly as they have been—at least for now. We've put agents all over the place, so if anything unusual is spotted, we'll be onto it immediately."

Gabrielle nodded, deep in thought. "Even if no one else is killed, these people have already won a big victory. Most labs are adding security, including guards, alarms, and even weapons. That will drive the cost of the research up and allow for less of it. If they catch these lunatics tomorrow, the research community will still feel the effects for years to come. Even though most biological research in general doesn't lead to a demonstrable advance in health, there are things we will never know without the use of animals."

She sat in her chair and swiveled it to face the agent. "What exactly is the FBI doing to stop these terrorists, Mr. Mason?"

He pulled out a notepad and flipped through it. "As of today, we have ten agents investigating, and they have already interviewed the top personnel in more than a hundred groups. There have been a lot of suggestions as to who it could be—everybody has an opinion, and we're following up every lead. Unfortunately, other than the woman who was killed at the medical school, we have no physical evidence. We combed the place for hair, skin, prints, anything off the other woman, but got nothing. It was complicated because Howard's blood was splashed everywhere."

Gabrielle winced. "So no real clues."

"Nothing yet, but I'm going to talk to my boss this afternoon about putting more agents on it. Also, even though the media's been all over this story, I want us to put out an alert to every laboratory—including the text of the ABP's threats."

Norton nodded. "Does the president know what's going on?"

"I'm not sure," Mason replied. "He knows, but the body count is still too low for him to make a public statement."

"Give it time, Mr. Mason."

Mason left, and Gabrielle went to her window. Plainclothes agents everywhere. Who were they? It could be that man crushing out a cigarette on the sidewalk, the woman hurrying out of an adjacent building. Any stranger out there could be an agent—or a member of the ABP, for that matter. *I can't obsess on this, or I'll never get anything done,* she thought. She went to her desk and picked up a stack of proposals waiting for her approval, forcing herself to put the matter out of her mind for the time being.

"I still think it's a few fruitcakes." James Garrow threw his feet up on his desk and chomped into an apple. He was the special agent in charge of terrorist activities in the Northeast. Garrow had a photographic memory and a cynicism that belied his thirty-nine years. Since rounding up the World Trade Center gang in relatively short order, he was very sure of himself.

"I don't think so, Jimmy. Three hits in a short period of time. They're pretty organized," said Mason.

"Attacks in the past haven't been clustered like this or directed at the scientists themselves. No one has actually been murdered up until now. It makes sense: start killing off doctors and lab techs, and after a short time, they're going to start thinking, fuck this, it's not worth it. Threats alone have already worked in some places. The chairman of the department of surgery at Cal-Irvine had a huge animal lab until he got a message that said, 'Dear Doctor: Close your lab, or we're going to kill you and your family.' It isn't like these doctors and scientists can't do some other kind of work."

"Even so, I'd imagine it would take at least a twelve-month uninterrupted siege on the scientific community before this group could absolutely put an end to animal research. To plan and coordinate an operation like that would take a huge amount of discipline, control, and funding," Garrow said to his younger associate. "These assholes don't seem to have that kind of organization. They already fucked up once, losing a comrade. They will fuck up again soon, and when they do, we'll be there."

Of the two hundred agents he commanded, Mason was

his favorite. Garrow had never seen a better investigator, and best of all, since he was unencumbered by a wife and family, Mason's time was the Bureau's time.

Mason flipped through his notebook. "PETA took in more than fifty million dollars last year, Animals International around twenty million, CARE about ten million. We have always suspected a relationship between the Animal Liberation Front, which has vandalized a number of laboratories, and one of these fund-raising organizations. The leaders of some large, well-known, supposedly nonviolent groups deny any complicity in the illegal stuff, but they usually don't disavow the violence explicitly."

Garrow chucked his apple into the garbage pail and took his feet off the desk. "I haven't even heard of half these crazies. Guess I'm spending too much time worrying about the towel heads and Allah."

Mason closed his notebook and pulled his chair closer to Garrow. "What if, as the ABP threatens, this is just the beginning? What if we start seeing copycats? What if every imbecile who thinks that dogs should have the right to vote starts getting into the fray?"

"Now, now, Mason, let's not be judgmental. Our job is to fight crime, not to impose our ideology on our fellow Americans."

Mason shook his head. "You're not taking me seriously."

"I take you very seriously. And so does the director, whom I have been on the phone with every day since the first attack in Vermont. I realize that there have been dozens of criminal acts against laboratories, yet there has never been a concerted, strategic attack on the entire institution of animal research."

"Until now," Mason insisted.

"Even if I accept your premise that the ABP has it in their heads to stop animal research completely, it will take considerable financial resources and professional expertise to accomplish it without getting caught. Their evil souls may be willing, but their tactical and strategic flesh is weak."

"You're not listening. I told you how much money these groups bring in from donations."

"That's true, but it would still be tough to divert enough money from PETA or Animals International or CARE's legitimate functions and not arouse a lot of suspicion. If a couple of hundred animal shelters stop getting their checks, a lot of people are going to ask questions, don't you think?"

"I agree," Mason admitted.

"From what we've seen so far, this could be a limited campaign by a few guys who've gone off the deep end."

"It's possible," Mason conceded.

"So let's not jump the gun on your theory just yet."

"Listen, I hope I'm wrong."

"No, you don't. You hate being wrong as much as I do. How about this? If I'm wrong, I'll buy us a couple of Kobe steaks to mark our deep respect for the animal rights movement."

Mason laughed. "I don't think eating steaks is what those people would have in mind."

"Do you know what a Kobe steak is?"

"No idea."

"It's a Japanese delicacy. They feed the cow a diet of special grain and beer and massage it every day, so by the time they slaughter it, the meat is so soft you can literally cut it with a fork. Can you imagine? Beer and a massage every day. I should be so lucky."

"How did you get to be such an asshole in just thirty-nine years?"

"My parents never got me a puppy. Look, go ahead and continue checking out your theories. But I don't want to hear about it until you have more to go on. I'm up to here with the real world," said Garrow, drawing his hand across his neck. "Every fucking disadvantaged group in the world is trying to get enough weapons-grade plutonium to blow up a few square blocks of Manhattan."

"If I'm right, I'm gonna need a lot of help. I think I'll need more agents on this."

"Beyond those guys you've got at NIH and the other

ten? I still don't know how you convinced me you needed that many," Garrow said.

"This Gabrielle Norton is getting all the letters. She seems to be a real focus for the ABP. I think it makes sense to cover our bases there. An incident at the NIH couldn't make anyone in the Oval Office too happy."

"Yeah, but the question is, would these fanatics go big-time like that?"

"Who knows? The MMC lab had a lot of people in it that day. They might be nuts enough to try something more ambitious."

"And Norton doesn't have any idea who this might be?" Garrow asked.

"She's been bombarded by zealots for years and wouldn't put it past any of them. She seems to be a pretty cool customer, the type that doesn't buckle under pressure," Mason said.

"Good. She may need her strength before this is all over."

75

10

Dr. Martin Anders, professor of physiology and chairman of the CHUA committee, called the meeting to order. Glen and Zach were both present to answer any questions about their project.

The Committee for the Humane Use of Animals met every other Friday. Its function was to ensure that animals used in research would be subjected to as little discomfort as possible. Any procedure that might cause pain to the animal needed to be done with anesthesia. If an experiment left the animal alive, provisions to ensure the least amount of postoperative discomfort were obligatory. The committee served a useful protective function, although researchers like Zach, who would have taken those measures anyway, resented the added bureaucracy.

The committee members included faculty from both the clinical and basic science departments, as well as a veterinarian who supervised the animal care laboratory. The veterinarian made certain that the animals used in experiments were healthy and well fed. After the experiment was complete, the animals were painlessly euthanized. In addition to the faculty members, a layperson from the community was included on the committee, a concession to pressure from animal rights groups.

Susan Holmes was UHC's concession to the animal rights lobby. She worked for the city as a social worker and held a master's degree in sociology, which most researchers considered odd qualifications for this committee. She was an attractive woman who presented herself well. She'd been on the committee for less than a month, but her dedication was obvious. Although she had no formal training in the sciences, she was an avid reader and prided herself on coming to the sessions well prepared.

"I've read the proposal. It appears reasonable and potentially important," Dr. Anders began. "I only have a couple of questions for the doctors. First, are you convinced that you can extrapolate the results of canine cognitive testing to humans?"

"Marty, you know that we can never be absolutely certain that two different species will perform similarly," Zach responded, wishing Casey, who was busy in the operating room, were present to field the psychology questions. "But I can guarantee you that no one is going to try this on a human until we have a firm grasp on its cerebral effects."

Holmes politely raised her hand. "I agree with Dr. Anders. It's naive to think you can compare human and dog brains."

"Obviously they're not the same, but we think the comparison will be valid," Glen returned. The other doctors around the table murmured their agreement.

Holmes rose from her seat. "Excuse me, but am I the only one here who fails to see the need for this line of investigation?" She had carefully reviewed the bibliography. "Hypothermic circulatory arrest has already been done hundreds of times in humans and in multiple clinical settings. This is just repetitive busywork and a waste of animals."

Both Zach and Glen were surprised by Susan's knowledge of the technique but annoyed at her leap to a conclusion. "With *no* due respect, Ms. Holmes," Zach said, "we are talking about a procedure that has never been done before, and we can't just get started on the next patient who is wheeled through our doors. It's obvious that your only concern here is to avoid using animals."

"Dr. Green, there's no need for the ad hominem attacks. We are here to discuss the merits of the research." Anders started nervously tapping his pencil on the table. He had seen Zach's act before—and the unpleasant aftermath.

Glen stepped up to bat, sensing that his friend was about to combust. "Ms. Holmes, if we thought we could do it another way, we would. And as we made clear in our proposal, circulatory arrest, a state of suspended animation, has not been attempted on a patient already in shock and near death. That's the difference here."

"But how many lives will this research save? How common is this injury?"

"Not all that common, but that isn't the point. It may be applicable to many other severe injuries. This kind of research is just a beginning. It could lead to other techniques of preservation in the moribund patient. No one knows where one discovery will lead," Glen responded firmly.

"It appears to me that more animals will die than the number of humans saved. I don't believe that the sacrifice of animals in this case is ethically or morally justified. I have spoken with Dr. Talarico, a member of your own surgery department, who agrees the research would be pointless."

Zach couldn't stand it a minute longer. He got up from his chair and pointed his finger at Holmes. "Listen, you idiot! No single dog or one hundred dogs are worth even one human life."

"Dr. Green, please sit down!" Anders had lost control of the meeting.

"It is precisely that attitude toward other living species that must be changed, and when it is, you people will have to answer for your acts," responded Susan Holmes, unintimidated.

Anders hated confrontations. Within minutes, Zach had turned this session into a shouting match. "Is it possible we can discuss this like adults?" Anders said, glaring at Zach.

Ruth Randolf, a psychiatrist, closed her folder and stood. "I think the cognitive testing methodology is sound, but in a sense, I agree with Ms. Holmes. I'm not sure I'd want to be the first human to have my vascular injury fixed that way."

"Ruth, the people who are candidates for this have a ninety-percent mortality," Glen said.

Randolf nodded and appeared satisfied.

A few of the other committee members had minor criticisms of the experimental protocol but not of the experiment itself.

Anders also knew that the project was sound and should be approved. "I am calling for a vote right now. All those in favor, raise your hands."

All but one hand went up.

"I'm sorry, Ms. Holmes, but the project is a reasonable one, and I'm sure the animals will be treated properly. Your dissension will be noted in the minutes."

"Treated properly for animals, right, Dr. Anders?" replied Ms. Holmes.

Zach and Glen thanked the committee and stood to leave. As they walked past, Holmes glared at them and said, "One battle, doctors; definitely not the war." She headed directly for a public telephone and called information.

"The number for CARE, please," she said, and then dialed. When a male voice responded, Susan Holmes angrily described the research proposal and the outcome of the committee's decision.

Outside, Zach looked at his friend and shook his head in dismay. "How the hell did she get appointed to the committee?"

"Good question. We could use a layperson with a little more balance," Glen agreed.

Anders bolted out of the room. "Christ, Zach, the project was going to be approved. Why did you have to bait her?"

"Let me ask *you* a question, Marty. Where did you find that woman? There must be a million citizens concerned with legitimate animal welfare issues, and you find a die-hard animal rights activist!"

"I didn't appoint her to the committee, but I do have to deal with her every week. You didn't make my life any easier."

"Yeah, how long has she been on your committee?"

"About a month."

"And how many projects has she been in favor of?"

"Not a single one," Anders admitted.

"Doesn't that tell you something? She's against all research on animals. What's the good of having her on the committee if she always votes no?"

"Most of the doctors vote yes."

"At least they're on the right side."

Nate Cohen chewed faster, swallowed, and in ten seconds the rest of his knish had made its way south. He was a big man—if you measured in an east-west orientation.

"Come in, Billy." He waved to his law partner as he gulped some Seagrams ginger ale. He reflexively buttoned his suit jacket, now a little tighter after his huge lunch. "Haven't seen you in a while."

William Vanderzell walked into Cohen's office, pulled up a chair, and sat. "I just got back from Florida."

"That's right, I forgot, another ACLU field trip to free a serial killer."

"Not free him, stay his execution," Vanderzell corrected. "He did the murders. We only wanted the sentence commuted to life without parole."

"And?"

"They pulled the switch yesterday at five in the afternoon. That redneck bastard appeals court judge in Georgia was our last hope."

"Sorry," Nate said.

"For whom, Toby Jackson or me?" Vanderzell asked.

Nate emptied the can of Seagrams and began to suck on a Twinkie. There were several chain-smokers in the office, but Nate Cohen was the only lawyer who chain-ate Twinkies. "Toby Jackson raped and slaughtered seven college girls. They should have electrocuted him one volt at a time."

"Actually, he murdered eight girls, but two wrongs don't make a right."

"That's the new math, Billy."

Vanderzell managed a smile. "That's your prosecutor mentality, Nate. He's no danger to anyone if he's stuck away in a maximum-security prison."

"That's true. But while the thought of that psychopath's ass getting more traffic than the Lincoln Tunnel is appealing, I would still feel much better with the fifty thousand volts."

"Someday I'll make a liberal out of you, Nate."

Nate chuckled at that. "Dinner tonight? I know you must be feeling a little down, with Toby Jackson being part of the ozone layer now, so I'll even let you rant about your animal rights nonsense."

Vanderzell grinned and got up to leave. "Sure. You're the only one around here who can cheer me up. I always know where I stand with you."

"Where to?" Nate asked.

"There's a new Ethiopian restaurant in the Village."

"Great. I can have a seven-course famine."

"Come on, Nate. We went to Sparks last time. All I ate was tomatoes and baked potatoes, while I watched you stuff an entire cow down your throat."

Nate sighed. "Fair enough. We should alternate our misery."

"She was my friend, too, Palmer. When she was wounded, I tried to get her out, but one of those bastards shot her again," Cecile said. A tear rolled down her cheek.

"I told you I should have come. If the three of us had been there together, this wouldn't have happened." Palmer flared out his chest and sneered. "A hundred will die for her."

Cecile sighed sympathetically. "I know you cared for her. But her death won't be in vain. Next week, we strike again. He's given us our next target. We'll be traveling a bit; it's out of town."

11

The morning Casey moved in with Daphne was beautiful and sunny. The humidity was mercifully low for July, which made the task almost pleasant. Casey didn't have all that much stuff to move. The two most difficult items were her bed and a large piano. The piano was impractical, but she'd moved it from her apartment in St. Louis to a warehouse in Manhattan, and she'd been anxious to get it out of storage. Daphne had been happy to make space in the living room for the new addition. Professional movers would pick it up and deliver it later in the week.

Casey had played since she was five years old and at one time had hoped to become a professional. Unfortunately, although she was very good, she realized she wasn't talented enough for the stage. She'd never stopped playing, though.

Daphne and Tim Adams, an intern who had a day off, helped her move the rest of her stuff. A small rented U-Haul easily carried all her possessions, and within four hours she was unpacking in her new home.

Casey put the sheets on her bed while Daphne straightened up her own room. After she finished, she went in to chat with her new roommate.

"All set?" Daphne asked.

"Yeah. I really think I'm going to be happy here."

"Great view of the alley, isn't it?"

"Well, a view isn't everything. It's light, spacious, and affordable, and that's what I needed. I don't know how to thank you. How about dinner sometime soon, on me?"

"Anytime, roomie."

While they were talking, Casey noticed a metal barrel protruding from under Daphne's bed. It was the end of a rifle. "Is that a gun?" Casey asked nervously.

"Yep," Daphne replied proudly.

"You keep a gun in the apartment?"

"Well, actually, I have three guns in the apartment," Daphne nonchalantly responded. She hoisted up the top mattress and produced a pistol. "See?"

"Do you have a license for those guns?"

"Of course not. Do you know how hard it is to get a gun permit in New York?"

Her Southern drawl was becoming more noticeable to Casey. "I can't believe you have guns here," replied Casey, visibly shaken by the discovery of her new friend's arsenal.

"Why not? There were a thousand murders, ten thousand rapes, and probably fifty thousand robberies last year. I was taught how to shoot a gun when I was five years old. Anyone coming into this apartment looking for trouble is gonna get it."

Casey looked at her and wasn't sure what to say.

"Look, I'm not going to wear a holster down Park Avenue, but if someone comes into this apartment who doesn't belong here, they are going out in a body bag. And that nonsense about getting shot with your own gun is *New York Times* liberal bullshit."

"I guess you're not a big fan of the Brady Bill," Casey retorted, trying to break the tension.

Daphne laughed. "I'm going to have to take you upstate sometime and show you how to handle yourself. You'll see the light."

"Listen, I've got to get back to the lab. I'm starting that research project today," Casey said, gathering up her coat and knapsack as she walked toward her new front door. "And I'm on call tonight, so I'll see you tomorrow."

Daphne waved good-bye.

Casey had just injected a female dog's intravenous line with thiopental. Within seconds, the animal was unconscious, and she placed it on a ventilator. She then took her scalpel, made an incision in its groin, and dissected out the femoral artery and vein. Finally, she began to remove blood from the dog to lower its blood pressure from a normal level of eighty mm Hg to thirty-five mm Hg. The dog was now in shock; the blood flow to its heart, brain, and kidneys was markedly diminished, simulating what actually happens after an injury.

This was the first experimental animal, and the protocol dictated a thirty-minute period of shock. During the entire procedure, Stu Keller, one of the lab technicians, monitored the dog's arterial and venous pressure, as well as the pulmonary artery and airway pressures. The levels were all recorded on a Hewlett Packard multichannel recorder.

"We'll be getting a load of data from this experiment," Stu said.

"Well, you never know what will be important, so we ought to record everything." Casey was preoccupied and hardly paid attention to Stu.

"Ya know, Doc, I could get the animals to sleep for you and put in the lines." Stu had been a lab tech in the surgery department for fifteen years and figured he had forgotten more about animal experimentation than Casey had ever known.

"I'd prefer to do the first few myself, until the project gets off the ground," replied Casey, this time looking up at Stu.

"Have it your way, Dr. Brenner," Stu said calmly. He knew that within a few weeks, she would be letting him do the surgery. They all did.

"Call me Casey. We're going to be working together a lot. I'm not much on formalities."

He brightened at this. A lot of the doctors tended to be

aloof and thought that their degrees and money made them superior to the rest of the staff. "This is some idea you have. Do you really think you can circ-arrest someone already behind the eight ball, fix their injury, and get their brain to work normally?"

"Well, it wasn't exactly my idea. I'm just helping Dr. Green and Dr. Brinkman. I *hope* it works. It would give the most severely injured patients, the ones who are nearly dead, a chance."

"I wouldn't want to be alive if my brain didn't work," Stu observed skeptically. He withdrew some blood into a syringe to measure serum electrolytes.

While the dog was in shock, Casey and Stu finished dissecting the femoral blood vessels and inserted the bypass cannulae. These were the plastic tubes that would bring blood to the heart-lung machine and then return it to the dog while it was being cooled. After thirty minutes had passed, Stu began the bypass machine. "OK, Doc, give me your venous flow."

Casey removed a heavy clamp device from the plastic tubing, and the blood from the dog flowed into the heart-lung machine. This pumped and oxygenated the blood and sent it back to the animal. When the machine had cooled the animal to twenty-eight degrees Celsius, the heart fibrillated and was no longer able to pump. The heart-lung machine took over the duty of pumping blood to the organs.

"How low are we going today, Casey?"

"I thought to seventeen degrees. That's the temperature the neurosurgeons like to use when they do their aneurysms."

"That's cold. You want me to pack his head in ice?"

"We should; it will give him even more brain protection."

Stu opened the freezer and hoisted out a big bag. He carefully surrounded the animal's head with ice. The colder the temperature of the brain, the lower its metabolic demand and the longer it could survive without blood flow. The dog's brain temperature, measured by a probe on its tympanic membrane, was now sixteen degrees. "I guess we're ready, Doc."

"OK. Stop the machine."

Stu drained the blood from the venous return lines, switched off the bypass machine, and started the stopwatch. The animal now had no blood flow to any organ. It was cold and dead. Within the next several months, they would learn whether a brain already deprived of blood from an accident could tolerate no flow at all to facilitate the repair of an otherwise irreparable injury.

"Thirty minutes to start with?"

"We'll start there," Casey replied. Looking at the dog lying lifeless on the table, it was impossible not to have doubts about the experiment. What if it weren't possible to use circulatory arrest in a trauma victim in shock? Was it worth all the work? And what about all the animals they would sacrifice?

Casey had never actually seen a retrohepatic vena caval injury. It would take only one case to erase her doubts.

The first day in the lab had gone well. Now, Casey was back in the real world.

The patient rolled into the operating room with Casey's right hand pushing on the young man's neck. Before this timely and simple maneuver, a red geyser had decorated the emergency-room ceiling.

"Stab wound to the neck. I'm sure it got his carotid. Tim, get on some gloves and hold right here," she said, pointing to the patient's neck with her free hand. The intern replaced her pressure on the artery. "Just prep with his hand in the field," she instructed the circulating nurse.

The nurse painted the wound, along with Tim's hand, with Betadine antiseptic while Casey went into the anteroom to scrub. Zach was already washing up.

"Bullet or knife?" Zach asked as he rinsed his hands.

"Ice pick," she replied. "It's in Zone Three."

"Great, that'll keep things interesting. Have you done a high injury to the carotid?"

"Not yet. But I've read about it." Actually, she had read

every article in the literature on penetrating neck trauma. Dozens of facts percolated in her head.

"Well, let's see what you can do, Dr. Brenner. I heard about that baby last week. Great save."

"It wasn't a big deal. Just a couple stitches in the ventricle." She was embarrassed by all the attention she'd received from that case.

Zach walked into the operating room, and the scrub nurse quickly gowned and gloved him.

"Is your hand tired yet, Tim?" Zach asked.

"A little."

"OK. Hold on." Zach quickly draped the patient's neck and then his lower leg in case they needed to harvest a piece of vein to repair the artery. He replaced Tim's hand with his own. By this time, Casey had been gowned and gloved and came to the table.

"Now what, Doctor?" Zach asked Casey, getting the suction and cautery ready to use.

"Get a Pruit shunt ready, please," she asked the circulating nurse. "Knife." She made the skin incision, curving it around Zach's finger. "Tim, go down to the leg and get me some vein." She then quickly deepened the incision and dissected down to the carotid artery.

"Are sure you haven't done this before?" asked Zach, observing her intense focus on the small operative field.

"The bleeding looks like it's coming from under the mandible. Can you move your finger up?" Casey asked.

"Your wish is my command. What's the plan?" Zach was impressed. The rumors were true. She had great hands.

Casey wanted to be ready to sew in a graft in case the injury was complex. "Tim, get the vein ready." She took it, reversed it so the valves would go in the direction of arterial flow, and placed the shunt through it. She looked over at Zach. "I'm assuming it's the internal carotid. If I can't primarily repair it, I can put the shunt in and sew in a vein graft around the shunt."

"Why not just clamp and sew it in? It's a lot easier than shunting," Zach asked.

"There's a twenty-five-percent chance he'll stroke out if I do that."

She had brains, too. "Sewing way up in the neck around the shunt is tough," Zach cautioned.

She looked up at him, and he could see the outline of a smile beneath her mask. "Just watch," she said softly.

Zach stared at her in disbelief for a split second, then returned the smile. *Pretty cocky,* he thought. *Cocky, smart, and beautiful. There is a God.*

Casey took her forceps and grabbed the distal artery while Zach took the proximal portion. At least two centimeters of the artery had been destroyed.

"The guy who stabbed him liked to twist. You'll never fix it primarily."

"No problem." Casey took the shunt with the vein over it, and within thirty seconds had placed it in the artery. Now she could sew in the graft with the patient still getting blood to his brain. "Six-zero proline on the smallest needle, please." She sewed in the distal graft, a real feat with the difficult exposure and a shunt in the way. It took her twelve minutes with Zach doing no more than following her suture and staying out of the way. She tested the repair by deflating a distal balloon.

"No leaks, Dr. Brenner. I'm very impressed." Zach paused for a moment. "For a fourth-year resident, that's excellent."

She looked up and formed another smile under the mask. "Could *you* do it faster?" She couldn't help herself—she knew Zach could dish it out; now she wanted to see if he could take it. If she had challenged any of the attendings in her previous program, they would have thrown her out of the operating room. Zach seemed to encourage it. What would he do?

Shirley, the scrub nurse, looked at Zach as she loaded up the needle holder with another 6'0 proline. "I think you've been challenged, Dr. Green."

"Ya know, Shirley, I think I may have met my match here."

Shirley shook her head. "She's awfully slick, Doctor.

And besides, you're on the downside of thirty-five now. Those hands aren't what they used to be."

"Every gunslinger faces that day, Shirley, but I'll go down like a man. Gimme the needle holder."

Zach sewed the proximal anastomosis. He started the running stitch and never moved his hands more than a few centimeters. The needle was perfectly set for each subsequent bite of tissue. He finished in six and a half minutes.

Casey had been a surgical resident for four years and had never seen anyone sew that fast. And yet his moves were not quick, just ergonomically efficient, with no wasted motion.

Zach looked up at Shirley. "Go ahead, Shirley. Let's hear it."

She looked at him and smiled but said nothing.

"Shirley."

"You're the best, Dr. Green," she replied dutifully.

"Come on, Shirley, you're not being truthful."

"All right, all right. You're the best *ever.*"

"That's better. Well, Dr. Brenner, why don't you close up?" Zach said as he pulled off his gown and gloves. "You were great," he said as he turned to walk out of the OR. Just before he reached the door, he turned back around. "But I'm unbelievable, so don't feel discouraged. You'll get faster," he said, and he disappeared out the door.

"That was some performance," said Casey. "He almost has a right to be so obnoxious."

Shirley nodded as she handed Casey the closing suture. "I'll tell you something, Doctor, I think he likes you. He was being a real gentleman tonight. Normally, he would have sewed really fast and tried to embarrass a resident who challenged him like you did."

"What do you mean? He did his anastomosis nearly twice as fast as I did," Casey replied.

"Did you notice anything unusual about the way he was sewing?" Shirley asked, handing Casey the suture to close the wound.

"Not really, just perfect technique," Casey answered as she began to suture.

"Yeah, that's true—and he sewed left-handed."

"Come on, he's right-handed?" Casey asked incredulously.

"Uh-huh. You should see him when he's in a hurry."

Her surgical preceptor in medical school had always told Casey that controlled arrogance was crucial to being a surgeon. But she'd never been around anyone quite so self-assured. Ever since she had started her surgical training, she had been put down by most of her attendings. Even the ones who let her operate sniped at her constantly. Part of it came with being a female surgeon, but there were times when it had given her real doubts about her abilities. Tonight, not only had she been good in the operating room, but she was actually told so by her attending, who was himself amazingly proficient. Maybe not anyone could have saved that baby.

Casey had a feeling she was going to be an excellent surgeon.

12

Ted Simpson greeted his guest at the door.

"Dr. Simpson, how are you tonight?" inquired Forrest Wells, doing his best Eddie Haskell imitation. "It's great to see you."

Simpson and Forrest Wells Sr. had been roommates in college and remained close friends until his death. Since then, both Forrest and his mother frequently received invitations to dine with the Simpsons, but tonight Forrest was there on his own. Forrest had gone to Dalton with Simpson's younger daughter, Emily. Emily was home from Brown, where she was a graduate student in medieval history. They had dated pretty seriously for a while, but Forrest, who was preoccupied with cars, expensive clothes, and drugs, was far from Emily's idea of a future spouse.

Her father was dismayed by the breakup and was certain that the fault lay with Emily, whose bohemian tastes had always disappointed Simpson. He couldn't understand why anyone would spend two years writing a dissertation on the Dark Ages, a term that Emily had told him she considered misleading about the period. He had always hoped to have Forrest as a son-in-law. But tonight, matchmaking wasn't what he had on his mind.

"So, Forrest," Simpson inquired facetiously, "have they made you a partner yet?" He had checked with a friend at the firm last week and already knew the answer.

"Not yet, sir. Things are a little tight at the firm. Hopefully soon," Forrest hedged.

Wells had been an average law student at an Ivy League law school. His father helped him land a job in New York that he otherwise never would have gotten. Wells looked the part of an Ivy League lawyer, although few in his firm considered his intellect anything extraordinary. Six-foot-three, with a narrow waist and shoulders, bright blue eyes, and a smile that bordered on a smirk, he looked like an ad for Brooks Brothers.

"Well, I have every confidence in you. If there is any way I can help, let me know," Simpson offered.

"Maybe you could send some malpractice work my way," Forrest added, not entirely joking. He never thought he'd end up chasing ambulances, but at this point his options were few. Everyone always told him what a good associate he was and how valuable to the firm he had become. But it was all bullshit. You didn't become a partner at one of Manhattan's best small law firms by doing good legal research. Paying clients, billable hours, publicity for the firm—that was what it took. Otherwise, he'd soon be looking for another job.

"I didn't know Cox, Durham, and Anderson went in for that kind of business," Simpson responded. *This might be easier than I thought,* he told himself.

"Money is money." Forrest shrugged.

"You'd prefer physician defense work, I assume?" he asked rhetorically.

"Money is money," repeated Forrest with a noncommittal grin.

"I'll see if I can help," said Simpson, pleased with Forrest's response. "Ah, here's Emily."

"I was just going to look for her. Good evening, Emily. How is life on the fief?" Forrest said snidely. Simpson excused himself to search for his wife, leaving them alone.

Emily was dressed in a plain, light blue faded jumper

with a white cotton blouse underneath. She was medium height and attractive, although she did little to embellish her looks. Since their breakup, Emily never felt entirely comfortable around Forrest. She couldn't believe she'd ever dated such a jerk. She'd only come to dinner as a favor to her parents, although she couldn't imagine why her father was interested in her old boyfriend. "Very funny, Forrest. Chasing any ambulances yet?" Emily shot back.

"Shall we at least try to be civil?"

"Fair enough."

"How long are you home for?"

"Just a week. I have a lot of work left on my dissertation."

He moved closer. "Maybe you could come over to my place some night. We could curl up in bed, eat some gruel, and read *Beowulf*. I know that stuff turns you on," he said. "Just seeing you gets my Grendel hard."

Emily recoiled and pushed him away. "You're really incredible. You nauseate me as much today as you did five years ago." How she could have lost her virginity to this pig still amazed her.

"OK, how about dinner? Lutece?"

"Forrest, how about you go fuck yourself?" Emily turned around and walked away.

Dinner that night consisted of the usual banal discussion of the cost of living in Manhattan, summer homes in the Hamptons, and, of course, what to do about the homeless. It had taken Simpson many years to nest in this privileged atmosphere, insulated from the poverty and violence just blocks from his home.

As usual, Victoria Simpson had spent most of the evening jumping up and down from the table, supervising the cook's presentation of each course. She rarely joined in the conversation except to scowl resentfully at her husband and cast knowing glances at Emily, who tried her hardest to ignore the tension between her parents. Forrest was used to the underlying animosity; Emily had bored him to death with stories of her father's extramarital adventures and her mother's ineffective and, in his opinion, pathetic acts of retaliation. He couldn't care less how Simpson's behavior affected Emily or her mother, but it did amaze him how oblivious Simpson was to Victoria's hostility. He treated her as little more than a well-dressed servant.

When the last course had been served, Victoria said, "Nice to see you again, Forrest," and left before he got the chance to thank her for dinner. Emily rose from the table and followed her mother without saying a word. Her father's treatment of his own family was somehow worse under the lawyer's gaze. Her older sister had stopped speaking with their father ten years earlier, cutting him off when she was barely out of high school. Emily wished she had the strength to do the same, but she was still financially dependent on him. For her mother's sake, she tried hard to maintain a superficial relationship with her father.

"Forrest, I would like to discuss some business that could be mutually beneficial to each of us. Shall we move into the library?"

"Sure, Dr. Simpson," Forrest replied, following him into the adjoining room.

Simpson closed the doors. "Would you be interested in some potential malpractice litigation work?"

"Are you being sued?" asked Forrest, somewhat surprised but excited about the prospect of new business. "I thought you had a lawyer."

"Of course not, Forrest."

"So, this is for one of your staff members?"

Simpson sipped his vodka. "Forrest, I don't know if you realize it, but medical care in this country is being rationed. There simply aren't enough resources to meet the demand for health-care services. I have dozens of patients who need coronary artery bypasses or cardiac valve replacements. They can't get into the hospital because of lack of beds and operating time or because some moron at an insurance company doesn't believe they need an operation. And Medicare and the insurance companies are always trying to screw doctors and not pay them, or pay them less. We're spending too much money on health care."

"I suppose the AIDS epidemic is the reason for the bed shortage at UHC," Forrest suggested.

"That is certainly a big part of it, but all the hospitals in New York are dealing with that constraint. The problem at UHC is the trauma center. We see more than two thousand gunshot and stabbing victims each year, and the number just keeps growing. I don't have to tell you that most of the people who suffer those types of injuries are not, shall we say, the upper crust of society."

"But I thought UHC was the best trauma hospital in New York. There must be an article in the paper about the place every week."

"We're too good at it. It's ruining my practice," Simpson growled.

"So bring your patients to another hospital."

"Forrest, open-heart surgery requires a team. I can't just pick up and go someplace else. Besides, operating time at other hospitals is tight. No existing staff at one of the other hospitals would grant me privileges."

"So we could sue them for restraint of trade," said Forrest naively.

"That would be a long and arduous fight. I haven't got the time or patience for a protracted legal battle. A case like that could be in litigation for years. The only winners would be the lawyers."

"So what do you propose?" asked Forrest, now totally lost.

"Son, this trauma crap is going to put me out of business. A business that has taken me more than fifteen years to build. The goddamned administration loves the publicity this shit brings to the hospital. But despite our reputation, a lot of these people still die or remain permanently disabled. Now, I'm not saying anyone else could do better. It's the nature of the disease. But publicity can work in two directions."

"Dr. Simpson, I'm still not following you. I'm a lawyer, not a journalist."

"Forrest," Simpson said softly, "there are some cases, some trauma cases, that I think are worthy of litigation."

"You want me to sue members of your own department?" Forrest asked with a quizzical smirk.

Simpson paused and looked him directly in the eyes. "I could get you the names of some patients who were crippled or died. You need to understand, many of these patients had multiple, extremely complex injuries; some spent months in the intensive-care unit, only eventually to succumb or suffer permanent disabilities. But there isn't one of these cases in which you won't find some mistake made. Those minor errors usually have no effect on the final outcome, but a clever plaintiff's attorney can often persuade an emotional jury that they do."

"What am I supposed to do, call these patients or their families on the phone, or go to their house and hand them my business card?" Forrest asked.

"Exactly, Forrest. I have some friends at your firm. Apparently, they like you well enough, but you seem to fall short in the billable hours department. This would give you a chance to get some big settlements, particularly for the disabled patients. The dead ones aren't really worth as much. In return, I could get some terrifically bad publicity for the hospital and get the administration to drop our Level One trauma designation."

"How do you get the names?" Forrest asked with increased interest.

"I'm the chief of surgery. I can get anything I want. I will give you names, phone numbers, and the basic information. You need to do the rest. If you approach the family and they want to go ahead, you can subpoena their medical records."

"What about expert witnesses? Even with unequivocal malpractice, it can be hard to get doctors to testify against one another."

Simpson smiled sardonically. "Forrest, I can find you some doctors who would testify that the earth was flat for a few thousand bucks."

Forrest pushed his chair back from the table. "When can you get me started with some names?"

"Tomorrow," Simpson said, looking at his watch. "Right now, I have to call it a night." He stood up and walked Forrest to the door. "I'll be in touch."

Emily saw her father at breakfast the next morning. Surprisingly, he thanked her for coming. "It means a lot to your mother and me."

"Sure, Dad," Emily said, knowing full well he didn't give a damn what it meant to her mother.

"How did it go seeing Forrest again?" he asked.

"It didn't go. I can't stand him."

Ted Simpson wouldn't push it. As it was, he'd expressed more interest than he really felt. "Fine," he said, and hesitated for a moment. "Have you heard from your sister?"

Emily nodded. "I speak to her about once a month."

"Do you think she'll ever talk to me again? It's been almost ten years."

"I thought she was going to come to see you. Last month, when I spoke with her, she told me it was time to try and patch things up."

Simpson shrugged. "I haven't heard a thing."

"That's funny. She said she wanted to come and surprise you, so I sent her my UHC ID badge so she could get in."

"Maybe she's changed her mind," he replied, not certain he would actually want to deal with the confrontation such a reunion would inevitably inspire.

Emily hugged her father good-bye. She still wanted to love him, despite his coldness and what he had done to her sister and mother. His abuse was subtle—he treated you as if it didn't really matter whether you came or went. "When you see her, just try to show her that you care."

"Of course, I'll try. But it's up to her to make it work," Simpson responded.

13

Once a week, the entire trauma team, or at least those who weren't busy taking care of patients, made rounds together. Today, Zach and Larry Gordon were the only attendings on rounds. Glen was in the operating room, and Ron was giving a lecture to the medical students.

They started seeing patients on the ward and ended in the intensive-care unit. Each patient's history was briefly presented by one of the residents, or by a medical student if he or she was exceptionally good. Double-oh-seven loved these teaching rounds because they allowed him to showcase his formidable command of the literature. Zach disliked these formal gatherings and Larry's pedantic, long-winded style. He preferred teaching in one-on-one situations, and only on his own patients. He usually let 007 drone on, commenting only when he thought an important point was being lost. The best thing about these rounds lately, he thought, was Casey Brenner. It had been four weeks since he had first met her, and he still got palpitations every time he saw her.

She was dressed in a khaki skirt about two inches above her knees and a white blouse that was just tight enough for Zach to make out the outline of her bra. He couldn't stop staring at her and wondered if she thought about him at all. *What's the difference anyway?* he thought. *I'm not about to get romantically involved with one of my residents. I'll get over it,* he told himself, but it was a struggle to keep his mind off her.

John Frank, a fourth-year medical student doing an acting internship on the trauma service, was presenting a patient on whom Gordon had operated four days ago. "The patient was shot in the left upper quadrant and sustained injuries to his spleen, pancreas, and colon. He underwent splenectomy, distal pancreatectomy, and closure of a hole in his left colon. He was doing well until this morning, when he developed fever, respiratory distress, and upper abdominal tenderness."

The medical student approached the patient and gently palpated his abdomen. The seventeen-year-old boy winced in pain wherever his belly was touched. The group moved away to continue the discussion

Gordon ran his fingers through his perfect hair. "He's probably developing a subphrenic abscess and a systemic inflammatory response. That occurs in twelve-point-five percent of patients after splenectomy with concomitant injury to the bowel. The other possibility is a leak from his pancreatic closure. Pancreatic fistulas occur in at least twenty-five percent of patients." Gordon went on for five minutes about the physiology of the spleen and the new drug somatostatin, which could close a pancreatic fistula in days. He even diagrammed the chemical structure of somatostatin.

Zach sized up the case, realized Gordon's diagnosis was wrong, and was about to impale him when Casey politely raised her hand to speak.

"Dr. Gordon? John said you closed a hole in the colon, but shouldn't there have been two holes?"

"Well, the hole was tangential to the bowel, so there was only one hole," he said confidently.

"It's just that he seems a little sicker than I would expect for an abscess or fistula. It looks like he has generalized peritonitis," Casey continued.

Zach smiled and nodded. "I think Dr. Brenner has zeroed in on the problem here, Larry. You missed a hole in his colon. He needs to go back to the OR. Four days is the classic time for a missed bowel injury to show up. The patient looks great for three days and then turns to shit, which is what you'll find his belly full of when you go back in." Zach looked approvingly at Casey, who returned his gaze.

"Well, I guess that's a possibility," admitted Gordon, a little less authoritatively than before. "Perhaps I'll scan him."

"Why, so the radiologist can make another payment on his Porsche?" Zach replied. "I'd just operate." Zach pivoted toward the group. "There aren't too many mysteries in surgery. If you do the operation right, the patient will usually do fine. Someone who gets better for a couple days after their injury and then crashes always has a complication. And remember," he said, looking at 007, "sometimes we're the ones that screw up, not the patient's immune system."

"You may be right, Dr. Green," Gordon said.

The group went on to the next patient, an eighty-two-year-old woman who had been hit by a car several days earlier. She had broken her hip and fractured two ribs. Except for some difficulty breathing because of the broken ribs, she was doing well. As the group approached her bed, she combed her thin gray hair back with her hands. "If I had known all these handsome young doctors were coming to visit, I would have fixed myself up a little."

"You look just fine, dear," replied Phillip Albert, her intern. He went to her bed and listened to her lungs.

"Am I going to live a while longer?"

"Don't worry, dear. You'll be fine," Phillip said absently as he returned to the foot of the bed.

Zach picked up the chart and scanned it for a few seconds. He sat on the woman's bed and held her hand. "You really got banged up, Mrs. Goldberg. But I bet you're tougher than all of us." He noticed a small yellow tattoo on her left arm. During her time in a concentration camp, she undoubtedly had suffered more physical and psychological pain than the entire group of doctors would ever know.

"So you think I'll make it to my grandson's wedding in October?" she asked hopefully.

"We'll have you out of here in a couple weeks," Zach responded as he squeezed her hand.

"Thank you, Dr. Green. If I were fifty years younger, without a bad hip, I'd be chasing you around the hospital."

Zach laughed and carefully got up. "You wouldn't have to chase me, Mrs. Goldberg. Now, I want you to work on your deep breathing, and in a couple days we'll get you to physical therapy."

Casey was impressed by Zach's unstrained gentleness with this woman. During the few minutes he spent with her, he made her feel as if she was the most important person in the world and didn't act as if he were doing her a favor by taking care of her. He was a natural at the bedside.

As they exited the room, Zach gave the intern the evil eye. "Phillip, do me a favor and don't call women, particularly women who are old enough to be your grandmother, 'dear.' I hate that. Gynecologists call their patients 'dear,'" Zach added.

"Sorry, Dr. Green, you're right," Phillip said.

Casey glanced over at Zach, who was already at the next patient's bedside. If he were a pig, it appeared he was a gentleman pig.

After rounds, the residents returned to the wards to finish the scut work—the dressing changes, blood drawing, line changes, and all the other details that translated into successful patient care. Zach returned to his office to do some paperwork, fighting the urge to daydream about Casey. Half his day was spent thinking about her. And it wasn't just her physical appearance. He liked her, at least as much as he knew about her from the hospital, and wanted to get to know her better.

His self-imposed taboo on dating surgical residents was

being sternly tested. Breaking this rule would be a violation of his principles. His grandfather had taught him that you only have your integrity once. But then again, his grandfather never saw Casey Elizabeth Brenner. He sat up at his desk, put down the disability forms he had just signed seven times—in the wrong place—and walked out the door.

Casey was changing the dressing on Timmy Sanders. Timmy had been playing baseball in the park when a fight broke out between two other teens. Shots were fired, and Timmy got a bullet in the leg, severing his popliteal artery. Glen had repaired the artery, but the leg had become so swollen that another operation was required to relieve the swelling. Timmy now had two large open wounds on his lower leg. The nurses were busy, so Casey hoisted his leg over her shoulder and began to change the bandage.

Zach returned to the ward and offered to help Casey. He held up the leg while she finished.

"Thanks, it was getting a bit heavy."

The kid started waving his hands at Zach. "Yo, Doc. Get out the way. You blocking my view of the lady doctor."

"How would you like an enema?" Zach teased as he turned to the side.

"Say, Doc," Timmy said to Casey, "when you're done wrapping my leg, why don't you sit down next to me for a few minutes?"

"Timmy, you already have a fever." Casey smiled as she finished the dressing.

"Will you change my bandage this afternoon?" Timmy asked.

"Sorry. Phillip will be doing the dressings then."

"Damn, but he's ugly."

" 'Bye, kiddo." Casey waved. "I have four more dressings to do. Thanks, Zach," she said, moving on to her next task.

"Hey, Doc," said Timmy as he beckoned Zach with his finger. "She's a babe. If I were you, I'd be trying real hard to get it on with her."

"You've got good taste in women, Timmy, my man. Work hard at physical therapy. I want you out of here in two weeks."

"Not soon enough for me." Timmy sighed.

Zach went around and saw some patients, biding his time until Casey was finished. When she finally started to leave, Zach sped after her, slowing down far enough away so it appeared as if he were passing her by chance.

"That was a good pickup on rounds today, Casey."

"Thanks, Zach, but it was pretty obvious the guy was sick."

"Not to Double-oh-seven."

"I've only been here a few weeks, but I don't think Larry Gordon is that bad. And he really cares about the patients," Casey said sympathetically. "When he had trouble last week with that aortic injury, he called Ron in to help him. He knows his limitations."

"When speed dialing is your strongest technical skill, there's a problem. Look, Larry is a smart guy and knows what to do—theoretically. But when there's an emergency, he gets flustered and thinks too much about the situation rather than acting instinctively. He makes the wrong decisions."

"Do you always make the right decisions, Zach?"

"Always," Zach said with a straight face.

"You're kidding, right?" asked Casey, hoping that no one could be that arrogant.

"Almost always," Zach replied.

"What do you do when you lose a patient?"

"Usually, I feel the need to punish myself, so I go home and read 'The Wasteland.'"

"Because of its hopelessness?" she replied, intrigued and surprised. Zach didn't seem like the T. S. Eliot type.

"No, because when I was in college, reading that poem was the worst possible form of torture. I couldn't understand one fucking sentence, and I needed to get a B in that English literature course to get into medical school."

"Did you get a B?" Casey asked.

"D, and I didn't deserve that."

"Well, you obviously got into medical school."

"Of course."

"But you said you needed a B in the course."

"I made it up over the summer. That's why I'm a trauma surgeon, not an English lit professor."

"So what's the moral of the story?"

"I could have read that poem for five years, and I still wouldn't have understood it. You have to recognize your talent and then develop and refine it. But if you don't possess natural ability, there are limits to what you can do." He paused and looked at his watch. "Do you want to get some lunch?"

Casey cocked her head and raised her eyebrows. "Isn't that a bit of a non sequitur, Dr. Green—from literature to the cafeteria?"

"Being pedantic gives me an appetite. Besides, it's almost noon."

"I have a case with Dr. Simpson this afternoon, but not until one-thirty. I'll change my clothes and meet you in the cafeteria."

Zach saw Glen, Ron, and a few of the residents eating at a table near the front of the packed cafeteria, but he wanted to sit with Casey alone. He spied a couple of seats to the right of the cashier's desk, bought a hot dog and a Coke, and sat down. Glen waved at him, but Zach wasn't paying attention.

"Does he need glasses?" Glen muttered.

"Fuck 'im," said Ron.

Casey walked into the cafeteria with a carton of yogurt and a peach she had brought from home. Zach stood up and waved, trying to catch her eye.

"Oh, here we go." Glen laughed as he saw Casey approach Zach's table. "Lover boy is at it again."

"He has the hots for our new resident? That's convenient. He wouldn't even have to leave work to get it," Ron added.

"I don't think it'll go that far. Zach's not going to date a resident."

"Bullshit. What about that skinny blonde, Daphne?"

"First of all, Daphne chased Zach. He's only human. And she finished her surgery internship on June 30. He didn't screw her until 12:01, July 1, when she was officially a psychiatry resident."

"Now, there's a man of integrity."

"You know, I think this is different; he really likes her," Glen replied.

"Zach? Give me a break. I'll tell you one thing, that babe isn't going to fall for his bullshit. I've seen her work. She's cool under pressure and slick with her hands."

"Ron, when Zach sets his mind on something, he's very persuasive," said Glen.

"You wouldn't want to make a little wager on that, would you?" Ron challenged with a grin.

Glen couldn't resist. "OK. If he isn't sleeping with her in six weeks, then I'll do your week of call in October. If he is, you take mine."

Ron looked over in Casey's direction. "Like taking candy from a baby."

Casey sat at the table next to Zach. "That hot dog looks like it's been sitting in water for hours. It's all shriveled. How can you eat it?" she asked.

"Should I dip it in the yogurt to make it healthier?" he asked, cramming about a third of it into his mouth.

"Sorry I brought it up. I'll mind my own business."

"I'll go work out tonight and dialyze the poisons. Then I can eat some more crap tomorrow."

"Not too worried about your arteries, are you?"

"I had three grandparents who lived to over eighty-five. I'm more worried about getting shot in this city."

"I haven't run since I started working here," Casey said ruefully. "I've gained five pounds already."

Zach resisted the urge to comment. She had a soft body, not skinny, but athletic and graceful. Sort of like "Venus on the Half Shell"—with a scalpel. "The beginning is always tough, especially on trauma. You'll have more time later in the year," Zach reassured her.

She put her spoon down and picked up the peach. "I was really impressed with the way you talked to Mrs. Goldberg. You seem to really enjoy talking to patients. Surgeons aren't usually known for their bedside manner," Casey responded.

"I was a doctor before I was a surgeon." He finished his Coke and began to suck on an ice cube. "By the way, you handled Timmy pretty well yourself. A lot of women doctors freak out when patients flirt with them."

"He's just a kid. It was no big deal."

"A kid with a testosterone storm brewing inside him," Zach corrected. "You threw it right back at him. I liked that."

"Thanks," Casey said. She looked away from Zach. "I have a case this afternoon with Dr. Simpson. I'd better get going."

"I didn't mean to make you uncomfortable. I'm sorry."

"Don't be," she replied. "I really do have a case with Simpson, and I'm a little nervous."

"You'll do fine. I'll see you around."

"'Bye." Casey got up quickly, threw away her garbage, and headed for the door.

Zach took a deep breath. He was becoming obsessed and needed some couch time at Debby and Glen's.

14

"We have as our guests today Mr. Greg Sandstone and Mr. John Power, president and vice president of CARE. Both are leading proponents of the rights of animals. They feel that any and all research that uses animals should be ended and have made their arguments all around the country. After I rake them over the coals for a few minutes, you can call in and lambaste them."

Brad Menchen, the third most popular radio host in the country, spoke into his microphone at the WKAT studio. Syndicated on five hundred stations with an estimated two million listeners nationwide, Menchen had grown from an obscure DJ in southern New Jersey into a radio icon. He was adored by listeners who thought Rush Limbaugh was too left-leaning. People either loved him or loathed him; his detractors favored suspending the first amendment in his case.

Menchen, tanned from a weekend in the Hamptons and dressed meticulously in a dark pinstripe suit, sipped coffee from a mug adorned with his picture. "I'm going to start with Mr. Sandstone. Correct me if I'm wrong, but haven't you been quoted as saying that animal-based medical research is immoral and should be stopped?"

Sandstone adjusted his earphones and microphone. "That is not only my position, but the position of a growing number of enlightened Americans. Since there is no moral distinction between pain-feeling animals, whether they are pigs, or dogs, or boys, using an animal in an experiment, for whatever means, is an act of murder."

"Let me get this straight," Menchen said. "If a scientist using animal-based research were able to discover a cure for cancer next week, you lunatics would oppose that?" Menchen loved to incite his guests. The madder they became, the more vitriolic the confrontation, the higher the ratings.

Sandstone stared at Menchen for several seconds before responding. With a tight-lipped smile, he replied, "We oppose animal research no matter what the ends. There are many doctors who unequivocally believe there are no further advances to be made through animal research. That it is a complete waste of money. Erica Talarico, a surgeon at UHC, is in the vanguard of physicians who have taken a stand against animal research. She is doing cutting-edge cancer research using modern techniques, not archaic vivisection. But frankly, even if advances were possible using animals, I could take no solace knowing that other living creatures were sacrificed to save the life of my son or my mother."

Menchen threw up his arms in disgust. "It is inconceivable to me that anyone would actually proclaim equality between a pig and someone's mother. The Lord made us the dominant creatures on this earth. We are the king of the beasts. Animals exist to feed us, to clothe us, and to teach us. Mr. Power, do you want to comment?"

"You are a speciesist, Mr. Menchen. By asserting your superiority, you are taking a position that is no different from the Nazis who butchered six million Jews." Power spoke gently but passionately.

Menchen couldn't wait for the call-in portion of the show. These fruitcakes were a gold mine. "My demented friends, how can you make the invidious comparison between six million innocent people and dogs?"

"Cannocide, poultricide, rodenticide—are all morally equivalent to genocide!" interjected Sandstone.

"Poultricide!" Menchen howled. "That's a good one. Frank Perdue would lose sleep over that. OK, let's say your house is burning down. Whom do you pull out first, your dog or your daughter?"

"Whoever is closer to the door," Power volunteered.

"Mr. Power, you need professional help, perhaps long-term commitment to an institution devoted to the treatment of the insane. Ladies and gentlemen of the listening audience, please send your contributions to the John Power Psychiatric Fund."

Power's face tightened, but he maintained a vacant smile. "You can laugh all you want. But the time will come, and sooner than you think, when equality among all living beings will exist. I really believe that, Mr. Menchen."

"Seriously, don't you people realize that you are the living embodiment of the lunatic fringe? Nothing but a part of the minuscule minority?"

"The majority can be made to see the error in their thinking." Power spoke without anger or rancor, only calm assurance.

Menchen shook his head in disbelief. "How would you respond to the recent murders of researchers?"

Sandstone knew this would come up, and he had practiced what he was going to say. But before he could start, Power jumped in. "I believe all life is sacred. Education, not violence, is the solution. You should know, however, that despite what the media would lead you to believe, the scientists who were killed were no closer to finding cures for anything than you or I. You just don't find a cure for human brain cancer by using cat brains as a model. The history of growing tumors in animals to mimic human cancers is repetitive. One failure after another."

"One of these days, those animal experiments may well provide a cure. I don't think the average citizen cares about how many rats, cats, or dogs it takes," Menchen insisted.

"Let me ask you a question. What gives you the right to kill an animal and eat it? Think about it. It's an easy question, Mr. Menchen," Sandstone said, his voice rising. He paused for a moment and looked Menchen right in the eye. "No one. You have no right. Animals feel pain. They have the right not to suffer. Animals are living creatures. They have a right to life. Why can't you see it? I have tried for years to make people understand that animals have the basic right to be left alone. That's all, nothing more. Just let them be." Sandstone stood up and walked out the studio door, leaving John Power to field the flood of calls lighting up the switchboard.

"Your boss is a little over the edge, huh?" Menchen goaded Power.

"He's as dedicated as they come," Power said.

Lew Mason sifted through the reports on his desk. He'd ordered them into stacks based on levels of credibility: his top three leads in the middle; to the right, the less believable but still possible; to the left, the more off-the-wall but still remotely plausible. In his mind, it all came back to these big organizations. They would have the money to fund the radical ABP.

His three best shots were Animals International, CARE, and a slightly smaller but way-out organization called Stop the Cruelty. Based in Seattle, Stop the Cruelty had a newsletter that went out to twenty-eight thousand members monthly. Mason had acquired the last twelve issues and had noticed the increasing hysteria of their tone. A phrase from one of the letters to Gabrielle Norton—"You have seen nothing yet"—kept cropping up in the newsletter's editorials. Could it be the same writer? Mason had called the editor, R. L. Burke, several times (his number was unlisted, but Mason had easily gotten it with one call to the Seattle operator) and had received no answer yet. He had on his desk copies of Burke's high school yearbook photo, his Mensa membership application (he was refused), and his traffic violations record (two speeding tickets in the past ten years). He had an agent on his way to

Burke's apartment, where Burke also worked, and would be anxious to hear about his interview.

What was really frustrating was that the traces on the packages sent to Gabrielle Norton had led to nothing. The packages had been sent from various locations on the East Coast, but they could have been mailed from another location—say, Seattle—to someone else and then Express Mailed from Baltimore or New York. They'd been unable to lift any identifiable prints, hair, or skin fragments off the interior contents. The exterior prints either led back to post office people, Gabrielle Norton, and her secretary, Marta, or were too broken up to get a complete set.

The second possibility was CARE. The leader of this group, Greg Sandstone, was definitely suspect in Mason's mind. He'd always advocated banning animal testing no matter what and had apparently had clashes with his number two guy, John Power, who seemed to advocate a more middle-of-the-road policy and a greater attention to fund-raising. Sandstone had devoted his entire life to CARE and made no bones about it. Power, too, was devoted and had been arrested while at college in Ann Arbor, Michigan, for breaking into a research facility and destroying property. Though this set off a trigger in Mason's mind, nothing else in Power's past or in his speeches (all of which Mason now had complete transcripts of) indicated that he was willing to kill. Sandstone, on the other hand, was more outspoken and unpredictable.

CARE also had huge funding, which could be used to front some of the raids. Since donations came into these groups every which way—people often gave cash and even willed them cars and paintings—it was notoriously difficult to account for every dollar taken in, despite what Garrow had said.

Mason had sent two agents to New York City to interview Sandstone and Power. Predictably, Sandstone had become enraged, and Power had placated him and replied to the agents' questions coolly. Of course, this good cop/bad cop thing could all be an act. Mason was going to have to get a subpoena to look into CARE and the other groups' financial records. And he wanted to interview these two clowns himself; there were certain things he didn't trust anyone else to get right.

Animals International was Mason's last organization of choice. This group was more than twenty years old, was also incredibly well funded, and had an aging hippie and a former TV actress as its founders and current leaders. He doubted Carole Reeves and Fred Baumgold had finally lost it—they might be flakes but were too high-profile to do anything as crazy as what ABP was claiming credit for. Carole's TV career as the heroine of *Apartment 1501* had made her famous worldwide; Mason himself had watched her on the show every week as a kid, and he used to fantasize about her. Now, she used her high "Q rating" to raise money for her pet project. If not her, perhaps one of her minions had gone berserk. His agents' initial interviews had come up empty, but again, Mason wanted to see for himself. He'd already booked his flight to New York and would kill two birds with one stone by seeing Sandstone and Power on the same trip. Besides, it would be fun to see Carole Reeves in the flesh, even though she was probably sixty if a day.

Mason thought about Gabrielle Norton at the NIH. Nothing of note had happened; his plainclothes people had seen nothing worth following up in the two weeks they'd been there. Of course, it was impossible to secure such a huge building with so many employees. If someone wanted to pull a stunt at the NIH, the best Mason could do was have his guys ready to pounce at the first shot.

ADVANCED BIOSYSTEMS, LANCASTER, PENNSYLVANIA

JULY 26

"What are you worried about, Jim?" Sanford Taylor asked. "I hired a new security guard and let go of the old fart we had. This guy is dying to use his gun."

Since ten million people contracted malaria each year, the first firm to manufacture an effective vaccine was guaranteed a huge market, and at least three other companies were working on a malaria vaccine. "We've got to finish these tests. But I'll tell you, all these attacks on labs have me spooked," Jim Haggerty replied.

Taylor frowned, took him by the shoulders, and marched him past the receptionist out to the entrance of the building. A man who looked like a cross between Pancho Villa and Hulk Hogan stood by the door. Though he was less than six feet tall, he weighed well over two hundred pounds. He had narrowly set eyes and a shaved head, and he cradled an assault rifle in his arms.

"Hey, Anthony, how did you get that scar?" asked Taylor, pointing to a jagged four-inch line across the behemoth's left cheek.

"Attica, 1994," he responded humorlessly.

"What about the guy who slashed you?"

Anthony flashed a large smile that made up with sinister energy what it lacked in teeth.

"Now, who's gonna fuck with him?" asked Taylor as they went back inside the lab.

"I guess we're all right."

Haggerty and Taylor had both worked for Merck, which paid its microbiologists terribly. It was Taylor's idea to leave and go out on their own, and Haggerty agreed it was worth a shot. Haggerty had been working on a malaria vaccine at Merck but could never identify the best protein of the protozoan to use. When he finally figured it out, he and Taylor decided to leave—with the secret. They knew from previous testing that the vaccine was efficacious, but now they needed to prove that it was safe.

"The techs have injected the rabbits today, and we should know soon," Taylor said. *If it works safely, we're set for life,* he thought. It was the perfect setup: a disease that infected millions but, as a bonus, only in Third World countries, which didn't have a couple hundred thousand underemployed lawyers waiting to pounce the first time someone who received the vaccine croaked. It was possible the American Bar Association could load up a few 747s and self-righteously descend upon the aggrieved parties, like at Bhopal, but he wouldn't think about that. It was a good vaccine, and both he and Haggerty thought it would be only minimally toxic. Well, they would soon see. That's why God invented rabbits!

Haggerty was in the animal lab, which was encased by glass partitions, when he saw the main entrance door swing open. No one came in, but the door remained ajar. He left the lab, walking past the technicians and staff, to find Taylor, who was busy at his computer.

"The front door is open, Sanford," Haggerty said anxiously.

Taylor peered out his door. "Must be a delivery. Anthony would have warned us if there was a problem." He walked the forty feet to the entrance and popped his head out the door.

The motionless, muscular ex-con had a knife driven through his left eye. Before Taylor could react, Ed Palmer pushed him back into the lab and shot him twice in the head. The gunshots resounded through the entire building. Scientists, technicians, and secretaries ran for the rear exit. As they opened the door, Cecile fired her Mac 11 until all seven employees were down. When one cried out or groaned, she fired more bullets.

Haggerty was in his office on his knees, begging for his life. "Please, they're only rabbits, for Christ's sake."

"You know, if you hadn't said that, I would have let you die painlessly," Cecile calmly replied. "But now . . ."

"Finish him, and let's get out of here," Palmer directed.

"Shut up!" she yelled. "Dr. Haggerty is going to play role-reversal with the rabbits now."

"I said we need to leave!" Palmer yelled back as he loped past Cecile and put a bullet into Haggerty's heart. Then he grabbed her by the arm.

She violently swung her gun at him, just missing his head. "If you ever touch me again, I'll kill you."

"Cecile, we need to get out of here."

Why can man not understand that there is certain
knowledge that should be forbidden? The last thing
this planet needs is a vaccine that will save millions of
human lives. This biocentric world was meant to be
inhabited by all creatures and will not sustain the
continued effluvium of human waste and destruction.
You leave us few options, Dr. Norton.

ABP

Gabrielle Norton had put her kids to bed, run four
miles on the treadmill, and made love to her husband for
fourteen minutes. Now, back to work. Fourteen people
had been murdered, and labs were starting to shut their
doors. Mason and the FBI had interviewed hundreds of
animal rights activists and still had nothing.

She laid out the letters from the ABP. She was disturbed
by the way they progressed from a focused message of
terrorism directed at medical researchers to the more
global environmental ranting. Their desire for a more
biocentric world, one in which all animal life receives
equal consideration, was becoming a common theme
among deep ecologists and fanatical animal rights groups
alike. A respect for all life was one thing, but in the hands
of fanatics . . . Did the ABP have an agenda that went
beyond animal research?

She nibbled at her Kit Kat bar and pondered what, if
anything, she could do.

15

Trauma was primarily a nocturnal specialty, although the violence was beginning to creep past dawn. Residents assigned to the trauma service were often asked to scrub in on elective operations during the day, if they weren't busy in the intensive-care unit or in the emergency department. Since operating was what surgical residents liked to do best, no one had to twist their arms.

Casey was excited about doing her first operation with the chief of surgery. The case was routine and straightforward: placement of a cardiac pacemaker. She joined Simpson in the scrub room, eager to make a good impression. The scrub, a surgical ritual, took five minutes if done properly. The purpose of this disinfection was to remove the bacteria from the skin surface to greatly reduce the chances of the patient developing an infection. It also gave the attending the opportunity to discuss the case with the resident.

"So, Casey, how have you enjoyed your first month with us?" Simpson asked.

"Quite a bit, sir. I've done more trauma surgery this past month than in my entire residency," Casey replied enthusiastically.

"There's a lot more to surgery than sewing up holes in drug dealers and addicts," Simpson replied abruptly. The last thing he wanted to hear was how much trauma was being admitted to the hospital.

"Well, it certainly gives me a chance to operate. The scary thing is seeing how many times it's an innocent bystander who gets shot."

"I have a very simple solution to the problem. Make the drugs available at little or no cost to whoever wants them. If someone wants to be a crack addict, let them."

"That's one argument, but you could also argue that would only increase the number of addicts," Casey replied, unaware that colloquy with the chief was supposed to be one-sided.

"Who cares?" he boomed. "As long as those people have the drugs, they won't shoot each other or assault innocent bystanders. And the police don't have to die trying to stop this nonsense. The police have no chance anyway. They are outnumbered and certainly outgunned."

"I guess so," replied Casey, who caught on quickly. One big problem with legalizing the drugs was the unknown number of additional addicts—not to mention babies of addicts—that decriminalization would produce. But Casey kept those thoughts to herself.

As they continued to scrub, Casey noticed that Simpson was looking at her. His eyes made several passes up and down her body. When she turned to speak to him, he quickly brought his gaze back from bust level to eye level. "What kind of pacemaker will we be placing?" Casey asked.

"This woman has occasional episodes of symptomatic bradycardia."

"Sick sinus syndrome?"

"Probably."

"So we can put in a single-chambered demand pacemaker," Casey responded confidently.

"No, actually, I think we'll place a dual-chambered model."

"But her EKG shows sinus rhythm. If she only has occasional bradycardia, why use the dual-chambered model? Isn't it much more expensive?"

"Both for the device and its insertion," Simpson replied calmly. "If you're through scrubbing, let's proceed."

They both held their wet hands up in the air to allow excess water to drain off. Casey preceded Simpson into the operating room. She didn't notice him staring at her rear end. The scrub nurse then dressed them, Simpson first, as was customary, in blue gowns and white surgical gloves. Casey positioned herself on the right side of the operating table.

"We'll be putting the pacemaker on the left side. I presume it would be easier to operate from this side of the table," replied the chief.

"Yes, sir!" Surprised to be allowed to do the very first case she scrubbed in with the chief of surgery, Casey moved to the other side of the table.

Shirley Parker, who had worked as a scrub nurse for twenty years, was also surprised. Simpson never let new residents do his cases.

The case went well. They were finished in under an hour, with Casey doing the whole case from skin to skin.

"That was an outstanding job," Simpson said as he removed his gown. "If you would just take care of the postop orders, I'll speak to the family."

"Of course, Dr. Simpson," Casey said, not believing her luck.

Rebecca and Rachel were lying on the floor, their eyes glued to the television. They were watching their *Cinderella* video for at least the hundredth time. Glen and Zach were sitting on the couch eating popcorn, while Debby was at the desk in the adjoining kitchen, paying bills.

Cinderella had just had her gown ripped off by her unpleasant and homely stepsisters. Things looked bleak for the ball. The girls' anxiety was apparent as Rachel looked back at the couch.

"But she'll go to the ball? Right, Daddy?"

It always amazed Glen that despite the fact that the girls had memorized the video, they still worried about the outcome.

"Don't worry, honey. She'll go to the ball."

"And meet the prince, right?"

"Right."

"And live happily ever after, right?"

"Definitely." Glen smiled and shook his head. "I don't understand why Cinderella doesn't go down the street, buy a Saturday night special, and blow those ugly bitches' heads off."

"But how would she get away with it?" Zach asked.

"Jury nullification. Look at that sweet face. They would never convict her."

"What about the prince? She might never meet him."

"So what? She sells that castle, gets an M.B.A., and makes a fortune in the commodities market."

"Shh, I can't hear," Rebecca begged.

"I think this city is getting to me. I'm starting to think like all those other psychos with guns," Glen said as he shook his head. He looked at Zach. "It's your influence. Seriously, though, Zach, isn't it getting to you? The same crap every day. Five or ten people shot, most of them our age or younger."

"We've still got the best job in the world," Zach said without hesitation.

"It has its moments," Glen admitted, "but do you ever think we're becoming a little bit twisted? Think about it, Zach. We spend sixty hours a week dealing with the results of violence, and then what do we do for entertainment? We go see violent football games, violent hockey games, and violent movies."

"What's wrong with violence?" Zach replied defensively.

Glen looked at his best friend incredulously.

Zach cocked his head forward and glared at Glen. "You know what I mean. Listen, it happens whether we like it or not. People get shot. Cars crash." He paused and grinned.

"People are thrown out of buildings. It's the way things are."

Glen shrugged and conceded the point. "It's just that I think we get desensitized to the awful things that happen to people. Sometimes I think I'm treating a bullet hole attached to a life-support system, not a patient."

"That's pretty cynical. You're starting to sound like me."

"I'm just being realistic. We treat the scumbags as well as the private payers. They're all the same to us."

"Look, I do it because it's right. It's why I'm a doctor."

"I've also seen you give a patient money for food and clothes."

"We make too much money anyway."

"Shh," Glen said, putting his hand over Zach's mouth. "Never say that. The AMA will have you killed."

"Hilarious. Come on, Glen. You know I'm right. The average surgeon makes two hundred thousand dollars a year. Some of the fucking heart surgeons, like Simpson, for instance, make over a million. It's immoral. I could live well on sixty or seventy thousand, even in this city."

"Wait till you have kids," Glen suggested.

Money was one of the few things that Zach and Glen didn't see eye to eye on. Zach changed the subject. "We have more pressing issues to discuss than violence and money.

"Dr. Brenner, I presume."

"Correct. There's no way I can go two years and not be with that woman."

Glen winked at Zach. "I figured you wouldn't last six weeks—in fact, I bet a week of call on it, so I *hope* the two of you can't resist."

"You bet on me sleeping with her?"

"You're my best friend! Of course, I bet on you."

"But I can't even go out with her; she's a resident."

"Oh, yeah, your prime directive. Remember the old *Star Trek* series? They had a prime directive, too. Kirk was always obsessing about messing around with other planets."

"There's a point here, but I'm not getting it."

"Well, the point is, they violated it if it was really important to the planet's development."

"And I'm the planet in this weak analogy?"

"In desperate need of development," he continued. "Casey is a mature, intelligent woman. She is capable of completing a sentence without using *like* or *I mean* five times. She doesn't chew gum. I suspect she's even read a book without pictures in the last year."

"She has awfully nice—"

"Her ass isn't bad, either," Glen interrupted. "So, Zach, forget the self-righteous 'I can't date a resident' crap, and go for it! If she's not interested, she'll let you know."

"I don't know. This would be the first time since Susan that I'd really give a shit if a relationship didn't work out. There's just something about her that gives me the shakes. When I'm in the operating room with her, I don't want the case to end. I just want to be around her. If she blows me off, the fantasy is over. And then, of course, marriage would be out of the question."

"What do you tell me when we go to the gym?"

"Yeah, no pain, no gain." He grimaced. "That much pain I don't need."

"Pretend you're on the river, rowing your boat."

"You wouldn't be encouraging me just so you won't lose your bet?"

Glen shook his head. "If I lose, you take the call. You'll be so depressed that sewing up a few holes in someone's heart will cheer you up."

"Who bet against me? Ron?"

"Yeah. He figured she was too classy for you."

"That cocksucker can be the ring bearer at the wedding."

16

Forrest Wells was in unfamiliar territory. He pulled a folder from his briefcase. Simpson had given him two names, and this was his first stop. Apparently, Mr. Melendez had won a pool bet, but instead of taking away ten bucks, he took away ten bullets. Now he couldn't walk, had lost a few points off his Stanford-Binet test, and would never work again. It sounded like a good start.

Forrest got out of the cab, looked around, and wondered what he was doing in a place like this. Dilapidated apartment buildings lined 143rd Street. Directly across from him was a bodega with a broken neon sign that looked as if it hadn't shone in years. A few drunken black men sat in front of the store gulping their beer. He spotted two figures in an alleyway exchanging money for drugs, and it occurred to him how lucky he was to be able to have his drugs hand-delivered to his apartment. He regretted not hiring a car service, since he had no idea how the fuck he was going to get out of this war zone. This wasn't a place most cab drivers would stop to pick up a customer, and he detested being here. However, he had billed less in the last six months than any of the other associates in his year. He needed to make this work.

123

Forrest walked down the south side of the street, trying to identify the numbers on the buildings. He felt the stares of the area residents, who knew that guys in thousand-dollar suits generally brought trouble. He found 357 West 143rd Street and entered the building, which at one time was probably a beautiful piece of architecture. Hector Melendez lived in 3S, but the elevator wasn't working. Irritated, Forrest walked the three flights and tried the bell. No sound. He banged on the door. A chunky woman in her fifties opened it. In the next room, visible from the doorway, a man sat in a wheelchair, smoking a cigarette. A blanket covered his lap. There were no feet resting on the base of the wheelchair. *That's my man,* Forrest thought.

"Mr. Wells?" the woman inquired softly.

"Yes, Mrs. Melendez," Forrest responded as he handed her his business card. "Thank you for seeing me. I think I can help you."

"I don't know, Mr. Wells. We don't have any money for a lawyer."

"As I explained to you over the phone, I do this type of work on a contingency basis. If there is a judgment in your favor, I keep one-third of the award, and you keep the rest."

"I still don't understand how you found out about my husband. We never thought of suing. I'm just glad his life was saved."

"I was alerted to your husband's tragic outcome by a concerned nurse at UHC who was appalled at the care your husband received," he lied with a straight face.

"The doctors told us that they couldn't fix the blood vessels to Hector's legs fast enough because of the other injuries to his heart, lungs, and liver. He was shot ten times."

"Of course, that's what they told you to cover up their own mistakes. If he was that badly injured, why didn't they call in another surgeon?"

"I asked them, and they told me that because of other patients, there was no one else."

"Mrs. Melendez, we pay taxes to subsidize these hospitals so that we can get the best medical care." *At least, I pay taxes,* he thought. "They should have called someone else in."

"Do you really think we have a case? It would be nice to get a little money since Hector can't work."

Like this guy ever made any money. "I wouldn't have come here if I didn't think we could win this case." *That's for fucking sure,* he said to himself.

"Well, what do we have to do?"

"Just authorize me to pursue the case. I'll file papers and get the ball rolling. I'll be in touch as soon as something develops," Forrest said, picking up his briefcase and starting to leave. "There is one thing your husband will have to do."

"What's that?" asked Mrs. Melendez, glancing nervously at her husband, who stared hard at the wall, ignoring their exchange.

"He'll have to testify in court."

"But he can't even talk! A bullet went through part of his brain," she added, now upset and uncertain. She didn't want to put her husband through any more pain.

"It doesn't matter if he can't speak," Forrest replied. "Can he grunt if asked yes or no?"

"But for what reason? I thought the facts of the case were clear."

"The truth is that the jury needs to see the horrible condition your husband is in to empathize with him. That's how we get the big money. It's essential that he testify."

Mrs. Melendez's eyes began to well up with tears.

"I don't want to be brutal, Mrs. Melendez, but unless the jury sees him struggle, we'll never win."

She thought it over. "I guess. Go ahead," she allowed, still hestitant and unable to look directly at her husband.

"I'll be in touch," said Forrest as he turned to leave.

Lenore Attenucci was puzzled. Two lawsuits, one on the heels of another, had been filed against two different surgeons at UHC: Zach Green and Ron Stewart, two of her best. The suits were filed by the same man, Forrest Wells. Attenucci had called Collier Phipps, a highly placed lawyer friend, to check him out; no one in Collier's circles had ever heard of Wells, and upon further investigation, it appeared he was a very low-profile guy at Cox, Durham, and Anderson who'd never done any malpractice work before. Apparently, Wells hadn't made partner and was hanging on for dear life at his firm. This was probably a desperate attempt to salvage his career, Collier had guessed.

Attenucci's phone rang, and her secretary buzzed her. "Woman on the line says she's calling about the lawsuits. Her English isn't too good—I'm sorry, but I couldn't get her name too well. Melendez, maybe?" said Rowena.

Attenucci grabbed her papers on the Melendez case and looked at them quickly. It must be the wife; she was the one bringing suit. "Put her on," she said.

The speaker light blinked, and Attenucci picked up and went directly to damage control. "Hello, Mrs. Melendez. I'm so sorry about your husband. I'm sure there's a way for us to discuss this and come to some conclusion without your having to go through the long process of a lawsuit. Would you like to come to meet with me here at the hospital? Or I could come to your home or somewhere nearby," she quickly added, "if it's more convenient."

"Oh, that won't be necessary, Ms. Attenucci," replied a crisp voice. "But I would love to stop by your office. It's Amy Mendoza from the *New York News*. I think your secretary had me confused with someone else."

Lenore scowled. "Ms. Mendoza, I don't appreciate your using tactics like this to get through to me. I have nothing to say on the subject."

"What subject? I haven't even asked you about the lawsuits yet. But I did hear something was up," Amy said slyly. "In fact, I'm going over to talk to Mrs. Melendez today. I just wanted to get your side of the story, too. You know, to be fair."

Lenore attempted to suppress her anger. Mendoza somehow always managed to get under her skin. But she couldn't afford to let her do that now. "Amy—may I call you Amy, and please call me Lenore," she began. "I don't want to waste your time by having you make a trip here to see me. Our record speaks for itself. We have an excellent group of trauma surgeons here. You know that. In fact, if I recall correctly, you've written several very complimentary pieces about their work. Frankly, I think this is a case of misguided enthusiasm on the lawyer's part. You might want to check him out," Lenore said. "I don't think he's ever done malpractice before, and he seems to have stalled in his career. But I'll leave all that to you."

"Thanks, Lenore. OK if I talk to Zach Green and Ron Stewart?"

Lenore gritted her teeth. "I guess I can't stop you, Amy."

"I just thought that as CEO, you should know all the details, Lenore." Simpson dropped a large folder with the bills of particulars for the lawsuits on Attenucci's desk.

"Try not to look so upset, Ted," she said. She skimmed the files and exhaled. "Did you review these cases last year?"

"Of course. As chairman, I review all the deaths and complications."

"Did your quality assurance process identify any problem with the quality of care rendered?"

"No," he admitted.

"Well, I'm having our people from risk management review the cases; they sound bogus to me. The lawyer appears to be an inexperienced ambulance chaser."

Simpson gritted his teeth but didn't change his facial expression. "I agree, Lenore, but that isn't the main issue, is it? Image is everything, right? Well, I doubt that two lawsuits, hot on the heels of each other, will be very helpful publicity-wise. Wouldn't you agree?"

"I really don't think a couple of silly lawsuits will affect our reputation."

"I certainly hope not.

* * *

Simpson walked back to his office, shut his door and took off his jacket. After lighting a cigarette, he dialed Forrest Wells's office and waited while Forrest's secretary tracked him down.

"It's Ted Simpson, Forrest. I have a few more names for you."

"Slow down, Ted. I'm only one lawyer," Forrest cautioned.

"Listen to me. Our CEO still isn't appropriately concerned with our wayward trauma service. We need to keep up the pressure. These cases are like SCUD missiles: not too accurate but quite destructive if one hits the target."

"I'll do the best I can. The first deposition is in a few weeks. What's Dr. Green like?" Forrest asked.

It bothered Simpson when he actually thought about Zach, the ultimate perfectionist, being sued. Zach had been his favorite resident, and Simpson had tried to coax him into cardiac surgery. "I'd be careful with him, Forrest. He's unpredictable."

"So, Emily," Zach said, holding the phone with his shoulder as he scanned the *Post*'s sports section for Mets scores. "I wish that I could never see a poem lovely as a tree."

"That's not Emily Dickinson, you goof," said Amy. "That's drivel."

"Gee, I always thought that was her line. Sounds like her," Zach said, grinning.

"Listen, I'm not calling to discuss literature. I just got off the phone with Attenucci. We were talking about these lawsuits."

"Oh," Zach said. Wow, this was hitting the press already? "How'd you hear about it?"

"I have my sources. So Attenucci thinks it's a bad lawyer run amok. What do you think?"

"I did the best job possible on Mr. Melendez. He came in like a piece of Swiss cheese, and I did everything I could for him. No surgeon could have saved his life *and* his legs.

I must have spent dozens of hours taking care of him. Sometimes you just can't win."

Amy clicked her tongue sympathetically. "Do you have any paperwork you could show me?" she asked. "To back up your story?"

"My story?" Zach pleaded. "It's not a *story*, it's the truth."

17

"Who is that?" Zach looked up from the chart he was
working on at the ward station during his afternoon
rounds and saw a tall, lanky, strawberry blonde stroll out
of a patient's room. She had a hospital name tag on, but he
had never seen her before.

Glen looked over. "Beats me," he said after glancing at
the woman.

"Look at those legs."

"Hey, I thought you were in love."

"I am, but since it's unrequited, at least at this point, I
have to keep my options open."

Glen groaned.

"Susie, who is that woman?" Zach asked the ward
secretary, a woman about sixty years old whom he had
known since he was a medical student.

"One of the nutritionists."

"She's beautiful."

"Forget it, lover boy. See the ring? She's engaged to Stan
Madsen."

"Madsen? Beautiful, but very bad taste."

Zach turned back to Glen. "She's engaged to Madsen."

"So?"

130

"He's that gynecologist who drives the Porsche with the license plate 'PELVISDOC.'"

"Oh, yeah, the guy whose usual indication for a hysterectomy is the presence of a uterus. A putz," Glen agreed.

Zach smiled as he got up and adjusted his tie. "Madsen doesn't deserve her," he said as he took off down the hall.

She was coming out of a patient's room, and Zach chased her down the floor. "Excuse me, but I noticed you were from the nutrition service, and I was wondering if you could tell me how much sodium is in a liter of Ensure. I have a patient with bad congestive heart failure who's not eating much."

She half smiled and pushed her long bangs off her forehead. Out of a briefcase, she retrieved a pamphlet that had the nutritional values of all the food supplements used at UHC. "About four hundred mg. It should be OK."

"Thanks," Zach said, and he turned and walked off in the opposite direction. He quickly reversed himself and followed her down the hall again. When he caught her, he tapped her on the shoulder. Her short-sleeved blouse exposed tan arms. Her back was narrow and muscular. "Excuse me."

"Yes?" She stopped and turned around.

"I lied."

"Huh?"

"I don't have a patient with congestive heart failure."

"Really." The half smile had evaporated.

"I just made it up so I could meet you."

"I have to go," she said, glancing down at her watch. She didn't leave.

"If I didn't make up that story, then we would have never met."

"We would both survive."

"My name is Zach Green. I'm a surgeon here." He held out his hand, and she shook it.

"My name is Karen Sherwood, and this is my engagement ring." She held up a two-carat heart-shaped diamond.

"Is it serious?"

"I'm engaged, you idiot."

"Have you set a date?"

"It's none of your business."

"Do you know that fifty percent of engagements never end in marriage and that fifty percent of marriages end in divorce?"

"Do you know that you're annoying?"

"Can I show you one thing?"

"What?"

Zach took her left hand and turned the engagement ring around so the diamond was no longer visible. "Can we have a drink later?"

"Do you think you're charming?"

"No, just persistent."

"That's for sure. Are you married?" she asked.

"To my work. Can I pick you up at eight?"

She wrote down her address, gave it to him, and started to walk back down the hall. Zach put his hand on her shoulder, and she turned back once again.

"Wait a second. You forgot to say, 'But only one drink.'"

"Maybe two." He saw the full smile as she turned down the hall.

As Zach walked back to the nursing station, Glen just looked at him, dumbfounded. "You amaze me. I can see your infatuation with Dr. Brenner was short-lived."

"Not at all. I'm in love with her. This is pure lust."

"How do you do it?" he asked, shaking his head. "I've seen you do this ever since college, and I've never understood the secret."

"No secret. You just have to be willing to strike out three out of four times."

"Yeah, but five hundred home runs gets you into the Hall of Fame."

Zach ignored that, thought about Casey, and took a slow, deep breath. "I don't want to strike out with Casey. On the other hand, I have no business going to the plate with one of the residents. Now I understand what cognitive dissonance is. I'll sort it out on the river. Need to work out before my big date tonight."

"Listen, Zach, you don't really know Casey Brenner that well. You may end up hating her."

"I don't think so. A mystical force is working there."

"Cut the Zen shit. I want full details of this one in the morning. My vicarious thrill tank is down two quarts."

"I'll bring the Polaroid. See you tomorrow."

The boat glided over the water, unaffected by the slight chop or the garbage that accented its surface. Zach had rowed five thousand meters and was still pulling at thirty strokes per minute; not bad sculling fifteen years after college. Complete solitude. It was the only time he felt totally free from the hospital, and the hour he spent on the East River three times a week was inviolate. He never carried his beeper, though there wouldn't be much he could do if it went off while he was rowing.

There weren't many places to keep a twenty-foot boat in Manhattan. He stored his shell in a crew house owned by Columbia. In college, he had rowed for Cornell on Cayuga Lake. His dream had been to row single sculls in the Olympics, but he was short about five inches and fifty pounds.

He had gotten to know the coach of the Columbia crew team after removing his daughter's appendix eight years ago. During his residency, Zach had gotten badly out of shape, and sculling again helped him get back into good condition, although he would never be the aerobic machine he was in college. In addition to the three times per week on the water, he did an hour a day on his rowing ergometer which occupied the center of his living room. This eight-foot-long monstrosity used a heavy flywheel attached to a bicycle chain for resistance. A seat that slid along a metal bar replicated the motion of sculling. This machine provided a brutal workout and was so popular among scullers and would-be scullers that each year in Boston, there was a contest to see who could row twenty-five hundred meters the fastest.

Compulsiveness and hard work were Zach's creed and his secret to being a great surgeon. Do it the same way every time. By his own estimate, he had missed only three days on the erg or the river in the past five years. He glided and looked at the city. Somewhere, a bullet or a knife was piercing flesh, but for one hour he didn't care. He guided the boat back in the opposite direction and began to pull. Could he break eight minutes for five thousand meters?

A goal. Without a goal, whether an A in organic chemistry, a sub-eight-minute five thousand meters, a flawless operation, or a beautiful woman, Zach was lost. When he became introspective, a rare indulgence, and pondered his goals in medicine, he realized that at times, the lives he had saved were secondary. The perfect technique, the fastest hands, the best judgment—sometimes those were his only goals. But wasn't the reason he became a doctor, his ultimate goal since he was a boy, to help the patients? He sometimes needed to remind himself of that, and he shouldn't have had to. His parents and grandfather had taught him what things were important. And what about a family? When he was with Rebecca and Rachel, he knew that's what he wanted. Unfortunately, he came up short on the wife requirement.

He strained as he crossed under the Fifty-ninth Street bridge and 3:59 flashed onto his watch. He increased his cadence to forty-one strokes per minute; he would have to maintain that pace to break eight minutes. Three minutes and twenty seconds later, he broke his previous personal best. Zach folded the oars up into his boat, coasted, and tried to catch his breath. Another goal attained. What next? Was it time to grow up?

Maybe after his date with Karen Sherwood.

They met at Cecile's apartment in Queens. There had been four attacks, reams of media attention, and the FBI and NIH had jointly issued an alert to all labs doing biomedical research. The net result of their efforts was that a disappointing eight percent of research facilities had closed. Cecile saw how agitated Palmer was. "What did you expect?" she said to Palmer. "Right now, the FBI has a few dozen agents trying to figure out which of the few hundred known animal advocate groups has finally gone off the deep end. They're calling around and sending agents out to interview all the people they can. They'll never catch us."

Ed Palmer shook his head. He was no more than five-foot-three but lifted weights obsessively and was powerfully built. He had a few strands of thin blond hair, which he combed forward, and delicate facial features. He worked at a bookstore and, like the others, was unmarried and lived alone.

Palmer had narrowly escaped having a criminal record. Last year, he had become so enraged during a protest at the Central Park Zoo that he ripped open the iron fencing that caged the monkeys with his bare hands. The cops were so busy catching the monkeys that he was able to disappear into the park. He had raged for years over the torture and murder that took place in thousands of university and industry-sponsored concentration camps. But now that fury was channeled. They were finally going to put a stop to it.

"I want more targets," Palmer said. "No matter how many researchers we eliminate, the ends are justified." For every human sacrificed, hundreds, maybe thousands of animals would live.

"You're right, Palmer," Cecile commented. "The effect of our early attacks hasn't been significant. We need to follow them up quickly."

The phone rang. Cecile picked it up.

"I'm calling from a pay phone, but your phone may be tapped, so be careful what you say," came a male voice. A subway thundered in the background, and the speaker had to pause for a moment. "I'm working on getting more money. With your help, I should have control of CARE soon. When I do, we'll escalate to stage two, just as we planned."

"We need to move faster. Thousands of labs remain open."

"Patience, Cecile. You know the plans, and remember who is in charge here," he barked.

"Okay," said Cecile, suddenly deflated. She slammed the telephone down. Why was it still so easy for him to put her in her place?

"What did he say?" Palmer asked.

"He's going to have more money for us by next week. Stage two begins," she said calmly.

"How can the three of us pull it off alone? The future attacks he's described will be even more dangerous. The planning will need to be perfect. We needed Sorrentino!" Palmer shouted. He couldn't get her out of his mind. She had been a soul mate and the first woman he ever loved. One of the doctors interviewed after the attack at MMC said he saw one of the terrorists shoot Sorrentino. None of the others in the laboratory could confirm it, and Cecile vehemently denied it. At first, Palmer didn't believe it, but after Cecile threatened him during the last attack, he realized it was possible.

"He hasn't told me," she admitted. Her stare bored into him. "Are you having second thoughts?"

Palmer didn't blink. "Not about our mission." He got up and walked to the door. "I'll see you here Saturday at two."

Cecile was twenty-eight years old and a dropout of Vassar College. In school, she'd majored in anthropology and now supported herself by working as a teaching assistant at PS 105. Sorrentino had recruited her for the group after witnessing Cecile bludgeon a woman wearing a mink who had unwittingly stumbled across an antifur rally in Central Park.

Because of the confusion at the rally, no one had identified Cecile as the attacker, and the case remained unsolved. Extremists declared the day a success, arguing that while one woman might not live, dozens of minks would be saved by the deterrent her attack created.

Cecile was estranged from virtually everyone she had ever known. Her own father, a research scientist, had planted the seed that grew into her commitment to animal rights. When she was eight, her father began bringing her to a lab where he was studying techniques to perfect liver transplantation.

Forever etched into Cecile's psyche was the memory of the innocent beagles shaking with rigors and cowering with pain as their own lymphocytes rejected the livers implanted in them. To make it worse, Cecile's father had become romantically involved with a lab assistant and often left her alone in the lab for what seemed like hours while he rendezvoused with the woman at a nearby motel.

The young girl struggled to calm the whimpering dogs, talking to them in the same quiet, doctorly tones her father had used when she'd had her tonsils removed. Months passed, and all the while Cecile believed that her father was working to heal the tortured animals. When she finally realized that he was the cause of their agony, she was destroyed, and it ended their relationship. Cecile never returned to the lab; the discovery came as a devastating betrayal and forever crippled her ability to trust or love.

Now when Cecile entered a lab, it wouldn't be the animals who suffered.

"We have Chuck from Arkansas on the line. Chuck, you are on the air."

Brad Menchen had received hundreds of calls after his interview with Greg Sandstone and John Power. At first, most of the calls echoed his own viewpoint, but in the last ten days a surprising number of people called in who sympathized with the animals. He had subsequently invited several other animal rights advocates onto the show and had spiked the ratings by making mincemeat out of each of them. In terms of raw, unadulterated insanity, Sandstone and Power had actually been mild. Menchen goaded two of his guests into suggesting he should be the next victim of the ABP. With these ratings, he was certain it would only be a matter of time before he had a television show. Brad Menchen was finally going to hit the big time.

"You know, Brad, most Americans agree with you about these animal rights nuts. The next thing you know, these commies are going to try to ban hunting and fishing. If a scientist wants to practice on a dog or rat or what-not, who cares?"

"Thanks for the call, Chuck. These people actually think that animals should occupy an equal footing with man. These miscreants, these self-hating, misanthropic fruitcakes, in an attempt to exorcise some inexplicable guilt from their psyches, somehow think that abnegation of meat, leather, and, worst of all, the pursuit of medical knowledge will lead to equality among the species. This is erroneous reasoning at its most outrageous. Human beings are king of the beasts. Animals were put here for us to use as we see fit."

"That goes double for me, Brad!" shouted the caller, not certain what Brad meant but thrilled at the sound of his own voice on the air.

Menchen was proud of his facility with the English language and thought his barrages of unintelligible verbal arcana added to his persona as an intellectual beacon of the right.

The calls continued, many on the animal rights issue, others on the poor, the homeless, gays, and any other group the average American perceived as dangerous in some way. After the show, Menchen said his good-byes to the crew and left the studio for dinner. He went to the parking lot where he kept his car, fantasizing about a chauffeur. He walked up the incline and saw his black Lincoln Continental, which Sam, the attendant, had ready every evening at eight o'clock. After starting the car and turning on the radio, he backed down the incline. He pulled out of the garage and headed toward the Palm, which prided itself on serving the largest steaks in New York. All this talk about animal rights had given him quite an appetite.

18

Casey was in Operating Room 7 with Simpson—to Bruce Evans's dismay. Evans, the chief cardiothoracic surgical fellow, had planned to do the quadruple bypass with Simpson. He hadn't done nearly enough coronaries as a first-year fellow, and this was his year to do more open-heart surgery. It was a waste for Casey to scrub in on a case she wasn't going to get to do. Fourth-year surgery residents didn't do coronary artery bypasses. Evans had made up the schedule, his prerogative as the senior fellow, but it had been changed by Simpson—his prerogative.

Evans had just finished doing a lung resection, an operation he hated and one that would have been more appropriate to Casey's level of experience. After downing a cup of tepid coffee, he went to the OR to relieve her and do the delicate anastomoses of the vein grafts to the tiny coronary arteries. When he walked into the room, he couldn't believe his eyes. Casey Brenner, a fourth-year general surgery resident, was on the right side of the table, the operating surgeon's side, doing a distal anastomosis. Once in a while, Simpson would let general surgery residents do a proximal anastomosis, just to throw them a bone. But never a distal, which was done while the patient was cross-clamped and time was crucial.

"Need some help, sir? I'm all done with the lung resection."

"I think we're OK here, Bruce," Simpson replied without looking up.

Evans walked out of the room shaking his head. He saw one of the perfusionists, Nick Rastelli, who ran the bypass machine, returning from a break.

"Can you believe that girl is doing the case?" Evans asked, disgusted.

Rastelli shrugged. "She's got good hands. Her first distal took nineteen minutes. It still takes you almost thirteen."

"That's beside the point. Since when does one of the general surgery residents get to do a bypass? I didn't do any until three months into my fellowship."

"Her ass is a lot nicer than yours," Rastelli replied.

"I guess so."

"Come on, Bruce, it's not Casey's fault. Simpson asked her to scrub. She's not going to refuse."

"Wait until she finds out what she has to do for him."

"That's another story," Rastelli admitted. "Ya know, I think he's either screwed or tried to screw every woman perfusionist who's worked here for me."

"His track record with female surgery residents and medical students is about the same. But Christ! Letting her do a bypass! I've gotta get another cup of coffee."

Rastelli laughed. He'd been at UHC for almost seven years. "You know, Bruce, I remember when you were a general surgery resident. You would have gladly fucked Simpson if he let you do a bypass."

"Blown him, maybe," joked Evans as he headed to the cafeteria.

Evans had taken only one bite of his doughnut when his beeper went off. It was the OR, and Simpson wanted him to come scrub. *About time,* he thought. *You need the senior fellow on these tough cases, not some pretty face.* He gobbled the rest of his doughnut, swished down some coffee, and returned to Room 7. As he walked in, he noticed that the patient was off bypass.

"Bruce, could you and the intern close the chest for me? I have a meeting to go to, and Casey has another commitment."

An order disguised as a request. He couldn't believe it: she did the case, and he had to close for her. "I'd be glad to," he said, grinding his teeth and wondering if being a heart surgeon was worth putting up with this indignation. Then he remembered the job offer he had lined up for a starting salary of two hundred thousand a year.

"Oh, I can close, Dr. Simpson," Casey quickly said, embarrassed by the uncomfortable situation.

"No, I need to speak to you. Dr. Evans can close."

Casey shed her gown as Evans walked by her. She shrugged her shoulders and rolled her eyes. "Sorry, Bruce, it's not my fault," she whispered.

He ignored her and went to the table.

"Nice job, Casey. I'd like to see you in my office in fifteen minutes," said Simpson as he exited to the men's locker room.

"Yes, sir," she replied.

As she changed, she saw Shirley Parker come into the locker room. "Shirley, can I ask you a question?"

"What's on your mind, honey?"

"Does Simpson usually let the general surgery residents do the heart cases?"

"Old Simpson could help a monkey do one of those cases. He can do a distal in under five minutes, so even if the resident does one or two and it takes a half hour, his pump run is still shorter than most surgeons'."

"You didn't exactly answer my question."

"Let the general residents do bypasses?" Shirley said. "Not in a million years. I'd be watching my flank if I were you."

During the walk to Simpson's office, Casey was haunted by recollections of her last surgery program, though she had suppressed that since she'd been at UHC. *It's going to happen again,* she told herself.

She made her way into the chairman's suite. There was no one in the outer office, usually occupied by his secretary. Simpson's door was ajar. Nervously, she approached it and knocked.

"Come in."

She entered to find the lights off and Simpson seated, looking at some angiograms. She saw a small circle of light flicker strongly and ebb as Simpson pulled on his cigarette. Clouds of smoke were visible as they drifted through the light beam of the film projector.

"Sit down, Casey." There was a seat to his left, which she quietly took.

"That was a very nice job today." He crushed out the cigarette.

"Thank you, sir."

"You can call me Ted, in here."

She wondered if the other residents called him Ted.

"Thank you for letting me do so much of the operation today."

"Well, you're here to learn. I think you'd make a fine heart surgeon. We have a spot open for a fellow in two years, when you'll be done with your residency."

"That's very flattering. I'll have to give it some thought."

"Of course, it's a big decision. I just want you to know, if there is anything I can do for you, let me know."

"Thank you. Is there anything else?"

"I know how busy you are. Have a nice day."

She got up from the chair, slightly relieved, but sensed his eyes following her out the door. She wouldn't think about it right now. She had to check on the animals and prepare herself for another long night. At least Zach was on call with her; that always kept things lively.

Stu and Casey operated on three dogs in two days. Casey had decided that the best time to test the dogs' intelligence was on the third postoperative day. By that time, the animals were pain-free and were acting normally. Casey had finished rounds at six in the evening and headed to the surgery animal care lab where the animals were kept. The first group of dogs seemed to act normally after they were subjected to the hypotension followed by a short period of circulatory arrest, but they would need to be accurately tested to determine if there was any significant change in their intelligence.

The animal lab was in the west wing of UHC. Casey took the tunnel to the new wing. There was no guard at night, and she used her encrypted ID badge to enter through the steel doors. Patricia Ascott, the chief veterinarian, was finishing up for the day. She made sure all the animals were healthy for the experiment and had adequate pain medication.

"Here to check your patients, Casey?" Ascott asked.

She nodded, though she didn't really consider the dogs patients. "And to do their cognitive screening."

"Interesting study," Ascott said noncommittally. "You are essentially putting the animals in a state of suspended animation."

"That's true," Casey said, "but you make it sound like science fiction. Hypothermic circulatory arrest has already been used in elective surgery. We're just trying to extend it to injured patients."

"You mean almost-dead ones," Ascott added. "That's a lot different."

"We understand that, but just think of the potential benefits if it's feasible. Eventually, we will be able to fix injuries in patients who currently have no chance."

"As long as the patient is just nearly dead, as opposed to *dead* dead," Ascott replied.

Casey nodded affirmatively. "That's true. Once a patient arrests from blood loss, it's almost impossible to get him back." Casey hesitated for a moment. "What do you think of the research?"

Ascott smiled. "You don't need my approval. If I had a problem with the protocol or your postoperative care, I'd let you know."

"I just wondered what you thought, from a veterinarian's perspective," Casey asked earnestly.

"I think it is methodologically sound but suffers from the same inherent weakness of all animal research. Can you infer from the results of your experiment that humans will be affected the same way as dogs?"

"What do you think?"

"You know as well as I do that a dog's brain is not nearly as complex as a human's. Your cognitive scoring may miss subtleties in a dog that could be profound in a man."

"That's why we're looking at the microscopic sections of the postmortem brain."

"Good idea."

"Pat, can I ask another question?"

"Sure, go ahead," Ascott replied.

"Does it bother you? All the animals that are"—Casey paused, searching for the best euphemism—"used here?"

"These dogs are my patients. I make sure they are properly cared for before the experiment, completely anesthetized during the procedure, and as free of pain as possible postoperatively. I get attached to some of the animals. But I believe that animal research is important." Ascott smiled warmly at Casey and put her hand on her shoulder. "Is your conscience clear now?"

Casey shuffled around. "As clear as it can be, I guess."

"If you didn't have some ethical and emotional qualms about taking the life of another living creature, then I would really worry about you," Ascott added sympathetically.

Casey hesitated. "You mean like Zach Green?"

Ascott laughed.

"Is he that bad?" Casey asked, remembering Zach's outburst the first day they met in the library to discuss the research.

"He's bad, all right. A pain in the ass is what he is. But when he actually conducts an experiment, he stays with the animal postoperatively to make sure it gets enough morphine. He says he doesn't trust us. He plays with the dogs like a five-year-old."

Big talker, that Dr. Green, Casey thought.

Ted Simpson unlocked the door of his Ferrari and sank into its leather seat. Simpson had more toys and gadgets than most men could dream of. He had slept with more beautiful women than he could remember. Unfortunately, the law of diminishing marginal return was universal, and each additional possession he acquired, each new woman he screwed, made him less happy.

Simpson had married young, poor, and ugly. Neither he nor his wife of thirty-five years had any money when they wed. Victoria had been a theater major at Yale, but her dream to be onstage was thwarted by an oversized jaw, weak cheekbones, and beady eyes, so she went for her teaching credentials. Simpson, no matinee idol himself, never had a date until he was a senior and met Victoria at a fraternity party. They lost their virginity together and were married the spring before graduation. She taught school and waited tables in New Haven so he could be third in his medical school class.

Early in his residency at Massachusetts General Hospital, Simpson discovered that attractive women who were repulsed by him just months before found the prefix *Dr.* irresistibly alluring. He lost his wedding band in the locker room one month into his training, got laid three successive on-call nights, and never put it back on.

An insatiable quest for material things and women governed Simpson's life. He wanted to own every expensive car, live in every mansion, and sleep with every beautiful woman he laid eyes on. And once he had what he wanted, he no longer wanted it. He was in perpetual need of a new car, a new woman, or a new house.

As he pulled out of the parking lot, Simpson looked back at the hospital where he had been a successful researcher and where he was now a respected cardiac surgeon. For him, the accumulation of material possessions had been a powerful addiction. When he was still in the lab, he had saved his modest salary for two years and bought a used Porsche. The novelty of that car, his first taste of the affluence that would eventually control him, lasted for several months. The power of the car, the admiring glances it received, the buzz from it were only transient. Soon, he had to have a newer car, a faster car. He couldn't control the desire. That was when he decided to leave research and become a cardiac surgeon.

One of his professors in medical school had warned him about the quest for money. Horace Verbock, an internist, told him that having too much money took your mind off what was really important. He reminded Ted that you needed only enough to have a decent house, eat well, take a vacation once in a while, and educate your children. Your family and your work were what mattered, and what you'd be remembered for. It was the best advice he never took.

It was ten o'clock, and Anita Diaz was sleeping in her bed along with her two sisters, Natalie and Ramona. Their apartment on 145th Street had only two rooms. The girls' parents slept in the combination living room-kitchen area. Luis Diaz was a janitor in another apartment building, and his wife, Maria, made some money cleaning apartments in the lower, more affluent part of Manhattan. Despite bringing home an above-average amount of money for that neighborhood, the small apartment was all they could afford. It was spotless and in good repair, unlike many other apartments in their building and the ones surrounding it. Luis was certain that pride in one's home and personal appearance was transferred into everyday performance at school or work.

Luis was pleased with his daughters. They all did well in school, and Anita, the youngest at eight, was considered gifted. He had read to the girls each night since they were infants and hoped the future would be brighter for them than his had been. His early involvement with drugs and gangs prevented him from fulfilling his potential. Luckily, although it didn't seem so at the time, he was shot during a dispute with a rival gang. His right leg had been amputated below the knee. This prevented him from keeping company with his dangerous companions, and perhaps from being killed on the street, like many of his friends. He had met Maria during his stay in the hospital, where she was a volunteer, and soon after that they were married.

Luis was saving his money so that he could move his family to a less dangerous neighborhood. Within a ten-block area, thirty-five people had been killed in the last year, and an uncountable number more had been shot.

Jamal Denzel was playing basketball in his new Air Jordan shoes. At fourteen years of age and five feet five inches in height, he could dunk a basketball forward, in reverse, and spinning around three hundred and sixty degrees. His friends called him the Rocket. The basketball courts were well lit at night, illuminated by both the streetlights and the lights from the cars moving down the FDR. The courts themselves were in poor repair. The asphalt was peppered with small potholes, and the netless rims were steeply angled downward from the strain of thousands of dunks and dunk attempts. The painted lines on the courts had eroded long ago.

There were six baskets, three on each side of the large playground. A few half-court games were being played, but Jamal wanted to practice his moves alone. Even though his interest in schoolwork was minimal, he hoped to get a scholarship to play college basketball and go on to the pros. If only he could grow a few more inches, he thought. He knew he would make it if he just got the chance.

Three older youths, whom he had seen before but did not know, approached him on the court.

"Yo, man, lemme have your shoes," commanded the largest of the gang, who was a full head taller and at least twenty pounds heavier than Jamal.

"Back off, man, I just bought these shoes; I worked for them," Jamal responded cautiously.

"Yo, bitch. Unless you want to get bucked, you best gimme your fucking shoes."

"OK, man, OK." Jamal sat down and pulled off his beloved Air Jordans; they certainly weren't worth dying for, he thought.

The crew leader picked up the shoes and winked at his friends. "Ya know, I think I'll get me a body anyway." Jamal was still seated on the ground when he realized what was happening. He pushed off the asphalt to run away. The older teen allowed him just enough time to get up before he unloaded a magazine of eight bullets. The first bullet literally took his head off; the next seven made his identification more difficult. As the dead boy lay in a spreading pool of blood, the teenagers ran off, certain that they wouldn't be caught.

The police came to the scene of the homicide minutes after an EMT, who had arrived by ambulance, declared the boy dead. Charlotte Raines had worked as an EMT for less than six months and was nearly ready for another career. She was getting sick of seeing children skeet-shoot at each other. The volume of violence was overwhelming the city's capacity to handle it. And the money to attack the social underpinnings of the carnage was forever lost to a three-trillion-dollar national debt. Hopeless? Charlotte had begun to think so.

The police were interviewing those witnesses who hadn't evaporated into the sweltering night after the murder. One twelve-year-old who lived in Jamal's apartment building identified the body and gave the police the boy's address. Terrence Wilson, the homicide investigator, was not surprised, however, when the witnesses could not or, more precisely, would not identify the murderers. He suspected this murder, like so many others, would remained unsolved.

Wilson filled out the paperwork and drove several blocks to Jamal's apartment. After several knocks, a black woman, who appeared less than forty years old, opened the door. She immediately sensed what had happened and was just waiting to find out which of her remaining sons had been killed.

"Are you the mother of Jamal Denzel?" Wilson asked softly.

"My baby!" she shrieked. "My baby is dead!" She fell prostrate to the ground and pounded the floor.

Wilson kneeled down and put his hand on her back. "I'm sorry," he said. "Do you know anyone who might have wanted to harm your son? Was he in any recent fights?" There were so many kids with guns that a minor school dispute that twenty years ago would have resulted in a few broken teeth and noses today generated dead bodies. "Miss Long, here is my card. If you find out anything, please call me." Wilson unfolded his wallet and handed the mother his precinct card. "We'll send a car so you can see your son."

The woman said nothing.

"I'm sorry," Wilson said. When there was no answer, he turned and walked back to his car.

"Bobby, your brother's been shot," shouted Keith Miller to Robert "Beaver" Denzel. A cigarette hung out of the mouth of the dead boy's sixteen-year-old brother. He was shooting a game of pool.

Beaver looked up from the table and threw down his cigarette. "Did he ask for it?" he asked in a controlled voice.

"No, man; he just playing hoops, and these three guys come steal his shoes. Then they just blow him away—for nothing."

"You know these motherfuckers?" Beaver demanded. Robert Denzel had no aspirations to play professional sports. He had been dealing drugs since he was eleven years old. At thirteen, he developed a rep for killing a rival drug dealer. By his own count, he had murdered five men since then; killing a man meant no more to him than killing rats in an alley to test out a new gun.

"I know the one who shot him," replied Keith, eager to please Bobby. "It was Thomas Bivens. He live up at the apartment on the corner."

Keith pointed to the building in which Luis Diaz and his family lived.

At midnight, just after Luis had checked on his daughters and gone to bed, Beaver broke into Thomas Bivens's apartment. He found him sitting up in bed, leaning against the wall that adjoined the Martinez bedroom. He was smoking a joint and wearing Jamal Denzel's Air Jordans.

"Those is my brother's shoes, motherfucker." Beaver pulled out a Mac 11 machine pistol and started firing. Thomas Bivens died as quickly as Jamal had.

Luis Diaz heard the gunfire, hopped out of bed, having already taken off his prosthetic limb for the night, and raced into his daughters' room. Ramona was dead, shot through the head at least twice. Natalie was screaming but uninjured. Anita, his youngest, was coughing up blood and gasping for air. There was blood pouring out of a wound in her arm. He ran to her and covered the spurting artery with his undershirt. Maria, who had realized what had happened, called 911. Luis clutched Anita, who wasn't crying. She was concentrating on breathing and barely succeeding. Maria entered the room and shook Ramona hysterically in a vain attempt to revitalize her. It seemed like hours before the ambulance arrived.

The EMT entered the room and quickly assessed the situation. Anita was in shock and acute respiratory distress. A bullet had entered her left pleural cavity, probably causing bleeding and an air leak inside her chest. The arm wound was bad but not life-threatening at the moment. The EMT knew she didn't have any time to spare. She quickly intubated Anita, placing a breathing tube in her trachea, so she could breathe for her. Then she deftly placed an intravenous line in Anita's uninjured arm to administer fluids until blood could be given at the hospital. The girl's blood pressure had fallen to sixty as the ambulance sped to UHC.

Casey Brenner was the only available senior resident when Anita Diaz arrived at UHC. The fifth-year resident was busy with another case. Anita was placed on the table in Trauma Bay 2.

"She probably has a tension pneumothorax on the left side," the EMT gasped as she helped the nurses get Anita's clothes off and place another IV. Casey listened for breathing sounds and heard none on the left side. She quickly placed a number 32 chest tube through the girl's chest wall and received a welcome blast of air, confirming the diagnosis of tension pneumothorax. With the air trapped around the lung evacuated to the outside, Anita's breathing became easier. But following the air out of the tube was a torrent of blood.

"BP is fifty," shouted the nurse.

"Get some O blood hanging, we're going to the OR. This kid is bleeding to death!" Casey shouted as she and the intern began to push the gurney out of the ER.

Whipping down the corridor to the operating room as fast as they could go, the child, shot by two bullets not even meant for her, grasped the rosary beads her mother had given her before the ambulance left and fought for her life.

Within minutes, Anita was placed on the operating table, prepped, and draped. Casey, who had no time to scrub, squirted some Septisol, an antiseptic foam, on her hands.

As she made the incision between the fourth and fifth ribs, Zach ran into the room. "What is it?" he asked as he peered over Casey's shoulders.

"An eight-year-old with a left chest wound and almost no BP."

Zach quickly scrubbed and came to the table. By then, Casey was in the chest. He could see that the girl was exsanguinating.

Casey had packed the chest, but blood continued to well up through the packs. Zach cranked the rib-spreading retractor up a few notches for better exposure. Casey cringed at the sound of the child's cracking ribs. Zach put his hand in the chest and compressed the hilum of the lung which contained the left pulmonary artery, vein, and bronchus. Most of the bleeding stopped. "Works every time," Zach quipped as he replaced his fingers with a vascular clamp. "OK, guys, fill this kid's tank. You have enough blood?"

The anesthesiologist was somewhat relieved as the child's blood pressure rose to fifty. "It's coming," he said.

"It's a good thing you were here," said Casey as the circulating nurse wiped her forehead.

"We'll see," said Zach. He knew they weren't home free yet. "What do you want to do now?"

Casey thought for a moment. "The injury is in the hilum. We will need to do a pneumonectomy."

Zach shook his head. "If you take out this girl's lung, she's dead."

"Why? We do pneumonectomies for lung cancer all the time."

"This kid has been in profound shock. Her other lung won't tolerate the extra blood flow, and her right heart will fail. Although I've never had the displeasure of doing a pneumonectomy on an eight-year-old, I've never seen someone with prolonged shock survive one. We need to fix the injury—if we can."

"Her blood pressure isn't going anywhere," warned the anesthesiologist.

"There's nothing else bleeding in the chest," Zach said calmly. "Where else did that bullet go?"

He lifted the left lung and saw a hole in the diaphragm. "She's bleeding in her belly. Gimme a knife." In about thirty seconds, he had her belly open. It was full of blood; there was a massive hemorrhage behind the liver.

"We're fucked," he said, shaking his head. "It's got her retrohepatic cava." He grabbed a half dozen packs from the scrub nurse's table and stuffed them into the right upper quadrant against the liver. "Sorry to steal your case, Casey, but I can't teach right now. I haven't got the faintest idea what to do myself."

"How can I help?" Casey asked, relieved that Zach had taken over. She was out of her league.

"Keep pressure on her liver. I'm going up to her chest to put in a shunt."

Zach extended the incision across the chest so he could get to the right atrium and place the shunt. First, he clamped the thoracic aorta to raise the blood pressure. Within three minutes, he had guided the shunt down the vena cava. "Can you feel it?" he asked.

"Yes, and I think it's above the renal veins," Casey responded.

"OK," he said as he inflated the balloon of the shunt. "Put a clamp across the blood vessels leading to the liver."

Casey placed the clamp without difficulty, stopping blood flow to the liver from the hepatic artery and portal vein. Zach came down from above, flipped the liver out of the way, and found the hole in the cava. There was still quite a bit of bleeding from the cava and liver.

"That's why these shunts aren't worth shit!" he yelled. "We lost ten units of blood placing the thing, and the fucker is still bleeding. OK, suture please, four-zero proline." He deftly sewed the two-centimeter tear and stopped the bleeding from the vena cava. The liver was still oozing, as was everything else. Anita was hypothermic—her body temperature was only ninety-three degrees, and blood didn't clot at ninety-three degrees.

"Zach, she's not doing well. BP is only sixty with the aorta clamped, and her oxygenation is getting worse. You have to get flow back to the other lung," said the anesthesiologist, who was the first to realize this had become a hopeless cause.

"Help me up here, Casey." Zach returned to the chest and took the pack out. He could see the left pulmonary artery completely divided. There was no choice. He removed the entire left lung. But Anita kept bleeding. He knew he had to get her chest and belly closed—the heat loss with two body cavities opened was massive, and the colder she became, the more she would bleed.

"She needs more blood, give her more blood!" he shouted at the anesthesiologist.

"Zach, there's no way—"

"Give her more fucking blood!" he screamed. "She's eight years old—you never give up on a kid!"

Casey had never seen Zach lose it in the operating room. He looked as if he was close.

The anesthesiologist took two more units of blood and some fresh frozen plasma and pumped them quickly through the blood warmers into the deteriorating child. Her blood pressure rose slightly—a Pyrrhic victory.

"I'm going to try packing her. Get me a dozen sponges," Zach asked. He knew he couldn't stop the bleeding with sutures and hoped to pack Anita's belly and chest full of sponges to compress the bleeding, get her off the table and into the ICU. If he could get her there and warm her up, she had a chance.

Zach quickly packed her belly while Casey packed the chest, but the child's blood pressure continued to drift downward. Even with more blood and the packing, Anita's blood pressure never climbed above thirty again.

There was no point in going to the ICU.

Zach and Casey watched over the child for ten minutes until her heart finally stopped beating.

The room was silent. Zach closed the incisions with a single suture through all the tissue layers and removed the drapes. The colorless child was unrecognizable, swollen to twice her normal size from all the fluid and blood she had been given.

"Sorry I lost my temper," Zach said to the anesthesiologist. He walked out the door.

Casey followed. "I'm sorry I wasn't very much help in there." Her lip was trembling. The sight of the dead child was too much for her. She burst into tears. "A baby. She was a baby."

As tears rolled down his own face, Zach put his arms around her.

"She had two fatal injuries. You did fine. Technically, we did everything we could have." He swiped at his eyes.

"How can you stand it?" she asked, crying on his shoulder.

Zach knew how she felt. Sick to her stomach. Useless. He rarely experienced those feelings anymore. He knew he did the best job that could have been done. When he first started out in practice, if a patient died, he would be depressed for weeks. But the more he saw, the shorter the length of time it took him to recover. A defense mechanism, perhaps.

Still, two things would always get him: if he made a mistake or misjudgment that killed the patient, which happened less often as he gained experience, or when the victim was a child or teenager, which was happening ever more frequently.

Zach looked at Casey. She had handled herself well. "We need to talk to the family," Zach said." If you want me to do it alone, I will."

"No, I'll go with you," she said, blowing her nose. "It's part of the job."

"It sure puts a different perspective on our research when you see the actual injury, doesn't it?" Zach said.

"The next time I see a hole in the retrohepatic vena cava, there's going to be a better way to fix it." Casey walked toward the waiting room and silently vowed to spend another night each week in the lab.

19

Brad Menchen poked a fork through the eye of the pig roasting on the barbecue spit. "Now, this should offend absolutely no one. The pig is already dead."

He smiled into the cameras gathered to cover his Animal Rights Fair. Dozens of people had come to see the show, while hundreds more protested at the periphery. He had set up thirty mock gravesites and placed the name of an extinct species of animal on each of the fake tombstones.

"With Animals Before People attempting to close laboratories violently, do you really think this is wise, Mr. Menchen?" Amy Mendoza asked. She'd tried to get a private interview with Menchen before the fair, but he'd refused to see her. He hadn't wanted to blow the surprise.

"Amy, I'm a social commentator, not a researcher, and I'm just trying to illustrate the sheer idiocy of this movement."

"Don't you agree that it's frightening, the number of animal and plant species we're losing each year?"

He flapped his hand at her. "Ninety-nine percent of species that have ever existed are now extinct. That's a fact. Dinosaurs lived here for thirty million years, and now they're gone. What's the big deal? The only species that we need to worry about is man."

"You're a brave man, Mr. Menchen. I hope that none of those protesters are ABP, or you could end up the next victim."

"I'd like to see some of those marginalized losers sign a paper that waives their right to any medical treatment developed through the use of animals. They'd be reduced to using leeches and high-colonic enemas."

Mendoza shook her head and smiled. "What's next for you, Mr. Menchen?"

"Amy, a talent for satire such as mine comes along only once every ten years. I'll be on network television and be as big there as I am on radio."

Menchen quickly turned away and began answering questions from a reporter for the *Post*.

Menchen's show had been a publicity extravaganza. Feeling smug, he picked up his black Lincoln Continental at the garage and headed uptown to his apartment.

"What the hell," he grunted as he heard a click. He turned his head around and saw a woman holding a 9mm pistol six inches from his head.

"I suggest, Mr. Menchen, that you turn around and drive where I tell you."

"If you want money, I have more than five hundred dollars in my wallet. Just take it," he pleaded.

"Keep your money, Mr. Menchen. Head for the George Washington Bridge."

"Where are you taking me? Please, I'll give you anything, just let me go." Tears were streaming out of his eyes, and he had just urinated in his pants.

The woman directed him up to the Palisades Parkway. He sobbed and begged to be let go. She directed him off the highway to Spring Valley, a small town in upstate New York, and to a small house on a sparsely populated, heavily wooded street. She got out of the car first, continued to point the gun at him, and pushed him inside the small house. Palmer was ready.

"What do you want with me?" Menchen begged.

"Mr. Menchen, I don't think you take me seriously. But that is going to change," Cecile insisted.

"It was all a put-on for ratings. Honest. I don't really believe that stuff. I love animals. Please let me go!" he screamed.

Ed Palmer grabbed Menchen's hands. Despite his attempts to resist, Palmer quickly bound his hands and feet. By then, Menchen was sobbing hysterically. As he lay on the floor, writhing to free himself, Cecile took an apple from her jacket pocket.

"Perhaps in death, you will be able to serve the creatures you have so defiled on this earth during your regrettably brief life," Cecile chanted.

"You're crazy. You crazy fucking . . ."

While Palmer held him still, Cecile placed a metal clamp on his nose to prevent him from breathing. Then Palmer took the apple, stuffed it into Menchen's mouth, blocking his breathing completely. As he lay suffocating on the floor, the animal rights advocates gathered around to watch him die, occasionally prodding him with forks.

"A pig is a dog is a man, Mr. Menchen. Now you'll know what it's like to be the pig."

Menchen's corpse, harpooned by a steel beam and suspended between two garbage bins, was discovered the next morning as it lay smoldering over a fire in an alley ten blocks from where he used to work. The initials *ABP* had been carved into his charred chest.

Gabrielle Norton had left work at ten before finishing the final budget estimates for the next fiscal year at the NIH. A Polaroid of Menchen along with yet another ultimatum from the ABP had wrecked her already fading concentration.

The light on her phone blinked; she always turned off the sound at night so it wouldn't wake her sleeping household. "Hello?" she said.

"Mom, sorry it's so late. I was going to call earlier, but

we went out for pizza." Brooke, her seventeen-year-old, was calling from New York, where she lived in a house with three other Bronx Science students and a dorm mother. Gabrielle had hesitated about sending her so far away for the summer program, but Brooke had begged, and the school was renowned nationwide for its excellent academics. Brooke was going to apply to colleges this fall and had every hope of getting into Harvard or MIT.

"No problem. I was going to call you tomorrow. How'd you do on your test?"

"I think I aced it, but I'll find out Friday. Mom, someone showed me in the paper about this animals rights group sending you letters. I'm worried about you. They've killed people! Maybe you should stay away from work for a while."

"Honey, nothing's going to happen to me. They wouldn't dare attack a government building. And there are FBI agents swarming around all over the place. I've been in touch with a top guy there, and he assures me nothing can happen."

"You trust those guys? What about after you leave work, are the agents following you home?"

"No, but I'm not worried," Gabrielle lied.

"They killed Tara McVey at home."

"That was different. She was a researcher. I'm just a paper pusher," Gabrielle said, trying to sound convincing.

"Well, I wish you'd just work at home for a few weeks till they catch those people. Isn't that why you got a fax for your study?"

"I'll be careful. What about you? You aren't taking the subway alone, are you?"

"I'm taking care of myself, Mom. Don't worry."

"How is Kim Lee? Do you see him at all anymore?"

"He hasn't called me since June. I think he's got a girlfriend; I see them in the library together all the time," Brooke said dejectedly.

"You could always call him. You don't have to sit and wait for a guy to call you."

"I know. I guess I just don't want to if he's seeing

someone else. There's a cute guy in my calculus class," she said, perking up. "But I haven't spoken to him yet."

"How are you liking calculus?"

"I love it! But the lab is still the best. The AIDS work I'm doing for the Rockefeller Institute is being presented at the Science Expo at the Javits Center. And guess what? They're going to let me present it. That makes me eligible for the Young Researcher Award." Brooke's premise was to increase the concentration of drug treatment to the white blood cells, the cells that carry the HIV virus, without increasing the dose and its toxicity. She proposed bathing the white cells in the drugs by using a phoresis machine to collect the cells and then return them to the body. Primates would be the best animals on which to test her theory. Her mother had no idea she was working on animals, and Brooke planned to keep it that way.

Gabrielle smiled. Her daughter was determined to defeat AIDS in her lifetime. With her youth and dedication, perhaps she had a shot.

"I bet you'll win it," she said.

"There's a lot of stiff competition. Don't be disappointed if I don't."

"I won't be. You never disappoint me, honey. Could I come up for the fair? I should be able to get away from the office for a couple of days. It would be great to spend some time together in the city, just you and me."

"Sure. I'll look up the exact dates and call you. I'd better go, though. Carmen is waiting to use the phone."

"I love you, sweetie. Thanks for calling."

" 'Bye."

"Oh, one more thing, Brooke. I don't want you actually working in animal labs until this business blows over, OK?"

"Do you actually think they let me do that good stuff, Mom? Get real."

Gabrielle sighed. "All right. I'll see you soon, honey."

Gabrielle hung up and looked at her reams of paperwork, suddenly exhausted. She hated that Brooke had heard about the ABP's threats and hoped Mason would find those maniacs soon so they could all focus on more important things.

Brooke kicked off her shoes, lay back on her bed, and opened her calculus book. Tomorrow she would be in the lab hooking the baboons to a phoresis machine to harvest their white cells. She felt guilty lying to her mother.

20

Casey finished rounds at eleven in the morning. She was free to go home. Her body felt heavy, and her legs were painfully stiff from standing most of the night. But Casey was thinking of Anita Diaz, and she made her way to the lab. She and Stu planned to work on a couple of dogs this afternoon.

"You look pretty tired, Dr. Casey," Stu said as he watched her head directly to the coffeepot. He was arranging surgical instruments that had just been cleaned in the autoclave.

"I'm OK, Stu," Casey said, pouring herself a large dose of caffeine. "I had a rough night of call."

"I don't know how you do it, Casey. You need to take care of yourself." Stu had seen lots of residents come through but never one as driven as Casey. Not a day went by that she didn't come by the lab for at least an hour or two.

"I'm OK, Stu. Without you, this project wouldn't be anywhere. You're better with your hands than half the surgeons I've seen."

"Thanks, Casey. That means a lot coming from you."

Stu hesitated for a minute. "What do you think about all these labs getting attacked?"

She took a gulp of coffee. "It's scary. I hope the FBI will catch them soon. Simpson hired some private security guards. I've seen them, and they look pretty tough. I feel safe here. How about you?"

Stu looked away for a moment. He seemed embarrassed. "My wife isn't too happy."

"Are you going to leave?"

He shrugged and said nothing.

"What would you do if you left here? You've worked in the lab for almost thirty years."

He grinned. "My wife says early retirement beats early death."

"Who's going to keep me out of trouble in the lab?"

"Look, I'm just talking. For now, I'm not going anywhere. What's the plan for today?" he asked to change the subject.

"I really want to extend the circulatory-arrest period."

"Well, the first four tolerated it pretty well," replied Stu, and he began preparing the operating table. "Their cognitive test was normal after the experiment, too."

She nodded. "The pathologists looked at the brain sections and couldn't find any histologic abnormalities. But a half hour isn't very long to fix such a bad injury, even in a bloodless field, and I also think a shock period of only thirty minutes is too short." By the time they got inside little Anita's belly, she had been in shock for almost an hour. A half hour would not realistically simulate the amount of time it took to get an injured patient from the field to the OR and on a bypass.

"If we shock the dogs for an hour, we'll have to repeat the thirty-minute circulatory-arrest times, too," Stu replied.

Casey nodded. Essentially, they would have to start over again.

"I guess that's OK, except it's going to take a lot more dogs. Prices went up again last week. Seven hundred bucks a pop."

"The price is irrelevant. We'll do what it takes to get the answer. Anyway, I think we have enough in our account to cover about twelve more animals. I'll run it by Zach and Glen." Seven hundred dollars for a dog, she thought. Without all the extra paperwork imposed by the government, the cost would be half that. But Zach was right. There was no equation to compute how many dogs equaled an eight-year-old child's life. "Today, let's start a group with an hour of shock and thirty minutes of arrest time."

It was already eight o'clock, and Casey hadn't eaten since noon. The hunger had kept her awake. She decided to go to the cafeteria for a quick sandwich before heading home. She was on call again tomorrow and needed to get some sleep. As she was putting away her laboratory notebook, the door opened and someone's head popped in. It was Zach.

"Late hours. How are things coming?" he asked.

"The results look pretty good. Look at this. After thirty minutes of shock and arrest, none of the five dogs suffered any obvious intelligence drop." She showed him the lab notebook. "But we need to extend the shock period to an hour before we prolong the circulatory-arrest time. Thirty minutes just isn't realistic."

"We should have enough money to add extra animals. Let me run it by Glen." He paused. "You've been working hard on this. Maybe too hard. Aren't you on call again tomorrow night?" Casey's eyes were underscored with dark circles, and she looked pale—like most surgical residents.

"Yes," she admitted. "I'm just going to the cafeteria for a sandwich before I go home."

"From the cafeteria? Nah, I have a better idea. Have you eaten in a good deli since you've been in New York?"

"No, I haven't," Casey responded. Her fatigue temporarily dissipated. "Do you have somewhere in mind?"

"The Second Avenue Deli. It's only a couple blocks away."

"Let's go!" As they walked out of the hospital together, they passed Simpson, who was on his way home.

"Good evening, doctors. Heading out on the town?" he quizzed.

Zach looked at him and chuckled. "Now, Ted, you know we work much too hard to do something like that. Actually, I was just walking Dr. Brenner to her car," he said. Where they were going was none of Simpson's business.

"See you tomorrow," Casey added as they continued on.

As they walked to the Second Avenue Deli, Zach wondered if Casey had ever eaten in a kosher restaurant before. He doubted it. She might order a BLT on white bread and a glass of milk. He laughed aloud.

"What's so funny?" Casey asked.

"Nothing. I just thought about a joke I heard today," he replied with a smile. He was happy to be with her.

"Tell me."

"Don't know you well enough yet."

They reached the restaurant on Tenth Street, and were seated in the Molly Picon Room, named after a star of the Yiddish theater. A middle-aged waitress, wearing a stained apron, brought them menus and a large dish of dill pickles. Casey, famished, devoured one immediately. She examined the expansive menu, and the waitress quickly returned to take their order.

"What can I get you, honey?" she asked Casey.

"Well, it all looks so good. Get me a bowl of matzoh ball soup, corned beef on rye, and some kasha varnishke. And I'll have a Dr. Brown's cream soda to drink."

"And you, dear?" the waitress asked Zach, who was staring at Casey in amazement. "Uh, get me a ninety-nine and a black cherry soda."

Casey caught the expression on his face. "What did you think I was going to order, muskrat on Wonder bread with a milkshake?"

"I'm just surprised. Kasha varnishke?"

"My grandmother was Jewish, and my roommate from

college was from an Orthodox family. I went home with her for a lot of the Jewish holidays. Her mother was a great cook and taught me plenty. My specialty is latkes."

"I'll remember that on Hanukkah."

Casey smiled. "Are you observant?"

"More than most of my Jewish friends but not enough to make my parents happy," Zach explained. "I grew up in a kosher house. I still go to synagogue once in a while."

"Religion wasn't too big in my house. We had a Christmas tree, but that was about it."

"I went to synagogue all the time when I grew up, but usually I just prayed that I would get into medical school," Zach added. "Probably not exactly what God had in mind."

"When did you decide to become a doctor?" Casey asked as she sipped her coffee.

"In utero."

"Come on," she responded.

He nodded. "My family had this general practitioner, Dr. Stein. I loved him. I remember when I was five years old, I had the flu or something, and my mother thought I was dying. Dr. Stein came to the house at two in the morning to see me. He carried this huge black doctor's bag, which was full of medicine and instruments. He examined me and told my mother I had pneumonia. I wasn't sure what that meant, but I was afraid he was going to give me a shot. I started crying and begged him not to. He held up his hands, opened them, and showed me that he had no needle. Then he had me turn over—I thought to take my temperature. Next thing I know, I get a shot of penicillin in my ass. To this day, I don't know where he hid the needle. He made house calls all the time. Can you imagine?"

"Not anymore," Casey admitted.

"He was my idol. I used to love going to his office, except for the shots. I paid attention to the way he examined me. I used to practice on my sisters. I can still remember the smell of his office, that old-fashioned combination of antiseptic and medicine. One time when I was in the office, I asked Dr. Stein if I could have a couple of empty medicine bottles so I could play doctor."

"That's how you played doctor when you were a boy?" Casey asked rhetorically. "We had a slightly different version where I grew up."

He shrugged his shoulders. "I was a nerd. What can I tell you? On my birthday, Dr. Stein's wife, who was a friend of my mother's, brought over this big package. Inside were about a hundred empty medicine bottles, all sizes and shapes. There were tongue depressors, and he even gave me a stethoscope. I was hooked. I never thought about being anything else but a doctor."

"So why did you become a surgeon? That's about as far from a GP as you can get," she said as their dinner arrived.

"I was going to do general medicine. I was a kid. I thought the doctor was a magician and that his stethoscope was his wand. But when I got to medical school, I realized that type of doctor didn't really exist anymore. At least, I never saw him. Dr. Stein did adult medicine, pediatrics, and delivered babies. He even took my tonsils out. You can't do that today unless you practice in the middle of nowhere. The people who go into family practice end up being gatekeepers for managed care. Can you imagine letting somebody who only trained for three years take out your appendix? It seemed to me that general surgeons, and particularly trauma surgeons, could do the most for their patients in the shortest period of time." He took a bite of his chicken with mushrooms. "What about you?"

Casey signaled to the waitress for some more coffee. "Most of my classmates thought I was crazy to go into surgery. The majority of the professors thought women should be internists or pediatricians. The usual sexist nonsense. But after my clerkship in surgery, I knew it was what I wanted to do. Actually, I didn't really decide to be a doctor until I went to college. My parents are both college professors, and I figured that's what I'd do. I just sort of fell into it. Not predestined like you. Were you always such a straight arrow?" Casey asked.

"Yeah, I guess so. I had a perfect childhood. My parents were crazy about each other and adored their kids. My grandfather lived with us and taught me how to think for myself and about right and wrong. He was a real Talmudic scholar. Mom never smashed me in the face with a frying pan, and my father never played hide the salami with my sisters. No Oprah shit."

She just laughed. "You have such a way of putting things."

"That's what people tell me. And were you a rebellious youth?"

"Not really." She paused and thought for a second. "Well, maybe by your standards. My mother and I didn't get along when I was a teenager. Typical stuff. Once she caught me and my boyfriend smoking a joint, and I thought she was going to kill me. She didn't talk to me for two months."

"Are you still a drug abuser?" he asked with a grin.

"Come on. Every kid I knew tried that stuff in high school. I think I used it three or four times in my life." She never knew when Zach was kidding, although she suspected he was now.

"I didn't."

"Why not. Weren't you curious?"

He cut his matzoh ball into four pieces, ate the first one, and sighed contently. "Best matzoh balls in the city. Tender but with a backbone. But I digress." He took another bite, savored it for a few seconds, and began again. "When I was four, I was curious about what would happen if you stuck your tongue into an electrical outlet, but I didn't do it. A little bird—kosher, of course—told me not to smoke, ingest, or inject addictive substances into my body."

"Your box of Crayolas must have been missing the color gray."

"Actually, my mom would never get me that big box, you know, the one with sixty-four colors. She bought me the box of eight and figured I could mix the other colors if I needed them. I don't like the color gray. There is black, and there is white." Zach cupped his hands under his chin and put his elbows on the table. He grinned. "I'm enjoying this metaphoric dialogue. Let's see if we can keep it going."

"Metaphor? I thought you were allergic to English."

"I love English. I went to a Catholic high school where the nuns pounded us with grammar and syntax. A dangling participle was the eighth deadly sin."

"But you're Jewish."

"My parents wanted me to go to private school, and they couldn't afford the secular schools. So I spent four years with the nuns. Wanna hear my Latin?"

"How many Jews were there in the school?"

"Me."

"Wasn't it tough being the only Jew?"

"I was president of the class."

"In a Catholic school?"

"Sure you don't want to check out my Latin?"

"Some other time, maybe. So you made up that story about T. S. Eliot," she said with a half smile.

"Not at all. I just never enjoyed reading literature or poetry. Particularly that anti-Semitic, nihilistic, expatriate scumbag Eliot. I usually read nonfiction. My favorite book is the encyclopedia."

"You read the encyclopedia?"

"Sure. If you know everything in the encyclopedia, you can infer anything else you might need to know."

"You never read the classics? Hemingway or Dickens or Tolstoy or . . ."

He shook his head no and made a face like a child taking medicine. "I did read *Candide*. My kind of novel. Violent, cynical, and short. Would love to have been on call the night of an *auto da fe.*"

"Are you really this weird?" she asked. "It's hard to tell

169

when you're serious. I read everything I could from the time I was ten years old. C. S. Lewis said you read so you know you're not alone."

"I wouldn't know about that, but talking to you, I don't feel the least bit alone. Do you?"

"Not right now, Zach. Lewis was speaking metaphorically. I enjoy being . . ." She stopped and corrected herself. "Talking with you, too."

Zach caught what she almost said. "Now, Casey, you would have to be with someone in order to talk to them. Otherwise, you'd run into a mind-body problem."

"Uh-huh."

"You see, that's where the encyclopedia comes in handy. The *World Book* has a great section on metaphysics."

She started to get up from the table. "This was wonderful, but I think I need to acclimate myself to you in small doses." She threw down fifteen dollars to cover her part of the bill.

He swigged down the rest of his Dr. Brown's and jumped up from his seat. "I'll walk back with you."

They caught each other's eyes for a second and quickly looked away. Zach opened the door for her, and they started toward the hospital.

Casey was lonely. She hadn't had a date in six months. *It's tough to meet anyone when you work all the time,* she thought. She recalled playing tennis, running, reading books, watching movies, and dating before her residency, but now all that seemed remote. Other than Daphne, whose social calendar kept her out five nights a week, Casey had no friends in New York. Zach was a guy she could learn to like. In fact, she already did. Too bad he was her boss.

I lust, therefore I am was Zach's version of Descartes. But this was more than lust.

21

The surgery department held a faculty meeting once a month to discuss problems within the department and to make important announcements. Simpson ran the meeting and attempted to make it as concise as possible. The average attention span of the surgeons was about fifteen minutes, if you didn't count Zach, who was limited to five. This day's agenda included one of the residents who had been written up by the nursing supervisor for verbally abusing an intensive-care nurse.

Charlie Mahoney had a history of losing his temper and getting testy with the nursing staff. His latest incident had been particularly obnoxious. One of his patients in the intensive-care unit had become disoriented during the night and pulled out his arterial line. The A-line, as it was known, was inserted into the radial artery of the arm and used for monitoring blood pressure and drawing blood. The patient, Mr. Shawn, had undergone surgery for a perforated ulcer nearly two weeks ago and hadn't done well. His major problem was sepsis, from an abdominal abscess that developed after the surgery. He required close monitoring and frequent blood chemistry determinations. When Mahoney was told the line had been pulled out, he went crazy and screamed at the nurse for ten minutes, using every commonly known obscenity and a few new ones that he had concocted.

"We will not tolerate this kind of behavior from our residents," Simpson said angrily. "It is not the image this department wishes to portray."

"It's OK to try to fuck the nurses, but don't yell 'fuck you' at them," Zach whispered into Glen's ear. Glen started laughing.

"Can you let us all in on the joke, gentlemen?" Simpson inquired, annoyed.

"I was just telling Glen that the language of some of our residents is shocking," Zach said in a mockingly serious tone.

"I'm glad you two think this is so funny, but let me assure you that the director of nursing does not."

"Ted, I'll talk to Charlie. He was exhausted, and the line falling out pushed him over the edge. He's a good resident, he just has a short fuse," said Glen in a conciliatory tone.

"You had better get him calmed down. I don't need the nursing administration on my back." Simpson shuffled some papers. He was going to mention the lawsuits but thought better of it. He wasn't in the mood for one of Zach's tirades.

"The next thing I want to talk about is this animal rights business and the wave of terrorism. I know many of you are involved in ongoing research work, and I urge you all to be extra careful."

"Why don't you all stop doing animal research? Be an example, part of the solution, not the problem," Erica Talarico blurted out.

"Erica, this really isn't the time to debate this."

"It's never the time, is it, Ted?" Talarico replied. She stood up and began pointing her finger at everyone in the room. "Why don't we try taking biomedical research into the twenty-first century?"

Glen looked over at Zach and anticipated some impending unpleasantness.

"What Erica really wants are donations for the UHC branch of Animals Before People," Zach told the group.

"You disgust me," Talarico replied. "You all know damn well that your animal work accomplishes nothing."

Simpson sensed a riot in the works and slammed his hand down on the table. "Fourteen people are dead, Erica. No one wants to hear this now."

"And that's a tragedy, but so is the murder of helpless animals."

"You ought to worry about the helpless people you murder in the operating room," Zach whooped.

"You bastard, I'll have you . . ."

"Both of you stop it," Simpson growled. "We all know what you think about animal research, Erica, but no one in this room agrees with you, and we're not going to debate it. Are we clear about that?"

Talarico glowered, picked up her briefcase, and stormed out of the room. She was sick of being ridiculed.

Simpson waited until the door closed behind her and continued where he had left off. "That incident at the Manhattan Medical College last month was gruesome," Simpson continued. "The dean's fund is spending four to five thousand dollars a month beefing up security around all the labs. More than a hundred labs have closed nationally. Some producers at CNN want to do a segment on animal rights and medical research. They have asked me if we would provide a spokesman for the animal research side of the issue."

One of Simpson's strong points as chairman was his legitimate commitment to research. The fact that he hadn't been in the lab for years didn't diminish his desire for the surgery department at UHC to be productive and respected in both basic science and clinical research. His materialism and avarice were tempered in part by this commitment, and he was generous when it came to departmental funding of research. Of course, this was predicated partly on the income limits at UHC. As a chairman at an academic institution, he was required to turn back any income that exceeded a million dollars. In the past ten years, he had billed almost three million dollars a year and grossed nearly 1.5 million. He turned over the extra half million dollars to the surgical research fund. But if his gross income fell below a million, the research fund would get nothing. He had no intention of taking a salary cut to support research.

"Ted, I'd be glad to do the show," Zach said.

"After your performance at the research committee last month, you must be joking," Simpson remarked. "Calling these people names, even if provoked, only makes us look bad. Thank you for the offer, but I think not. Glen, I want you to do the show. You can present the case for animal research as well as anyone I know."

"Sure, I'll do it. But do I get a bulletproof vest?" Glen responded glibly.

"Don't joke. The way things have been going, anything is possible," Simpson warned.

"Well, I'll try hard not to piss them off. But it's important to show how ridiculous their arguments are."

"Just make sure you have plenty of facts to back up what you say. Some of these people are very intelligent."

"That may be true, but their reasoning is based on misrepresentation, half-truths, and lies. I've read Singer and Regan's polemics. They don't even agree with each other on the subject of animal rights."

"That's true, Glen, but they still come to the same common conclusion: using animals is wrong."

Glen was surprised that Simpson had read Singer and Regan. Most physicians railed against the assault on research without understanding the arguments. "I didn't know you were into philosophy, Ted."

"I have many talents, Glen. Just remember, if a lie is outrageous enough, people tend to believe it. History has proved that sad fact," Simpson lamented. "The show is next week. I know you can make the proper points, but no matter how provocative your opponent, don't lose your temper."

* * *

CARE Bylaws, Section 7

The election of officers, including the president, shall be conducted yearly during the month of August. Any member of CARE in good standing shall have the right to run for office. An election shall be considered valid if thirty percent of the electorate votes by proxy form, and victory shall be determined by a plurality of votes.

During the months of May, June, and July, more than two thousand phone calls were made soliciting votes for John Power. His fresh leadership, they emphasized, would do even more than Gregory Sandstone's to improve the lot of animals. Power was portrayed as a moderate voice on animal issues, and most of the members who voted had no reason to doubt it.

"Our own incorporation certificate is very clear, Greg. You've been voted out. I'm the new president." John Power stood in front of the desk which he was soon to occupy and handed Sandstone the printout of the proxy vote.

"Only thirty percent of the membership voted, and ninety percent of those have been members for less than a year," Sandstone complained.

"The charter, which you wrote, required only a thirty-percent vote and made no reference to length of membership." Power put a hand on Sandstone's shoulder. "I just hope that you'll continue to work with me. The organization still needs you. We just can't continue to bludgeon people with controversial philosophy."

"Animals do not need our pity. They need us to empower them, to assert the rights that are theirs. I could challenge this in court," Sandstone said.

"That's our system," replied Power before his predecessor left the room.

John Power believed in democracy. A trillion animals that depended on a rapidly shrinking ecosystem outvoted the world's five billion humans who continued to destroy it. He was now their representative. He finally had what he needed to implement the plan he had nurtured since his days at Ann Arbor: the legitimacy of a mainstream humane organization and its coffers.

"Once again, William, a magnificent job," said Power.

Just like at Ann Arbor. Vanderzell held his tongue. Even when he had saved his ass, when the trial was all over, all Power had said was that it would be good for his career. Which in retrospect was true. "It was really no big deal. The charter and bylaws are pretty explicit," Vanderzell replied. It was still hard for Vanderzell to figure why Power had joined CARE to become a relative moderate in the animals rights spectrum. Power's views on animal rights were hardly compromising. He had a mesmerizing gift for rhetoric and came off as reasonable and moderate, but the few who really knew him always wondered. "So what now, John? Do you still think you can change the average person's mind? Beyond the reasonably humane treatment of animals, most people simply don't care."

"Everything is subject to change, William."

"Even you, John?"

Power forced a smile. "Why should there be compromise on something so morally obvious? No reasonable individual suggests that under certain circumstances the sacrifice of humans is acceptable. Why should I concede that it's ever right to take an animal's life?"

"I disagree. We concede human life all the time. It's called war. It's called ethnic cleansing. It's called unnecessary famine."

"It's a shame that your prosaic, pro forma liberalism doesn't extend to nonhuman animals," Power said, now without a hint of the fleeting smile Vanderzell had seen.

Vanderzell groaned. Power was as exasperating now as he had been at Ann Arbor. "We've been through this for fifteen years. I agree with ninety percent of what you say. Christ, my whole family is vegetarian, we don't wear leather, and I think most of the animal research done is useless bullshit. But I don't think it's possible, practically, ethically, or legally, to equate animals and humans."

"Its entirely possible, William, if one renounces species-ism, which is more pernicious to our world than sexism and racism."

"So, now it's worse than other discrimination? Fifteen years hasn't curbed your tendency toward hyperbole."

"Time has only clarified my positions," Power said calmly. "This society becomes unhinged because there aren't more black lawyers, doctors, judges, and baseball managers. But it ignores the cataclysmic truth that the human species continues to expand at an unsustainable rate and in doing so has mutilated the planet."

"John, I agree we have been ecologically irresponsible, but—"

Power raised his hand and interrupted. "Spare me. Not recycling your aluminum cans is ecologically irresponsible. The human species has wantonly destroyed this world, at the expense of millions of other species, each one of which has an equal right to exist. We were never intended to become the dominant species on this planet, and in becoming so we've ruined this world."

"John, you are a visionary. I really believe that. You look at things differently from 99.99 percent of the rest of the world. But why must you be so intransigent? It's like abortion. There needs to be some compromise."

"I used to think that was possible. To compromise. I've tried for fifteen years—and failed. Maybe what we need is the retroactive abortion of three billion people," Power said, and suddenly once again broke into his version of a smile.

Vanderzell didn't know what to say. He truly believed that the world needed men like Power to create a balance, to pull the center of the debate to the left. No, the world needed men like him and Power to be different. Within reason. "That's a little extreme, even for you, John."

"Just a little hyperbole, William. Lighten up. At least I'm not out killing researchers."

Vanderzell reluctantly nodded. "What else can I do to help you?" he said as he looked at his watch.

"Right now, not a thing. Being the new president of CARE will help me reach more people. I'll be in touch," Power said as he took another sip of his tea and got up and walked away. It was a strange habit. Power never said good-bye. Whether it was a meeting, like now, or on the phone, he'd finish what he had to say and just leave or hang up.

Vanderzell remained seated and took a bite of his fruit. Power inspired him. He often made him feel guilty about joining an establishment law practice, as much as he enjoyed the job. So he made time for activist, pro bono work—to the dismay of his partners, most of whom measured a lawyer's worth by his billable hours—and made time for his family. But Power also scared him. Power had crossed the line before—for the greater good, he had assured him—and although he had subsequently toned it down, Vanderzell wondered, and worried, if he would cross it again.

No one is born a zealot. The path toward advocacy and activism is a combination of nature and nurture, but the willingness to cross, violently if necessary, commonly accepted boundaries of behavior to redress a wrong requires an extraordinary stimulus.

John Power's junior anthropology seminar at the University of Michigan featured a trip to central Africa. The central African rain forest, which occupies a constantly diminishing parcel on the map, is home to the largest number of living species on the planet. It is a primordial soup of biological activity, and as the rain forest recedes, societal pollination with heretofore unknown forms of life should have been expected.

To many living in the Congo region of Africa, the baby monkey is a gastronomic delicacy. As the primate colonies are raided, the mature monkeys, grizzly and unappetizing, are killed, and their succulent offspring are then raised by the natives. Power thought the sight of the African women wet-nursing baby monkeys was the most perverse scene he had ever witnessed.

That was until he saw those primates being decapitated by their surrogate mothers so the tribespeople could feast on their meat. The sights and sounds of the squealing babies and the images of the natives drenched in the blood of their evolutionary predecessors prior to devouring them proved to be John Power's extraordinary stimulus.

When he returned to Ann Arbor, he began his mission to fight the senseless extermination of living creatures whose only crime was to belong to the wrong species. After his near-criminal conviction for breaking into a lab, he tried to moderate his politics. No one would listen.

Fifteen years later, man's evil and unnatural exploitation of animals and the environment continued. True, it was harder to use animals in experiments, but the experiments were still done. And humans continued to eat meat, drink milk, wear leather, and exploit animals in every possible way. The perfidious Judeo-Christian ethic taught that man was special, rather than just a cog in the web of life. Humans had become the biggest blight on the earth.

Power had picked four special people who understood that only by animal rights superseding human rights could the proper balance return to this world. It was his version of affirmative action for animals. The goal was attainable. The first stage had little impact, but soon a fortified ABP would strike again and again until animal experimentation became a historical footnote. With time, the world would revert to the state the true Lord had intended before the domestication of animals, the beginning of man's dominion, and the destruction of the ecosphere.

It would succeed. The world was ready.

And if it didn't? He tried not to think of it, because stage three was too terrible to contemplate.

22

"What do you think of those angiograms?" Simpson asked.

"Ninety percent LAD, plaques in the circumflex, and less than fifty percent in the posterior descending—single-vessel coronary artery disease." Casey sat next to Simpson in his dark office, looking at film for the third time in a week. "What's her aortic gradient?"

"Almost eighty millimeters. What do you think we should we do?"

"Fix her valve, and do a single graft to the LAD."

"Exactly. That's our case for tomorrow."

"Well." She hesitated. "I'm supposed to close a colostomy on a patient who was shot a few months ago. One of our few elective cases."

"Can't the attending do that with one of the junior residents?" Simpson asked. He sounded more disappointed than annoyed.

"I really should be there."

"You're right. It's just that I've enjoyed working with you. You're quite talented." He turned his chair toward hers, took her hand, and began rubbing it. "I've become quite fond of you."

Casey could feel herself turning red and started shaking as she pulled her hand away. He put his arms around her.

"Don't do that," she insisted. She pushed her chair away from his, got up, and headed for the door.

Simpson jumped from his seat and blocked the door. "Casey, I'm sorry. I don't want to offend you. But I simply have these feelings toward you that are difficult to control. I'm just asking for a chance." He embraced her again.

"You're married," she said as she removed his hands from her shoulders. On his desk was a picture of his wife and two daughters. Did they know what a creep their husband and father was?

"Not in any meaningful sense of the word."

"Please let me go." She bit her lip and wouldn't cry.

"I'm not going to pressure you. There's no quid pro quo," he said, moving away from the door.

"That's just great." She raced out of the office.

"I still want you to scrub with me," he shouted after her.

Casey arrived home from the hospital at eight o'clock. Daphne had already eaten and was doing some reading at the kitchen table. Casey muttered hello and plopped into the recliner. She still wore her bloodstained white coat.

"Bad day?" asked Daphne, seeing that Casey looked upset.

"I can't believe it happened again," she said, staring at the ceiling.

"What's wrong?" Daphne asked.

"What is it about female surgical residents that brews a perpetual testosterone storm in married middle-aged men?"

"Simpson, I'll bet," Daphne responded knowingly.

"How did you guess?" Casey asked.

"The man is a slimeball. He'd try to screw anything with a set of ovaries."

"Thanks for the compliment," Casey said with a muted laugh.

"That's not what I mean. The guy is a lech. He's tried to sleep with every resident, medical student, nurse, and technician with two X chromosomes. He tried it with me."

"You're kidding. What did you do?"

"When I was a surgical intern, he called me into his office to discuss my progress. He told me what a good surgeon I'd be, that I was a little weak in the academic stuff, but with some help from him, he was sure I'd be asked to stay on."

"I can imagine what that entailed."

"Well, he didn't know that I had already decided to go into psychiatry and didn't give a rat's ass about being a surgeon. So he gets up out of his chair and comes around behind me. Then he puts his hand on my shoulders and starts rubbing them. Next thing I know, his paws are heading toward my breasts."

"Jesus, what did you do?" asked Casey incredulously.

"I tilted my head back—that asshole thought I was trying to kiss him—and I told him if he ever put his hands on me again, I was going to get a gun and blow his balls over to Staten Island. Then I just got up and walked out."

"What did he do?"

"Not a thing. I was going into psychiatry, whose department chairman, incidentally, is a woman. What was he going to do, tell her that I wouldn't screw him?"

"Why didn't you report him for sexual harassment?"

"I probably should have, but really, it was his word against mine. I didn't want to go through all of that, so I let it go. It's really too bad, because he's a great surgeon."

"I've heard he was tops in the lab before he became a heart surgeon," Casey added.

"All true. But it doesn't excuse his behavior."

"My situation is even worse." Casey sighed. "I do want to be a surgeon, and this is my second program. I won't get another chance. Besides, there's only one woman department chairman in surgery in the whole country."

"What did you mean, this is happening again?" Daphne asked.

"This happened to me before. I didn't exactly leave my

last program voluntarily. The chief of surgery, who was also married, pulled a similar stunt to Simpson's, although he was more subtle. While I was rotating on his service, he treated me well. He allowed me to do all his operations and never yelled at me, which was unusual for him because he could be a terror in the OR. He even helped me with some of the scut work. I had gone three years without anyone telling me I was any good, so it was nice for a change."

"You must have known something was up."

"It really never occurred to me. I was younger and more naive. But soon the other residents on the service pointed out, not so subtly, that the reason for his preferential treatment had more to do with my breasts than my being the next Michael Debakey."

"So when did he make his move?" Daphne asked.

"At the end of the rotation, he told me he was having the team over to his house for dinner."

"Let me guess. No one else showed up, and you were supposed to be the main course."

"You got it. He started in with the crap about he and his wife living separate lives, about how much he could help me with my career, and, surprise, how no one need know about our relationship."

"Classic."

"It gets better. I had been dating one of the junior faculty members. I actually thought we were going to get married. So I told the chairman I was involved with Bob and couldn't really see dating a married man."

"I suspect he didn't take that well."

"Well, I was surprised. After I told him about the other relationship, he apologized and said he understood perfectly. I had been off his service for about a month when he called me into his office. He told me that the faculty had voted not to renew my contract for the next year. It came as such a shock to me because my evaluations were always very good. I never thought I would get cut from the program. When I accused him of orchestrating my dismissal because I wouldn't sleep with him, he looked me in the eye, laughed, and told me not to flatter myself. I left his office and didn't know what to do." Casey's voice cracked. "It was the lowest point of my entire life. Objectively, I saw no way that creep could unilaterally throw me out. I wanted to see Bob, but he was in the OR, so I went to talk to Patricia Scott, the only female surgeon on staff. She told me that at faculty meetings, most of the surgeons would agree with whatever the chairman said. He had a lot of power, and people were scared of him and always kissing his ass. He also had a three-million-dollar NIH grant, so naturally the administration loved him, too. At the meeting discussing resident promotions, he made his recommendation that I be cut. Apparently, Pat was the only one to speak on my behalf. Bob, the man I thought loved me, didn't even stick up for me."

"What a bastard."

"I didn't know what to do. When I saw Bob that night, I told him I had been cut."

"What did the asshole say?"

"He lied. He told me he did everything he could to fight for me. It turned out that he was up for promotion to associate professor and wouldn't go against the chairman."

"The dog!" exclaimed Daphne. "What did you ever see in him?"

"You get lonely. I was working all the time and never had the chance to meet anyone. Basically, I guess I settled for someone who, deep down, I knew wasn't right. Anyway, I moved out of his apartment. He never said a word. He knew I knew. The next day, I went to see the chairman and told him that I would leave quietly if he didn't interfere with me being accepted at another program. If he tried to blackball me, I told him that I would go to the dean and charge him with sexual harassment."

"Well, it worked."

"Eventually. He tried to scare me. His word against mine, you know, the usual stuff. But he saw I was serious and probably figured it wasn't worth the risk. So here I am."

Daphne frowned knowingly. "I feel guilty about not going after Simpson, but I just didn't want to go through the process of being put on trial myself."

"I know how you feel, but we're going to have to stick up for ourselves sooner or later. There is some justice, though. Bob didn't get promoted. I guess the chairman thought a man who would sell out his own girlfriend was too big an asshole to tolerate." She paused and took a sip of the zinfandel. "You wouldn't really have shot Simpson?" Casey asked.

"Honey," Daphne responded, her Southern accent purposely exaggerated, "if that man ever touched me again, he'd be grabbing air when he went to scratch his balls. But if that's too extreme for you, I know a lawyer who might help you out if Simpson doesn't back off."

Casey downed the rest of the wine and pensively stared over at Daphne.

23

The trauma service was unusually quiet, and Casey had a free morning which she had intended to spend in the lab. Unfortunately, Erica Talarico had different ideas.

"To take out a right colon," Casey rhetorically repeated over the telephone to Talarico's secretary. "What does she need me for?" Casey had heard some horror stories about Talarico and had no desire to witness any firsthand. Talarico was a surgical oncologist by training but an angel of death by reputation.

"Perhaps you would like to ask her that yourself, Dr. Brenner. She would like to see you in her office in five minutes."

Casey hung up the phone and took the stairs to the fourteenth floor to Talarico's office. She entered the front office, and the secretary pointed her to the chair to sit. "The doctor will be with you in a minute," she said curtly, and returned to her typing.

Casey couldn't understand why Talarico was wasting her time or what was the big deal about removing a right colon. It was a case for a second-year resident. She and Zach had taken one out three nights ago in seventeen minutes for a gunshot wound.

186

"Go in, Dr. Brenner," said the secretary.

Talarico was sitting at her desk and working on her computer. "Just finishing up a grant, Dr. Brenner. Sit."

Casey sat there for at least five minutes, while Talarico continued working, and grew angrier by the minute.

Finally, Talarico shut down the computer and looked up. "The reason I asked you to help me today is that I know you're new here, and being stuck on the trauma service with those adolescent male cretins who pretend to be surgeons is simply unfair. Since we are both in the same boat, being women and unmarried, I mean, we should do some female bonding. Get to know each other. I'm the only woman on staff here."

"Well, it's just that I'm a little busy between the trauma service and the research," Casey said. *This is going to be big trouble,* she thought.

"No offense, Casey," Talarico said smugly, "but that research you're doing is garbage. Bleeding and freezing a few dogs. To prove what?"

"It's important work and could very possibly—"

Talarico didn't let her finish. "Casey," she said, shaking her head at her as if she were a four-year-old, "animal research is crude and inefficient. And more importantly, it's cruel and immoral. Don't you understand that abuse of animals and abuse of women are similar evils in this patriarchal society? There isn't anything that can be learned from animals that can't be gleaned through other methods. My research uses cell cultures and will provide more answers about cancer than all the animal research ever done."

Casey sat dumbfounded. How could any medical doctor, let alone a surgeon, believe that? Common sense told her to be quiet and let Talarico rant, but she couldn't. Not after already spending dozens of hours in the lab. "We are looking at a way to save patients who are exsanguinating. You can't answer that question with a cell culture," she said firmly but respectfully.

Talarico swatted her like a bug. "Do you know I have an

M.D. and a Ph.D. from Harvard? More than fifty publications in peer-reviewed journals and twelve book chapters? I don't really think you're in a position to debate me on biomedical research."

Casey didn't know what to say. Talarico was pretty, but she had an obnoxious countenance punctuated by a nose so turned up that Casey found herself searching for a cable suspending it from the ceiling. "Zach Green thinks it's a good project, and that's good enough for me," she said, regretting it the minute it spun off her tongue.

"That misogynist pig is no researcher," she brayed painfully, as if Casey had just begun a root canal on her. "Listen to me. Trauma surgeons are simplistic, linear-thinking hacks. Today I'm going to demonstrate to you the difference between a Harvard-trained oncologic surgeon and that puerile fool Green. Do you know that imbecile watches the Three Stooges?"

"So what?"

"He's a pig. His brain functions like an eight-year-old on testosterone shots. He's an anachronism. Women—strong women like us—need to penetrate this male-dominated world. And to do that, we need to stick together."

"He's a total gentleman around me, and besides, he's not married, so who really cares about his love life?" she replied, conceding to herself that maybe she did.

"Come on, Casey, you're smarter than that. Married, unmarried, what's the difference? Men exist to exploit women."

"I guess I don't see it that way."

"Are you trying to tell me that Simpson hasn't tried to proposition you?"

Casey noncommittally shrugged her shoulders and decided that Talarico wasn't anyone to confide in.

Talarico looked at her and responded fiercely, "If he didn't, you would be in a minority. We have to stick together, Casey. If I can get enough women together, we can drag him down." Her tense face, which had ballooned out in anger, temporarily softened. "I could become the next chairman. Wouldn't that be a whole lot better than working for him?" Talarico paused. "I'll expect you in the OR in fifteen minutes."

Casey left wondering which was worse, being harassed by her or by Simpson.

The case was going as she had expected. Talarico was shredding every tissue plane they encountered, and the anatomy was obscured in a miasma of bright red. The anesthesiologists had already hung three units of blood for a case that shouldn't have required any transfusion at all.

"I don't see why we are going all the way down to the superior mesenteric vessels," Casey said as Talarico yanked up on the mesentery of the colon. "The tumor is small. What's the point?"

"This is how a cancer surgeon takes out a colon," she replied. "Now, I almost have it up." Talarico grunted and jerked up on the colon like a tree surgeon extracting a stump from the earth.

"Be careful, the vein is . . ." Casey attempted to say.

It was too late. The blood welled up faster than they could suck it or soak it. It was as much blood as she had seen from any gunshot wound. The key to salvaging this patient, as Zach, Glen, and Ron had told her repeatedly, was to stay calm, put your finger in the dike, and make a plan. The calm in the room dissipated immediately.

"Give blood, give blood!" Talarico screamed at the top of her lungs. Her arms flailed around while she pointed at the anesthesiologists and then started jumping up and down, at least two feet from the table. "Pump that blood, you stupid bastards!"

"We know how to pump blood, Erica. Maybe you need to get someone to stop the bleeding for you," said the anesthesiologist, as sarcastically as he knew how.

"Shut up, you pig. You bastard. I'll have you fired. You're killing my patient." She was now wildly gyrating around the room, knocking over everything that got in her way. A Tasmanian Devil in scrubs.

Casey watched her pathetic decompensation and realized if the patient were going to live, she would have to take over. She guided her finger onto the hole that had been ripped in the superior mesenteric vein. That's all it took to stop the bleeding. "I controlled the bleeding, Dr. Talarico. Maybe you could come back to the table and help me sew up the hole."

"That's nice, Casey. You rip a hole in my patient's vein, and I have to clean up your mess," Talarico said as she came back to the table.

"I didn't rip—"

"I heard you were better than this, Casey. You need a lot of work if you're going to finish this program. And just remember, you need to be twice as good as the men to get half as far. I'm living proof of that. You need plenty of work," she repeated vacantly.

Casey looked at the anesthesiologist, who just rolled his eyes and shook his head in a way that said, *Don't even bother arguing.*

"I'm going to make you fix your own mess," Talarico said. Her hands shook so much, she broke scrub and had to leave the room.

Casey looked at the scrub nurse. "She just walked out of the room while her patient was exsanguinating."

"Actually, today was a good day, Casey. Here's the suture. Do us all a favor. Sew up that hole, and get the rest of the colon out before she comes back."

The patient miraculously reached the recovery room alive. Talarico came back just as Casey was about to close the skin to tell her that she would do whatever it took to make her into a surgeon and quickly ducked back out.

After changing into her street clothes, Casey went to the lab to pick up some data to show Zach. She knocked on his door.

"Who is it?"

"It's me."

A second later, he opened the door. "I'm disappointed in you, Dr. Brenner," he said seriously.

What did I do wrong now? she thought. "Why?" she asked.

"You said, 'It's me.' It should be, 'It is I.' *Is* is a linking verb, and you need to use the predicate nominative."

"Did anyone ever tell you that you can be annoying?" she replied.

"Never. Now, what do you have there?"

She showed him the data on the cognitive screen for the group of animals shocked for an hour and arrested for thirty minutes.

"It looks good so far. Now we need to extend it to an hour."

"We're going to start the forty-five-minute circulatory-arrest group next week. By the way," she continued, "what did you do to Talarico? She hates your guts. Did you and she date?"

Zach gave her a wide-eyed gaze of amazement. "I think I have one Y chromosome too many for her."

"I guess that's a no. How about her academic credentials, though? Fifty-nine papers in five years, that's pretty good." She couldn't help smiling as she said it.

"I understand you did a little case with the doctor today."

"That is true."

"And how did that case go?"

"It was a bloodbath."

His mouth and eyes enlarged in mock amazement. "What a surprise. Let me tell you something: Talarico would have to improve tremendously just to become inept. And can I tell you something else?"

"I'm sure you will even if I say no."

"First, this is not a woman thing. I abuse Double-oh-seven much more than her, and he's ten times better, if you can believe that. Second, I admit that Talarico has ten or twenty points of IQ on me. She does great research. But if you can't operate, at least with a minimal degree of competence, then you are not a surgeon. She hides behind that 'I'm a woman' crap. Can I tell you one more thing?"

"You're going to anyway."

"She's a disgrace to surgery and a disgrace to women."

"So I guess you're going to have to be my role model," Casey said.

"There are worse."

She agreed but just smiled. "I defended you today, you know. Talarico isn't too enamored of the Three Stooges. I have to agree with her on that one."

"Have you ever watched the Three Stooges?"

She shrugged her shoulders and replied, "Maybe a couple times."

"Then you can't understand the depth and importance of their social commentary, the way they represent the ethos of the common man of the depression era, or their satirical lampoon of class struggle," Zach said, keeping a poker face.

"And what about them do you like the best?" she asked suspiciously.

"Probably either when Moe smashes Curly in the head with the crowbar and it bends to the shape of his head, or when he does a creative combination. Ya know, like eye poke, face slap, roundhouse to the top of the head."

"That's what I figured," Casey replied.

Her lab coat was riding up over her neck, and the collar was folded backward. Zach took a step toward her and gently straightened it. She moved a half step closer to him. "You know, Dr. Brenner," he said as he continued to adjust her collar, "I realize I have a lot of bad points. I'm not well read, overly aggressive, impatient at times, and uncritical in most of my thought processes. But I make up for all of that with a keen sense of self-awareness."

"You're a nut, Zach. It's not that I don't appreciate"— she paused and smiled sweetly at him—"and enjoy you fixing my lab coat for ten minutes, but I have ICU rounds."

"Lunch later?" Zach asked.

"I'll be in the lab. Come get me," she replied as she hurried down the hall. She looked forward to it.

Casey had lunch with Zach and had a great time as usual. He was certainly different. She noticed that he dressed meticulously but always in the same kind of clothes. A pair of khaki pants, a white button-down shirt, and a tie. He told her that he owned five pairs of khakis for the summer, five pairs of corduroys for the winter, and a dozen white shirts. He had one sport jacket that he wore only when coerced, and the only item of clothing he owned that cost more than fifty dollars was his shoes, because his grandfather had told him shoes reflect a man's character. You could see your reflection off his brown loafers.

Unfortunately, she had to check on the patient she had operated on that morning and do the cognitive screen on the last dog she and Stu had done. She made her way through the security door that led to the laboratory and animal care wing and got the dog out of the cage.

"Come here, girl," she said to the two-year-old beagle. The dog hopped out of the cage, shook its tail, and started licking Casey's hands. The dog rolled over on its back to let Casey pet its belly. "Glad to see me, huh?" she said.

The dog's incisions looked well healed, and it didn't appear to be in any pain. Casey took out her checklist and prepared to evaluate the animal's intelligence. The previous experimental animals had lost nothing from one hour of shock and thirty minutes of circulatory arrest. This beagle, however, had undergone a forty-five-minute period of circulatory arrest, fifty percent longer.

The dog was up on all fours, and when Casey looked up from her checklist, the animal looked her in the eyes. She rubbed the beagle behind its ears. "Good thing you don't know what's coming in a few days, girl." On day five, the dog would be put to sleep—permanently—and its brain would be sectioned for the pathologists to examine.

Casey had no doubt that what she was doing was both ethical and necessary. It also made her sick.

Lew Mason deplaned last, an old habit acquired in his FBI training; he always checked to see if anyone had left any suspicious bags behind. It gave an edge to his ride, wondering if he'd find a bomb intended for the next flight. Of course, he never did, but he always scanned each row as he walked down the aisle. He'd returned a lot of lost purses to their owners, if nothing else.

He went straight to the taxi line with his small leather valise; he never checked luggage. Tomorrow he'd wear the suit he wore now and would have the hotel do the shirt he had on while he wore his spare. Mason believed in packing light and always being ready to move quickly. He'd been on the scene for too many airport messes not to have learned that.

The taxi line inched forward. Finally, Mason got into a cab and headed for the city. The turbaned driver drove like a madman, and Mason fastened his seat belt. You didn't want to comment on their driving; he'd made that mistake once, and his driver had turned around to argue with him, completely taking his eyes off the traffic.

Mason came to New York City infrequently, avoiding it whenever he could, but when he did, he always marveled at the ethnic consistency of his cab drivers. This time, they'd all be Indian. The last trip, every driver in the city seemed to be Senegalese. Before that, it was Nigerians. *Must ship them over by the truckload,* he thought. The INS up here could use some looking into. But hell, it wasn't his concern.

By the time he was deposited at his hotel, he felt slightly nauseated from the raspberry-scented air freshener on the cabbie's dash. Taking deep breaths, he waited in another long line and was finally checked into his room by nine P.M. He did one hundred push-ups, showered, and got into bed.

Brad Menchen's murder had increased national attention to the case exponentially, and Lew had finally gotten the extra agents he needed. He was in the city to interview the leaders of Animals International and CARE, and he wouldn't spend a minute longer here than he had to. From bed, he reached into his bag and pulled out a James Ellroy thriller. Twenty pages later, he was asleep.

In the morning, he called to confirm his first appointment and was soon hurtling down Seventh Avenue to the SoHo offices of Animals International. He was a little psyched about meeting Carole Reeves, he had to admit. But it was Fred Baumgold who let him into the loft that was their headquarters.

"Carole said she'd be back in a bit," said Baumgold, a paunchy, balding man wearing gray pants and a black shirt sporting a CK logo. He'd probably been sponging off Carole for years, Mason thought.

"That's fine. I'll start with a few questions for you, and she can join in later. You founded Animals International how many years ago?"

"Twenty-two. We started it after Carole came back from India. Her guru—she did actually have one back then," Fred said, smiling, "suggested she not eat meat. It made her think about our whole lifestyle. We went vegetarian, stopped wearing leather and fur, and started Animals International a year later. Of course, we never realized what it would grow into," he said modestly. "We're very proud of our work. But I have to tell you, Mr. Mason, we are not into violence. In fact, our whole thing has been antiviolence, even back in college in our protest days. Anyone who knows us, or our organization, would tell you that."

"I did do some checking, and that's what we've been told. But is there anyone in your group—your inner circle—who could've gone over the edge? I know it's hard to pin down, but has anyone in the organization acted strangely, off the wall lately, uncharacteristically angry or out of touch, blown a fuse or seemed oddly focused on the recent murders? Anyone leaving the office late at night?"

Fred Baumgold smiled. "Not to be disrespectful, Mr. Mason, but if our volunteers weren't a little off the beam, we'd have no staff whatsoever. This is an entirely thankless task; it's all volunteer—no pay—and beyond a desire to help animals, it's hard work for no reward. Sure, we have our share of quirky people, but they're nice. No one I know of could be behind the killings."

As if on cue, the door opened, and Carole Reeves walked in, flashing that famous toothy smile. "Oh, Fred!" she exclaimed. "You let me be late for Mr. Mason!"

She walked toward him, extending her hand. Up close, she looked amazingly fragile, her huge brown eyes now framed in wrinkles, but still beautiful. Mason was tempted for a moment to ask how Charlie, the grumpy character on her TV series, was doing. He blinked a few times and shook her hand. "Nice to meet you, Ms. Reeves. I'm a big fan," he said before he could stop himself. Damn! What was he doing? This was supposed to be an investigation.

"Please sit down. Did you offer Mr. Mason some tea, Fred?" Carole asked, looking askance at her husband.

"I'll make some right now," Fred said.

"Oh, no, I'm fine. Nothing for me. I was just asking Mr. Baumgold whether he'd noticed anything odd in any of your members. Any strange behavior, obsession with the recent slayings . . ."

"Please call us Carole and Fred," she said, smiling.

"And please call me Lew." *Now, where did that come from?* he asked himself. Fred came back and placed a mug filled with steaming, almost clear liquid in his hand.

"Thanks," he said, and took a sip, scalding his tongue.

"It's hot, watch out," said Fred. "So, Mr. Mason—"

"He wants us to call him Lew," said Carole.

"Lew, what else can we help you with? Other than noticing strangeness in our extremely strange staff," said Fred, sinking back into a black leather couch.

Suddenly, Mason's questions disappeared from his mind. Putting his tea on the table, he reached into his pocket for his notebook. Finally, he found the right page. It wasn't like him to be this disorganized. "Have you noticed anything unusual in your financial accounts lately?"

"Other than that we always seem to spend more than we earn, no matter how much we earn?" Carole laughed huskily. "Not really. But we could put you in touch with Bill Sievold, our finance guy. He could answer any questions you'd need to know."

"Thanks. I'll take his number," Mason said, writing as Fred recited it to him. "Do any of the other animal rights groups seem predisposed to violence? Anyone you could see having done this?"

"I can't think of anyone I know who'd commit murder, even to stop animal research," said Carole. "Can you, Fred?"

"Certainly not. But if we come up with any ideas, we'd be glad to call you."

"Let me leave my card," Mason said, handing it to Carole. "I'll be back in my office by tomorrow afternoon. Thanks again for your time. It was great to meet you in person. I was always such a fan of *Apartment 1501.* I watched it every week as a kid." Mason realized that Fred and Carole were looking at him expectantly. "Well. Do call if you think of anything," he concluded gruffly, and let himself out the door.

"Asshole," Carole Reeves said as she listened to his steps clomp down the stairs. "Be a doll, Fred, and pour me a drink."

Mason cursed himself as he took yet another cab with yet another turbaned driver uptown. How could he have let his professional demeanor drop like that? *Oh, well,* he thought, *it's not like she's going to call Garrow and tell on me.* "I always loved you in *Apartment 1501.*" Jeezus.

As they crawled up Sixth Avenue—whenever he was in New York, Sixth seemed to be under construction— Mason pulled out his notes about CARE, his next destination. Sandstone seemed to be a loose cannon; he'd mouthed off to the press on numerous occasions, had been in lots of protests before becoming president of CARE, and while he had no known history of violent behavior, he had Mason's vote for Most Likely to Be ABP. Plus, CARE had the big bucks to finance something like ABP if someone at the top got bold about embezzling. It would be interesting to meet Sandstone in person, and also to see John Power, his number two.

The cab lurched to a halt in front of a nondescript building on West Forty-eighth Street, almost hitting a woman who was trying to pull a yelping little dog out of the gutter. Mason paid the guy, took the receipt, and stepped right into a pile of dog shit.

"Goddamn," he muttered. Hastily, he scraped his heel on the curb, trying to get the stuff off his shoe. Great timing. Why couldn't this have happened on the way to his own office in D.C.? Didn't New York have a pooper-scooper law? When he was pretty sure he'd gotten most of it off, he went into the lobby and up to the fourth floor. Unlike Animals International's slick offices, CARE's were much more functional and plain. Cardboard boxes full of papers lined the hall the receptionist led him down. "Greg," she said, "here's Mr. Mason."

Sandstone stood to shake Mason's hand. "You find me in a bit of disarray. John Power just got voted in as president, and I'm cleaning out my desk. Twelve years as president has left me with a lot of junk," Sandstone said, picking up a pen and motioning Mason to a chair. "Sit down and tell me what you want with us. No one in CARE has had anything to do with these murders, although, personally, I can't say I'm sorry."

"Really, Mr. Sandstone?" said Mason. "Tell me why."

"I'm sad for the families of these people, but I'm also sad for the thousands of animals who are killed or maimed for research. Do I agree with murdering the researchers? No. Do I think this might be the one thing that will finally get America's attention and wake the country up to the horrors going on in these labs? Possibly so."

"But aren't donations to your groups down as a result of the killings?" Mason asked.

"Yes, actually, they are. For the moment. But I have no doubt they'll pick back up again," said Sandstone.

"Do you have any idea who the ABP are?"

Sandstone did an interesting thing. He dropped his pen—Mason was sure on purpose—and fumbled under his desk for it for at least ten seconds. "No, I don't have any idea," Sandstone said. His eyes were fixed on Mason's face, but they wavered. "None at all."

Maybe he does know something, thought Mason, *or maybe he's just nervous.* He heard footsteps behind him. "John Power, Mr. Mason." Mason turned toward the voice behind him. "Don't get up. We don't stand on formalities here," said Power, pulling up a chair. "Has Greg given you all the information you need?"

"He's been very helpful. I hear you're now president of the organization," Mason said, eyeing the two men. Power sat back relaxed, and Sandstone sat tensed on the edge of his chair. Perhaps the succession hadn't been too amicable. "What do you plan to do differently, if anything?"

"Oh, we have lots of plans," said Power. "One is to step up our fund-raising. I'd like us to be the number one fund-raising group this time next year, instead of always being number two or three."

"And will you hire more staff? What will you do with the extra money?" Mason asked.

"Oh, no extra people. We always maintain a lean staff here. The money is for more ads, more phone campaigns, more publicity for our cause. Our goal is for every American to think before eating or wearing any part of any animal or participating in any animal's abuse or extinction."

"A very far-reaching goal," said Mason. "Do you think these murders are going to turn people off to your cause—or turn them on?"

Power gazed at Mason calmly. "I have no idea," he said, "but I think whoever's behind it has to be stopped. In the long term, there's no doubt it will hurt us."

"Any idea who it could be?" Mason was sick of asking this question, but protocol demanded it. He was starting to feel like a bad *Columbo* rerun.

"None at all," Power said. "But I'm sure you guys at the FBI will find them soon."

"Well, call me if anything occurs to you," Mason said. Sandstone had been strangely quiet the whole time Power was in the room. Mason left and decided to walk the twenty-three blocks to his hotel rather than risk his life in another taxi.

"Did you smell that?" Sandstone asked Power after Mason had gone. "I thought I'd tracked dog poop into the room. I even looked under the desk at my shoes, but they were clean. I felt nauseous by the time he left, it was so strong."

"Must have been the Fibbie," said Power. "They always were full of shit."

Sandstone looked at Power. "Do you realize we're suspects in all this?"

Power shrugged and looked at his watch. He didn't want to miss his meeting. The concern over a few dead scientists and that fool Menchen was touching, but it hadn't made any significant difference in the amount of research being done. They had tried it the easy way. Now things were going to get mean-spirited. "Don't worry about it, Greg. I have a plan."

John Power seethed; he couldn't understand it. Maybe it was some perverse heroism, but only a few hundred labs had announced plans to end animal experiments. He was about to go to stage two of his plan, but he still prayed that he wouldn't have to implement stage three. With Lonergan's help, the body count would soar. It was true, with a lot of work you could find anything on the Internet. Now CARE's money would finally be put to good use.

"The per contract price won't be negotiable." Lonergan held on tightly to the aluminum bar as the Number 4 subway slowed at the Fifty-ninth Street stop. Business had been bad. The days when a professional terrorist and assassin could name his price were over. Terrorists were being homegrown now, and he had to supplement his income with the drug trade. He still had more than three million in various bank accounts, but with his lifestyle, that wouldn't last forever.

Power, who grasped the adjacent pole, waited until the subway had accelerated from the stop before he spoke. "How much are we talking about?"

Lonergan could barely hear him, but that was all right because neither could anyone else. He shook his head at Power. "If you want my help, I'll expect half a million each time." Lonergan's face was expressionless. The ideology of his employers had never really concerned him, and, in fact, he had on occasion worked both sides of the street. But to be reduced to killing scientists who experimented on animals in labs was almost too much.

"I will get the money," Power said.

Lonergan got off at the next stop, and Power continued on to the bank.

"I'm very sorry, sir, I can't do that," the bank teller replied after looking at his computer screen.

"Is there a problem with my identification?" Power asked.

"No, but to withdraw this amount of money, Mr. Sandstone must also provide his signature."

"There must be a mistake. I was recently elected president of CARE. Mr. Sandstone no longer runs the organization."

"No mistake, Mr. Power. If you would like to speak with my supervisor, I'll get her."

He grimaced, shook his head no, and headed out the door. He would have a talk with Sandstone. Lonergan expected the wire transfer, and he would have to stall him. Without him, their war would fail.

Power bounded up the five flights of stairs and burst into the CARE offices. Sandstone was behind his desk in the front office, and Power immediately confronted him. "I just went to the bank," he gasped, still breathless from the five-flight ascent.

"And you found out that you needed my signature to withdraw funds," Sandstone replied with a minimal attempt to conceal his glee. "Actually, John, that's only if you need to withdraw more than ten thousand dollars."

"Sign over the account," Power replied tersely. "It isn't your money anymore."

"It never was my money, John, and it certainly isn't yours," Sandstone said as he put his feet up on his desk. "It's CARE's."

"I am the president," Power sharply responded.

"That's a very bad Nixon imitation, John."

"Listen, Greg, I have ideas for the money. We can make a bigger impact."

"Well, John, I have a surprise for you. You may be the president of CARE, but if you look at the incorporation certificate, I am still the head of the board of directors. And guess what the head of the board has control of? You can make all the policy decisions you want, but if you want more than ten thousand dollars in cash, I have to approve it. And I'll tell you something else. We disburse millions of dollars a year, but I have rarely spent more than ten thousand in one place."

"You donated more than a million dollars to that zoo for its elephant breeding program."

"That's true," Sandstone admitted proudly. "It was an incredible success. Two African elephants have been born in four years."

Power had regained his composure and didn't want to provoke Sandstone. He needed him. Without the money, without Lonergan, it was just a question of time before they would be caught—knocking off a few researchers at a time. There was no use arguing now. There had to be a way to get at the money. He nodded his head imperceptibly, went into his office, and dialed Vanderzell.

"Technically, he's right, John. The way the bylaws are written, you can't make any cash withdrawal greater than ten thousand dollars without his approval." Vanderzell's trained eyes scanned the document one more time before he laid it on the table.

"William, you were first in your class in law school. I'm sure you can figure out some way to get around this problem."

There probably was some way to get around Sandstone, Vanderzell thought. The trouble was Power. What did Power need with half a million dollars in cash?

24

It was almost nine before Zach and Glen had finished for the day. Ron was on call. "Let's stop by the lab and see how things are going. Casey and Stu are staying late tonight," Zach said.

"Interested in the experiments or the experimenter?" Glen teased.

"Gimme a break. It's all business."

"Not if you had your way."

"You question my ethics, sir?"

"No, Doctor, I question your willpower."

"Come on. Take a walk with me."

"What do you need me for?"

"Moral support."

"Listen, Zach, you're treading dangerous water here," Glen said seriously.

Zach lost the smirk and looked at him. "What do you mean?"

"Come on. You know exactly what I mean. You've said it a million times. Casey Brenner is your student. So if you go for it—and I told you that I have no real problem with that—you had better be sure. I know I joked about it before—the bet with Ron, I mean. But that was before I got to know her. This woman is not another trophy. Don't fuck with her life."

"I told you, the minute I saw her, she was the one. Nothing over the past couple months has changed."

"Just be honest with yourself, Zach. Will you love her when she's too tired to screw you, or when she's eight months pregnant and can barely get into the car, or when she's so busy at work and with the kids that you only talk to her five minutes a day? Because that's what being married is."

Zach nodded. "Sure, I've thought of all that, and I'm still crazy about her. But do you think she's interested? I don't deal well with rejection, you know."

"Well, if it means anything, when we're doing a case together, all I ever hear is 'Zach does it this way' or 'Zach said this' or 'Wasn't Zach funny in conference today?' Sort of pisses me off."

Zach smiled broadly and exhaled. "I don't think she's going out with anyone, do you?"

Glen shrugged. "When? Christ, she's working more than a hundred hours a week. She's practically sleeping in the lab since we lost the little girl, and there are only so many hours in a day."

"Good. Come on, let's get going," Zach urged. "I want to catch her before she goes home."

They headed for the lab. As they entered, Casey was making notations in the laboratory book. An anesthetized dog was hooked up to a myriad of tubes, as Stu oversaw the experiment.

"I see you've recognized Stu's talents," Glen said to Casey.

As Stu had predicted, Casey was letting him do most of the animal surgery. His speed was amazing. "I'm a quick learner. Stu's the greatest."

"Thank you, Dr. Casey. After thirty years, I ought to be fast."

"If I ever go into private practice, I'm taking Stu with me as my physician's assistant," Glen said, patting Stu on the back.

"Private practice, don't make me puke," Zach commented.

"There's more to life than trauma, Zach."

"Taking out gallbladders all day, no thanks. That's not you talking, it's Debby."

"Anyway," Glen said, trying to change the subject, "how are we coming, Casey?"

"Fantastic. The last four dogs have tolerated an hour of shock and thirty minutes of circulatory arrest without any cognitive changes. We did one with forty-five minutes of arrest the other day, and this is the second one in that group."

"How about the histology in the thirty-minute group?"

"So far, OK," she replied. "The neuropathologist thought maybe there was a little swelling but decided it was just artifact."

"How far out should we go?" Glen asked.

"An hour, I think," Zach responded. "A really bad injury could take that long to fix."

"Even longer if the liver is real mush too," added Glen.

"I guess," responded Zach, "but I think if the liver is involved as well, the patient is hosed."

"Probably true." Glen looked at his watch. "I'm going home to my wife and kids. I'll see you guys later," he said as he left the room.

"Dinner, Dr. Brenner? I'm starving," Zach said.

"Sure," Casey replied happily. "Where to?"

"Where else?"

Zach was eating a corned beef sandwich; Casey some split pea soup. The manager of the deli practically knew them by name—it was the fifth time they had been there in two weeks.

"You know, Zach, there are about a thousand restaurants around here. We could try another one," Casey said.

"The soup's no good today?"

"The soup is fine. Why not try another place?"

"For what reason? The food here is great, the service is fast, and there are fifty million things on the menu."

206

"You don't get sick of it?"

"The hospital food makes me sick. This is like having your grandmother cook for you. Why switch?"

She smiled and shook her head. "You are a creature of habit."

Sheila Downey, one of the pediatric residents, walked in and waited for a table. Casey waved at her, and Sheila responded with a wink as she pointed to Zach, whose back was turned. The implication was obvious. The hospital was such a small world. She and Zach eating together, particularly outside the hospital, would be construed as a date. It was the last thing she needed.

"I think that people might get the wrong idea seeing us together like this," Casey said hesitantly.

"Do you care?" He dipped a piece of rye bread into his matzoh ball soup.

"No, not really. I guess eating together isn't a date."

"Now, if we ate and then slept together, that would be a date," Zach said as he took a bite of his sandwich.

She put down her spoon, stared at Zach, and feigned confusion. "Wait a minute. Let's say we went to dinner, say someplace where you didn't order with a number, and then went to a movie."

"I'm with you."

"Now, after the movie ends, we walk out, and I say, ''Bye, Zach, I had a nice time, I'll see you tomorrow.' Wouldn't that be a date?"

"Maybe."

"Maybe? What does sleeping together have to do with it?"

"Intent. If this were a date, I'd be trying to get you into bed, which I'm not. We are just eating and talking. Like two guys. Teacher and student."

"Nice try, but I'm not a guy."

"That's obvious."

"Nice of you to notice. The problem is, Zach, if we didn't have the professional hospital relationship, this would be a date," Casey said. She looked at him for a second, wondering if he was as interested as she was. He flirted with nearly every woman he saw, even patients in their eighties. "Sort of," she added, almost shyly.

"But I don't date residents," he said half-heartedly. *It's not as if she's a fucking vestal virgin*, he thought to himself. *Would it be so wrong?*

"And I wouldn't date one of my attendings," she replied defensively.

"So, Dr. Brenner, we are back where we started: dinner. Let's eat." Zach took another bite of his sandwich. This was a game he enjoyed. "What if I wasn't one of your attendings?"

She frowned at the question, and he figured he had stepped over the line.

"Zach, don't. You've been a good friend and mentor and, despite your abominable reputation, a complete gentleman. But I've been through this before. I was in a relationship with someone I worked with, and it was a disaster."

"What happened?" he asked, trying not to show his disappointment

"Long story. Basically, a similar situation, but Bob let me down. He didn't stick up for me when I needed him, and I really thought I knew him." Casey realized that Zach was very different from Bob but kept it to herself.

"Well, Casey, I'm glad to be your friend and teacher, and it's obvious that I like you a lot, too," he admitted, surprising himself. "But as far as sticking up for you, I really don't think that will be necessary. You are a bright, compassionate doctor and gifted in the operating room. You'll be better than I am soon."

"Do you really believe that?" she asked eagerly.

"Nah, it's just a figure of speech. No good surgeon thinks someone else is better than them. I've always known I was the best."

"What are you going to do about this self-esteem problem, Zach?"

"Just kidding."

"No, you're not," she retorted.

"OK, have it your way, I'm the best. But believe me, if

you weren't a good resident, I wouldn't be eating with you all the time."

"As usual, I don't follow."

"If you were a rotten resident and there was a chance you wouldn't last here, our being together could be construed as your attempt to gain my favor—a basic ass-kissing maneuver—or my attempt to take advantage of someone in a subordinate position. But since you are a great resident, you have no need to seduce me, unless, of course, you want to. And if I tried to proposition you, you could tell me to fuck off without worrying about getting dropped from the program. In short, there is no reason for sex to come into play here."

"Has anyone told you that your mind is twisted, probably beyond help?"

"Everyone who knows me, but if it's any consolation, you're the first today."

Casey finished her last spoonful of soup. She got up, left ten dollars on the table, and put on her white coat. "I've got a case in the morning. See you tomorrow. And Zach, I think that maybe you are trying to get me into bed," she said as she turned and walked out.

No question about that, Zach thought, while he sat and finished his sandwich.

Casey sat in the lounge chair trying to read as Daphne came out of the bathroom dressed in a skintight bodysuit underneath a very short skirt. "I'll see you tomorrow, Casey."

"Big night out?"

"One of the ortho residents. A real specimen. He played football at Northwestern. You know, Casey, you ought to get out once in a while."

"I guess so," Casey said. "I've been in New York for two months, and I haven't had a single date." On the other hand, she thought, Daphne had a continuous renewable source of attractive men. She almost never slept in the apartment, which was probably fortunate. The last time Daphne and one of her friends stayed over, they went at it till four in the morning. Casey went to work at five-thirty, tired, lonely, and envious.

"Well, you could always relent and give Simpson a break."

"Very funny."

"What about Zach? You and he are together a lot. You two must have a reserved table in the cafeteria. I see you there every day for lunch."

Casey laid her surgery atlas on the couch. "Well, you were right about him, he's a great guy. But he's my boss, and besides, I'm not sure he's interested in me other than professionally."

"Casey, trust me, he's interested."

"How do you know? He flirts with everyone."

"You're his type—smart, pretty, talented—and besides, he wouldn't be eating with you every day if he weren't interested."

"And what gives you this insight?"

"Well, your personality is much different from mine, and when we went out . . ."

"You went out with Zach? I thought he had a rule about dating residents," she asked anxiously.

"Surgery residents, not psychiatry," she said, sitting on the couch and sipping some coffee. "I knew he was hot for me, always flirting, but he never made a move my whole surgery internship year. Then, at about two minutes after midnight, July 1, I hear my bell ring. It's Zach with a bag of cookies and a pint of ice cream."

"Ice cream and cookies?"

"You've been with him; he's obsessed with food. Anyway, we never got to the ice cream; it melted."

"You slept with Zach?" Casey replied, half incredulous and half jealous.

"Sure," Daphne replied nonchalantly. She noticed the strange look on Casey's face. "Hey, it wasn't like I just found him in a bar. I had known him for almost a year. Anyway, it didn't last too long. I wasn't really his type."

"Well, it's all a moot point. I'm going be a surgery

resident for the next two years, and it's going to be all business," Casey said resolutely while wishing the opposite.

"Maybe not. I know Zach. Most of these male doctors can't stand intelligent, successful women; they feel threatened by them. They look for someone to idolize them. Zach is the opposite. He has more confidence than anybody I've ever met."

"So I've noticed, but from what I hear, a lot of the women he dates aren't Rhodes scholars."

"Don't judge him by that. Look, he's the paradigmatic surgeon. Aggressive, driven, and horny, particularly after doing a long stretch of operating. You have to understand the mentality. After these surgeons finish a long, hard case, they have this tremendous energy, this feeling of power. They need to sublimate it, and sex is the perfect outlet."

"Are you trying to tell me that there is some connection between sex and removing a ruptured spleen?"

"My observation is that for most of these guys, surgery is an aphrodisiac. I would love to measure their testosterone levels after surgery. My bet is that they would be off the scale. So Zach, like many of his colleagues, has this hormonal imperative."

"Tell me, Daphne, what did he do for foreplay, whack out your gallbladder?"

"Come on, don't be mad at me. It's just my observation as a psychiatrist."

"That's depressing. Now, why is it that you think that this overflowing bag of testosterone with a scalpel is interested in me?"

"He respects intelligence and competence; he just hasn't found the right woman. Supposedly, he had some girlfriend in medical school who dumped him, and he hasn't had a serious relationship since then. I think he knows exactly what kind of woman he wants, but he's scared to get burned again. I know some of the women he went out with. They were no more interested in a real relationship than he was. Like me," she added.

"And if I wasn't around after he fixed a ruptured aneurysm, I suppose he'd be screwing the nearest candy striper."

"Other than my daddy, Zach Green is the straightest, most ethical person I have ever known. If and when he commits to someone—admittedly a big if—that will be it."

"Well, I'm a perfectly well-adjusted woman. After I finish a late night in the OR, all I want to do is go to bed—alone."

"That's a resident thing. It's tough to be horny when you work more than a hundred hours a week."

"Daphne, your insight is amazing. All I can say is that if your theory of hormonal determinism is true, then I must be totally resistible to Zach Green, because other than a little flirting, he's the perfect gentleman around me."

"I'm telling you, he just doesn't want to give the appearance of impropriety. He's such a boy scout." She giggled. "To him, it's a battle between his ethics and his balls. If you weren't his resident, he'd be at the door with a gallon of ice cream right now."

Casey shrugged her shoulders. "I could use some ice cream. It's been a long time."

25

Glen adjusted the knot on his tie for the third time.

"You look fine. Hurry up, or you'll be late," Debby urged.

The preinterview portion of CNN was at seven-thirty, even though the program didn't begin until nine-thirty. At the CNN studio in Manhattan, all participants for that evening's show were given a general idea of the questions the host would be asking and were quizzed about the types of responses they would give. Naturally, the topic and the guests' responses would dictate the actual flow of the program.

"I hope this Bill Courier can stay objective. All I need is to be debating two hostile people," Glen said nervously. "At least, with someone like a Ted Koppel, you know he'll be objective. Courier, I don't know. Being a contrarian is a great way for a host to make himself look good."

"Don't worry, you'll do great. You're the most persuasive person I know. You got me to marry you, didn't you?" Debby said as she hugged her husband.

"That didn't take much persuasion."

Debby patted him on his rear end. "Get going," she ordered.

"You think the girls will stay up to see their dad on TV?"

"Are you sure it's OK?" Debby asked.

"Why not? They won't know what we're talking about; they'll just get to see me on the tube." Glen looked at his watch. "My taxi should be here. See you later."

"Knock 'em dead."

Glen unbolted the two locks on the door, kissed Debby, and walked down the hall to the elevator. It didn't come right away, so he took the stairs down to the lobby. The cab was waiting. Hank, the doorman, opened the heavy glass door.

"I hear you're gonna be on TV tonight, Doctor," Hank said. "On the operations channel?"

"No, CNN," Glen said. The kids must have been talking about it in the lobby.

"I'll be home to catch it. Good luck, Doc."

"Thanks."

The twins were still up at nine o'clock. Debby had made some popcorn, and the girls were munching it in the living room. "When is Daddy going to be on TV?" Rebecca asked impatiently.

"In ten minutes, sweetheart. Be patient." Just then, the doorbell rang. Debby looked through the peephole, but it was blocked by a nose. "Zach, cut it out," Debby said, and let him in.

"Hi, gang. I thought you would be up."

The girls jumped up and down on the couch, ecstatic to see him. "Come sit with us," Rachel begged.

"Just a second, kids. Debby, I need to talk to you."

"What's wrong?"

"I'm in love."

"Yeah, sure you are," she said as she shook her head. "How many times have I heard that?"

"This resident at the hospital, Casey Brenner. She's smart, beautiful, compassionate. Just like me. There is only one problem."

"Which is?"

"She probably won't go out with me," Zach said.

"Glen told me all about her. I thought you wouldn't date one of your residents."

"I may have changed my mind. I have to be flexible."

Debby laughed. "You're the most inflexible person I know."

"That's true, and I need to be more flexible about my inflexibility," Zach responded with a straight face.

"You're crazy. Maybe she feels uncomfortable about dating one of her attendings."

"So what should I do?"

"Keep trying. I doubt she'll be able to resist you for long. I can't wait to meet this one."

"You might get a chance next week. Our abstract on fixing the vena cava during circulatory arrest was accepted. Casey did most of the work, so we're going to let her present it. The meeting is at Mohonk Mountain House, up in the Shawangunk Mountains."

"Jesus, Glen never told me. I hope my parents can babysit; then we can all go up for the weekend. I've always wanted to go there; I hear it's beautiful."

Zach glanced at the TV. "Uh-oh, it's starting." He sat on the couch next to the girls, who cuddled up against him.

Glen was seated next to John Power in a studio down the hall from where they had been interviewed. "It's a pleasure to meet you, Mr. Power. I've read a few of your books."

Power extended his hand. "I'm surprised, Dr. Brinkman. Is there anything we agree upon?" he asked.

Glen smiled. "Well, I agree that there is quite a bit of bad and unnecessary animal research done. But for me, the moral implication of allowing humans to suffer and die outweighs any wrong done to animals, as long as the research is competent and the animals are treated humanely."

"So you agree that there is a moral cost to using animals?"

Glen nodded. "But an acceptable cost."

Power patted Glen on the back. "Then let's see who can be more convincing. Good luck, Doctor."

The studio contained several TV cameras and a separate room for the director and other technical staff. There was also a monitor so the guests could look at the host.

The director counted down. Glen heard the theme music and Courier's voice in the background. What he saw on the monitor distressed him.

"Should animal research continue . . . ?" Bill Courier introduced the show with a videotape backdrop. It was footage taken by animal rights activists of dogs having their heads smashed in to study the consequences of head trauma. Glen had seen the tape before and, like many researchers, had been appalled. This out-of-context, particularly violent, and apparently egregious example of research had been shown hundreds of times before. It was typical of the animal rights activists to use one horrific example of research to draw a faulty conclusion. It was a bad start.

Rebecca and Rachel were frightened. "Is that what Daddy does at work?" Rebecca asked. "He hurts puppies?"

Debby held the girls. "No, Daddy doesn't hurt dogs. He helps people." Partially true, Debby thought to herself. "I think maybe you girls should go to bed."

"No, we want to watch Daddy." They settled in to watch after hearing Debby's explanation.

"Uncle Zach, do you hurt puppies?" Rachel asked.

Zach was unsure how to respond. Four-year-olds were not going to understand animal research. "Everything your dad and I do is to help people who are sick get better." He looked at Debby and rolled his eyes. Well, it was true, if not completely so, he thought.

* * *

"Tonight we will look at both sides of the animal rights controversy. Is animal research moral? Is it useful? And what about the tactics that some animal rights activists use?" Courier turned away from Camera 1. "Mr. Power, if experiments on animals can save human life, why should we forgo those advances?"

"Mr. Courier, one of the great canards of the last fifty years is that animal research has improved or prolonged human life. Nothing could be further from the truth. There is no conclusive evidence that animal research has done anything but slaughter and torture millions of animals."

"But," protested Courier, "aren't there really many examples of useful research? What about the polio vaccine, insulin, open-heart surgery, and organ transplantation?"

"The medical establishment would have us believe that life has been improved and extended by these things—this is not so. Polio was on the decline before the vaccine, and even that vaccine could have been produced by using cell-culture techniques. Diabetes is by and large a preventable disease, preventable by the proper diet. Open-heart surgeries, those bypass operations that enrich the surgeons, are completely unnecessary. The most recent studies suggest that they don't prolong life, and once again, if people ate a diet free of animal fat, there would be no need for bypass operations. As far as organ transplantation, I have two comments. First, heart and kidney failure are the result of poor nutritional habits. Second, and perhaps Dr. Brinkman can enlighten us, if animal experimentation was so important, why did the first hundred or so liver recipients die from their transplants? I'd also—"

"Why don't we give Dr. Brinkman a chance to respond? Isn't it true, Doctor, that we humans are our own worst enemies?" Courier asked.

Glen sat up straight in his seat, took a breath, smiled, and looked directly into the camera. "Mr. Courier, before I answer your question, which is a good one, I must say that the sermon that Mr. Power just gave is nonsense." He looked over at Power and winked at him. "Mr. Power knows that research helps humans. He just doesn't like it. We should all eat less fat in our diet, no question about it. But to suggest that diabetes and heart disease are completely nutritionally related is naive. Four-year-old children don't get diabetes from eating at Burger King. Diseased heart valves and congenital heart defects are not caused by a corned beef sandwich. And organ transplantation has saved thousands of lives and has improved the quality of thousands more. Mr. Power's suggestion that animal experimentation is unnecessary given the initial high mortality of liver transplantation is foolish. If the techniques hadn't been practiced on animals first, the number would have been ten times higher, and most likely liver transplantation never would have become common practice."

"Please, Doctor," Power interrupted. "You scientists just don't understand that you can't extrapolate animal data to humans. More people have been killed than saved using misleading animal experiments."

Glen nodded at Power. "I agree that we can't always jump from animal data to humans. But every kid in college biology knows that. You seem to want, for obvious ideologic reasons, to portray a comic-book scientist that doesn't exist."

Power was taken aback. Glen was sharper than the usual representatives sent to debate him. He wasn't going to win with a utility argument and decided to switch tactics.

"Even if the lies of organized medicine that Dr. Brinkman regurgitates were true, the fact is, we must protest the use of animals because it is morally wrong."

Courier was determined to remain evenhanded. "Dr. Brinkman, what gives you the right to use animals for human purposes? Do animals have any rights?"

Glen considered the question but already had his answer. "No," he replied thoughtfully, "I don't think that animals have rights. They are not moral agents. They can't understand what a right is and therefore cannot claim any. A lion never considers a zebra's rights before munching on it for dinner, but it does no wrong in doing so. We do, however, have obligations to animals, laboratory animals in particular. We need to treat them humanely. But let me ask Mr. Power a question." Glen turned and looked at Power. "Since the notion of rights is a human concoction, how can animals possess what they don't understand?"

Power swiveled his chair toward Glen. "Well, Doctor, since babies and the retarded can't understand rights, either, why don't you use them in the lab?"

Glen knew that argument and had his medical students debate it. It was a reasonable philosophical question, but not on national television. It was time for a low blow. "Mr. Power, if you don't believe there is a difference between a rat and a baby, then I think you just lost this debate."

"That's not exactly what I—"

"I have to agree with Dr. Brinkman, Mr. Power. You are beginning to sound like Dr. Mengele." Courier smelled blood and decided to rip off a hunk for himself.

Power calmed himself. "I simply meant that all life needs to be treated with respect. The wholesale destruction of animals and our ecology threatens us all. What is going on today in the labs and on the farms represents another Holocaust."

"What would you say about the recent violent attempts to stop research, Mr. Power?" Courier asked, now clearly on Glen's side.

"Violence directed at any animal, human or nonhuman, is simply wrong. And my organization, CARE, has donated twenty thousand dollars to the families of each victim."

"We're just about out of time. Any final comments, Dr. Brinkman?"

Time for one last low blow, Glen thought. "I wasn't going to bring this up, but Mr. Power brought up the Holocaust analogy, so I'll respond." Glen looked at Power and then back into the camera. "'We shouldn't feel superior to animals, we have no reason to.' This is a direct quote from the vegetarian head of state of the only twentieth-century nation to outlaw vivisection. His name was Adolf Hitler, and we all know who he experimented on."

"And you, Mr. Power?" Courier asked perfunctorily.

Power had lost the battle, but he was determined that his small army would win the war. "I believe we owe it to ourselves to treat all life with respect, and to do less diminishes us as humans. I—"

"I'm sorry, Mr. Power, we are out of time. I must say, Dr. Brinkman, you erased many doubts that I had about using animals for research," Courier said, having given up the pretense of objectivity. "For our audience, a copy of the transcript is available for three dollars. I would make it required reading," he added.

The producer came out and unhooked Glen and Power from their microphones. Power rose and shook Glen's hand. "You were very well prepared, Doctor. I congratulate you," he said, managing a forced smile. "I hope we can debate again someday."

"Thank you, Mr. Power. Even though you probably don't believe me, most of the people who do animal research are trying to find other methods, and we really do treat the animals well."

"I'm sure you do," Power replied as he walked away. He had to meet Lonergan at ten o'clock.

"I had some trouble getting the money," Power admitted.

Lonergan moved away and shuffled through the crowded subway car.

Power followed him and grabbed his arm. "I'll get it. I just need some time."

Lonergan looked through him icily, and for a moment, Power thought his life was over. But a smile slowly appeared as he removed Power's arm. Lonergan had done some work for farmers from Colombia, as well as in Turkey. They were always looking for more convenient avenues to launder the proceeds of their businesses.

"This group you work with. It is a registered nonprofit company?"

Power nodded, but he didn't know what Lonergan was getting at.

"Perhaps we can do business, Mr. Power. I'll contact you about my requirements."

26

"What's this 'we're looking into it' crap, Ted?" Zach asked. He was standing over Simpson's desk after declining his invitation to sit. It wasn't enough that researchers had become the world's newest endangered species. Now he had to waste three hours for a deposition, with God knows how many more to come, and the chairman wasn't even backing his own surgeons. Zach saw the article in the *Post* that morning

"Zach, sit down," Simpson said firmly, and pointed again to the chair. "I never said anything was done improperly, I merely said that we are reviewing the cases." Simpson had leaked word of the malpractice deluge to the media and had four interviews during the past week. His defense of his surgeons could be charitably described as lukewarm.

Zach continued to stand. "Ted, you know goddamn well those cases are bullshit. There's no malpractice."

"Look, I have a responsibility as chairman to make sure things are running up to snuff on the trauma service," he replied calmly.

"Things are running fine on the trauma service," Zach said loudly, then paused and looked up at him. "Ya know,

222

Ted, don't you find it funny that these cases are all being handled by the same scumbag lawyer?" He sat in the chair and leaned back.

"What's your point, Zach?" Simpson opened up his desk drawer, grabbed a pack of Camels, and lit one.

Zach waved the smoke out of his space and moved his chair a foot back. "Well, Ted, wouldn't it be convenient if, for whatever reason, we lost our trauma designation? Hell, five or ten more bypasses a week, and you could go out and get another beach house, or Mercedes, or who the fuck knows what."

"Are you accusing me of something, Zach?" Simpson puffed calmly on his Camel.

"I don't know, Ted. Are you so greedy that you would sell out your own partners?" He shook his head in disgust, not letting him respond. "What happened to you, Ted? Some of the guys in the medical school said you were smart enough to have won a Nobel prize. You gave that up to sew vein grafts into hearts?"

Simpson flicked his ashes into the air. "And you patch up the scum of the earth so they can go out and beat, rape, or rob someone else. I wouldn't be so self-righteous."

"The only thing I'll ever be invited to Stockholm for is a porno movie festival. Being a clinician is what I do best. But you had a special talent, a gift."

"I also had a talent for heart surgery. It was my choice."

Zach nodded because that was undeniably true. "But you chose it for the money. There are lots more people who can cut and sew than can do original research."

"What is it with you and money, Zach? There is nothing wrong with money."

"It's a drug, Ted, and you have been addicted for a long time."

Simpson said nothing for a long moment. "Good luck with the deposition, Zach." He hated what he was doing, but it was necessary.

"When we get in there, just answer their questions truthfully. Don't volunteer any information. And whatever you do, no matter how much he provokes you, don't lose your temper." Nate Cohen had reviewed the case with Zach for about an hour and wished he could give him some Valium before they went into the deposition.

"Do you know what a fucking waste of time this is? I saved that bastard's life, and now he's suing me."

"You're in good company, Zach. There are two suits against the trauma surgeons here, and we've just received notification that there are four more going through. The only one who hasn't been sued yet is Dr. Gordon."

Here was irony. The worst surgeon of their group had managed to escape this litigation epidemic. And how? Every single one of the lawsuits was on a damaged but alive patient. When 007 fucked up, the patient usually ended up in the morgue. Zach's lawyer, Cohen, had explained that the payout to a successful plaintiff would be much higher when the victim was chronically disabled. Zach chuckled but said nothing. He would only bad-mouth Larry to his face. "We go years here without getting sued, and now all of a sudden we're inundated. And by the same fucking lawyer."

Cohen nodded. "Sometimes it's a snowball effect: one or two patients sue, and suddenly everyone tries to get into the act. If it's any consolation, the case I'm handling for you is nearly groundless."

"Meaning what?"

"We should win it, or if we settle, it won't be for much."

Zach pounded on the table. "I'm not settling a fucking thing! I didn't do anything wrong!" he shouted.

"Let's see what happens," Cohen said.

"Hey. This is my reputation. If I settle this case, it goes into the national data bank and labels me forever. If they want to go to court, let's go."

"You never know what a jury will do, Zach," Cohen said cautiously. "I will tell you that Wells doesn't appear to be a very good malpractice lawyer. His strategy seems to be to drag a couple of these questionable cases into court and pray for a sympathetic jury."

Zach slumped back into his seat. "At least, if I get hit by

a stray bullet like most of our patients, it will probably be quick and relatively painless. With you lawyers, it's just slow torture."

"Zach, I only do physician defense work. I'm a good guy."

"Don't take this the wrong way, Nate, but you are all bad guys."

"May I talk to you for a minute, Greg?" Power asked as he gently knocked on Sandstone's door.

"Come in, John. Sit down," Sandstone offered,

Power took a seat and folded his hands on Sandstone's desk. "I need to apologize for my behavior last week."

Sandstone nodded but said nothing.

"We need to work together, Greg. We both want the same thing, but we go about it differently."

"What did you want a half million dollars for?" Sandstone asked firmly.

"If we want to make a difference, we need money," he replied nonresponsively.

"You're president of the third-largest animal rights group in this country, John. We have money. But I need to make sure it's used wisely. And reasonably. We don't want to be lumped together with these terrorists."

"Heavens no. But I'm talking about big-time money. To reformat a society's ideology is expensive."

"How then?" Sandstone asked suspiciously.

"I want CARE to be in the health products business— health food, cosmetics, those kinds of products. Make people realize they don't need to eat animal products or use animal-tested cosmetics."

Sandstone shrugged. "That's not what CARE has been about. And besides, there are already a million health-food stores."

"Not like the ones I have planned. Please, Greg, I'm the president. Give me a little latitude," Power begged.

"How much money would you need to start up?" Sandstone asked.

"No cash at all, Greg. Just be a signatory on a loan from the bank."

"Do you think you can make this work?"

"I'm going to make CARE rich and famous. And when we raise enough money, my plan is to build an institute devoted to developing alternative research methods."

Sandstone smiled and felt relieved. "You're starting to think like me, John."

"Oh, Greg, I almost forgot. I will need a hundred thousand dollars," Power added.

"Christ, John, I thought you . . . ," Sandstone said tensely, realizing what he had just heard was too good to be true.

Power interrupted and smiled at him. "It's for a fund for the families of the victims of the terrorists. The least we can do, don't you think?"

Sandstone exhaled and relaxed. "Maybe that will convince the FBI that we're not involved with those terrorists."

Nate Cohen was relieved. Zach had done a terrific job at the deposition. He never raised his voice, and his responses to Wells's poorly framed questions completely frustrated the lawyer.

"We're off the record now, right?" Zach asked.

The transcriber nodded.

Before Nate could grab him, Zach walked over to Forrest and stood four inches from his face. "I hope you get shot someday soon, you ambulance-chasing motherfucker, so I can operate on you and sew your ass to your mouth. That way, the shit can get out quicker."

Nate bit his lip to stop from laughing and pulled Zach away. The cases were weak, but he would need to be a magician to make them all go away.

Zach zipped back to his office to check his phone messages, then took the stairs to the lobby to go to lunch. When he emerged from the stairwell, he was blinded by an incandescent arsenal of camera lights.

A reporter stuck a microphone in his face. "Dr. Green, what's going on at UHC? I thought this was supposed to be the best place in the city for trauma care. With all these malpractice suits, it looks more like the *Killing Fields.*"

Before he could answer, he was barraged with five more questions. "The trauma care here is the best around," he responded over the noise.

"Apparently not," another reporter fired back.

Zach wasn't sure what to say; he felt like hiding. This wasn't his usual captive audience of medical students, residents, or surgical peers. Here, he wasn't in control.

Suddenly, Larry Gordon appeared at Zach's side. His Armani suit hung perfectly, and he smoothed down his jet-black hair. "One question at a time," he commanded. Calm was restored in a flash.

"To what do you attribute the recent downslide in trauma care at UHC, Dr. Gordon?" a reporter asked.

"What downslide? There have been no trials, no settlements, and I assure everyone here that we're still the best." The cameras flashed and captured Gordon's perfect smile.

"Have you been sued, Dr. Gordon?" asked another reporter.

"As a matter of fact, I haven't. We're only taking depositions, and it appears they will go nowhere." He became serious and moved a step closer to Zach. "The only thing I'll add is this: if any of you are ever unfortunate enough to be injured, you should pray that you're lucky enough to have Dr. Green operating. He's the best."

The questions kept coming, but Gordon calmly led Zach out of the lobby back to their offices.

Zach stopped in the hall and put his hand on Gordon's shoulder. "Thanks, Larry. I didn't know what to say, and knowing me, it would have been the wrong thing."

Larry smiled. "It's the least I could do after all the times you've bailed me out in the OR."

Lenore Attenucci sat in her office, having her fifth cup of black coffee of the day. She had been spending too much time defending her hospital's trauma service, and she shouldn't have had to. She knew it was the best in New York City. But image was everything. No one would remember all the previous publicity and praise if this negative press continued. Over the past week, she had fielded a dozen calls from members of UHC's board of directors. *What is the problem?* they had asked.

There was a problem, but her instincts told her it wasn't with the trauma service.

27

Xenograft.

To animal rights activists, Pearl Harbor, the sinking of the *Maine,* the assassination of the archduke of Serbia, the Alamo, all historic *causa belli,* were no greater provocations than the use of xenografts for human organ transplantation.

The use of an animal's organs to replace nonfunctioning human organs was a transplant surgeon's dream come true. The well-documented shortage of human organs was too familiar to the thousands of dying patients in need of a new kidney, heart, liver, or pancreas. But the success of transplanting animal organs, usually those of primates, had been poor, because though chimpanzees were close antigenically to humans, they were not close enough. Inevitably, rejection prevented long-term success.

The explosion of knowledge in molecular genetics, however, provided a potential solution to that problem, particularly in light of the recent cloning of a sheep in Scotland.

The scientists at the Institute for Applied Genetics on Long Island, owned by a small biotechnology company called Retrogene, were working on a simple premise. If the

DNA of a chimpanzee was different from human DNA, they would change it. For almost three years, the scientists had been attempting to infect the animals with a very special adenovirus. It could insinuate itself into the DNA of its host, causing it to alter its protein synthesis. Special proteins—the HLA antigens—on the cell surface were responsible for rejection and varied between people and between species. If the scientists could infect the chimpanzees with the properly altered adenovirus, which would code for the human rejection proteins, the patient's immune system would think that the animal's organs were human and would eliminate the rejection response. The technology could allow the creation of a designer heart, kidney, or liver for anyone who needed one, and since the organ could be coded with the recipient's own DNA, there would be no rejection.

This was a great theory but extremely difficult to put into practice. The funding for this ambitious undertaking was private. Retrogene had borrowed heavily to provide the capital. Its motivations were not totally altruistic. If they held the patent on the proper adenovirus, it could be worth billions of dollars.

"This will be the most important day in the history of the struggle for equality," John Power said triumphantly. The new "businesses" had already paid Lonergan's fee for at least two missions. On paper, Eat Right and Body Beautiful barely broke even, but a series of shell corporations layered millions of dollars of cash from the Caymans to the Netherlands. The connection to CARE would be untraceable. The group had bitterly resisted using a mercenary like Lonergan, but Power realized that to carry out attacks on the scale needed—and not be caught—it was the only way. Lonergan had already provided maps and blueprints of dozens of potential targets.

"If we intercept the truck on the way from the airport, there will be very little security," Lonergan said.

"The animals must not be harmed, under any circumstances, Mr. Lonergan."

"I'll do the best I can, but I can't make any guarantees."

"I'll make sure," Cecile said confidently.

"I hope she can handle herself, Power," Lonergan muttered. He preferred to work alone or use his own people, but Power had insisted she be involved.

"Just make sure you can take care of yourself," Cecile spit back.

His face tightened, and his back arched. Who did she think she was talking to, he thought, and momentarily considered killing her. He calmed himself and decided it could wait. "I assure you a very bloody result," Lonergan promised.

"For what we're paying you, I would hope so. Tomorrow is the day, then. Good luck, everyone. God is with us."

"If this comes off, it won't be luck or God, it will be meticulous planning and execution." Lonergan had maimed and murdered on nearly every continent and was certain this was the strangest group he had worked for. But for a three-percent cut of the money laundered through Eat Right and Body Beautiful, he could put up with it.

Power made his way carefully out the door. He felt guilty about not physically participating in the war but couldn't risk being caught. The FBI would eventually try to follow him, and he was ready for that. Without him, there was no chance of success.

The final chimpanzee was loaded into a white panel truck with the Retrogene logo.

"Jesus, those things stink," said Mike Nelson, the driver.

"Just get them out of here," said the worker standing on the loading dock at the JFK freight terminal. "They're noisy and smelly." He handed the driver the invoice to sign and gave him a receipt.

The driver got into the truck and began the ride out to the tip of the Island. *The trip from the airport shouldn't be too bad now,* he thought as he drove toward the airport exit. He was picking up speed, when he saw flashing red lights behind him. He looked at the speedometer and saw he was only doing thirty miles per hour.

Once the truck stopped, Lonergan, dressed in a police uniform, approached it. He looked around to make sure no other cars were nearby. When he scouted this mission, he realized as busy as JFK was, the access roads from the freight areas were usually not busy at this hour.

"I wasn't speeding," Nelson said as he rolled down his window.

"Could you open the door, please?" Lonergan replied.

The driver opened the door. The last thing he saw was a silenced 9mm Ruger pointed at his chest. Three quick shots didn't even give him time to scream. Lonergan hopped into the truck, shoved the body onto the floor, and drove out of the airport, confident no one had seen what had happened.

He drove east and exited. A car was waiting in a garage. Cecile helped drag the dead driver out and got into the truck. She was already dressed in a Retrogene uniform, and Lonergan quickly donned his. They pulled out of the garage and headed toward the laboratory complex.

As the truck arrived at the loading dock, the doors opened and Larry Kilmer, the head animal keeper, appeared. He looked annoyed. "You're an hour late," he yelled angrily, before the truck doors even opened. There were three other men to help unload the animals and get them set in their new environment.

Before Kilmer had finished his sentence, he realized there were two people in the truck, neither of whom he recognized. Lonergan jumped out of the front seat with an AK-47 assault rifle and picked off Kilmer with one shot which left virtually nothing of his head. Cecile, out the other side, sprayed the three other men with her Mac 11.

"OK, let's get to the lab," Lonergan directed. They made their way from the loading area to the third floor where the animals were kept. When they entered the elevator, two secretaries were on their way back from the cafeteria. The women noticed only the familiar Retrogene logo on their clothing and not the guns.

"Do you know what they do here?" Cecile asked the closer of the two women.

"Some sort of research on monkeys," the secretary answered slowly.

"Doesn't that bother you?" replied Cecile.

"Not in the least," the woman said nonchalantly.

"It should," Cecile said as she pulled out the Mac 11.

"No!" screamed the woman as Cecile grabbed her throat, pushed her into the wall, and fired three rounds into her torso.

"And what do you think of animal research?" Cecile asked the other secretary.

"Please," sobbed the other woman, who pulled a family picture out of her purse. "I have three children."

"Answer the question."

"Bad, it's bad," she pleaded.

"I don't believe you," Cecile said as she shot the woman in the head. The elevator opened, and they exited.

Lonergan looked down the hall. "Let's go. We have ten minutes left."

Lew Mason toured what was left of Retrogene. Fifteen other agents were searching for anything that resembled a clue. Thirty cops helped identify the victims. The media, blocked from the building by more police, were in a frenzy.

In all, thirty-two bodies were removed, but residual blood and bits of human tissue randomly dotted the floor and corridor walls. The terrorists had planned every detail of their entrance and escape. There was no video film—the cameras had been shot out—but the timer mechanisms survived and showed the entire elapsed time from arrival to departure was fifteen minutes. They knew exactly where to go. Every person who had come into contact with the group had been shot dead. No witnesses.

Thirty-two people—scientists, lab techs, secretaries, and administrators—were dead. The message was straightforward. *If you are involved with research on animals, we are going to murder you.* ABP had kept its promise.

Mason looked down and saw a bullet-riddled photograph of three small children. The mother of those children had begged for her life. He understood two things with absolute certainty. The killers behind this were sociopaths. And they had a good source of money to accomplish such an organized attack. Maybe the other attacks could have been carried out by determined amateurs, but not this one. He simply had to get that subpoena for these animal rights organizations' financial records. More reports kept coming in about their personnel, and Mason had grown tired of sifting through them. Of his three top choices, R. L. Burke of Stop the Cruelty in Seattle had turned out to be a benevolent wacko; he had solid alibis for all the dates of the murders and didn't seem to have the funding they would have required. Mason had scrutinized the arrest records, tax filings, and other minutiae of the minions at Animals International and had no strong leads from workers at that source. He was still looking into CARE's staff, including the two at the top. Perhaps it was time to make another trip into the city.

"Your Honor, we are in the midst of an unprecedented spree of terrorism against the research community of this nation. The nature of the crimes, particularly the last one, suggests professional terrorist involvement. We strongly believe that the financing of these attacks must be through one of the well-funded animal rights groups."

"So, if I understand you correctly, you want me to allow you fellas at the FBI to rummage through the financial records of the SPCA," Judge Stanley Gradinger said as he skimmed the twelve-page brief.

The sarcastic tone was not a good sign but not unexpected. Paul Hortenza, the assistant U.S. attorney for the Second Circuit, knew they were in trouble. "Actually, Your Honor, the SPCA is not on our list. The groups we have listed are not animal welfare groups that advocate the humane treatment of animals. They are groups that profess more radical or extreme philosophical beliefs. We believe that one or more of these groups is at least financially responsible for the ABP wave of terrorism."

"And are you going to share your evidence of this cabal with me?" the judge asked impatiently while he fiddled with his gavel.

Hortenza paused and swallowed. "There is no direct evidence, Your Honor," he admitted. "But the attack at Retrogene was a logistically perfect terrorist strike. We aren't dealing with angry pet owners here, sir."

"Well, Mr. Hortenza, in case you were out hunting the day the Fourth Amendment was discussed in law school, let me refresh you. You need some probable cause to get me to allow you to rummage willy-nilly through the bank records of a half dozen nonprofit organizations. Maybe these attacks were professional, but on the other hand, last year some kids in Syracuse, New York, built a bomb like the one used in Oklahoma City with information they got off the Internet. Don't waste the court's time. Get me some evidence, Mr. Hortenza. Court adjourned." Judge Gradinger stood and headed back to his chambers.

28

Bruce Evans had two rules about the open-heart surgery cases he chose to do as the senior cardiothoracic fellow. First, he only wanted to scrub in on cases the attending would let him do, because as far as he was concerned, after six years of residency, his days of watching were over. And second, there was no use in scrubbing in on cases that he wouldn't be doing in private practice. He was about to violate both his rules on one case.

The American Board of Thoracic Surgery, in its wisdom, required that all surgeons perform or first assist on at least twenty-five cases of congenital heart surgery before they could sit for the cardiothoracic board exam. Bruce had always avoided the congenital stuff and was short by about twenty-three cases. Very few private-practice groups, his future group included, did complex congenital surgery. It was very difficult surgery, often in sick premature neonates with other congenital disorders, and a large percentage of the babies were retarded. If that wasn't bad enough, the reimbursement was terrible because many of the sickest patients had parents without health insurance. It was the valves and bypasses that brought in the money, and that's what he cared about. Worst of all, the attending,

Dr. Delaney, required the resident or fellow who operated with him on the baby to sit by its bedside all night and fine-tune the physiology. Fuck that, he thought.

He had come to the OR reluctantly to assist Dr. Delaney on a Norwood procedure. It was the most difficult operation in pediatric congenital heart surgery, and that was saying a lot. Delaney never, absolutely never, gave those cases away. He usually wouldn't even let the residents close the skin.

Evans stood across from Delaney as the first assistant while Casey was tucked out of the way to hold retractors if necessary. "So, Bruce, why don't you tell me everything you know about a Norwood?" Delaney was a terrific teacher if the residents acted interested, and like every pediatric heart surgeon, he was a magician in the OR.

Evans couldn't believe he was quizzing him like a medical student. He was the chief resident. He also didn't have a notion about the details of the operation. "Well, it's a staged procedure for the correction of a hypoplastic left ventricle—very high mortality," he said, going into his bullshit mode.

Delaney was getting the four-pound baby on bypass and didn't even look up. "That's a great answer—for a first-year nursing student. I can see how well you prepared. I know the cardiac fellows don't like to scrub in on these cases because I don't let you do them, but sometimes you can learn from watching," he said. "If you understand what I'm doing," he added.

Casey could just catch a glimpse of the heart. It made the one she sewed up last month in the ER look gigantic. She had never seen any neonatal cardiac surgery before and wished she had a better view.

"Dr. Brenner, what do you know about the Norwood procedure?" Delaney asked.

She had stayed up until two in the morning reading about it. "It's a three-stage procedure for hypoplastic left-heart syndrome. Most of the babies have a small or absent mitral and aortic valve and a rudimentary left ventricle, so they die as soon as their patent ductus closes. The first stage involves hooking the pulmonary artery to the aortic arch to establish systemic blood flow, followed by a BT shunt. When they are bigger, you go back and do a staged Fontan procedure."

He looked up at her and nodded. "Bruce, switch places with Dr. Brenner."

"I don't think that's . . ."

"Move, Sonny. Now!" Delaney barked.

Casey looked into Evans's eyes and could see the hate as she took his place across from Delaney.

The operation was going well. Casey was transfixed with Delaney's gentle but lightning-quick technique. She was following his sutures, careful not to pull too hard on the tiny, congenitally mangled heart. They were down to the last anastomosis.

"Very good, Dr. Brenner," he said softly. "I hear you had some experience with baby hearts."

"Oh, I just put a couple stitches into the right ventricle, and luckily the baby lived," she said modestly.

He stopped sewing and looked over at her. "Casey, there is no such thing as luck in surgery. And besides," he added, "you have to start somewhere. Could you do this half of the anastomosis?"

"Sure," she said in a state of shock as he handed her the needle holder. He followed her suture, and she meticulously completed the last anastomosis. Then he let her close the chest.

As the final skin suture went in, Delaney took off his gown and gloves. "I'll expect you to stay with the patient tonight."

"Of course," she said, bobbing her head like a six-year-old. She would adopt the baby if that's what he wanted. Now she knew what kind of surgeon she would become. Zach was right; it was instinctive.

The patient was tucked away in the pediatric unit. Casey headed to the ER to see what was going on when Evans accosted her from behind.

"You fucking cunt! Who do you think you are?" he screamed, before she could even turn around.

"Excuse me, Bruce," Casey said to her livid senior resident. Her voice was weak and shaky. He looked as if he were going to hit her.

"First you steal a bypass from me, and now you try and make me look like a moron in front of Delaney!" He was hyperventilating, and his beefy, sweaty face had turned an unattractive shade of purple.

Casey had been a surgery resident for more than three years. She had been verbally abused too many times to count, sexually harassed, and physically worn to a nub, and she wondered if it was worth it. Then she remembered how she had saved that baby in the ER, all by herself. Zach had told her how good she was, and she was beginning to believe it. Today had been an epiphany. It was also a crossroad. Zach was right; she didn't need anyone to stick up for her. "I didn't steal anything from you. Simpson just let me do the cases, and so did Delaney," she said, not backing down an inch. "And you definitely don't need me to make you look like a moron." Her voice was soft and controlled but no longer shaky.

He sneered and ignored the remark. "Do you really think you can fuck your way through this program? Give it up, Casey. Get married, have a few kids, and work in the peds clinic a few hours a week. You have no business being a surgeon."

She looked at him and laughed. "Bruce, I'm three years behind you, and already I can operate better than you. I know it, you know it, and anyone who has operated with us knows it."

A crowd of at least ten nurses, respiratory therapists, and pediatricians had gathered as the confrontation escalated. They ogled the combatants: Bruce and Casey having it out after class.

Bruce stood there speechless, a bully who had his nose bloodied. He didn't know whether to keep going and get whacked again or give up while he was still standing. It was a combination of both weakness and common sense that catapulted him silently down the hall, licking his deep, salt-filled wounds.

By morning, the baby looked terrific. Casey adjusted the drips and the fluids all night, and it paid off. It was seven-thirty, and she wanted to be in the OR by eight. Delaney had asked her to help with another big case. She headed for the shower after gulping down her ninth cup of coffee in the last twelve hours.

Simpson caught her as soon as she came out of the women's locker room. "Casey, you're scrubbing with me on the mitral valve this morning," he said tersely.

"But Dr. Delaney is doing a great vessel switch today," she replied. "It's such a rare operation—I didn't think you would mind." She had hoped that after the episode in his office, when she had made it clear that she wasn't inter-ested in him, he would back down.

He grabbed her arm, more firmly than he had intended, and led her into an empty conference room. He let go as soon as they were inside. "Why would you want to watch an operation on some retarded baby with a rat heart? I'm doing a mitral valve today. I'll let you do it." He was almost pleading.

"The baby is not retarded, and I would appreciate it if you would let me go in on it," she said firmly.

"OK, OK," he quickly agreed. "Then how about dinner tonight? I checked the schedule, you're not on call." Her lipstick was fresh, and all he wanted was to kiss her. He grabbed both her arms and pulled her toward him.

She pushed him hard, and he quickly released his hands. "Dr. Simpson, I thought you understood that I am not interested in having an affair with you." She wished someone would come into the room and extract her from this awkward and sickening situation.

He looked at her with a childish sadness, and then suddenly his eyes focused and became angry. "I think you should reconsider," he said coolly, and walked out.

It was strange, but it didn't even bother her anymore. Ted Simpson was a pathetic old man, and she pitied him.

She had tried to convince him he should leave her alone, and he just didn't get it. Fine. Now she was ready for him.

"What do you have, Lew?" James Garrow asked Mason, who'd just come back to Washington. The Retrogene massacre had gotten Garrow's attention even before a call from the president's chief of staff.

Mason exhaled and shook his head. "We're up against a dead end with the money trail unless we come up with more evidence. Judge Gradinger stonewalled us."

"You've investigated all the groups that have enough dough to pull off a hit like the one at Retrogene?"

"Sure, they all tell me how terrible this violence is, and how it hurts the movement, etc. . . . I ran background checks on three or four dozen of the major players in the animal rights movement. About half of them have been arrested at least one time for some protest—antifur, antimeat, antiresearch."

"Anything violent?"

"Lots of damaged labs, but other than pelting some scientists and fur store owners with red paint, not to people. I went back to New York City to see Greg Sandstone at CARE again. I wanted to surprise him, but he wasn't in the office, wasn't home, and no one, including Power, the new president, knew where he was or when he'd be back. I talked to Power again, got nothing. We aren't going to find what we need without that subpoena."

"Where we going with this? At this rate, they're going to blow up a whole fucking medical school soon. We're taking incredible heat from the president, and two thousand labs have closed since Retrogene. These bastards are actually pulling this off. I don't like it when the bad guys win, Lew."

"I'm doing everything I can. We just need a break."

"I'll give you twenty more agents. Go make one."

Gregory Sandstone was ambivalent about being in the health products business. Power didn't really seem the entrepreneurial type, but it looked like a good move for

CARE. If the Eat Right and Body Beautiful stores were successful, then CARE wouldn't need to depend solely on donations to fund animal welfare projects. And a research institute devoted entirely to alternative medical research was an inspired plan. Power had been so sure of the success of their enterprise that he had employed an architect to draw preliminary plans. Although it hurt to admit it, maybe CARE needed new direction after all these years. The initial outlay of cash was minimal, and Power, who appeared consumed by this new endeavor, never again mentioned the half million dollars he had wanted. Sandstone looked at his watch and decided to check out what Power had said would become the finest chain of health-food emporiums in Manhattan.

Sandstone walked to Eat Right, but it was just after seven o'clock, and the store was closed. He had taken a key and decided to go in just to look around. He unlocked the door and entered. A light was on in the back storage area, and he heard Power's voice.

"You have your money. Is the strike on for next week?"

"The details have been all worked out. You'll be pleased with the outcome. There ought to be more than a hundred people in the building when the bomb goes off," Lonergan said.

Lonergan had already laundered more than three million dollars through the stores. The FBI and Treasury would figure it out sooner or later, but by then he would be on to something else.

"And you're sure the animals are kept in the other building?" Power asked.

"Don't worry," Lonergan responded.

Sandstone stood frozen in place. He wasn't sure what to do but figured he should get out fast. He tiptoed, then accelerated toward the entrance. He was about twenty feet from the door when his foot caught a stack of cardboard boxes, which came crashing down.

Lonergan and Power bolted from the warehouse into the retail area as Sandstone made his way out the door.

"Do you know who that was?" Lonergan asked.

"We have a problem," Power said. He had recognized Sandstone's jacket.

"I'll take care of it. Who is he?"

Power pounded his hand into the wall and shook his head. "Greg Sandstone. My predecessor. If you kill him, that's all the FBI will need."

"Don't worry. This is a dangerous city. Where does he live?" Lonergan asked.

Greg Sandstone headed west on Twenty-second Street, not sure what to do. There was no benign interpretation of what he had heard an hour and a half ago. He decided to go home, lock himself in his apartment, and call the FBI.

Which was exactly what Lonergan had figured.

Three buildings down from his co-op, a man waited with a duffle bag. He was shuffling from foot to foot and appeared nervous. Sandstone didn't sense the other man about ten feet behind him but realized someone was there when the man with the duffle bag looked past him and signaled at the guy trailing him. Sandstone figured it was a drug deal in progress and began to cross the street. Before he reached the curb, he was shoved into the man with the duffle bag, who was as surprised as he was. The gunman pulled out his 9mm and calmly pumped a half dozen bullets into the heads and chests of Sandstone and the drug dealer, grabbed all the cocaine but a few grams, with which he dusted the dealer, and quickly took off.

The EMTs brought in Sandstone while giving him CPR, but after a few agonal breaths, there were no signs of life. Zach was already in the ER evaluating a patient with a gunshot wound to the neck, when a flock of doctors and nurses flew to Sandstone's gurney.

In less than two minutes, he was intubated, had two IVs, a nasogastric tube, and a urinary catheter. Unfortunately, he remained dead. The second-year resident opened the thoracotomy tray, preparing to fillet Sandstone's chest, but Zach stopped him.

"How long has he been out?" Zach asked the EMTs as he stepped between the resident's scalpel and Sandstone .

"About eight minutes," replied the EMT, looking at his watch.

"Forget it, Tad," Zach said. "No signs of life, no vital signs, for eight minutes. It's useless. Call it."

The resident, more disappointed at not getting to open a chest than at the sight of the dead man in front of him, reluctantly complied.

A nurse pulled a curtain around Sandstone's cubicle and covered him with a sheet. "Do we know who he is?" she asked.

"Name is Gregory Sandstone," replied Lieutenant Wilson, NYPD, who was at the main desk with Sandstone's wallet in his hands.

Zach appeared from behind the curtain and saw the detective. He knew him from at least a couple dozen other shootings and stabbings the police detective had investigated. "Hello, Lieutenant. Haven't seen you in a while."

"Lucky for both of us, Dr. Green. How you doing?" He looked at the closed curtain behind Zach. "Nothing you could do, Doc?" he asked.

Zach frowned and shook his head. "Newton's law. A dead body tends to stay dead."

Wilson chuckled, being as immune to the everyday violence as Zach. "Too bad. He was a good guy. It looks like he got in the middle of a contentious business transaction."

"Drug deal?" Zach replied knowingly.

Wilson nodded. "Probably," he said slowly. "Third mushroom this month, and it's only the twenty-fourth."

Zach shrugged. "It gets worse every day. Businessmen, mothers, kids." He paused and looked at Wilson. "Cops," he added.

"You're right, Doc. At least, we have you guys here at UHC to patch us up if we go down. Wouldn't go anyplace else."

"Well, thanks, detective, but I hope you never need me."

* * *

Mason hopped off his Schwinn and logged onto his PC. Scrolling quickly through the headlines, he nearly missed it: "**Leader of animal rights group caught in drug crossfire.**"

He double-clicked the headline and read the details. Why in hell did he have to find out from a newspaper? Goddamn it, they were the FBI.

Not a week went by in New York City when some poor bastard didn't manage to be in the wrong place at the wrong time. Mason hated coincidences.

"Do you have a minute?" Vanderzell poked his head into Nate's office.

"Sure, Billy, what's up?"

Vanderzell sat on the corner of Nate's desk. "You remember that group I represent, CARE?"

"Yeah, and I'm not giving you any donations. Scientists are dying like dogs, if you'll forgive the expression."

Vanderzell nodded somberly. "The former president of CARE was killed yesterday."

"I saw that in the paper this morning—got caught in the middle of some drug deal. I think it was God's wrath."

Vanderzell shook his head. "Greg Sandstone was actually a reasonable guy. Just committed."

"Is that something like a moderate Iranian?"

"Come on, Nate. The maniacs doing all this killing don't represent the mainstream of the animal rights movement."

"Whatever you say. What's bothering you?"

The new president, John Power, had tried to get half a million dollars out of the CARE account. Sandstone had blocked it.

"What the hell did he need with half a million dollars?"

Vanderzell said nothing.

Nate unwrapped a Twinkie and inhaled it. "You think your buddy might have something to do with all this nonsense?"

"I doubt it," Vanderzell said wishfully. "He's a mild-mannered guy, soft-spoken and brilliant. Respect for all life. That's his motto. I've known him for fifteen years." He suppressed the lab incident at Ann Arbor.

"Well, Sandstone wasn't eaten by a pack of stray dogs, he was shot by a few stray bullets. It happens all the time."

"True, I suppose. But the other thing that's a little strange is the stores CARE has opened—health food and beauty supply stores."

"Everything you guys do is a little strange to me, Billy."

"Maybe the stores are connected to all this. Maybe Power has found another way to get the money. Maybe . . ." He paused and didn't finish the thought.

"There are ten million stores like that in New York. Do you know how much business you need to generate to show a half million profit? Let me check those places out."

"Don't, Nate. Let me do it."

Nate chuckled. "You may know contracts and the constitution, Billy, but leave the crooked stuff to me. I'm a savant."

"Forget it, Nate. It's my problem."

29

Casey asked Zach several times what he did to keep in such good shape. Finally, he told her he'd show her, but it meant they had to get together on a Saturday. Casey happily said yes. At last, they were moving beyond a forty-five-minute lunch at a deli.

"Zach, I have to ask you something," Casey said as they drove up the FDR in his Honda Civic. "A personal question," she added.

"Anything." *Please let it be whether I like to be on top or bottom,* he thought.

"It's a weird question, but it's been driving me crazy. What's that cologne you're wearing? I've smelled it before, but a long time ago, maybe when I was a kid."

He looked over and smiled. "Do you like it?"

"Yes. It's different from the usual men's stuff."

"Pinaud Lilac Vegetal—been around for a hundred years. Not many men wear it anymore. When I grew up, my grandfather used to take me with him to the barber every three weeks. Not one of those unisex places, but a real, if you'll excuse the expression, men's barbershop. My grandfather would always get a shave, and afterward the barber would douse on the stuff."

"Lilacs, that's what it smells like," she said.

"It's all I've ever worn since I was thirteen. I had a girlfriend once who didn't like the smell and bought me some expensive designer cologne crap from Bloomingdale's. I returned it, took the money, and got about a ten-year supply of Pinaud."

"What about the girlfriend?"

"I returned her, too."

She laughed and took his hand. "So where are you taking me?" she asked as they turned off the FDR and headed to the Columbia boathouse.

"Are your shorts waterproof?"

She saw the boats in the background and figured it out. "We'll find out, I guess."

He turned into the small driveway of the boathouse. There was an old A-frame building with a newer garage attached to it. Inside were about a dozen sculls. He parked the car, and they both got out. Two enormous men were carrying their double scull back into the boat room.

"Cutter, how ya doin'?" one called. "And more important, who is your lovely companion?"

"Casey Brenner, meet Wiley Worthington. And this other behemoth is Judd Iverson," Zach said, pointing at the two land masses to their right.

They were big. Worthington was six-foot-five and went about two hundred thirty-five pounds. Iverson was just slightly smaller. They both shook hands with Casey after they put the scull back in its place.

"They call you Cutter?" she asked, smiling at Zach.

"Everyone here has a nickname," Zach replied. "Judd over there is Tumbles, because the first few times he tried to row, he fell out of the boat. That was a long time ago—now he's been invited to the Olympic trials. And Wiley is Loaf. You don't want to know why," he quickly added.

"You gonna teach Casey how to row, Cutter?" Worthington asked.

"Yeah. I need to use that wide double. She's never rowed before."

"Casey, you're the first woman he's ever brought up here."

Zach and Casey looked at each other for a second before Zach responded. "Casey's one of the surgical residents at UHC."

"A lady surgeon. I guess we'll call you Blade," Worthington suggested. "Yeah, Blade and Cutter; I like that." He and Iverson went and got out the double scull and the oars.

Zach pulled off his T-shirt, and Casey did a double-take. Under the tank top was a smaller version of the two college boys. Not an extra ounce of fat; a perfect body.

Zach caught the stare. "Not bad for an old man, huh?" he said.

Casey gave him the biggest smile he had ever seen. "Not bad at all, Cutter," she said as she stripped to her tank top.

Loaf and Tumbles could barely contain themselves at the sight of her. They held the boat while Zach helped Casey in. Loaf handed them the oars, pushed them off from the dock, and waved good-bye.

"Fucking Zach. Way to go," Loaf said.

They started slowly, but Casey caught on quickly. Soon they were gliding down the Harlem River.

"I can see why you love it," Casey said, feeling a little winded.

Zach lifted his oars and let the boat coast. "It's almost a religious experience." *Like being with you,* he thought.

After they came off the river, they sat in Zach's car talking for two hours. Neither of them wanted to leave.

"I wanted to be a concert pianist," Casey said. "I've been playing since I was four years old."

"You must be great. I took trumpet lessons for a few years. My dad called me a lease breaker."

She laughed and smiled. "I was very good, just not good enough to be at Carnegie Hall."

"I'd like to hear you play sometime," Zach asked.

"Sure, anytime."

"How about now?"

She thought for a minute. It was getting late. Bringing Zach back to her apartment didn't strike her as a very good idea. If he came up, something was going to happen, and despite the fact she was close to being in love with him, there was still the major problem of twenty more months of residency. Nothing was more important to her than becoming a surgeon. Yet . . . maybe she could control the situation. "OK," she replied. "Let's go."

"Is Daphne home?" Zach asked nonchalantly.

"No. She went on a fishing trip with her dad."

"Will you feel uncomfortable if I come over?" There was a question he had never asked anyone.

"Should I?" she asked.

Zach shook his head no.

"Then I wouldn't be uncomfortable at all."

As they walked back to her apartment and talked and laughed, it occurred to Zach, physical attraction aside, how much he enjoyed being with her. There was probably some operation he would rather be doing, he joked to himself—a brain transplant, maybe. But it was a close call.

They walked up the three flights of stairs. Casey opened the door and turned on the lights. The piano occupied half the living room.

"Take a load off your feet," she said, pointing to the sofa.

He sat down as she made her way to the piano.

"That's some piano," Zach said. "Baby grand?"

She nodded. "My parents bought it for me when I graduated from college. It got me through some tough times. What would you like to hear?"

"Surprise me."

She began playing the "Moonlight Sonata." To Zach's untrained ear, she could have played at Carnegie Hall. Though he had operated with her before, he had never really looked at her hands. They were small, but her fingers were long and slender. It almost seemed a sin that tomorrow they might be scooping shit and blood clots out of some drug addict's belly.

250

"You're unbelievable. That's the most beautiful playing I've ever heard."

"Thanks," she said as she got up from the bench and sat next to him on the couch. She always felt a little awkward talking about her playing. She leaned back into the sofa, took one of the pillows, and held it to her chest. Zach wanted to trade places with the pillow.

"So, Zach, what makes you happy besides operating and rowing?" she asked, changing the subject.

He wanted to tell her that she did but didn't want to chance ending the fantasy. "Being with friends, especially Glen and Debby. And their two girls; they're a lot of fun. And my family," he said seriously. He hesitated. "And you," he added.

Casey's heart skipped a beat. "Really," she said, searching for words.

"Don't tell me you're surprised," said Zach.

"Nooo. I guess not."

"And are you happy being with me?" Zach said.

"Yes. You're a good, good friend," said Casey, suddenly shy.

The dreaded *friend* word, not what he was looking for. He looked at his watch. "Hey, it's late. I'd better be going." He stood up and headed toward the door.

"Zach?" She wanted him to stay overnight.

"Yes?" He stood about a foot from her. Looking into her eyes and hearing her voice, all he wanted to do was hold her.

"I had a nice time."

"Me, too."

"I mean, I *really* had a nice time," she said emphatically.

"I'll see you tomorrow," Zach said as he closed the door behind him.

Casey took a deep breath. She tried to recall if she had ever felt this good about any other man, but she couldn't remember. Still, she had to remind herself, nothing was more important than becoming a surgeon. And this was the same scenario that almost ended her surgical career a year ago.

Zach walked back to his car. When he was a teenager, he'd asked his grandfather how he would know when he had met the right woman. "You will be consumed by a passion that, no matter how hard you try, you will not be able to resist," his grandpa had answered in his half-English, half-Yiddish dialect.

Consider yourself consumed, Zach.

"There is a Lenore Attenucci here to see you, Mr. Wells."

The name sounded familiar to him. He had seen it before but couldn't place it. "Does she have an appointment?" he asked.

"No, sir, but she said to tell you that it has to do with some of the cases you are handling."

"Christ, I'm swamped. Send her in, and interrupt me in ten minutes with an emergency."

A tall, expensively dressed woman walked into his office. "Mr. Wells, I'm Lenore Attenucci, the CEO of UHC. Do you mind if I sit down?" She took a seat and crossed her legs.

"I really can't talk about any of my active cases, Ms. Attenucci," Forrest said, trying to remain calm. He had the big honcho in his office, ready to beg. What a rush. *This could mean a big fucking settlement,* he thought.

Attenucci grinned at him and leaned forward. "Mr. Wells, do you know that I have worked my whole adult life at UHC? I'm not married, and that hospital is like my family."

"Well, Lenore—you don't mind if I call you Lenore, do you?"

"Not at all," she replied.

"Lenore, every family has problems, and I'm afraid one of your children, specifically the trauma service, has a serious one," he oozed.

"Forrest, today is your lucky day."

It has to be at least a few million, he thought. He almost had to restrain himself. "How much?" he asked.

She clapped her hands together. "Here's how much,

little boy. If you advise your clients to drop these ridiculous lawsuits, I won't move to have you disbarred."

"Don't threaten me," he hissed. "My responsibility is to my clients." His stomach knotted up, and he felt sick. He should have stuck with one or two cases. *Damn Simpson,* he thought.

"They weren't your clients until you approached them. Ever hear of solicitation? It's a crime, and it doesn't just apply to prostitutes on the street but also to whores with offices on Park Avenue."

Forrest sucked on a mint and tried to calm himself. "All of these patients were injured, Ms. Attenucci. They have a right to their day in court."

"You have a partner at UHC, Mr. Wells, and I'm pretty sure I know who he is. You and your partner are guilty of conspiracy. Check your case law. What you have done is illegal."

Three years ago, she had spent almost ten million dollars to computerize the byzantine medical records department at UHC. With the new system, it had taken her about ten minutes to find out who had reviewed the charts of these plaintiffs. All physicians at UHC had a medical records number and were required to log in to review charts. Ted Simpson had reviewed these malpractice cases. Since he was the chairman of surgery, that would have been fine, except that he had gone over them before the claims had been filed.

"What are you going to do?" asked Forrest.

"I may not do anything, if you drop these lawsuits. I'd prefer to let this nonsense die quietly. But if you don't, I'll call my old college friend in the DA's office, and I'll destroy you."

"What if my clients won't drop their cases?" he whined.

"That's your problem. You talked them into it." She stood up. "Tell me, Forrest," she said, leaning over his desk. "I want to hear it from your own lips. Who's your partner in this? Who at UHC is setting up his own colleagues?" She wanted to hear it from Wells.

Forrest gulped. He held out for thirty seconds, then caved. "Ted Simpson," he said.

Sonofabitch, Lenore thought. "I was right," she said briskly. "Not a word to Simpson, or the whole affair gets turned over to the DA," she added before closing the door.

She couldn't wait to drop the ax on Simpson's bald head, but she'd let him sweat it out for a while first.

"Sit down, Dr. Brenner," Simpson ordered. He was sitting at his desk writing and didn't look up until he finished the note he was working on. "So, Casey," he said nonchalantly, "I was wondering if you would reconsider our spending some time together outside the hospital."

Casey sat erect in the leather chair at the side of Simpson's desk. Her heart was pounding and her hands sweaty. "Dr. Simpson, I'm very flattered, but I don't go out with married men. I wish that you would respect that."

Simpson pushed back his chair as he took a deep drag on his cigarette. He exhaled quickly and put it out in an ashtray. "Casey, as I've explained to you, my wife and I have an—"

"I know, an understanding; you've told me. Well, I want you to understand this: leave me alone." Her voice was shaking.

"Casey, I'm not sure you understand the conditions under which I accepted you into this program. You have been, since you weren't one of our own handpicked residents, under a form of probation ever since you arrived here. That being the case, if the attending staff feels that you aren't performing up to par, you can be terminated." At a conscious level, he didn't even realize how pathetic he had become. But the angelic beauty who sat across from him had become unattainable, and that was unacceptable. She was different from the rest; he might even consider leaving his wife for her, despite the steep price of a divorce.

"My performance has been more than adequate. You yourself have let me do quite a bit in the operating room,"

Casey said more firmly. Her nervousness had abated, replaced by disgust.

"I have let you do quite a bit—more than a fourth-year resident should expect—and I believe I deserve some consideration in return." If she would give him a chance, he would make her happy. She just needed coaxing. He needed to be firm with her.

"So I guess what you're saying," Casey said softly, almost inaudibly, "is that if I don't sleep with you, I'll be thrown out of the program."

"I always get what I want, Dr. Brenner, and trust me, I have had very few complaints from my female companions." He had an apartment on Fifth Avenue, a place in the Hamptons, the Vineyard, and Naples, Florida. It could be a great life.

Casey put her hand into her purse for a second, got up, walked around to Simpson's side of the desk, and sat on its edge, facing him. She put her hands on her lap and smiled at the chief of surgery.

"Dr. Simpson, I suspect that the reason that no one complained about your sexual prowess is that you asked before you paid for the service. If you had asked afterward, I'm sure the woman would have told you what a revolting pig you are."

Simpson jumped up from his desk. "To whom do you think you are talking? You are dismissed, and trust me, from more than this meeting." He didn't want to do this, but she was being unreasonable. He deserved a chance.

She didn't move from the corner of the desk. "I am talking to a lecherous old man who is a disgrace to the medical profession. I am talking to a man whose execrable behavior should be reported to the Board of Professional Medical Conduct. I am, sadly, talking to a man who instead of being content with being a fine surgeon and a superior teacher, spends his afternoon trying to coerce a woman young enough to be his daughter into sleeping with him," she said, pointing at the picture of his two daughters on top of his desk.

"Good-bye, Casey, I believe I dismissed you. Now get

out of this office," Simpson said calmly as he walked to his door. "And make sure that you let everyone know about this conversation. I'm sure they'll believe you," he added.

Casey got up and left. Simpson had no idea why she was smiling. It didn't matter much. He always got what he wanted.

Casey walked out the door, confidently cradling a tiny tape recorder in her hand. Technically, it would be blackmail, but she didn't care. Daphne had suggested getting a lawyer if Simpson wouldn't back off. Casey considered it, but she didn't want the publicity. Besides, this way was cheaper.

Simpson was the last person, male or female, who would push her around. She was good in the operating room, and the research was going well. Maybe she could become a chairman.

If the research didn't get her killed, she thought as the reality of being under siege returned to her jumbled mind.

30

MEETING OF THE DOWNSTATE TRAUMA ASSOCIATION, MOHONK MOUNTAIN HOUSE
AUGUST 24

Casey was relieved to be finished with her presentation. It had gone well, and more than three-quarters of the audience believed that their technique could work in humans. Glen and Zach were also pleased with the reception it had received. The media, which always attended this meeting, was enthralled with the notion of *killing* patients to save them. She was lying down in her room when she heard a knock.

"Hi. Would you like to play some tennis?" Debby called. "Zach and Glen are out on the golf course."

"Sure, let me get my racket." Casey reached into the closet and retrieved it. "Let's go."

"Before the twins, I was a decent player. Now I play about four times a year," Debby said as they walked to the court.

"I played in high school, but only once in a while since then," Casey said.

They began hitting balls. Both women were above-average athletes. Debby had a better stroke; Casey was quicker on her feet. They hit for about ten minutes and played a couple of sets, which they split. Both were ready to collapse after the second set.

"How about playing the third set tomorrow?" Casey huffed between deep breaths.

"Fine by me. Let's get something to drink," Debby said.

They went into the gift shop, bought bottles of water, then went out on the veranda. The hotel grounds were beautiful. There were expansive flower gardens and large old oak trees which could be seen from the porch. A lake that appeared to be carved out of the mountain rock glistened in the afternoon sun. Debby and Casey collapsed into a couple of white Adirondack chairs.

"This is the life," Casey said dreamily as she took a sip of her water. "I haven't had a real day off in almost two months."

"I thought the new regulations had improved your work hours."

"Well, they're better, but you still work pretty hard. Besides, it's different being here, away from the city. But you don't get a break with the twins, either, do you? That must be harder than any job."

"Not all women who work outside the home realize that. They think that moms lounge around all day and watch soap operas. I'll go back to work full-time when the girls are in school."

"I want to have kids before I'm too old to enjoy them," Casey said.

Debby laughed. "How old are you, twenty-eight? You have plenty of time. What are you going to do about working when you have a baby?"

"It's tough. You can't just take a few years off from being a surgeon. I guess I'd take a few months and then try to work part-time. It isn't easy to get that kind of arrangement, though."

"It should be. Once you've finished training, there's no reason you should have to kill yourself trying to work full-time and never get to see your children," Debby responded sympathetically.

Casey frowned. That was true in theory, but no surgical group was going to hire a woman part-time, she thought.

"Maybe as more women surgeons are trained, I can find another woman to split a job with," she said hopefully.

Debby could see why Zach liked Casey. She was smart, down-to-earth, sensitive, and, as Zach had said, very attractive. Best of all, she was a grown-up.

"Casey, I want to tell you something that's really none of my business. Just tell me to shut up if you want, all right?"

"What is it?" she asked curiously.

"Well, in case it's not obvious, Zach has quite a crush on you. Now, I've known him for seventeen years, and I can tell you that it isn't one of his usual adolescent infatuations. He talks about you all the time. And don't take this the wrong way, but more with respect to your mind and personality than your anatomy—which, to be honest, is unusual for him."

Casey's face began to flush. She was pretty sure that Zach was interested in her. After all, they had spent a lot of time together. But to hear someone else say it felt good.

"We've spent a lot of time working together, and I'm very fond of him. The problem is that I just don't think this is a good time. He's my attending, and I'm not sure our getting involved right now is in anyone's best interest." All true, she thought, but becoming increasingly irrelevant.

"He said the same thing. Personally, I think you're both crazy. I can tell you that, except for being a little immature at times, you cannot find a better guy."

"I'm very attracted to him," Casey admitted. "Maybe in a little while the time will be right. He's lucky to have friends like you and Glen who care so much about him."

"I think he would be lucky to have you as a friend." Debby smiled and got out of the chair. "Oy! I'm stiff as a board. Let's get ready for dinner."

As Debby and Casey were heading back to their rooms, Glen and Zach, having finished their golf game, came walking up. "How did you do?" Debby asked.

"We did OK, considering we haven't played in more

than a year," Glen responded. "Zach was his usual calm self—he only smashed two golf clubs."

"It's a very frustrating game. What can I tell you?" Zach was a little embarrassed.

As they walked back to their rooms, Debby whispered to Casey. "Like I said, he's not perfect." They both started laughing.

During dinner, which was mercifully free of medical discussions, Debby let Casey in on some Glen and Zach history.

"I thought they were gay. The first time I saw them, I was walking by their dorm room, and they were in bed together."

"That's not true," Zach protested. "I was on his bed watching Johnny Carson. We watched it every night; he owned the TV. What was I supposed to do, lie on the floor?"

"The two of them were maniacs. They would study together for two straight weeks during final exams. I mean, they didn't sleep. They didn't shower. They didn't do anything but study. Thank God they calmed down a little in medical school."

"After you and Glen got married, didn't they spend less time together?" asked Casey, amused and impressed by this special friendship.

"A little. But Zach still occasionally came over and watched Carson in bed with us. The only time we didn't see as much of him was when he was dating Susan."

"We don't really need to go into the details here," Zach protested.

"Oh, I'd love to hear that story," Casey said.

Debby related the incident, while Zach rapped his fingers on the table and blushed.

"The CT scanner. You poor thing." Casey took Zach's hand in hers and squeezed it.

Zach looked at her and smiled. He got palpitations the moment her hand touched his. She was wearing a flowered, loose-fitting dress over the body he hadn't stopped fantasizing about. Her normally fair complexion was a shade darker after a few hours in the sun. She was the most beautiful woman he had ever seen. He couldn't take it any longer. "Would you like to take a walk?" he asked.

"Sure." They got up and left the dining room, barely saying good night to Glen and Debby.

"I think the surgery department paid for one room too many," Glen said.

Debby agreed. "I don't think he'll be over to watch TV tonight."

As they walked around the gardens, Zach put his arm around Casey's waist. The mountain air was cool, and she leaned closer to him. "This place makes you not want to go back to the city," she said, looking up at stars that could never be seen in Manhattan.

"That's for sure." Zach stopped walking and faced her. He put his hands on her shoulders and looked at her face in the moonlight. "I've waited so long for this," he said, and kissed her.

If there were an emotion that encompassed the ideal proportion of love, respect, and uncontrollable lust, this was it. He kissed her again and felt the warmth of her body against him. After a few minutes, their embrace became almost frenetic.

"Zach, they're going to arrest us," Casey whispered, biting his ear. "You know, I've read a lot of things about you in the women's rest room. Let's see if you can live up to your reputation."

"At least there's no pressure," he said as he took her hand and headed back to the hotel.

"You told me you do your best work under pressure," she replied as they stepped up their beeline to the bedroom.

Casey turned on a small lamp on the dresser. As she approached Zach, she unbuttoned her dress and let it slide to the floor. He took off his shirt and walked toward her. As he touched her soft skin and caressed her body, which was even more beautiful than he had imagined, she kissed him and unhooked his belt. "I haven't made love to anyone in a long time," she said.

Zach loved women. He loved sex. But there was only a faint memory, a distant frame of reference, for this kind of ecstasy and contentment. Emotionally, he had been treading water for years. The times he had slept with a woman since his breakup with Susan had been physically pleasurable experiences but emotionally neutral at best. Being with Casey felt natural to Zach; it felt right.

At four in the morning, Casey awoke, lifted her head off Zach's arm, and saw that he was also awake. She kissed him and rolled on top of him. "Anything wrong?" she asked softly.

He kissed her neck and firmly pushed against her. "You seem too good to be true," he said.

She put her cheek against his. "Zach, you'll never find me in a CT scanner with anyone else."

As she put him back inside her, he was sure that he'd found the woman he was meant to be with.

The waiter was mildly annoyed when Zach and Casey came to breakfast the next day five minutes before the dining room was supposed to close. They saw Glen and Debby finishing their meal.

"What kept you two, early game of tennis?"

Debby kicked Glen under the table. "Ouch! What did you do that for?" protested Glen.

"Because you have a big mouth."

Casey and Zach just smiled. The waiter brought juice and coffee. "Do you want something to eat, Casey?" Zach asked. "I'm starving."

"Me, too. Are we going to finish our tennis match, Debby?"

"Absolutely. When are you guys playing golf?" Debby asked.

"We're supposed to tee off in half an hour, if Zach can round up enough clubs," Glen joked.

"All right, Casey, I'll meet you at the court at eleven o'clock."

"I'll be there."

Debby and Glen got up and went back to their room.

"Zach, I hope we didn't make a mistake," Casey said softly after they left.

Her words interrupted the euphoric state he had been in since last night. He tried to smile. "We'll do better next time," he said.

Casey pushed her chair closer to his and hugged him tightly. "You know what I mean. I'm not sure it's a good idea to continue a relationship now. Technically, I'm your student. We're both so busy. This isn't great timing."

Zach clasped his hands around her neck and touched her forehead with his. "With the exception of knowing I wanted to be a doctor since I was a kid, I have never been so certain about something in my life." He paused and kissed her. "Casey?"

"Yes?"

"I love you." The words came easily, because they were true.

"Me, too." She kissed him softly on his eyelids. "We have half an hour before we meet Debby and Glen. Let's go back to my room."

On the way back to the city, Glen and Zach sat in the front seat singing their scatological version of "Anything You Can Do, I Can Do Better."

"You guys are gross," Debby moaned.

Casey just laughed. "Are they always this disgusting?"

"Usually worse. I think they're toning it down for you."

"Glen, I saw your performance on CNN last week. Virtuoso." Casey clapped her hands.

"Yeah, it went well."

"How did your opponent take it?" Casey asked.

Glen shrugged his shoulders. "He was a gentleman. We may debate again sometime."

31

Nate Cohen didn't buy it for a minute.

Today, he was going to find out more about Eat Right and Body Beautiful. Vanderzell was in court, and he grabbed the addresses of the places off his desk. He would find out more about these joints in an afternoon than Billy would in a month.

He walked out of the lobby and crossed Park Avenue. He headed east on Forty-fifth Street, dropping a dollar into a cardboard box that contained a young woman who looked pregnant. Since he had no more idea what to do about the homeless than anyone else, he frequently gave out money. It didn't do a thing for the problem, but it made him feel better.

He walked up Lexington and then took the subway to Eighty-sixth Street. He hurried up the stairs and crossed the street. He was hungry, bought a falafel at a little stand on Lexington, and ate as he walked toward Third Avenue. The store, just around the corner from Eighty-sixth, had a large sign taped to the inside of the window. It was painted, not printed. The inside of the store looked like any other health-food store. It did not appear to be a place able to generate a half million dollars in a year.

He entered and noticed only a few customers. There was a young man, probably in his early twenties, behind the juice bar and a teenage girl at the cash register. He picked out a candy bar, or the health-food equivalent, and went to the register to pay.

"Two dollars," she said, looking up from her *People* magazine.

"For a candy bar?"

"It's not a candy bar. It's a Power Bar. Only two grams of fat and ten grams of protein," she replied.

At two dollars a pop for a candy bar, maybe this place can make money, he thought. He gave the girl a twenty.

"Do you have anything smaller?" she asked. "I don't have change."

And then again, maybe not, he corrected himself. He dug around in his pockets and found two dollars in change. "Here. So, how's business?"

"Not great. I've been working here for a month, and it's been slow the whole time. But they pay me every week, so, like, who cares?"

"Where's the manager?"

"Back there." She pointed to the man behind the juice bar.

He looked at the emaciated spook busy concocting some tasty potion and decided that a conversation would be unrewarding.

He left and headed to the next store on the list. As he walked across Lexington, the aroma of a bakery sent out its tractor beam. *The chances of that Eat Right place being able to generate enough business to net a half million are about the same as me being able to pass up this bakery,* Nate thought. He would have to check out the other places—after a treat. He looked through the glass enclosures at the shelves of desserts, and the saliva welled up in his mouth.

"Are those filled with chocolate?" Nate asked, pointing to the oversized croissants on the top shelf.

"Chocolate mixed with raspberry," replied the woman behind the counter.

"Unbelievable," said Nate, who could hardly control himself. "I"ll take half a dozen."

"They're pretty rich," she admonished.

"I hope so."

"That will be fifteen dollars, with tax. Would you like a box?"

"No, thanks, just stick them in a bag so I can get at them."

The woman complied and wrapped each of the pastries in a separate piece of tissue and carefully placed them in a bag. He handed her the money and took the bag. "Enjoy."

"Don't worry about that," Nate said as he reached into the bag and extracted one of the croissants. Before he was out the door, half of it was gone.

By the time he reached Body Beautiful, he thought he was going to puke. The walk to Seventy-fifth and First lasted forty minutes, and only two of the croissants were left. He entered the store, which sold cosmetics and bath products. Like Eat Right, it was conspicuously empty. He browsed through the aisles of products whose labels all boasted that they had not been tested on animals.

He picked out a bar of soap and walked to the cashier. "Business not too swift, huh?" Nate asked as he pulled out a twenty.

"Not today," answered the attractive teenager behind the counter. "Do you have anything smaller?"

"Yeah, sure." Another Walmart, he thought as he dug out a five-dollar bill. "Can you handle this, sweetheart?"

"Thanks."

"Who owns this place?"

"Beats me," she replied. "Do you know you have some chocolate on your face?"

Nate swiped his sleeve across his mouth. "Did I get it?"

"I could have given you a napkin. That's a little gross."

"You should see me after a full meal," Nate said as he exited the store. *Smart-ass kid,* he thought. He considered finishing the other croissants but was still feeling a little queasy. He walked back down First Avenue, toward his apartment. The third store was on the west side. After what he had learned this afternoon, he surmised what he would find.

Nate laughed to himself. CARE. Supposedly one of the good animal rights groups. *There's an oxymoron,* he thought. Billy Vanderzell had said his buddy, Power, wouldn't hurt a fly. Nate figured he was a hypocrite, like most guys with a cause, and probably needed money for drugs, gambling, or broads. The normal reasons.

"Lew Mason from the FBI, Mr. Power."

Power opened the door. "Our receptionist has been out sick this week," he said. "Things are a bit chaotic. Come on in."

"I appreciate you seeing me on such short notice."

"Why wouldn't I? With what's been going on lately, if there's anything I can do to help, I will. We're all in shock over Greg's death. Can I get you some coffee or tea?"

Mason shook his head, sat down, and pulled out his notebook. "You recently became the president of CARE," he began.

Power nodded. "Very close election, but yes, I won."

"How did Mr. Sandstone feel about that? He was the founder of this organization."

"That's true. Greg and I agreed on many things and disagreed on a few. Have you ever had someone with whom you competed but still remained the best of friends? That was Greg and I. He understood."

"If you agreed on so many things, then why did you challenge his leadership of CARE?"

"I felt we needed a change. Greg had hung on for twelve years, but he wasn't fresh anymore. We needed new ideas, new input. A lot of our members had said so for a while."

"And how did he take all of this?"

"If you are trying to imply that I had something to do with Greg's death, I am insulted, Mr. Mason," Power gasped.

Mason held up his hand. "I never said that, Mr. Power.

As far as the police are concerned, Greg Sandstone was an innocent victim in the wrong place at the wrong time. He didn't use drugs, did he?"

Power sighed. "Not to my knowledge. This is a brutally violent world, Mr. Mason. Look at this city alone—more than a thousand murders a year. But is it surprising? The way we treat animals mirrors the way we treat one another. Research laboratories, farms, many industries—they all brutalize living creatures. We have all become inured to the violence."

"So you would unconditionally condemn ABP," Mason said.

"I believe that all violence is wrong. But I also believe that violence comes in many different forms, and humans tend to recognize only that against other humans."

Mason looked around the messy office. "I still think that whoever is behind the terrorist attacks has lots of money. The carnage at Retrogene convinced me of it, and that's why I am trying to subpoena all the major animal rights groups' financial records."

"With little success," Power added.

Mason gave a slight nod. "So far, that's true."

"Mr. Mason, even though I am under no legal obligation to give you anything, you can have our records. I am sick of the innuendo that this one small group of fanatics has cast on the hundreds of innocent animal rights groups." He and Lonergan had created a dozen separate offshore shell corporations in three countries that were financed by cash laundered through Eat Right and Body Beautiful. There was no linear connection to CARE. Mason wouldn't find a thing.

"I appreciate your candor," Mason said wryly.

"Do me a favor, Mr. Mason. Find these people. They've been bad for business."

Vanderzell sat at his word processor, redoing a brief, when Nate rolled into his office. He looked up as Nate buried himself in the couch. "Hi. What's up?"

"Billy, I think you have a problem—a significant problem."

"Go on; I'm all ears."

"I took a gander at a couple of your pal Power's Fortune Five Hundred companies a few days ago."

"Christ, Nate, I told you to stay out if it."

"Well, I'm a bad listener. Let me tell you something. If he's pulling big money out of those joints, then in addition to a misunderstanding about the hierarchy of the food chain, he's a crook."

"What do you mean?"

"I have seen kids with lemonade stands that look more profitable than those outfits."

"So they aren't making any money, so what?" Vanderzell replied defensively.

"OK, Billy, here's the important question, which I'm sure you must have asked yourself. What did Power need the half million for?" Nate popped a few Junior Mints into his mouth, waiting for an answer.

Vanderzell couldn't rationalize it anymore. He had to admit that Power could be responsible for the terrorism. "But Nate, he never got the money from CARE, and as you point out, it couldn't have come from the stores."

Nate snickered. "Let me just review what has transpired in the past month. Your friend essentially takes over a very well-funded animal rights group. He tries to get a half million dollars out and is stuffed by the previous president. Then, all of a sudden, he decides to become a businessman—and, from what I've seen, a bad one. And coincidentally enough, the previous leader ends up as a piece of swiss cheese. An accident, of course."

"We don't know anything for sure, Nate." Vanderzell fumbled with a pencil, and it dropped to the floor.

"Jesus, Billy, wake up. Something is fishy. I suspect your buddy is running a Laundromat."

Vanderzell buried his head in his hands and quickly looked back at Nate. *I need to do something.*

* * *

"They got my bad side," Zach complained.

Ron laughed. "They're all bad, Zach."

"That's a compliment coming from a *meskite* like you."

"I know what that means," Ron returned.

"I forgot you're the only two-hundred-twenty-five-pound black man in the whole world who knows Yiddish."

"It's some article," Glen said after reading the story in *Newsweek*. The national magazine had picked up on the story after its science editor had heard about the research presented at the meeting last weekend. The same reporter had caught Glen's debate on CNN and thought it had the making of a great piece.

"We needed some good press after all this malpractice crap," Zach said. "Thank God those lawsuits got dropped." Zach had received a call from Nate Cohen that morning. Both cases against him had been dropped, and he reminded himself he had to go to Nate's office to pick up some anatomy books he had lent him.

Glen, Zach, and Casey didn't make the cover but were featured in the lead article in the science section. According to *Newsweek*, Glen gave a "virtuoso performance" on CNN, and their research "could revolutionize the science of resuscitation."

"We're keeping up the tradition at UHC. If our idea works and we actually save someone from bleeding to death using hypothermic arrest, we'll stay among the top medical schools in research in the country," Zach said.

"If you all don't get your miserable heads blown off," Ron added.

"Ron, no one is getting into our labs or offices without an ID card. The doors to the wing are six inches of steel, and the only way to open them is with the goddamn cards, which are specially encrypted to prevent some budhead from forging one," Zach said dismissively.

"Zach's right, Ron. Besides, the FBI will nail these guys soon."

"Now, if you'll excuse us, an interview with Channel Two awaits."

Cecile sat in front of the television and watched the bastards bragging about their work. UHC's evil legacy continued, always at the leading edge of atrocity. Once she had been helpless and unable to combat the unspeakable acts, some of which she had witnessed herself. No more. The research chimera had multiple heads, but none figured more prominently than UHC's.

32

"We need to discuss, as a department, what we are going to do about these threats by the . . ." Simpson hesitated for a moment and glanced at a notepad he held. "Excuse me, the ABP."

"What do you mean, what are we going to do?" Zach said. "Do they really think that everyone in the whole country is going to close their labs?"

"Zach, calm down, and let's try to have an intelligent discussion about this. We're all as mad as you are."

Glen spoke up. "Obviously, one group of terrorists is not going to continue to shut down thousands of labs, but how will the people who choose to do research be protected?" Debby asked him that question every night and had begged both him and Zach to stop working in the lab for now.

Simpson put his hands into his pockets and grimly shook his head. "There aren't enough law enforcement agents in the country to protect everyone. The hospital and the department of surgery have hired around-the-clock armed security guards. As you all know, without your encrypted ID badge, you can't enter our research wing. But the truth is that if these people really target a particular lab or researcher, a couple of guards may not stop them. There was a meeting last night among the heads of all the academic departments in the New York area. The police, FBI, and some people from agencies I've never even heard of briefed us on this ABP group. It was a short meeting; they still don't know anything about them."

"Is it the group that tried to blow up the president of U.S. Surgical?" Ron asked.

"Afraid not. That was attributed to the Animal Liberation Front. Actually, the FBI thought that was a rather inept attempt. This ABP group, according to the FBI, seems to be better organized. The bottom line, though, is that most labs are staying open. However, until this blows over, any of you who wants to stop your research or put it on hold is welcome to do so."

"What if it doesn't blow over?" Glen asked.

"The police and FBI think that this is a very small group, and while they may have the capacity to kill efficiently, their scope is limited. The ABP theory seems to be that if they can scare enough people, they can shut down everything. The problem will be tracking down such a small group that no one knows anything about. They have left few clues."

"Screw those assholes. I'm going to my lab," Zach said as he got up.

"Zach," said Simpson, who would have probably said the same thing twenty years ago, "and this goes for everyone: you need to be careful. Any suspicious characters, new faces, anything out of the ordinary needs to be reported."

"Yeah, right. I have a feeling these guys aren't going to wear black lab coats," Ron said.

"Just watch it," implored the chief of surgery.

Erica Talarico sat silently at the back of the room. What could she say? She was rooting for the other team.

Glen, Zach, and Ron walked out of the room together.

"Heavy shit," Ron said as they walked down the corridor. "Can you believe these crazy motherfuckers? We have millions of people dying each year from diseases we can't do anything for, and these guys are worried about a bunch of rats."

"I agree, but they have a logical argument if you accept their basic premise that all animals have the *right* to life," Glen responded.

Zach broke stride, stopped, and looked at Glen. "Man, I love you like a brother, but sometimes you are so full of shit," he said, exasperated. "These assholes threaten to whack anyone doing research, and you try to play fucking Plato?"

"Come on, I don't agree with them. You know that. But you have to understand their viewpoint to argue with them effectively."

"Glen's right," interjected Ron. "If you accept the notion that all life is equal, then we shouldn't be using animals for anything."

Zach eyed his partners. "My dear intellectual associates, let me present you with the world according to Zach. Their arguments are sophistry. Animals are not equal to humans. Period. *A priori. Prima facie.* No proof necessary. And seeing as these cocksuckers have already murdered at least forty people, it seems that they put animal life *above* human life. When they're caught, I would take them to the Bronx Zoo, cover their peckers with meat tenderizer, and throw them in with the polar bears. Then they'd discover that the polar bear does not share their egalitarian view of the sanctity of life."

"Zach, you are the John Stuart Mill of scatology," Glen replied.

Zach chuckled. "Thanks, pal. Let's discuss this over lunch. Where do you want to go?"

"I'm not in the mood for the cafeteria slop. Let's go to the deli," Ron said.

"I'll meet you guys there. I left my wallet in my office," Glen said.

"I've got money, come on," offered Zach. "I'm starving."

"No, I need some slides for a lecture this afternoon. I'll be there in a few minutes."

Casey had arrived at the hospital at four A.M., rounded on forty patients, and then she and Stu completed the last dog experiment using shock times of one hour and circulatory-arrest times of forty-five minutes. So far, the animals had looked fine after the cognitive screens, although necropsy of the brain revealed minor swelling. But the real test would be at the more clinically practical time of one hour of circulatory arrest.

She had a case at noon but needed some more coffee. As she was about to pass through the steel door, she saw a plain woman with short hair and glasses who already had used her encrypted ID badge to open the metal barrier. Casey thought she looked familiar but couldn't exactly place the face. She carried a large briefcase. One of the administrators in the surgery department, she thought. They exchanged smiles and passed in opposite directions.

Glen went to his office as Zach and Ron went on to get a table at the restaurant. He reached into his pocket for his keys. As usual, they weren't there. He checked all his pockets and then remembered he had left the keys in the operating room. As he walked back down the hall, he saw a security guard coming toward him. "Hey, Sal," he asked the middle-aged custodian, "could you let me into my office?"

"Sure, Doc." He unclipped a large key ring with at least twenty keys on it from his belt. "Let me see, I think it's this one." Sal tried the key in the lock, but it wouldn't turn. "Hmm, let me try this one," he said as he inserted the key into the lock and turned it. "Got it," he said as the key twisted.

The instant he pushed the door open, a deafening explosion blew the door off its hinges and into pieces. The lower half of the door flew up and struck Sal in the front of his neck. The force crushed his trachea and snapped his vertebral column and spinal cord. The dead man was catapulted back into Glen along with the other half of the door, which struck him in the leg. Glen's head smashed into the opposite wall, and he crumpled to the floor. His left femur was split in half, and one of the divided ends had slashed his femoral artery. Glen lay in a stupor on the floor, a column of arterial blood spurting from the open fracture.

The first person to arrive at the scene was Glen's secretary, who was returning from lunch. She resisted the urge to scream and quickly grabbed her phone. "Code red, third floor, room three forty-two," she said as calmly as possible to the operator, who automatically beeped the members of the trauma team.

Within a minute, at least fifty people were gathered around Glen. Joe Farrell, the surgical chief resident, saw the open femur fracture gushing blood and quickly compressed the artery with some gauze, temporarily stopping the bleeding. Another resident put an IV in Glen's arm and started to administer Ringers lactate solution.

Glen groaned and called out Debby's name as other IV lines were placed. The head nurse from the emergency department placed a blood-pressure cuff on his arm and got a pressure of only seventy. Given the red color of the floors, walls, and ceilings, she wasn't surprised.

Blood was soaking through the gauze. Farrell replaced it, positioning the intern's hand over the wound. "Don't move your hand," he commanded. He quickly examined Glen and put an oxygen mask over his face. There was a gaping scalp laceration which wasn't bleeding much. He listened to his lungs and heard good breathing sounds. His abdomen didn't seem tender.

"Jesus, this blood just keeps soaking through!" yelled the intern.

"Pressure is only fifty," said the nurse.

"Let's get him to the OR—now. Make sure the blood bank has eight units of blood for us." Farrell and the others lifted Glen onto a gurney, carefully holding his neck until they could be sure it wasn't broken. "Somebody page the attending and tell him to meet us in the OR."

"Let's order, I'm starved," Ron said.

"Where the hell is Glen?" Zach moaned. "I have a case in twenty minutes." Just then, his beeper went off. He pushed the recall button and saw 2222. "Oh, shit, I'm out of here—code red. They're starting early today." The 2222 meant "drop everything and come to the operating room; someone is bleeding to death."

"Have fun," Ron said. "Do you want me to bring you anything?"

"Corned beef and a black cherry soda. And tell that asshole Glen he made me miss my lunch," Zach said as he ran out.

Zach ran up the three flights of stairs to the operating room and quickly changed into his scrubs. As he trotted into the foyer of the operating suite, he saw about twenty-five people gathered there. "Who got shot, the fucking mayor?" Zach asked, whizzing by the crowd.

As he entered OR 7, all he saw was a mound of drapes covering the patient. The anesthesiologists were squeezing in blood. The monitor showed a blood pressure of fifty. "All right, what's the story?" Zach said as he put some antiseptic foam on his hands.

"Zach, it's Glen!" Farrell yelled. "A bomb went off in his office."

"Oh, God," Zach said, almost in a whisper.

"Are you OK? Can you do this? We have to move!" said Farrell.

"I'm fine. Let's get going," Zach said grimly. He was damned if he'd let anyone else operate on his best friend. The nurse quickly gowned and gloved him, and he sprang to the table. "What's he got?"

"His femoral artery and vein were cut in two, and his femur and acetabulum are mush."

Zach looked down. Farrell had put vascular clamps on

the divided ends of the blood vessels. Except for the oozing bone, there wasn't much bleeding. "How much blood has he had?"

"Six units," Hal answered.

"Then why the fuck is his pressure still fifty?" Zach asked, looking at the arterial line tracing. "Joe, how were his chest and belly?"

"We didn't have time to do a tap or chest X-ray. His lungs sounded good."

"He's got to be bleeding from somewhere else. Farrell, do you think you can manage to sew these vessels back together without screwing it up?"

"No problem."

"On second thought, narrow the artery a little bit; it will slow him down next time we play tennis." *Please let there be a next time,* he prayed.

The people working on Glen laughed a little at Zach's bad joke, which was a good thing. Everyone needed to treat Glen as if he were another patient off the street. The VIP treatment would kill you every time.

"All right, I'm going up top." Zach ripped open the drapes that covered Glen's abdomen and chest. In less than a minute, he had put a chest tube in each side of Glen's chest. No blood came out. Zach knew the bleeding had to be coming from his belly. He zipped open his friend's abdomen, and the blood flowed out in a torrent.

"Fuck, look at this. Get me the suckers." While the nurse was sucking out the blood, Zach stuck his hand into Glen's belly and felt around. "Liver is OK, but his spleen is a piece of dog meat." He grabbed what was left of Glen's spleen and delivered it into the wound. "Give me a big Kelly clamp."

Shirley snapped the clamp into his hand. He put it across the splenic artery and vein, cut across them, and threw the spleen onto the Mayo stand. "Bleeding stopped," Zach said. "Everyone relax." He tied off the vessels and made his way back to the leg.

"The pressure is much better." Hal sighed with relief.

"OK, Farrell, now see if we can sew these vessels a little quicker," Zach said as he grabbed a forceps to help.

Other than requests for instruments, the room was in stunned silence, finally coming to grips with what had happened. Their colleague had nearly been blown up in his own office.

"Was his head OK?" Zach asked as he finished the vein repair.

"I think so," Farrell replied. "He was mostly out of it, but he squeezed my fingers before we started. We'll scan him as soon as we're done. The orthopods said it will take another couple of hours to fix his fractures."

"All right, thanks, everybody," Zach said to the OR staff. "You were great. This is the greatest fucking place in the world to be blown up." He ripped off his gown. The easy job was over. Now he had to tell Debby what had happened.

"Are you sure he's OK?" Debby asked for the tenth time. The screaming and crying had finally stopped.

"Debby, he'll be all right. His hip and leg are really smashed, but the pods say they'll heal. He can do without his spleen, and his head is fine. He already asked about you."

"I'll be there in an hour. The kids are with my parents. Damn you, Zach. You two wouldn't listen. Those people said they were going to do this, and they did. I want him out. And you, too. No more macho crap. Do you hear me? Fix hernias, take out gallbladders, but quit the research."

"Debby, you're right. Don't think about it now. Can I pick you up?"

"I'll take a cab. Stay with Glen until I get there. They may try to finish the job." She started crying again.

"Don't worry about that. There are cops all over the place."

"Yeah, they did a great job of protecting him."

There was no reply.

"And Zach?" she added.

"Debby . . ."

"The violence isn't so entertaining when it's someone you love, is it?"

"That was stupid, Cecile. Stupid and unnecessary," Power said.

She sat stone-faced and said nothing. It was worth it, she thought. UHC had always been at the frontier of animal abuse and Glen and Zach's preening interview had infuriated her. It was justice. Eventually, she would get them all.

"What were you thinking? We can't waste our time with personal vendettas. The stakes are too high now to go after one person. The next attack will kill hundreds. We can't blow it now. If you had been caught, the whole plan could have been jeopardized." Power stayed calm but realized he had a problem. The group was small, and needed to be. The coming attacks would be devastating. The research establishment would reel, collapse, and die. But they needed to act as one. No freelance emotional displays outside the structure of the plans he and Lonergan had created.

"I would have never given us up," Cecile replied sullenly.

Power softened. At this point, it was too late to recruit anyone new, and he would need her in the future. "Please, Cecile, just stick with our plan."

"And if it doesn't work? If it doesn't end?"

"More than half the labs have closed now. We're winning," Power said with less enthusiasm. He knew the FBI was watching him, and he knew he was fortunate to have slipped by them today.

"Are we? The labs that have remained open will become more impenetrable. Have we just selected out the most intransigent vivisectors?"

Power nodded. Cecile grasped what he had understood long ago. Like a virus that mutates and becomes stronger, he thought. "There is a final contingency," he said absently.

* * *

280

After the others left, Power decided to make certain that his final contingency was still available. There was one member of the ABP who didn't live in the New York area, and he truly hoped he wouldn't need her. Victoria Dunn had a Ph.D. in virology and was Power's most lethal ally. When she had told Power she would do anything for the cause, he understood what she meant. But there had to be a way short of biological Armageddon.

"You will be able to get it for us, Victoria?" he asked.

She was silent.

"Are you having any doubts?" Power asked.

"No, John. If we need it, I can get it. With my clearance, I can get in without arousing any suspicion, and if I substitute the vial, they won't find out until it's too late. But if I steal it, I'll need a place to escape."

"Don't worry, Victoria. I'll take care of you."

Power hung up the telephone and reviewed Lonergan's plans for the attack on the Philadelphia Project. The six medical schools in Philadelphia had pooled millions of dollars in research money from public and private sources to form a consortium whose exclusive purpose was to find a vaccine and a cure for AIDS. Located off the Schuylkill Expressway, just west of Center City, the Philadelphia Project had been making significant progress, especially on the development of a vaccine using primate models.

Bombs were Lonergan's specialty, and in a few days, hundreds would die.

"Sorry about your friend, Zach," Nate Cohen said softly. He'd offered to have his secretary bring Zach the papers to sign and return his anatomy books, but Zach had insisted on coming himself.

"Thanks, Nate. He'll be OK," Zach replied. "So I'm all clear now. Nothing on my record," he said as he signed the official deposition transcription and the document that would officially expunge any reference to the dismissed litigation.

Nate nodded. He was as shocked as Zach that the lawsuits had been dropped.

Zach looked over at Nate. "I had to get out of the hospital for a while. Glen's wife, Debby, got to the hospital, and she's pretty pissed off at me."

"It's not your fault, Zach. These people are sick."

Zach glanced out of Nate's office, and his gaze drifted across the hall to Vanderzell's office. He immediately recognized the man speaking to Vanderzell and clenched the arms of his chair. "That's the fuckhead Glen debated on CNN. Don't tell me your firm represents that piece of shit." Zach started to get up, and Nate grabbed him.

"Don't bother, Zach. We already gave the FBI some interesting information on him."

"Do you think he could be behind all this?" Zach yelled.

Nate hesitated. "There's some fishy stuff . . ."

Zach began to get up again. "How about if I just beat his fucking head in until he talks?"

Nate groped to restrain Zach. "Let the FBI do it, Zach."

So far, the FBI had done zero. Zach knew a pushy reporter who would love to get a shot at figuring things out.

33

Except for Erica Talarico, every member of the department of surgery was present for the meeting. Zach, who never made more than one out of ten, was there first. Both the NYPD and the FBI were represented. Whiteside, the cop, was upper-echelon brass and predisposed to sound bites and platitudes. Lew Mason was all business and didn't try to underestimate the gravity of the situation.

"We have twenty-five detectives investigating this tragedy as we speak," Whiteside said. "I have no doubt we'll find the guilty parties, and soon." He had a red nose and bloated belly from too much beer, and although he usually managed to be sober at work, it was a struggle.

"The FBI is dissecting the bomb debris as we speak," Mason said grimly.

"These criminals will make a mistake somewhere along the line, and when they do, we'll be there," said Whiteside.

"I'm not really interested in any of my faculty being the next mistake," Attenucci responded.

"Security will have to be tightened," Whiteside added.

"There is only one entrance to the research and office wing from the outside, and we have an armed guard. The corridor that connects to the main hospital has another armed guard, and you can't get through without an ID card," said Simpson.

"Who has ID cards?" Mason asked.

"Anyone who works in the hospital. But to get to the offices and labs in our wing, there is a special code on the ID. It can't be forged, and only members of the surgery department have them."

Mason shook his head at Simpson. "The point is, Dr. Simpson, in such a big hospital, it's still possible for someone to get in who doesn't belong. Your colleague's attack proves that."

"We still think that this attack, as horrible as it is, is the work of a few lunatics," offered Whiteside, who couldn't stand the imperiousness of the FBI. His department didn't need their help. Who knew more about violent crime than the New York Police Department?

"Well, fuck these assholes. I'm not closing my lab, and if I get lucky and find one of these pricks, I'll shove a live rat up his ass," Zach said, pounding on the table.

Attenucci wanted to bury her head. She never understood how someone so talented could be so profane, so unpolished. "This is Dr. Green, Dr. Brinkman's closest friend. He's understandably upset."

Mason looked at Zach sympathetically but said, "I understand how you feel, Doctor, but listen to me carefully. I can guarantee that if you run into these people, they won't be fighting by the Queensbury rules. Your twenty years of education will be blown out the back of your head and splattered on the wall." The tendency for people who were successful in one field to think they could transpose that talent to law enforcement always galled him. In his several dealings with physicians, he had found them to be particularly guilty of this misjudgment.

"We appreciate that the police and the FBI are doing everything possible," said Simpson, who desperately needed a cigarette. He had run directly to this meeting after his bypass operation took longer than expected, and he was getting fidgety. "What can you do to protect us?"

"The NYPD will place full-time plainclothes officers at the main entrance and around the corridor to the research wing," Whiteside offered.

"The problem that I see, doctors, is that while I'm sure the police can protect you while you're here at the hospital, the terrorists may strike in other places," Mason said.

NIH
SEPTEMBER 4

Man has become the enemy. Beyond the labs, he poisons the world as he expands and exploits without thought or reason, destroying a universe created for all. Our resolve is unlimited. Stop the research. Prove to us that man is remediable. There isn't much more time.

ABP

Gabrielle Norton read the latest letter a dozen times. "If it's possible, Mr. Mason, I believe this group is crazier than I thought."

"Forty people are dead, Dr. Norton. What's the encore?" Mason asked.

She rose from her chair and sat on her desk. "Where the radical animal rights people and fanatic ecologists merge, there are those who believe that man is the ultimate evil force, no more important than any other species of plant or animal on the earth."

"The implication of that being what?"

"I can't answer that with certainty, but I suspect that our terrorists may be natural fundamentalists."

Mason imagined what his boss would be saying now. Garrow hated fundamentalist anything. "And what does that mean?"

"Basically, they believe that all life-forms are equally sacred. That man has multiplied out of control, disrupted the web of life—as they would put it—and ruined the world."

"Come on, Doctor. You are telling me that there are

human beings who really believe that all life is essentially equal?"

"I'm not sure *equal* is the correct word. All life, and in particular all animal life, is sacred and matters. Animals count. Darwin himself said that animals differ in degree, not in kind."

"Next time I watch *Inherit the Wind,* I'm rooting for William Jennings Bryant. So where are we going with all this?"

Norton shook her head. "I'm not sure. Maybe if we stop the animal research, it will all go away. But if you follow the theory to its logical conclusion, man will need to be subordinated to some undefined will of nature. And with five billion people, that will be a hard sell. To the hard-core fundamentalist, biomedical research on animals is wrong both because it uses animals against their will and because it allows man to survive and multiply at the expense of other species."

"But it seems to me that man's main survival advantage is his intellect. So why is it wrong to use it to cure diseases? Didn't Darwin preach survival of the fittest?"

"Obviously, I agree with you, Mr. Mason. But not everyone would."

"So what are you saying? They are going to blow up the world and start over?" Mason chuckled.

Gabrielle said nothing.

"Maybe you ought to keep those thoughts to yourself when you talk to the president today." Mason rubbed his eyes. "On a somewhat less depressing note, what do you know about John Power at CARE? We have some information on him, some suspicious money dealings. A lawyer who has worked with CARE and knows Power quite well tipped us. Power had given me CARE's records, but it's what he isn't showing us that I want to know. And his compatriot, Greg Sandstone, who was killed a few days ago, well, it seems too coincidental. He could be the one. Since Sandstone's murder, we've had two agents on Power almost constantly, but he's been very careful."

"To answer your question, I've never met Mr. Power, but I've heard him on the radio. He sounded sane enough. I've never known anyone who knew him. Researchers don't tend to hang out with animal rights people," Gabrielle said wryly. "I wish I could help you, but I don't know a thing about the man."

"Well, if Power so much as double parks, my agents will grab him," said Mason. "And good luck with the president."

Gabrielle Norton had met with President Daniels a few times but never really had a conversation with him, and certainly not in the Oval Office. She had been appointed by the previous president, although she was ideologically more compatible with this one. She was joined by the director of the FBI and the president's chief of staff.

"Thank you for coming Dr. Norton," Samuel Daniels said.

Norton looked at the president. He was more handsome in person and seemed completely relaxed. "Of course, sir."

"The casualties keep mounting," he said solemnly. "What should we do?"

She couldn't believe he was asking her that question. Research and its administration were her jobs, not counterterrorism. "Mr. President, I don't know," she said truthfully, "but I can tell you that if it doesn't stop soon, you will be able to use the NIH research budget for deficit reduction."

He turned up the right corner of his mouth into a truncated smile. "How many labs have closed down, Gabby?"

He even knew her nickname. She was impressed. "Of NIH-funded labs, more than half. That probably mirrors the figure in the privately funded arena. And each day, the number grows. I predict with a few more attacks, animal-based research in this country will become a historical footnote."

"I can't say I would blame anyone for quitting," he said, looking at William Hurley, the director of the FBI. "William, anything?"

"The attacks are quite professional and not many clues. Our best bet is the money trail, but the courts are holding things up. The federal judge in New York County has a thing about these not-for-profit organizations."

"I appointed him, didn't I, William?"

"I guess so, sir."

"We all make mistakes," he responded, to break the tension.

Norton had planned not to mention her theory that she had discussed with Mason but changed her mind. "Mr. President," she interjected, "I think it is important to add that the most recent communiques have become increasingly bizarre."

"I find the whole matter bizarre, Dr. Norton," the president replied dryly.

"What I mean, sir, is that instead of focusing on animal research per se, the message is becoming more generically ecological. I don't know what to make of it."

"Are we going to round up these nuts, William?" the president said, ignoring her last comment.

"We just need a break."

The president sat up straight in his seat and folded his hands across his chest. "In the meantime, Dr. Norton, I have a way to restore the confidence of our scientists and to clearly send a message to these terrorists that we will not be intimidated."

The chief of staff looked over at Daniels and smiled proudly. He had worked for him since he was a first-term congressman and always admired the way he took the bull by the horns, even if that probably violated the bull's rights.

The cameras rolled in at eleven in the morning. Glen had begun physical therapy—just some passive stretching of his shattered leg—and was exhausted, but he had agreed to the interview and wanted to complete it. It had been five days since the attack. He had developed a painful new perspective on the abdominal incisions he had made in others, hundreds of times before, and would never again underestimate the dosage of pain medication his patients might need.

His room looked like a florist shop. He was getting extra special treatment from everyone in the hospital and was as comfortable as he could expect five days postoperatively, but he was lonely for Debby, Rebecca, and Rachel. At least he felt safe. There were two cops outside his room and another four prowling the floor.

As the television crews were checking their connections and John Edwards from CNN, Sally Hargraves from NBC, Timothy O'Brien from CBS, and Matt Broder of ABC entered, Glen began to appreciate the irony of the situation. The attack had given him the ability to speak out as never before. Lying in bed with a smashed leg and ruptured spleen, he should be able to evoke plenty of sympathy. He was a page one story that, for once, made doctors sympathetic, and he planned on milking it as much as possible.

"Are you sure you're up to this?" asked Zach, who had stayed with Glen almost nonstop since the attack.

"I'm fine. I just had a shot of Demerol. You look worse than I do."

"Don't worry about me. When you get tired of these assholes, let me know, and I'll throw them out."

"Be nice. This is going to play to our advantage. This is a national crisis, and we're the good guys."

Zach nodded and sat over in the corner of the room with his arms folded and an unpleasant scowl on his face.

The four reporters from the networks were joined by representatives of the major New York papers. They sat on metal chairs that formed an arched row in front of Glen's bed. Of course, Amy Mendoza elbowed her way into the first row. She turned around and winked at Zach, who responded with a morose wave. A technician placed a microphone around Glen's neck, and the producer counted down to air time.

Each journalist was allowed to ask one question and a follow-up. Sally Hargraves from NBC began.

"First of all, Dr. Brinkman, thank you for permitting us this time, and we all wish you a speedy recovery. The group Animals Before People, which has claimed responsibility for your attack and the other recent murders, state that they demand an end to all animal-based research. Doctor, are you going to stop?"

"Is my wife listening?" Everyone in the room began laughing. "I don't want to be a hero, but I also don't think a misguided group of zealots should be able to dictate the scientific policies of this country. Having said that, I plan to be very careful until this group is rounded up."

"Doctor," Tim O'Brien asked, "the ABP has made it clear that it has only begun its fight. What do you anticipate will be the response by the scientific community as a whole?"

"I would hope that most researchers would continue, but I wouldn't blame anyone for stopping. As I said, it would be a tragedy if, in the world's largest democracy, an infinitesimally small percentage of the population dictated the scientific policy of the nation."

"But, Doctor," O'Brien continued, "isn't that an exaggeration? Are we really dependent on animal research? Far more reasonable heads than the ABP have spoken out against the usefulness of animal research. In fact, the Physicians Committee for Responsible Medicine is adamantly opposed to it. And one of your own associates, Dr. Erica Talarico, is a member."

"First of all, Mr. O'Brien, someone listening to this interview would assume, incorrectly, that the PCRM is made up of physicians. There are actually very few doctors in that group. And Dr. Talarico is entitled to her opinion even if she is woefully mistaken. Most American doctors understand the need for, and support the use of, animals in the laboratory. Second, I think the phrase *dependent on animal research* is misleading. A lot of biomedical research is not dependent on the use of animals. Molecular biological techniques, cell cultures, and computer simulations are responsible for many of our most important advances. But it's naive to believe that animals are never necessary. How does one simulate a new surgical technique on a computer? For example, we now remove most gallbladders using a laparoscopic camera and four small incisions. The postoperative pain and disability are minimal compared to the old way. This procedure wasn't tried out on humans first. I practiced on pigs until I felt comfortable doing it on a patient." Glen was on a roll. He decided to give the audience a little of the Lyndon Johnson treatment.

"So, Mr. O'Brien, would you rather have your operation with a few poke holes in your belly or through an incision like this?" Glen lifted up his hospital gown and displayed Zach's handiwork. Half of the assembled reporters closed their eyes, and the other half groaned. Zach, sitting in the corner, could hardly contain himself.

"I get the point, Doctor."

"The truth is, Mr. O'Brien, we still need to use animals for research. I know many of the animal rightists claim that animal research is no longer needed, and in fact, some claim that it was never needed. The manufacture of insulin for diabetics, numerous vaccines, open-heart surgery and transplantation, to name a few advances, would have never occurred or would have been delayed for years or decades without animal research. There is no question that if we forgo animal-based research, we will also miss out on significant future medical advances."

Matt Broder from ABC began a question about duplicative medical research, but Mike Lepkowitz from the *Post* jumped up from his seat and addressed his colleagues. "I think we are getting way off the track here. Dr. Brinkman was nearly blown to bits by these terrorists, and we're asking him to justify what he does. Come on. Let me ask Mr. Mason if he has any leads in this case."

Mason stood slowly and turned to the press. "The FBI currently is following several leads, but I can't really discuss them at this point."

"So, you have nothing."

"We have dozens of agents on this case, and we're evaluating the data."

"Like I said," Lepkowitz huffed, and sat down.

"Amy Mendoza from the *New York News*. Hi, Glen." She smiled. "I think you're a hero, and sure, we need to use animals for research. What bugs me are the horror stories you always hear about the way the animals are treated."

"I think the humane treatment of animals is our sacred obligation," said Glen. "Animals feel pain, just as we do, and every experiment must be done with that in mind. At UHC, as in most labs, we only do painful experiments on anesthetized animals. We have full-time veterinarians. The animals are exercised and well fed. But let me make this clear. The fanatics in the animal rights movement don't care about the humane treatment of animals. They consider animals our equals, subject to the same right to life that we, as humans, have. They can provide logically consistent philosophical rationale for their beliefs. But when I see a child who is alive because of a liver transplant that would not have been possible without animal research, my conscience is clear."

Zach saw that Glen was beginning to tire, and he stepped over to the bed. "I think we'd better end this session for today."

"Are you his doctor?" Sally Hargraves asked.

"As well as his partner and best friend."

"So you and Dr. Brinkman work in the same lab?"

"We do. We are trying to perfect a surgical technique to fix an injury that dusts about ninety percent of the people who suffer from it."

"I'm sure the animal rights groups would point out that it kills one hundred percent of the animals that you experiment on," Matt Broder commented.

Zach smiled. He had promised he would be good. "I gather, Mr. Broder, from your question that you sympathize with the animals. Now, that is certainly your business. But I see you have on leather shoes. And since you've got three chins and your belly hangs, I'd say, eight inches over your belt—a condition medically known as morbid obesity and not usually linked to a vegetarian diet—I wonder if you are being somewhat hypocritical."

The media loved it and roared, particularly Amy, who had worked with Broder on the paper before he made the network news and knew what a pompous ass he was. Broder harrumphed and sat back down on his pork butt.

"Perhaps a closing comment, Dr. Brinkman?" Hargraves asked.

Glen was ready. "Virtually every person watching this interview wants the advances in medicine, which we have automatically come to expect, to continue unabated. If this issue were put to a public referendum to be democratically decided, an overwhelming majority would choose to continue the necessary animal research. As a society, we cannot allow a small, nihilistic minority to dictate our future.

"Computers, cell cultures, and molecular biology will provide many of the advances, but the use of living animals will be necessary for the foreseeable future. Our responsibility to treat animals humanely is inviolate, but as you hug your children, kiss your spouse, or honor your parents, let's not lose perspective on how singularly important human life is."

The camera panned Glen's broken body and closed in on his face. The room was silent.

"When I get out of this hospital, I will continue both my clinical and research duties. I have no doubt that the FBI and police will catch these terrorists."

"Dr. Green, do you have anything to say?" Hargraves added.

"Is this live television?"

One of the producers nodded. Glen cringed.

"I could never be as eloquent as Dr. Brinkman, but I would just like the evil, sick, misguided, pig pederasts who did this to know my plans for the afternoon. I'm going to put on my new leather shoes, go and eat a half pound roast beef sandwich for lunch, and return to the lab and continue our work. Then I'm going to row my scull, sitting on its calf-hide seat, and after I'm done, I will take a shower and put on deodorant that was undoubtedly tested on animals. If anyone has a problem with that, they can kiss my . . ."

The camera and microphones turned off, and the feed went back to the local stations. Most of the reporters were hysterical. The NBC cameraman fell down laughing.

Many of the reporters filed over to Glen's bed for more questions.

"Pig pederast?" Glen repeated. "Do you sit up at night thinking up these things, Zach?"

"They just come to me. Your closing soliloquy was something special."

"I wrote it last night." Glen showed Zach his wrist cast, which had his closing remarks scribbled on it.

"Well, from a public relations standpoint, it couldn't have gone better."

"Yeah, I guess so, but I can't help feeling like we're preaching to the choir. Most people don't have to be persuaded that it's all right to use animals in research, as long as it's for a reasonable project and the animals are treated OK."

"Unfortunately, the ABP isn't most people."

Cecile Morgan shut off the television. UHC and its doctors evoked her only expressible emotion: rage, now uncontrollable. Through her whole life, UHC always seemed to be the epicenter of the battle against the rights of nonhuman species. Every aspect of its history, beginning with its early transplant programs to more recent transgressions, resulted in more animal carnage, more innocent victims. Brinkman, Green, and all the others were the second-generation sadists he had trained.

Thousands of institutions had closed. But one still hadn't. She couldn't bear it. Lonergan and Palmer could get along without her in Philadelphia. To hell with Power.

34

John Power looked blankly around his office and then at the television on the credenza. He looked at his watch. There would probably be a news flash within the next hour. Palmer and Lonergan were in Philadelphia, and the bomb would detonate any minute now. Would this finish it? With fifty percent of the country's labs closed, the imminent devastation might finalize what he had begun only ten weeks ago. He knew now he was right to have hired Lonergan. It was after the attack at Retrogene that the majority of research facilities had closed. Lonergan had been able to acquire blueprints of their targets and precisely plan the attacks. After Sorrentino was lost at the medical school, he knew it would be necessary. True, Lonergan was a money launderer for drug dealers, a soldier of fortune with no real beliefs other than the pursuit of riches, but he was effective, and that was all that mattered.

Power poured some tea and looked out his window at the tens of thousands of people who blanketed the streets. Of course, they were the root of the problem. Unchecked and relentless human proliferation was the common denominator. Did he have the will to use the weapon that Victoria Dunn could obtain? Perhaps the mission in Philadelphia would make it unnecessary.

His watch beeped, and he smiled serenely. Palmer and Lonergan had attacked and would soon make their escape. A sense of tension suddenly grabbed him as he remembered that Cecile was also to have joined the mission, but he hadn't heard from her since yesterday. Where was Cecile?

It was cloudy and looked as if it might rain as Zach pulled his boat at a leisurely twenty-eight strokes a minute. He had rowed hard the past few days and just wanted a light workout. He passed under the Queensboro bridge and brought the scull around to return to the boathouse. At seven o'clock, the traffic had slowed slightly. He was as relaxed as he could be. Glen was getting better, their research was progressing, and he was sure he was in love with Casey.

The speed of sound is about seven hundred miles per hour. The muzzle velocity of an AK-47 assault rifle is about eighteen hundred feet per second or around twelve hundred miles per hour, so it wasn't surprising that Zach saw a hole rip through the hull of his boat before he heard the repeat of the shot.

He dropped his oars and instinctively, if not logically, covered his head and crouched down in the boat. A stray bullet was his instantaneous assessment of the situation. Three more bullets hitting the boat negated that theory.

He was being shot at, and judging from the holes in his boat, by a powerful weapon. Reflexively, he capsized the boat and dove underwater. At least five more bullets hit the boat and the water, one of which grazed the top of his head. He swam about twenty-five yards underwater before surfacing for air and immediately dove again. He headed toward the shore two hundred yards away. The stench of the East River didn't really bother him until he was about fifty feet from the riverbank and started vomiting. Zach climbed out and traversed the FDR. He was a mile from UHC, and in his condition, no cabs would pick him up.

When he walked into the ER, blood was streaming down from his scalp laceration onto his face. He smelled worse than the derelicts who lived in boxes outside the hospital grounds. The cops recognized him and helped him into the ER. Inside the trauma room, Ron was seeing a patient.

"Zach, what the hell happened to you?" Ron ran over to him, dropping a clipboard onto another patient's gurney.

"I was taking a swim in the East River, and I hit my head on a rock."

Ron helped him over to a gurney and lifted him onto it. He quickly examined his head. "That's no damn rock cut."

"Brilliant, Ron. You're fucking Quincy."

Ron held his nose and stepped back two steps. "I've got to be honest with you, Zach, you smell worse than a bathroom at the Port Authority. You OK, other than that cut?"

"I'll live."

"Then take a shower before I sew you up."

He slowly got off the gurney and headed toward the shower across the hall. One of the nurses grabbed his left arm to help him.

"I'm OK."

Ron finished sewing Zach's lacerations in time for the beginning of the evening festivities. A paramedic crew brought in what was left of a nineteen-year-old Dominican who had tried to siphon off some of the cocaine he was supposed to be selling. He told his boss that he had been shorted, and the wanna-be kingpin made up the shortfall with the contents of a Mac 11 clip. There were three wounds to the left chest, suggesting that this had not been intended as a warning. The patient's blood pressure was barely palpable as the trauma team went into action.

Zach bolted off his gurney to enter the fray, but Ron grabbed him. "Get your white ass out of here, you psychopath." Zach had grabbed a chest tube and was ready to start putting it in before Ron physically threw him out of the ER.

"I shall return," Zach protested after Ron sent him down the hall.

"Go home." Ron pivoted and returned to the ER.

When he saw Zach, Mason chased after him down the floor. "Doctor, I need to talk to you," Mason said as he finally caught up.

"I'm fine, just a few scratches." Zach kept walking down the hall.

"Dr. Green," said Mason sternly, "I need to talk to you now. Why don't you tell me exactly what happened?"

"Well, let's see," Zach said. "I was rowing my boat, and somebody tried to blow my fucking brains out. And what are you guys going to do about it? We're going to run out of surgeons here soon."

"Did you see anything?"

"Yeah, my life passing before my eyes. Christ, when I'm rowing my boat, the only thing I think about is my next breath."

Mason smiled. The guy had balls, if not brains. "Doctor, to be honest, you and your pal Dr. Brinkman are not helping yourselves out. Your partner is getting more air time than the mayor, and you practically begged them to come get you."

"I think that it's important for the public to understand the threat that this situation poses."

"Well, we can protect Dr. Brinkman in the hospital, but you are a more difficult problem, though I doubt that they'll try to get you again."

"That's nice. Why not?"

"Because they have bigger fish to fry."

"That was an insensitive metaphor, Mr. Mason."

Mason shook his head and smiled. "Doc, you're a character, but I'm telling you that we're not dealing with run-of-the-mill psychopaths."

Zach straightened his bandage. "There are a hundred and fifty thousand people doing animal-based research in this country. They can't kill them all."

"They won't have to. Most people aren't as stupid as you."

"I'll take that as a compliment."

THE PHILADELPHIA PROJECT,
PHILADELPHIA, PENNSYLVANIA
SEPTEMBER 5

The AIDS research facility had two buildings, only one of which, according to Lonergan, contained animals. That three-story brick structure and its inhabitants, both animal and human, were to be spared. Ed Palmer and Lonergan each drove a car, and Lonergan had left his vehicle, containing the bomb, adjacent to the other building.

They rejoined in Palmer's car and prepared to speed away from the impending five-megaton explosion. "Step on it. We've got two minutes," Lonergan commanded.

Palmer accelerated and gazed at the building that would soon be rubble. He slammed on his brakes when he saw them.

"What the fuck are you doing, Palmer? Get out of here," Lonergan hissed.

"You said there were no animals in that building. Look over there!" Palmer screamed. On the second floor were at least a half dozen cages containing chimpanzees. "You have to stop it. We can't kill the animals."

Lonergan grabbed the wheel and stepped on the gas pedal, but Palmer, who was at least as strong, braked again. Lonergan pulled out his gun and smashed Palmer across his face. With Palmer stunned, Lonergan opened the driver's door and shoved him out. His car sped off, away from the imminent explosion.

Palmer ran to the car in an attempt to drive it away and save the animals. He opened the door and hurried in but never had a chance to turn the key before the car, the building, and its one hundred inhabitants were fragmented into an unidentifiable pile of rubble.

Lonergan looked back with pride at the devastation. It had been a particularly good bomb. ABP, however, was another issue. He knew of Palestinians who had wrapped themselves with explosives and then proceeded to die for Allah. Very romantic, but as far as he was concerned, not a desirable trait in an employer. Power and those maniacs were going to get caught, and he didn't plan to be around when it happened. A tidy sum had been made with the laundering scheme, but that, too, wouldn't last forever. Time to get out.

One last detail. Power and Cecile could identify him. That condition was one hundred percent fatal.

"It's Zach." Casey buzzed open the door, and Zach strolled into the foyer. He took the elevator and two minutes later knocked on her apartment door.

She opened the door and hugged him. It took her a few seconds to notice the bandage on his head. "What happened?"

"Bad haircut."

She knew instantly. "They tried to get you, didn't they?" she said as her heart began to pound. She hugged him tighter. "They tried to kill you. First Glen, and now you."

"I'm fine. My skin is still crawling from a swim in the East River, but I'll live."

"They shot you while you were rowing? What are we going to do?" She took his hand, led him to the couch, and sat him down.

"How about some dinner?"

"Cut it out, Zach. They tried to kill you."

"The only thing they killed was my scull."

"That's not funny. We have to stop the research, at least for now."

"As far as you're concerned, that's right. But I'm going to keep going until that miserable project is done."

"If it's so safe, then I'll keep working, too. No one even knows who I am."

"Just in case, why don't you stay away?"

"Zach, you have been the quintessential feminist around me, so don't ruin it. If it's OK for you to be in the lab, it's OK for me."

He reluctantly nodded and held her hand, noticing that she was braless beneath her T-shirt.

"Where's Daphne?"

"On call tonight at the hospital."

"Really? Lucky us." He inched closer to her and kissed her cheek. His hand slid up her T-shirt.

She pulled him closer. "I suppose you're going to tell me how nearly getting murdered makes you horny."

"I finally found a woman who understands me," Zach said as he wriggled out of his clothes.

"Scary thought." Her cutoffs flew to the floor.

Feeling her warm mouth and soft body, he wondered if the bullet had killed him after all. He was in heaven.

The next morning, neither of them said much on the way back to the hospital. The news of the explosion at the Philadelphia Project was the only topic of discussion on the radio that morning. Zach cursed the traffic, using a creative new combination of expletives, and Casey stared out the window.

"Zach, what would you want to do if you knew you were going to die?" Casey asked.

He stopped for a light, put the car in neutral, and looked over at her. "Make love to you and fix a ruptured aneurysm—not necessarily in that order." The light changed, and he gunned the Honda.

"No kidding. I'm really worried about you. They might not miss the next time."

He drove with his left hand and massaged her leg with his right. "If we aren't executed by these lunatics," he asked, "will you marry me?"

She squeezed his hand. "How could a woman turn down a proposal like that?"

Zach pulled up in front of the main entrance to UHC and put the car in neutral.

"Why are you stopping here?" Casey asked.

"I have a few errands to run," Zach replied as he looked at his watch.

Casey frowned. "You have a look on your face that tells me you are about to do something stupid—or dangerous." At least four cars were blasting their horns for Zach to move his car.

Zach saw the traffic jam behind him, kissed Casey on the forehead, and reached over her to open the car door. "Not me. I'll call you tonight."

Casey reluctantly got out, and Zach pulled away.

They pulled up in front of CARE headquarters, and Zach parallel-parked the Civic. "Let me do it, Amy," Zach pleaded. After seeing Power at Nate's firm, he had called Amy, who had talked him into this foray which he was beginning to think he would regret.

"Forget it; if Power is there, he'll recognize you." Amy replied. She adjusted her Staples jacket and cradled the box of pens, printer toner cartridges, and other assorted office material.

"Maybe we should just wait for the FBI," Zach replied cautiously.

"No way. Those guys have this obsession with the Fourth Amendment. I'm not waiting for some judge to get off his fat, liberal ass and sign a warrant."

Zach nervously nodded his head, and Amy bolted out of the car. She took the elevator to the fourth floor, took two lefts, and opened a darkly stained door that framed a semitransparent plate of glass stenciled with the letters "CARE." Amy knocked on the door and thirty seconds later, after she received no reply, walked in the door. There was a receptionist's desk about ten feet from the door but no receptionist. Hearing no voices, she quickly moved down a hall, where she spotted two doors. The door on the right had John Power's name on an embossed brass rectangle. She looked around again and, seeing or hearing no one, marched into Power's office. On a couch, she saw a pile of blueprints. After putting the office supplies down on Power's desk, she began to rifle through the blueprints.

"Jesus," she said aloud as she perused the floor plans and elevations for Retrogene, the Philadelphia Project, and dozens of other medical research facilities and government buildings. She began photographing the blueprints when she heard the front door open. She wildly snapped a half dozen more pictures, opened the window, and shot down the fire escape.

President Daniels awaited his signal to begin. The message would be broadcast on all four networks as well as the cable news channels. He had cursed himself for waiting so long. Those men and women in Philadelphia should have been protected.

"My fellow Americans, we have all come to routinely expect that as each decade passes, our lives and our life expectancies will improve. This has been, in no small part, due to research conducted on animals in the laboratories of this country. In the last three months, our laboratories have become a war zone. One hundred and sixty-one researchers have lost their lives attempting to defend their fellow citizens, not from foreign enemies but from disease. But because of the ruthless and demented terrorists who aim to stop them, these selfless men and women have had to fight this war on two fronts.

"To these heroes, I respond, it is time for us to protect your flank. Therefore, I, as commander in chief, will order the armed forces of this nation to protect and defend the laboratories that are being drenched in blood. Every facility that engages in biomedical research shall be protected with the full force of the United States National Guard. Terrorism on American soil will not be tolerated."

The camera panned in and caught the president's intense glare. "And to the evil perpetrators of these high crimes, let me assure you that your capture is imminent and your punishment certain."

"Have you heard the president? He's going to use the National Guard," Cecile said in disbelief. They sat in the third row of the two-fifteen showing of the Bruce Willis film *12 Monkeys*. Two FBI agents were parked outside the theater.

Power said nothing for a moment and collected his thoughts. He was confused. His premise was so simple. If the doctors and scientists understood that doing research was a death sentence, they would stop. But now the military was involved, and the doctors and scientists were heroes. He had never really thought it would come to this. There were other conventional targets, but Palmer was dead and Lonergan had disappeared. Stage three would be necessary.

"We must keep it up. There are still hundreds of targets. They can't all be protected," Cecile whispered.

Power sighed. "We could, Cecile, but it won't be enough. Palmer is dead now. We could go on this way, until we are both caught or killed, but man will go on butchering. Butchering the animals and butchering the world. The God who created this world never intended for humans to become the dominant species. We have reached out and taken that which is not ours to have. There is no balance." His expression was morose, his blue eyes no longer piercing but cloudy and moist. "Nature is strong. It has tried to halt a human blight that has grown to over five billion. Black death in the Middle Ages, smallpox and diphtheria in the eighteen hundreds, influenza, tuberculosis, and polio in the first half of this century. Nature is strong, but not strong enough. Man always finds a way to overcome its will and repopulate, destroying more of the nonhuman species and the world along with them. AIDS offered a glimmer of light, a ray of hope, but its creeping pathway toward death will allow man to defeat it."

"What are we going to do?" Cecile asked, herself

struggling to hold back tears. "We can't give up. I won't." She clenched the armrests and shook them.

Power regained his intensity and rose from his chair. "We have another ally. I haven't mentioned her to you, because, frankly, I had hoped it would be unnecessary."

"Who is she?" Cecile asked, "and what can she do that we haven't already attempted?"

Power spoke softly, almost inaudibly. "She will help end it."

"How?" Cecile hopefully asked.

Power hesitated and then huddled with Cecile. "We ourselves may not survive," he said as he looked unflinchingly into her eyes.

Cecile nodded her head, and Power went to the phone to call Victoria Dunn in Atlanta. He would have it hand-delivered within a day.

> We regret your decision to reject our demands, and now must take the only remaining avenue open to us to prevent the carnage of nonhuman species and the further degradation of this world. We have provided ample warning, and your decision to ignore obvious, self-evident truths will now hasten the destructive forces that man himself has begun.
> "And the meek shall inherit the earth."

They couldn't be that crazy, Gabrielle thought after she received the fax. The ABP seemed to want to take down all of mankind. But how? Mason seemed to think Power was behind the ABP. Had his past left any clues?

She decided to search Medline, which referenced journal articles published in the medical literature. Maybe she had missed something the first time she looked. She searched the databases all the way back to 1981. Power would have been a freshman at the University of Michigan then. The computer came up with nothing. Power was no different from any of the other extremist animal rights activists—at least on paper. But mainstream medical journals wouldn't publish way-out animal rights theories.

It wasn't science so much as philosophy. What about the philosophy literature? She switched databases and accessed the Philosophy Index.

Once there, she again typed "John Power" into the author field. There was one reference by Power, J. A.—in the *Journal of Applied Philosophy*. The coauthor was Victoria Dunn. Gabrielle moved from her office to the library, and there she found it. She skimmed the article and skipped quickly to its conclusion:

> *In summary, the return to a biocentric world in which man does not pervert the will of nature may require radical remediation. If man cannot willingly accept his place, beside and not above other creatures, and does not cease, at least as a start, his irrational practice of vivisection, then draconian measures should be undertaken. Ironically, the solution to man's impudence may ultimately be found within the forests and jungles which he rapaciously violates.*

Gabrielle thought for a moment. When her brain made the connection, she felt sick. Victoria Dunn had applied for an NIH grant as a researcher at the CDC. Her specialty was Level 4 viruses.

35

The telephone rang, and Mason picked it up before the first ring had ended. "Thank God," he said, and exhaled into the receiver.

"They found her?" Gabrielle Norton asked hopefully.

Mason nodded. "She hadn't actually stolen anything but was on her way into a Level Four area. She wasn't scheduled to be there today and had switched shifts with an associate. When my agents told her that they had telephone records that showed conversations with John Power, she caved and admitted the plan."

"I thought the judge wouldn't give you warrants?"

Mason put a stick of gum in his mouth. "He didn't. We lied to her."

Gabrielle managed a smile, something she hadn't been able to do in a while. "So is it over?"

"My guys have been following Power. We'll pick him up." He smiled at her. "You were on target about that fundamentalist business."

Gabrielle picked up her briefcase and shook Mason's hand. "I hope the next time I see you, Mr. Mason, it's at some festive occasion."

"Where are you off to?"

"I'm flying up to New York. My daughter is participating in a science symposium at the Javits Center."

"Following in her mother's footsteps?"

"You never know," Gabrielle replied proudly.

"She'll have a tough act to follow," he said, glancing at his watch. "We may be on the same flight. I want to be there to interrogate Power."

"Mr. Mason, please," insisted the woman on the phone.

"Can I ask who's calling?"

"Amy Mendoza from the *New York News*. But please tell him I'm not calling for an interview. Tell him I've got some important—no, make that *urgent* information about the ABP attacks."

"He's actually going to be in the New York office this afternoon. He just flew out this morning. He has a full schedule, but I imagine he'll call in before noon."

"This can't wait—can I have the New York number?"

"I can switch you there, but I doubt you'll get through to him. Hold on a minute."

Amy waited while the call was transferred. Mason picked up the line brusquely. "Ms. Mendoza, this is Mason. What can I do for you?"

"This is urgent—at least, I think it is. I recently came across some blueprints belonging to John Power. Guess what of? How about Retrogene and the Philadelphia Project? And dozens more research facilities."

"And tell me, Ms. Mendoza, how would you know that?"

"You don't want to know, Mr. Mason. The Fourth Amendment doesn't apply to the fourth estate."

Mason held back but let out a chuckle. "Well, I'm glad you're on our side, Amy. But we already know it's Power, and my agents are picking him up now."

"Come on, Mason, this could be my ticket to the *New York Times*."

"There's a press conference in half an hour. Be there, and I'll make sure you get in the first question."

"How about the last as well?"

"Don't push it, Amy."

Special Agents Sisini and Foster each opened a door of the maroon Chevy they had parked out in front of CARE headquarters, spilled the remaining coffee from Styrofoam cups onto the street, and prepared to take John Power. They finally had the go-ahead. Judge Gradinger had signed the warrant ten minutes ago.

Victoria Dunn was to have called at exactly three o'clock, and when she hadn't, Power suspected what must have happened. He had noticed the Chevy outside the office during the day and outside his apartment at night for the last week. When the agents got out of their car, each carefully repositioning his shoulder holster, he was sure of what was happening. His hands were sweaty, but he calmly pondered his options. Getting away, at least temporarily, wouldn't be a problem unless the FBI knew that the buildings on each side of his were connected underground. He had only one place he could go.

Mason stood at the podium and shielded his eyes from the lights and flashes that emanated from his audience of several hundred reporters. "I have a brief statement, and then I'll be glad to answer questions."

He unfurled an eight-by-ten sheet of printer paper and began. "This afternoon, the Federal Bureau of Investigation has obtained a warrant for the arrest of John Power. He will be charged with one hundred sixty-eight counts of murder and be prosecuted under the 1996 Terrorism Act. We believe he and a small number of accomplices are responsible for the recent attacks on medical researchers." Mason rested the paper on the podium and looked out at the audience.

Amy Mendoza jumped up, and Mason pointed to her. "Mr. Mason, what gave you the break?"

Mason didn't want to get into the details of the near disaster at the CDC, although he knew that eventually it would come out. "Dr. Gabrielle Norton, director of the

NIH, should win the Presidential Medal of Honor. Her intuition, instinct, and medical detective abilities enabled us to identify a potential target and intercept one of Mr. Power's accomplices, who then confirmed our suspicions. Without her help, we would still be investigating."

"Where is Dr. Norton?" Amy continued, a little annoyed. After all, she had risked her life figuring out it was Power. If only she had figured it out a day earlier, she would be up there with Mason.

"Right now, Dr. Norton is attending the International Scientific Symposium at the Javits Center in which her daughter is a participant."

The questions came as fast as Mason could blurt out his vague answers. He wanted to end the session and pointed to Amy for the last question, but another agent had jogged to the podium and whispered something into Mason's ear.

Amy was close enough to see the color drain from Mason's face. Mason abruptly ended the press conference and stalked off through an arched entryway to the right of the podium. While most of the other reporters were typing onto laptop computers and placing calls on cellular telephones, Amy bolted up from her seat and followed Mason. She ran up behind him and two other agents and caught on immediately.

"How the hell could it have happened?" he said as he balled up his press conference notes and threw them at a wall. He was disgusted with himself for going public before he actually had Power. He would be back at a desk for the next five years.

"Nice work, Mason." Amy swung her bag over her shoulder. "What now?"

"Ms. Mendoza, leave," Mason said sharply as he turned once again to leave.

Amy grabbed Mason's arm. "Don't you think he'll go for one more attack?"

"Are you deaf?" Mason said, pulling his arm away.

"Did you see the blueprints in his office? There are more than thirty targets!" Amy shouted to his back.

Mason looked at his men, who were staring away from him. "Did you get the blueprints?" he fired at them. The lack of eye contact gave him his answer. "Jesus Christ!" Mason shouted.

"They weren't there," one of the agents replied weakly.

Amy smiled coyly. "I took pictures."

Mason's expression didn't change as he slowly pointed his finger at her. "I want them. Now."

"Of course, Mason. But I don't have them here. They are digital images, and the computer disk is back at my apartment."

Mason grabbed her arm and dragged her out the door. "Let's go, Amy."

Power sat in the only chair in Cecile's apartment, staring intently at the television. He thought from the outset that Gabrielle Norton might listen to reason. She was reputed to be brilliant. How ironic that Norton, the nation's vivisector in command, had a daughter training to become a second-generation murderer.

"Cecile, how much explosive do you have here?"

"More than enough."

Amy scrolled though the digital images of the blueprints on her Macintosh, while Mason's brain whirled. He saw research facilities and private and governmental buildings all over the country, though mostly in the northeast. That narrowed it down. He had no doubt that Power would attempt one last violent statement to trumpet his cause. The Bureau's psychological profile of him, based primarily on the letters that Norton had been receiving from the outset of this nightmare, strongly suggested that he was not the type of criminal who, when faced with capture, would go gently into the night.

When the image of the Javits Center came up on the screen, Mason remembered his effusive praise of Gabrielle Norton at the press conference and felt sick.

"Shit, Mason, you probably should have kept Norton's

schedule to yourself." Power was going to try to blow up the Javits Center, and without her, the FBI would have never known. *Pulitzer prize, here I come.*

Mason said nothing for a moment, got up, and walked to Amy's door. Before leaving, he stared gravely at her. "Listen to me very carefully, Amy. Unless you want to spend most of your thirties in Leavenworth, you are not to say or write anything about this situation until it is resolved." He left without salutation before she could respond.

"Whatever you say, Mason," she said to the slammed door. She waited five minutes, ran down seven flights of stairs, and caught a cab to the West Side.

"Look at these lines! I'm glad we got here early—this place is going to be a zoo today," Brooke remarked to her mother as their cab pulled up outside the Javits Center. There was a convoy of yellow buses unloading kids from regional schools, and swarms of people were approaching on foot from the nearest subways.

Gabrielle smiled at her daughter's excitement. It was great to spend time with Brooke; she'd really missed having her daughter at home. And great to have the crisis over, she thought. "I'm so proud of you, sweetheart. Coming up with the idea of using a phoresis machine in that way was brilliant. You're going to make a terrific researcher."

"Thanks, Mom." Brooke rolled her eyes. "But even though it was my idea, there were also about ten other people at the Rockefeller Institute who worked on it. It was great that they let me present it here for the competition." Brooke had always respected her mother, but after seeing how hard research really was, she was even more impressed. "And I'm sorry I lied about working on animals."

They got in line behind a large group of older women who were obviously well acquainted. "We're retired librarians from northern Michigan," one of the women told

Gabrielle. "Every year, we attend a conference together where we figure we'll learn something. We thought this would be a great way to bone up on some science without having to plow through a bunch of technical journals." Gabrielle and Brooke introduced themselves and talked with the women as the line inched its way forward. Buses and taxis kept pulling up to the curb, letting off groups of students interested in science, researchers and marketers who'd flown in to see their exhibits, and tourists who were simply curious. There were three different entrances to the main hall, and each one had a line of people snaking through its own maze.

Once inside, Brooke marveled at the breadth of the conference center, with its enormous windows that let in light from every angle. Twenty-five tons of glass and steel formed ceilings more than two hundred feet high. Fifty-foot glass panels formed the center's walls and defined each wing. The Javits Center resembled an ultramodern greenhouse covering a football field. They presented their tickets at the turnstile, moved slowly through the entrance, and then attached their ID badges. Each of them received an expo directory, which was the size of a small phone book. Brooke scoped out the huge room, her eyes widening at the sheer number and diversity of displays. Exhibits featuring research breakthroughs and promoting universities and corporations ran the length of eighty rows, each neatly numbered. There were categories for medical research, proposals for outer space exploration, displays of plant ecology, veterinary science, and agricultural experiments. Concession stands selling all manner of food and drink were set up at the ends of the aisles. The noise level was starting to rise as the crowd began to pour in. Brooke and Gabrielle searched their programs for her team's research entry and found its location on Aisle 27, situated on an entire row of exhibits dedicated to AIDS research.

"Let's go find your entry first," Gabrielle suggested, "and then we can browse through the rest for as long as we want."

They headed down Aisle 27, but Brooke got sidetracked when she ran into a group of Bronx Science students. They were excited to meet Gabrielle, and she responded warmly to their questions. It was great to see Brooke among a group of young people who shared her passion for science. A reporter recognized Gabrielle and asked her for a short interview. Gabrielle looked at her watch. She had a few minutes. Why not?

By the time they started off again for Brooke's exhibit, the crowd had filled the hall to near capacity. It was a gorgeous New York summer day, and the light hitting the Hudson River reflected off the west wall of the center, flashing an unnaturally bright light over the vast hall.

"Where to?" asked the cab driver.

"The Javits Center," Power said. Cecile had taken another cab and was probably already there.

Brooke was thrilled—all those months of hard work had culminated in seeing her team's research proposal displayed at the expo alongside those of eminent scientists from all over the country. The loud buzz of the crowd was infectious. She was literally beaming as Gabrielle took a picture of her standing beside their original draft of the notes for the experiment and the enlarged photographs of a chimp's white blood cells. A thin woman with glasses and short hair, wearing a safari vest, stepped aside with an annoyed look as the flash went off.

"You're the person who thought up this research project with the chimpanzees?" she said to Brooke.

"Well, I was part of a team," Brooke said humbly, although at that moment she was bursting with pride.

"Have you considered the consequences to the chimps if anyone ever acted on your proposal?" the woman asked pointedly.

Gabrielle turned quickly from the exhibit to face a woman staring hard at Brooke, as her young daughter struggled to respond. She stepped forward protectively. "Are you interested in this kind of research?" she asked, placing herself squarely between her daughter and the woman.

"Quite interested," the woman said with a thin smile. "You aren't by any chance Gabrielle Norton, are you?"

"I am. And who might you be?" Gabrielle asked, now on the offensive.

"Oh, I've never been of any consequence to someone like you. Is this your daughter? You must be quite thrilled to have the acorn drop so close to the tree." The woman sneered.

As Gabrielle turned her head to check on Brooke, the woman quickly darted into the milling crowd.

"Wow, what a weirdo," Brooke commented as they continued down the aisle. "What did she want from me?"

"Don't dwell on it, honey. Nothing you could have said would have satisfied her," Gabrielle replied, still concerned. She glanced around but could not see the woman. She'd keep an eye out for her; she didn't want her anywhere near Brooke again.

Amy's heart raced when she caught sight of the lines snaking into the conference center. She'd prayed it would be too early for much of a crowd to have formed, but her hopes were in vain. What if Power and his group had already planted the bomb?

Amy ran to the turnstiles and flashed her press card to bypass the line and go directly into the hall. Thousands of people were meandering through the exhibits: senior citizens, junior high school students, even parents with small children found something to spark their interest.

On the north wall of the center, Amy caught sight of four men walking with two huge hounds. The animals sniffed avidly, heads down—neither the dogs nor the men were distracted by the random patterns of the crowd. Several people turned to look at the dogs, but no one except Amy had any idea how important their work was at that moment. She turned to the east wall and saw a similar group of men and dogs working their way determinedly from the perimeter of the hall toward its center. *A bomb!*

Amy wanted to scream. Why didn't Mason just evacuate the place? She began to wonder if the story was worth risking her life. What kind of reporter would she be if she didn't stick it out?

Power entered the Javits Center through a loading dock at the rear of the building. He moved quickly down an aisle to the centerpiece of the expo, the installation of an Imax theater with seating for fifteen hundred people, set up in the middle of the main exhibit hall. A twenty-foot-high, four-color poster advertised the featured film on the vanishing wildlife of Brazil's rain forest. "Please enter, moving as far forward as possible, and take your seats," a piped voice announced melodiously over a looped tape. "Our first showing will start in fifteen minutes." Power stepped inside the theater, where the first twenty rows of seats were already filled. Glancing around, he moved down the left side aisle to the front of the theater and slipped behind a curtain to the back of the huge projection screen. He placed the leather bag at its base. By the time the clip started running, all fifteen hundred people would be seated, forming human dominoes in the face of the explosives. Power estimated that the bomb had enough power to shatter the windows of the entire main hall. Those who survived the blast's impact were unlikely to escape the shrapnel of flying glass.

Mason went inside to check on the progress of his agents, but so far no one had sighted Power, and the dogs had barely begun to cover the hall. He had a very, very bad feeling about all of this.

Cecile patted the gun inside her vest. Large crowds always made her nervous, and today she was practically undone by the tension. She had taken out a security guard at the delivery dock at the rear of the building, to ensure that Power had no trouble gaining entrance to the expo with the explosives. She would track Power as he planted the bomb, prepared to intervene if he encountered any

unforeseen obstacles. They would then meet at a designated spot just outside the center, watch the explosion
from the other side of Eleventh Avenue, and cab it back to
Power's hotel room to watch the news stations picking up
on the disaster. Spotting Gabrielle Norton with her daughter was the icing on the cake.

Power had insisted that he be the one to plant the bomb.
Cecile smiled bitterly at the thought of Norton and all the
eminent researchers who were gathered within these walls
of glass. Too bad her father hadn't stayed in that line of
work.

Amy positioned herself near the entrance to the Imax
theater and suppressed the urge to shout a warning to a
bunch of giggling high school students entering the theater. They were followed by two women pushing strollers.
One stopped to retrieve her son's pacifier. "We're going to
see a movie about pretty birds!" she exclaimed

Suddenly, a familiar face passed by. Amy stared in
horror as a man in a blue workshirt and khakis exited the
theater.

"Mr. John Power, I . . . I thought I recognized you." For
the first time in her life, Amy struggled to get out the
words. The nightmare had begun. "Amy Mendoza from
the *New York News*." She picked up speed. "You're a hard
man to track down. I've left messages at your office, and
you haven't returned any of my calls."

Power looked around, clearly agitated. "I'm busy. I've
got no time to talk." He turned and began walking away
from her toward the entrance to the building.

Amy ran to keep up, scanning the crowd for a blue
uniform. "Mr. Power!" she called loudly, her mind racing.
If she could just get the attention of a cop or one of
Mason's men—by now, they had to be on the lookout for
Power. "I just need a minute of your time, Mr. Power!"
She grabbed his sleeve and held on. Power whirled around
to face her.

"What do you want?" he hissed.

"I'm surprised to see you here, given your opposition to research. Are you here for information for CARE? Do you guys have a protest planned?"

"We have nothing planned. I'm here as an observer."

"Mr. Power!" she shouted even more loudly, vainly hoping someone would recognize his name. "I called you to get a quote about the ABP. Surely you can help me? I'm doing a big piece on them, and I needed—"

"I have no comment," Power said, and hurried away.

"But Mr. Power!" Amy screamed frantically, running after him. "Mr. Power! How do you feel about all the recent attacks, about Greg Sandstone's death, and about . . ."

Finally, a cop in the middle of the next aisle had heard her. Amy saw him glance at a photo in his hand and move toward them. Power noticed the cop and turned back on Amy. "Mr. Power, I just wondered . . ." She faltered.

"Shut up, you bitch!" Power said, grabbing her arm. The policeman was now jogging toward them. "You're going to tell this cop you're feeling faint," Power said, "and that I am helping you to a cab."

The policeman approached, but he wasn't interested in questioning Amy. "NYPD. Are you John Power?" he asked.

"Never heard of him," Power replied, moving with Amy toward the exit.

"None of you are going anywhere until I see some ID," the policeman said. As he closed in behind them, Power suddenly swung his gun away from Amy's ribs and pointed it at the policeman. Terrified, Amy jerked her arm free and grabbed for the gun as the policeman tackled Power. The struggle seemed like forever but was only a matter of seconds, when the gun exploded with a deafening bang and the policeman hit the ground. He didn't move.

There was a moment of utter silence. Then a thin blond woman on the aisle pointed at Power, screaming, "He shot that policeman!" Pandemonium erupted, and people catapulted away from Power in a 360-degree spread of chaos. Amy, stunned at the sight of the policeman's body, hesitated before moving away. Taking advantage of her lapse, Power grabbed her from behind and put the gun to her head. Amy was seized with fear as she saw people desperately trying to escape, trampling the displays, smashing racks and signage as they ran toward the exits. A young woman fell and never got up under the stomping of panicked feet.

Amy knew if she was taken hostage by the ABP, she'd never survive—and Power clearly needed to get out of the building.

Inside the theater, Gabrielle and Brooke sat in the darkened room and waited for the film to begin. The walls of the installation were heavily soundproofed to eliminate noise from the crowd outside while the film was playing. An older man accompanied by a young boy leaned over, holding his program. "What time do you have?" he asked. "I thought this was supposed to start soon. We wanted to make it to the Circle of Life display after this. They're doing a demonstration of how larvae hatch into butterflies, and my grandson here really wanted to see it."

"My watch says it should be less than five minutes," said Gabrielle.

"Thank you." The man smiled and leaned back in his seat.

"Nice to see so many laypeople at the expo," Gabrielle said.

"Yeah, more than I would have thought," Brooke agreed.

Mason watched in horror as the melee in the middle of the conference center spread. From what his men could gather, at least two people were down, but they couldn't get near the shooter. There was a general stampede for the exits, which made it impossible for them to get close enough to take out the gunman. Inevitably, people were getting hurt as they were shoved aside by the strongest, most aggressive members of the pack.

Mason could hear shouts of "A gun!" mingling with

cries and screams as people were stomped on, shoved, and brutalized. He managed to push his way into the aisle where the commotion had started, unable to help as two women were repeatedly trampled. "Stop! Police!" Mason shouted vainly, but the crowd just kept surging forward.

He began grabbing people and shoving them out of his way. After glancing at the blueprint, he'd directed his men and the bomb squad with their dogs to get to the Imax theater, no matter what. He could see some of them as they tried to push through the crowds. However, only one of the large hounds had the discipline to keep moving forward through the mob. The other dogs stopped in their tracks, baying in terror and confusion.

Mason blasted forward a few more feet. Now he could see into the eye of the storm, and sure enough, there was John Power holding a gun to Amy's head, searching frantically for a way out.

Amy tried desperately to get away, but Power had an arm around her throat, and he wasn't letting go. "You put us here, and you are going to get us out, you bitch!" Power screamed into her ear. They had only minutes before the bomb would explode, and Power needed her to get past the cops he knew were waiting outside. He violently shoved her toward the north exit. She could see two cops trying to channel people to keep them from knocking a large display into another group of people in the next aisle.

Amy knew she could never match Power's strength. She paused for a moment to let him walk right into her and came down with all her might on his instep, grasping his forearm with her two hands to loosen his choke hold and bending forward to throw him off balance. It worked. As Power tumbled forward, Amy slipped out of his grasp. "Get the fuck away from me!" she cried, quickly moving away from him. Power screamed in fury and leveled the gun at her again. Amy ran but didn't get more than ten feet before she hit the back of the crowd and was forced back toward him by a phalanx of people who were blockaded by a group of cops. "Stop moving right now! Stand still in your tracks. There is no danger," came a voice over a bullhorn. "You will hurt yourselves. No one has a gun. There is no danger," the voice lied.

Special Agent Doug Hanson urged his dog through the frenzied crowd. Over and over, when Hanson was convinced Max wouldn't continue, the hound would put his big nose to the floor and unflinchingly move forward. Even when he got kicked or stepped on, the dog would simply whimper and keep on going. Finally, they reached the entrance to the Imax theater. The agent swiftly opened the door, and Max scooted in.

"Quiet, boy," Hanson urged, bolting the door behind him. "Find the ticker. Find the ticker, boy. No barking."

Max looked up at Hanson, snorted, and began lumbering down the hall. Hanson could hear the murmurs of the audience waiting behind the curtain. Max made a right turn, hesitated, then turned around and headed back down another hallway. He came to a stop behind a huge projection screen, where he scratched excitedly at its base. Hanson knelt quickly. Sure enough, a black leather case lay underneath. Hanson cautiously pulled it out and slid open the zipper. There lay the bomb, its timer indicating there were only a few minutes to go. Hanson thought of all the people sitting just a few feet away in the theater. He didn't have time to get them out; he'd just have to go to work and hope he'd be fast enough. "Good boy," he said to Max as he began to dismantle the intricate wiring system.

Cecile was posted by a door leading back to the loading dock. Power was late; the bomb was set to blow any minute now. There was a major disturbance in the main hall, and she knew he must be involved. She glanced at her watch again. "No, I can't wait anymore," she muttered to herself, and slipped out the side exit.

Amy scrambled to make some headway into the crowd, away from Power's line of fire. Out of the corner of her eye, she saw Mason moving toward Power, pushing people out of his way. Power was still trying to reach her, but she had a small buffer between them. Each time he held the gun up, trying to squirm through to her, people would panic more.

Finally, Mason was almost beside them. "You're under arrest!" he shouted, aiming his gun at Power.

Power turned and broke for the theater. "Get him!" Amy screamed. Mason was close on his heels until an older man stumbled into his path, and Power took the opportunity to slip inside the theater. Amy heard a loud click as Power locked the double doors from inside.

Mason yanked desperately at the doors. Two more agents came running up. "Check the other entrances to see if they're locked!" Mason shouted. The agents sprang around the sides of the structure.

"He's got a gun—he could shoot people!" Amy cried.

Mason stared at her. "He's more likely to take hostages," he said.

Power caught his breath and looked at the people waiting to see the film. There was no escaping now—he couldn't have defused the bomb if he wanted to. He felt calm and peaceful. He was prepared to meet his fate. He walked down the aisle of the dimly lit auditorium and stood right in front of the screen. Murmurs arose from the crowd.

"I have an announcement to make!" Power shouted, waving his gun. "You—all of you—are participating in horrible acts of torture and murder of animals, every single day. You don't have to be a researcher. If you've bought a lipstick or deodorant that was tested on an animal, you've participated. If you've eaten beef or veal, you've participated. If you've had a vaccine that was tested on animals, you've been a part of it. Even now, thousands of animals are being victimized needlessly for obscure purposes that will never forward any medical knowledge."

A terrified Brooke turned to Gabrielle. "Mom . . . ," she began.

Gabrielle felt numb. It was actually happening, what she'd feared all these months. The ranting madman at the front of the room had to be ABP.

"Some of you may even be unaware of this," Power continued, "but that's not my problem. You should have been aware. And if there are any researchers present who have used animals in experiments, I'm happy to say you won't be doing that anymore. Everyone in this room is going to die—"

Screams and cries broke out among the frightened audience. Gabrielle took her daughter's hand. "God, no," she whispered.

Hanson could see the outlines of the madman through the screen. Power might be getting ready to start shooting people, but Hanson couldn't stop now to nab him. He had to get this thing defused. He looked down at Max waiting expectantly.

"Go get 'im, boy," he whispered, and Max darted away.

Mason and his men stood outside the locked theater, debating what to do. They could break down the doors, but would Power start firing into the crowd if they did? "Get on the PA system and tell him to give up," said one agent. "Call a hostage negotiator. There's a good one here in the city," offered another. Mason stood undecided, wishing Garrow would arrive.

John Power paced the front of the room, fervently delivering his message. "In thirty seconds," he shouted, looking at his watch, "this whole place is going to blow! You're all going to pay for the atrocities you've committed against cats, chimpanzees, rats, chickens, dogs . . ."

As if on cue, a huge bloodhound dashed out in front of the screen and leaped up at Power's throat, knocking him to the ground. Power tried to push the dog away, but it held on tenaciously. Moments later, a tall man ran out and held a gun to Power's head. "Stay still! Stop moving. Now! You're under arrest," said Hanson. "OK, Max, you can back off. Back off, boy." The dog gave Power one more shake and returned to Hanson's side.

Power glared up at the agent. "Too late. I've set a bomb!" he cried furiously.

"And I've just defused it," said Hanson. Holding the gun on Power, he turned to the frozen audience. "It's all right. There was a bomb, but you're safe now. Please stay seated. Everything is all right."

A crash sounded in the hall, and Mason and four agents came running in, guns drawn. "I've got Power here. The bomb's defused!" Hanson shouted. "Someone cover him while I pack up the evidence."

Mason strode forward. He pulled Power to his feet, and the other agents cuffed him and dragged him, shrieking obscenities, out of the theater.

Gabrielle hugged her daughter as she sobbed. All around them, people were in shock, either crying or staring forward, still afraid to move. "It's okay, honey," she said, patting Brooke on the back. "It's over. We're all going to be fine," she continued, expressing a confidence she didn't feel.

Amy was still trying to catch her breath when Mason made it back out of the theater and over to her. "Did you get him?" she asked.

"Yes, and one of our guys defused the bomb. It was a close call," Mason said, shaking his head. "Turns out you averted quite a disaster."

"Wow," Amy said shakily.

"Well, we've got them now," said Mason.

"Can I interview this asshole before you cart him off?" she asked.

"I'm sorry, but I really can't let you interview the suspect," Mason said. "But I'll be happy to talk to you all you want. Come with me, I want you to meet my boss."

"You're not gonna talk to any of the other papers, right? Because I've gotta get this out first. I need all the details."

"For what you did today, you've definitely got an exclusive," Mason said.

The next day, Cecile turned off the news in disgust. The Javits Center operation had been a disaster. Eventually, they might find her, but she wasn't quite finished. She gave Otto a steak bone and loaded her gun.

There was really no chance Cecile would ever identify or describe him to the FBI, so truthfully, he didn't need to be there. Lonergan rarely killed for pleasure, but today he would allow himself a treat—a going-away present. He had picked the lock and stood in the living room as Cecile exited from the kitchen. "Hello, you pig-fucking, ugly bitch," he said as he grabbed her by the throat.

He drew his fist back and with surgical precision drove it into her mid-face. The blow shattered her nose and left cheekbone, but she remained conscious as he had planned. Blood gushed from her mouth and nose, and she fell to the floor. "Get up. I'm not done. I have ninety minutes to kill before my plane leaves." But before he could strike again, Otto had left his meal and leaped across the room.

Although Otto's overall genetic percentage of Staffordshire terrier, or, as it was more commonly called, pit bull, was unknown, his teeth and jaws were one-hundred-percent pit bull. The crushing force that animal can deliver with its teeth, thanks to its overdeveloped masseter muscles, is twice that of the next most powerful breed.

Lonergan had no time to react to the missile of muscle and teeth that had locked onto its target. A gaping cavern of knives set in concrete closed around his throat before his brain's impulse to avert could reach his limbs. As the animal's jaws slammed shut, Lonergan's cervical spine, trachea, esophagus, and carotid artery were simultaneously transected. His head had almost been ripped off. The frenzied animal continued its attack, sequentially shredding and avulsing all four extremities of the almost headless torso. Within sixty seconds, Lonergan and the piece of steak and bone that Otto had been eating were indistinguishable, except that the remnant of steak was smaller and more well done.

Cecile went to the bathroom to wash away the remnants of blood. Her off-center nose and fractured cheek were throbbing, but she would not stop until she was finished with them. She put the ID badge in her pocket and left.

36

Ted Simpson sat down at his desk and opened a small package marked "Personal." Inside was a tape and a letter. He put on his reading glasses.

Dear Dr. Simpson:

Enclosed is a tape recording of our conversation in your office last week. I really should hand it over to the dean, if only to make a statement about the kind of crap that goes on all the time. It might save some other woman from the same indignities, but I'm selfish and don't have the time or energy to go through any legal hoops. So if you are a good boy and leave me alone, after I have finished this program, I will send you the original tape.

Incidentally, I've decided to become a pediatric heart surgeon. You know, to operate on those useless rat hearts, as you put it. My in-service test scores are 99th percentile, and I have great hands, so I trust with all your connections you can get me a spot at Columbia.

Casey Brenner

P.S. I know that recording our conversation without telling you is illegal. So if you have a problem with that, sue me.

He slumped back in his chair, threw his glasses on the desk, and attempted to rub away the headache that had only just begun.

Bypassing his secretary, Lenore Attenucci strode into his office, with poorly concealed glee.

"What do you want, Lenore?" Simpson demanded.

"A little riddle, Ted. What do you call a chief of surgery who tries to get his partners sued?"

He said nothing.

"It's easy, Ted. The ex-chief of surgery. You have a week to get out."

"You can't do that! I have tenure!" he cried.

"You don't anymore. Forrest Wells ratted on you. I have to say, Ted, even I didn't think you'd sink that low. Give me your resignation, or I'll turn the whole disgusting affair over to the DA," she said.

Simpson lit a cigarette and looked out his window. He felt like jumping.

"One week, Ted," Lenore repeated, and walked out.

The last dogs had tolerated sixty minutes of circulatory arrest after an hour of shock without an obvious drop in intelligence, but the microscopic picture was a different story. The nuclei of the brain cells looked swollen, and many were obviously dead. Those changes could profoundly affect a human's intelligence, even though the dogs appeared normal. It looked as if an hour was the limit, at least at fifteen degrees. This afternoon, they planned to use even deeper hypothermia, to a tympanic membrane temperature of twelve degrees Celsius. The dog was already on bypass, and Casey immersed the animal's head in packed ice. "What do you think?" Zach asked. "Sixty minutes is a long time to be dead, even at twelve degrees."

"I think with the extra few degrees, we'll be OK," Casey

responded. "I wonder, though, if we can cool the animal down any faster. With a real patient who has continued bleeding, I'm not sure we can afford such a long cooling period."

"If this works out, we can try to cool the dogs quicker next week. I can't wait to try this out on a victim. A cop killer or rapist would be a great start," Zach said.

"Before we do this to a human, or even a subhuman, we need a lot more work. What's the rush?" Casey asked.

Zach walked over to Casey. He put his arms around her and hugged her. "Why don't we drive to the beach this weekend?" He began to kiss her neck.

"I'd like that," said Casey as she pressed up against Zach. "It would be nice to spend some time alone, relaxing together."

Zach put his hands on Casey's waist and began to move them up toward her breasts as he looked around the room. "How about relaxing together right here?"

"Are you crazy?" She laughed, making no attempt to stop him. "What if someone comes in?"

"Don't worry," he said.

"Zach . . ." She moaned softly and kissed him. As she began to unbutton her lab coat, a noise that sounded like thunder reverberated through the lab. She felt Zach's body tighten and lurch forward. He looked up at her as he collapsed to the floor. Blood oozed from the front of his shirt.

"Zach!" she screamed hysterically. She fell to her knees and grabbed him.

Behind him stood Cecile Morgan, holding a 357 revolver.

"This is a really special scene. While an innocent dog is being tortured, you two are fucking. Now, you tell me, who's the animal?"

Zach's head was in Casey's lap. "You insane bitch!" Casey screamed.

Zach was too weak to move. He knew that he was bleeding to death.

At that moment, Simpson, who had been wandering around the building in a daze, ran into the lab. "I heard the noise. What the hell . . ." He stopped, frozen in his tracks. He looked in horror at Zach lying on the floor and at the woman who held the gun.

"Carol! What on earth?"

"The name is Cecile now, Father," she said without emotion.

"You're involved with those terrorists?"

"No. You bastards are the terrorists. I am a liberationist. And you can thank yourself, dear old Dad. The times you forced me to watch those atrocities in your lab showed me my mission."

He moved toward her to take away the gun. "You stupid little girl. Because of those experiments, tens of thousands of people have new kidneys, livers, and hearts."

"And hundreds of thousands of animals are dead. Who the fuck gave you the right to decide life and death?"

"You've lost your mind. Now, put down that gun and let me take care of this man. He's dying."

"And so are you." Without a trace of hesitation, Carol Simpson a.k.a. Cecile Morgan put a bullet through her father's head, splattering the wall with bone fragments, blood, and pieces of his brain.

Casey suddenly realized that this was the same woman who had passed her in the hall before Glen's attack. She rolled away from Zach behind the lab counter. Her briefcase was in the lower drawer; hands shaking, she pulled it out. After Glen and Zach had been attacked, she took Daphne's advice and borrowed one of her handguns. She just wished that she had fired it before.

"You're dead, too, you fucking slut." Cecile stalked around the lab counter, ready to finish her mission.

Casey's first shot only grazed Cecile's left arm when she appeared from behind the lab counter. But before an astounded Cecile could get off a shot of her own, Casey had pumped five more bullets into her chest. The impact knocked her off her feet and onto the lab table countertop, where she died seconds later.

Casey ran to the telephone on the wall. The operator didn't answer until the tenth ring, which seemed like hours. "Code A! Room Twelve-fifty." She then quickly dialed the operating room. "Get the trauma room ready. Dr. Green has been shot."

She ran back to Zach. He was alive, but barely. She could feel only a faint pulse in his groin. She pulled his shirt off. The bullet had entered his back and exited from his right upper quadrant, where the liver and vena cava were located. She cupped her hands around his face and kissed him. "You'll be OK," she said, attempting to hold back her tears.

"Who's on call tonight?" Zach asked in a barely audible voice.

"I think Gordon," Casey replied.

"Get Ron. I don't want that asshole operating on me."

"Ron's out of town."

"I'm fucked." Zach attempted to smile.

"Don't worry, I won't let him touch a sharp instrument," Casey said in the most encouraging voice she could muster. "Just lay back. I promise you'll make it."

"It's *lie* back," he said, almost inaudibly.

"I love you, Zach."

Those were the last words he heard before he lost consciousness.

At least ten people rushed into the room and began to work on Zach. Within two minutes, there were two intravenous lines in his arms, a catheter in his bladder, and a tube in his stomach. A nurse attempted to take his blood pressure, but she couldn't hear it.

Casey thought quickly. She called the operating room again. "This is Dr. Brenner. Have the heart-lung machine ready, and stat page Dr. Gordon to the OR." Maybe Zach was right—maybe it was time to try their experiment on a human being. But Zach's blood pressure was much lower than the animals they had used in their experiments. Would he tolerate the circulatory arrest and have a normal brain afterward? Maybe he would have an easily repairable injury, but she doubted it. The trajectory of the bullet and his profound shock suggested a bad liver injury or major vascular injury. The major blood vessel in the path of that bullet was the vena cava.

Casey ran to the operating room. Larry Gordon was already there.

"What's going on?" Gordon asked.

"Zach's been shot in the right upper quadrant. He has almost no blood pressure. I want to try to fix him with circulatory arrest."

"Are you fucking nuts?" Gordon screamed. "This isn't a goddamn dog lab. No one has done that on a human being before."

"Larry, he has something terrible in his belly, and he's almost dead. If it's his retrohepatic cava, we'll kill him for sure trying to fix it. When was the last time you had a survivor of that injury?" *When was the last time you had a survivor of a hernia?* she thought.

"Let's at least see what he has," Gordon insisted. "Maybe it won't be so bad." But he knew better.

The gurney rolled by them and into the operating room. "I'll meet you in the room," Casey said.

They went to their respective changing suites and quickly donned their scrubs. When Casey reached the OR, the anesthesiologists had Zach intubated, and a nurse was painting his abdomen and chest with Betadine antiseptic. The perfusionist, Tammy Hart, rolled the heart-lung machine into the room.

"Are you sure you want to try this?" Tammy asked. She wasn't used to putting nearly dead people on bypass.

"Just have the machine primed and ready to go," Casey said as she dried her hands and gowned.

Shirley had already placed the sterile drapes over Zach and was gowning Larry Gordon.

"You'd better get going. His pressure is thirty, and we're hosing in the blood," Hal, the anesthesiologist, said nervously.

"Knife." Shirley handed Casey the scalpel, and she made the incision from the top of Zach's sternum to his pubic bone. Gordon assisted; he knew deep down that Zach would be better off if Casey operated on him.

A torrent of blood gushed out of Zach's abdomen. "Get the suckers going!" Casey screamed. She could see the blood welling up behind the liver. She stuffed about ten large pads up against his liver and held them tightly. "Larry, push down on the aorta at the diaphragm." Between the packing and the aortic compression, Zach's blood pressure rose to ninety. "OK, Hal, see if you can catch up with his blood loss. It's slowed—a little."

"Pumping it as fast as I can."

After five minutes, Zach's pressure was still less than a hundred, and the packs were soaking through. "Let's take a look up there," Larry said.

"I think we should put him on bypass now. You know the bullet has to have gotten his retrohepatic cava," Casey said.

"Look, he's more stable now. Let's see if we can fix it." Before Casey could say another word, Larry pulled out the packs. The bleeding was audible. His pressure dropped to forty in less than thirty seconds. No one could see anything in the river of blood. "God, Larry, are you trying to kill him?" Casey yelled. She replaced the packs, and although the bleeding slowed, it did not stop. "Larry, we are going to put him on bypass, or I am going to put this knife through your hand." She was serious.

"He's dead anyway, go ahead," Larry responded, shaking his head.

Casey put sutures in the aorta and atrium, then inserted the plastic cannulae that would connect Zach to the bypass machine. She had him on bypass in less than five minutes. All those cases with Simpson had helped. "OK, Tammy, start cooling him down. I don't want to stop his circulation until his tympanic membrane temperature is less than twenty degrees." *Please, God, let him be all right*, she thought.

"The heparin is in, and he's on bypass," Tammy said. "I'll transfuse some more blood through the pump."

"His perfusion pressure is only thirty, even on bypass. You need to stop the bleeding," Hal said.

"He isn't cold enough yet to stop his circulation," Casey argued.

"His tympanic membrane temperature is twenty-four degrees," Hal said.

"Tammy, cool him faster."

"I've never done it that way before. The brain only cools so fast."

"Get some ice and pack it around his head," Casey said.

After another five minutes, which seemed like five hours, Zach's tympanic membrane temperature was fifteen degrees. "OK, exsanguinate him, and stop his circulation."

Zach Green was dead—but only temporarily, Casey prayed. If someone hooked him to EEG, they would have seen minimal brain activity. His brain's metabolism was slowed to a fraction of its normal rate, protecting it from cellular damage. Casey knew that Zach's prearrest shock had been much more severe than in any of the experimental animals. Furthermore, with the extra-rapid cooling, the effects on his brain might be devastating. She couldn't allow herself to think about it.

"It's eight thirty-seven," Hal said. "I'll call the time every fifteen minutes."

Casey removed the packs and explored his abdominal cavity, now dry with the exception of some old blood, which Casey evacuated. With Larry's assistance, she mobilized the liver to expose the injuries. It was even worse than she expected. Seventy-five percent of the wall of the retrohepatic vena cava was destroyed, as well as the veins that drained the right liver. "We're going to have to put a graft in the cava and resect the right lobe of the liver," Casey said desperately. Dejection was setting in. She had never even seen a hepatic resection before, and this was a bad time to learn.

"Jesus!" exclaimed Larry. "Let's get going. Shirley, get some twenty-two-millimeter Gortex." While the circulating nurse went for the Gortex, a leak-proof polymer that would replace Zach's irreparably damaged vena cava, Larry began to use his fingers to fracture through the pulverized liver, tying the blood vessels as he went along. "At least this part is easy when there's no bleeding."

Casey couldn't believe it. Larry was resecting the liver—expertly. She realized that while he couldn't operate worth a damn when constant bleeding obscured the surgical field, in this absolutely bloodless environment with perfect exposure, his technique was excellent.

"Thirty minutes!" Hal shouted.

"Larry, we have got to go faster. We haven't even started the repair of the vena cava. The dogs that were arrested more than sixty minutes suffered brain damage, and they underwent less shock than Zach!" Casey cried.

"If we don't do this properly, he'll bleed to death after we restart his circulation," Larry said, without stopping.

Casey realized Larry was right. After another ten minutes, they had the right lobe of Zach's liver out and were ready to start the repair of the cava. "Get me a five-zero proline suture," Casey asked. Shirley had it ready, and Casey began to sew in the piece of plastic to replace the vena cava. As Casey began the second suture line, Hal noted that the circulatory arrest time was an hour. She was sewing as fast as she could, and the repair took another ten minutes. "OK, Tammy, let's start the pump and warm him." Casey had no idea what Zach's neurologic function would be, or if they would even be able to get him off bypass.

"I can't believe how well that went. We should use this technique more often," Larry said.

"What good is it if he is a vegetable afterward?" Casey replied. An hour and ten minutes of arrest time, she thought anxiously, remembering the histological changes in the dogs' brains at one hour. The pathologists weren't certain if the swelling and destruction of brain cells were real or artifact.

"Well, Zach always said you don't need to be very smart to be a surgeon," Larry replied, trying to cheer her up. Casey tried to smile, but tears rolled down her face instead.

"We're on full bypass, and his temperature is twenty-nine," Tammy said.

Casey and Larry carefully inspected the abdominal cavity. With the exception of some minor oozing from the suture lines and the edge of the liver, things were dry.

"His temperature is thirty-three now. Why don't we defibrillate him?" Hal requested.

"All right," she responded. Hal switched on the defibrillation unit, and Casey applied the paddles to Zach's heart. Twenty joules of current shot into his heart as it jerked and then spasmed.

"Come on, Zach," Larry murmured. Zach's heart began to beat, irregularly at first, but within a few minutes, the rhythm was normal.

After the last staple was placed closing Zach's abdomen, Casey looked at Larry Gordon, put her hand on top of his, and squeezed it. "Thank you, Larry. I didn't know you were such a good liver surgeon."

Larry gulped. "Neither did I."

Twenty-four hours postoperatively, Zach was still not awake. Casey, who had not left his bedside, was despondent. One reason he was still out could be all the drugs used during the operation; large amounts of narcotics had been given. But whether he was sleeping or in a coma because of neurologic damage was unclear.

"Dr. Brenner, you have to get some sleep. I'll call you when he wakes up," an intensive-care nurse said as she placed her hands gently on Casey's shoulders.

"Thanks. I appreciate it, but I think I'll stay." Casey sat in a chair and laid her head down on Zach's bed.

She awoke to a hand brushing against her head. She jumped up and saw that Zach's eyes were open. He couldn't talk because the endotracheal tube used to breathe for him still was in place. Her entire body shaking, she sprang out of the chair and touched his unshaven face. "Zach, do you know who I am?" she asked. *Please let him know me,* she thought.

Zach curled his index finger, beckoning Casey closer. She sat down beside him on the bed. Then he lifted his left hand and slid it over her breast.

A nurse who stood ten feet away observed the scene and became hysterical. "Same old Dr. Green."

Casey gently took Zach's hand and removed it from her breast. She kissed him and whispered in his ear. "Can you wait until you are off the ventilator?"

He shook his head no.

The day Zach was moved out of the intensive-care unit, Debby and Casey met in the hospital gift shop. Glen wanted some candy, and Zach a newspaper. Zach had asked to be put in a room with Glen.

"When is Glen getting out?" Casey asked.

"Phillip said he can leave in a day or two. He's going to need a lot of physical therapy before he walks normally again, but Phillip thinks with time he may not even limp much."

"Are the girls OK?"

"Yeah. They miss their dad, but they know he's going to be all right."

"Zach should be out in a week. What is Glen going to do after this?"

"We haven't really discussed it." Debby hesitated. "I want him to get a job somewhere upstate. I want out of this crazy city."

"What does Glen want?" Casey asked.

Debby laughed. "What do you think?"

"He and Zach are both out of their minds, you know," Casey said, shaking her head. "I walked into the intensive-care unit yesterday, and I saw Zach scribbling on his bedside chart. I guess the nurse, who has more common sense than he does, wouldn't give him any paper. Do you know what he was doing? He was writing up a case report for the *Journal of Trauma*. Guess which case?"

"He is unique." Debby laughed. "What about you?"

"I'll finish my residency here and then go to Columbia for pediatric cardiac surgery. Oh, I forgot to tell you with all the craziness lately. Zach and I are getting married. He said he's going to have a ring made for me from the staples I closed his belly with."

"Hold out for a diamond," Debby said, beaming as she hugged Casey.

Debby and Casey walked down the hall to the elevator, and took it to the fifth floor. "I'll meet you in their room," Debby said. "I just want to give this box of candy to the nurses." Casey continued toward the room.

When Debby arrived at Glen and Zach's room, she noticed that Casey was standing outside the door. "What's the matter?"

Casey put her fingers to her lips. "Look at this," she whispered. Glen was lying on Zach's bed watching television. It was a special retrospective on thirty years of Johnny Carson.

Debby looked at Casey and put her arm around her waist. "Now you know what I put up with. Get away from him while you still can."